I0772731

CELESTIAL DESTINY
BOOK TWO

SARA PUISSEGUR

For everyone battling their own monsters.
Don't be afraid to fight for yourself.
You deserve to live in the light.

KINGDOM OF DENORFIA
KINGDOM OF NYZENARD
Graynor
Lettras
Jessirae
Murmont
KINGDOM OF HYROSENCIA
Marlto River
Axys
Morlerae
ELJICOY LAKE
Ramdemoi
CELESTIAL DESTINY SERIES
Eldawia River
Kypno
Ewiajoy
Durmak

THAMAR
OUNTAINS
Silvermane
Symptee
NEW
HYROSENCIA
Lexilor
Avoika River
Faswyn
LESTERA
SEA
Estivor
Lei'wana
Noomi
Envyre
VALLEY
OF
NORLEE
ORD
METSIILVA
Sarklii
Monteris

CONTENTS

1

RELENTLESS

"Harder," Cole snapped, lunging toward Serena. "Don't hesitate!"

She huffed, blocking his attack with the wooden training staff. "I'm doing my best," Serena said through gritted teeth. The sparring stick felt unnatural in her hands after wielding Sannarvin for months. The stick was lighter, easier to swing around, but somehow, she felt like she was moving in slow motion against her Elven instructor.

Cole was unrelenting. He gave Serena no time to catch her breath between his barrage of attacks. She swung her weapon around over and over, barely blocking each move. Sweat dripped down her temples as she panted. After an hour of practice, her muscles were screaming for her to quit.

A bell chimed from the citadel tower, signaling the top of the hour. Serena groaned. Usually, that sound meant it was time for her to clean up and rush to morning tea with her aunt. Using her momentary distraction to his advantage, Cole knocked Serena's feet out from under her body, and she slammed hard on her back on the lawn. The grass did nothing to cushion the impact. Peering up at the clear blue sky and the looming brick towers of the magnificent fortress she now called home, Serena clenched her jaw. Now, all she could see was a prison with an unyielding taskmaster and no way out. *Some haven*, she thought.

"Try not to kill her, Cole!" Xandra called out, rushing to her aid.

Serena sat up and glared at her opponent while rubbing her lower back gingerly. "I'm fine. Let's go again," she spat, swiping the sparring stick from the ground beside her. Her chest constricted as she fought back the tears that glistened in her tired eyes. She refused to give her rigid mentor the satisfaction of seeing her give up.

Cole lowered his arms and dropped his signature smirk, recognizing the pain in her face. "I think we're done for the day, Princess," he declared, turning his back on her. "Wouldn't want you to be late for tea."

Serena stepped toward him and shouted, "No, I can keep going!"

Cole turned with a spark in his eyes and bounded toward her. Serena lurched out of his weapon's path and grimaced, unable to stifle the pained squeak that escaped from her lips as she swung her weapon back toward him. Cole caught her training staff in one hand and shook his head as her emerald eyes locked onto his. "I said you're done." With a quick jerk, he snatched the staff out of her grasp.

"Great work, Alarcole. You've injured her again," Crystal grumbled, pushing herself off the grass. She stomped over to Serena and yanked up the back of the girl's cream blouse wordlessly. "Elara's going to behead us if you aren't careful."

"Hey!" Serena shouted, twisting free from her grasp and tugging down her shirt. "Not out here. Elara would kill us both."

Crystal rolled her eyes and gently reached her left hand under Serena's blouse to feel her lower back. Heat radiated from a sensitive knot to the left of her spine. "Might have broken a rib," the guardian muttered, fixing her icy glare on her brother from over Serena's shoulder. With a frustrated exhale, Crystal pressed her other hand to the front of Serena's hip to steady her hold and began muttering in the ancient language. A familiar tingling sensation bloomed through her back, and Serena sighed as her friend's healing magic flowed through her, mending her bruised ribs.

If only it could mend her bruised ego as well.

Cole barked, "Really, Crys? You can't heal every little scrape on Her Royal Highness. She has to learn to take a hit." Xandra shushed him, shoving his arm.

"I don't need Elara breathing down my neck any more than she already does," Crystal snapped back, trying to focus on her patient. Leaning over Serena's shoulder, she whispered, "If it's broken, I may not be able to heal it in one session. You should see the physician later."

Serena rolled her eyes and exhaled loudly. "I miss when you didn't coddle me." She frowned at the citadel as Crystal's glowing hand continued to press against her injured back. "I'm not a child."

"No, you aren't," Crystal replied, pulling her hands off Serena and wiping them on her own blouse. "You're the heir to the throne, and Elara would not be pleased if you died while training."

"You don't have to remind me." Serena reached around to press her back cautiously. The swelling and pain had lessened, though the area where she had landed was still tender. She sighed, dropping her head back in defeat. "Every second of my life has been dictated since we got here. Etiquette lessons, sword training, tea, knife skills, fancy dinners—she wants me to be two different people, and it's pulling me apart."

"Serena," Xandra whispered, stepping closer. The warrior reached out to comfort her but was stopped by an agonizing scowl. "This is new territory for all of us, but we are here to support you through it."

Serena kicked the pile of weapons beside Xandra. The sudden clang of metal made the guardian jump. "I don't know how to accept this fate," Serena said, running her hands over her braided hair.

"You're young," Crystal said, patting her ward on the shoulder. "No one expects you to save the kingdom anytime soon. Stop worrying over it."

"*The man who stole his crown shall meet his fate when the true heir fights for their rightful throne*," Serena quoted, her tone laced with spite. "How could I not worry when such a fate is being forced upon me?" Cole clenched his jaw and raised his eyebrows at the other guardians.

"Your destiny is to fight, but it doesn't say you must fight alone," Crystal declared, squeezing the girl's arm.

She inhaled deeply, holding her breath for a moment before exhaling slowly. "You're right," she murmured. "Thanks."

"I think what you really need is a break," Xandra added, wrapping an arm around Serena's shoulders. "Luckily, the tournament begins today, so you'll have plenty of time to sit and rest."

"I still think she should have entered the competition. Would have made great practice," Cole said, not hiding the grin that made Serena's blood boil.

"So you could beat me in front of a crowd? No, thanks," the princess huffed.

Crystal exhaled, taking the training staff from Cole. "Much as I hate to agree with my brother, he's right." She paused to gather their arsenal from the ground and stuff each piece into a large tote.

"Seriously?" Serena huffed. She crossed her arms and glared at the guardians.

"Elara's told everyone you're the daughter of Sir Nathan Fritz. We're out here training daily. It would have made sense to test your progress against fresh blood," Crystal added.

"And what if I had beaten them?" Serena asked, narrowing her eyes. Her statement was ridiculous, of course, and Cole did nothing to stifle his laughter. They all knew she wouldn't defeat anyone who had spent a decade training at Envyre Academy. Not without Sannarvin in her hands.

As Cole had suspected, historians in Symptee were able to confirm that the Heir's Blade was imbued with divine magic, improving the strength and skills of its one true owner when they alone wielded it. That was why she had been able to kill the soldier in the mountains. She wasn't a super soldier, just the last in a bloodline blessed by Divinity. With Sannarvin in her hands, it was like pure magic radiated through her body, strengthening her muscles and washing away her hesitation. Without Sannarvin, she was just a girl with basic sword skills and a desperate desire to survive. That desire had gotten her this far, but it wouldn't help her defeat Antoine Rexton and his army.

Flexing her tired fingers, she examined her calloused hands. Scars and fresh cuts wove through the creases of her palm like an intricate spider web. She clenched her hands and muttered, "Thanks for the vote of confidence."

"Come on." Xandra tossed an arm around the girl's shoulders and turned her toward the citadel. "It's too early to be moping. Besides, we get a front row seat for the event of the year! It's going to be a great day."

Cole wiped his forehead with a towel and took a swig of water from his canteen. "Indeed, it is," he said with a grin. He was in a far better mood than usual, though that had no impact on his training methods. He took the bag of weapons from Crystal and followed them toward the citadel's entrance.

"You're just looking forward to fighting the new graduates," Xandra said, shaking her head.

His smile broadened as he swung an arm around her, quickly glancing around their surroundings before pecking her on the temple. "You're right about that, sunshine. It's a highlight every year."

Crystal and Serena rolled their eyes as they passed beneath a stone arch, the grassy exterior giving way to a smooth stone path. They navigated from the western entrance of the citadel through a labyrinth of halls until they reached the Guard's wing. Cole promptly saluted with two fingers and made his way into the men's quarters.

As per their morning ritual, Serena followed Crystal and Xandra through the ladies' quarters into a communal lavatory equipped with several large tubs. Three tubs filled with warmed water awaited them; the warm coals beneath the tubs sizzled softly.

Serena dipped her fingertips into the middle tub and smiled; the water was not yet cold. Glancing to the side, she noticed Crystal and Xandra were already busy shedding their sweaty practice clothes. She pulled her drenched layers off one by one and quickly climbed over the tub's ledge. The warm water sloshed as they each settled into their respective tubs with contented sighs.

Serena unbraided her hair, fluffing out her frizzy waves before leaning her head back against the edge of the tub. She inspected her pale skin through the clear water. Her hands weren't the only scarred parts of her body. Her arms and legs held an array of bruises ranging from deep purple to faded yellow. Training had taken its toll on her over the past few weeks, but she was determined not to slow down. Too much was at stake. Her eyes caught the faint white scar on her thigh. She stroked her thumb over it, remembering the men who attacked them outside of Noomï. The way one man's sword ripped through her flesh moments before she skewered another with her own blade to save Will's life.

Will. Her cheeks warmed as she closed her eyes and pictured his face. She hadn't seen his warm brown eyes in over a week; he had been working overtime at the forge to finish his apprenticeship. She knew he was lucky to be able to find a master in Symptee, but that did nothing to quell the ache she felt from his absence. She ached to see the dimpled smile that always set her heart racing. His arms were far warmer than the bathwater, and she yearned for him to hold her like he had in the mountains when her world had fallen apart.

"Do you think we'll see Will today?" Serena asked, her voice quiet but hopeful.

Xandra grinned at her, her messy bun bobbing as she shifted to sit up in the tub. "It's highly likely! The blacksmith is usually at the games working as weapons master, ensuring everyone has the appropriate tools. I'm sure he'll bring Will to help."

Serena nodded, picking up the bar of soap beside the tub and beginning to scrub herself. It had a mild floral scent. She hoped the guardians didn't notice the smile that she couldn't hold back. "And what of Rigel? I haven't seen him in a couple days either."

"Oh, he'll be there. Like my brother, he wouldn't miss this for anything," Crystal noted, working the soap between her hands until it lathered.

"I think Rige will also be mediating the tournament, making sure everyone follows the rules," Xandra said, rinsing the layer of soap bubbles from her skin. Serena noticed the way the guardian shivered a bit as she dipped lower in the water.

Turning her attention back to her own tub, Serena took a deep breath and plunged her head into the tub, scrubbing the soap from her hair while underwater. Elara expected her to smell like a spring garden when they met for tea, not that Serena cared for her fancy etiquette lessons. But if she was going to see Will today, that was different. For Will, she wanted to dress up, wanted him to see her as a young lady. So today, she planned to look her best.

Serena settled into her seat to Elara's right, surveying the arena before them. The sun burned bright in the sky above them, and she was thankful their chairs were set up under a massive gold canopy. To Serena's right sat Crystal, Xandra, Sir Alexander Stanton, and several other members of the War Council. To the queen's left sat her new husband, Gerard Stirling, and a dozen nobles. Elara had introduced Serena to enough new faces over the past few weeks to make her head spin.

Today she was grateful to have Crystal beside her to answer any questions about the tournament and keep her from being sucked into an excruciating conversation with her aunt. The guardian leaned toward her and whispered, "The sword is arguably the most important part of the tournament, which is why everyone turns up to watch."

Serena pressed her palms against her chiffon skirt. She leaned over in her chair to peer past the canopy in hopes of catching a glimpse of a certain young man. As her eyes scanned the bustling arena, bright red hair caught her attention, and she realized that Rigel was waving at them. She nudged Crystal with her elbow and pointed before waving back.

Elara cleared her throat, and Serena sank back in her seat, wide eyes cutting to her left. Jewel eyes that matched her own stared down from her raised seat, brows lifted slightly.

"If you must wave, just lift your hand like so," Elara instructed in a whisper. The queen plastered on a polite smile and lifted her right hand to face-level as two competitors stopped to bow before heading into the arena.

The princess snorted, adjusting her back to sit up straighter. "My apologies," she mumbled, turning her eyes back toward her friend. Cole had joined Rigel at the edge of the arena. They chatted enthusiastically as they watched the eight competitors warm up. Rigel looked well, considering he had nearly died six weeks prior. Thanks to Crystal and Ismenia, his arm seemed to have healed quite nicely on the outside—though he did complain of soreness when he overworked it. Serena smiled as she watched him rake a hand through his shaggy hair, her heart swelling with joy knowing they had all survived the harrowing journey together.

Xandra giggled, and Serena glanced over, noticing the way her eyes lit up as she watched Cole's every move. Xandra was so clearly in love she was practically glowing; it was almost sickening. Almost. Yet as Serena watched Crystal and Xandra laugh, she couldn't help but smile, too. Seeing her guardians—her friends—at ease after the intensity of the crossing made her happy, and she'd do anything to keep things the way they were.

"Oh! There's your blacksmith," Xandra declared, pointing to the far right of the field.

Serena's smile faltered, and she nearly fell out of her seat. Catching herself on the guard rail, she leaned her head over in search of him. There he was, standing beside a stocky man inspecting a competitor's blade. The man said something to Will before passing him the blade. Will balanced it on two fingers and nodded. As he turned back to face his master, Serena got a glimpse of the winning smile that made her day.

"Ahem," Elara said. Serena winced as she stepped back and turned to face her aunt. Elara exhaled loudly as she tapped her fingernails on the armrests of her chair. The sides of the massive wooden piece were carved with the Garrick family crest: a massive white oak with stars above it. Though this chair wasn't as grand as her throne within the citadel, it was still majestic, keeping the queen perched a few feet higher than the rest of her entourage. "Perhaps you should take your seat, my dear."

"Yes, Your Majesty," Serena said, hurrying back to her designated seat. She wished more than anything that she could fling herself over the guard rail and join the others out on the field. Anything would be better than having her every move scrutinized by Elara's judging gaze.

Horns resounded, and everyone turned their attention to the center of the arena. One of Elara's Commanders announced the start of the tournament, introducing the first two competitors as Heath Grange and Kieran Brooks. Serena narrowed her eyes, focusing on the young men. They were both dressed in cream tunics, loose pants, and boots. The first had brown curls that covered his neck while the other had jet-black hair slicked back out of his face.

"The one with the dark hair is Kieran. He's the son of the late Earl Valen Brooks of Axys, who died in the first rebellion. Kieran and his mother joined us many moons ago. I have no doubt he'll quickly rise to Captain in the Guard," Elara informed her.

Serena watched as Kieran twirled his sword around his knuckles. When his bright blue eyes met hers, she raised her brows as his mouth hitched in a broad grin. A face like that could be dangerous. She flushed, turning hastily to face Crystal.

"Don't be fooled by a charming face, Serena," the guardian whispered to her. "He may have grown up kissing the queen's rear, but he was not well loved in Envyre."

Xandra bit her lip, glancing sheepishly at them. "He may be elitist, but he was a damn good kisser back in our youth," she said with a shrug.

Serena gasped, and Crystal quickly covered her open mouth for her. "When the humans hit their teenage years, it felt like everyone was kissing *everyone*. It was terrible."

"Oh, hush," Xandra hissed, lightly slapping her friend's arm. "It's not that big of a deal. It was just a kiss."

"So how did Cole compare?" Serena asked, grinning at the way both guardians reacted.

Crystal moaned, covering her face. "I do not want to hear this. Can we just watch the competition?"

Serena snickered at the guardian's clear discomfort. Xandra winked, leaning in closer to whisper, "Cole did not have to kiss a dozen frogs to know what he was doing. It's just another thing he's naturally talented at."

Crystal gagged, wrinkling her nose as she shoved Xandra out of her personal space. Serena laughed at their antics. Crystal loved them both and supported their relationship, but Serena could understand why the archer did not want to hear the details. She wouldn't have wanted to know who her brother was involved with either.

Her thoughts drifted to Cameron, and she clenched her hands in her lap. His face often came to her in dreams, sometimes playing in the woods and others, scowling at her in the mountains. Though her friends always reminded her that she had killed him in self-defense, the burden was still there, simmering beneath the surface along with her rage toward Rexton.

Serena shook her head, eager to shake his face from the forefront of her memory. The fight was in progress. The two young men charged at each other; each sought the other's weakness. As she watched them circle each other in a lethal dance, the clash of metal ringing in her ears, she wondered how they could put aside their camaraderie and face each other as enemies competing for the same prize. That was something she still struggled with while practicing with the guardians. She didn't want to hurt anyone. She never had. And after everything she'd been through, everyone she'd hurt with her own two hands, it still didn't feel natural to wield a weapon against anyone, especially a friend.

It wasn't long before she realized these men were built differently from her. Like Cole, there was a cold determination in their eyes, a complete lack of empathy for their opponent. They rushed at each other, arms swinging swiftly with reckless abandon. Neither blinked when their opponent's blade came dangerously close to their extremities. They reveled in the danger, spurred on by the crowd's cheers. The one with the long curls, Heath, barely winced as Kieran's blade cut through his shirt sleeve; Kieran's blue eyes darkened as he watched blood trickle from Heath's forearm to the ground. There was something beautiful about the ruthless glint in his eyes; Serena couldn't help but stare at him. She wished she could feel that kind of confidence when she fought.

"He's gotten much better over the past year," Crystal said, her voice tinged with surprise. "Perhaps third time's the charm."

Serena peeled her eyes off the fight, convinced Kieran was close to clinching his victory. "Did he compete last year?"

"Yes. He graduated with us," Xandra noted. "But Rigel knocked him out of the competition. He was not pleased about that."

"Kieran's always thought too highly of himself. Noble blood and all that," Crystal said, wrinkling her nose. "Instead of taking a position as a guard for the outer ring, he went back to Envyre to train harder."

"So did Rigel win the tournament last year?" Serena asked.

The guardians chuckled to themselves, exchanging glances. "He did. The year prior, that honor went to Crystal, who smoked all of us in archery and bested Rigel in the final duel."

"Really? I don't know if I've ever seen you fight with a sword," Serena said.

"Then we will have to change that," Crystal replied, her lips curled into a smug grin.

Xandra leaned over her friend, whispering low, "If you think she's a force with her bow, just wait until you see her with a blade. She's just as powerful as her brother."

"I still prefer the bow above all," the elf noted, her irises bobbing as she followed the match.

Serena glanced back at the arena just as Kieran sliced through Heath's shin. The bystanders winced as the young man went down on his knees. She held her breath as Kieran stepped toward his opponent, flourishing his weapon around his knuckles. His gaze shifted to the tent behind Heath, and she thought he winked at her. Or perhaps he was winking at her friends. They knew him from the Academy. Kieran placed the edge of his blade on Heath's shoulder, and Serena sucked in a breath. It looked as if he was preparing to behead his fallen comrade. She gripped the armrests of her chair, her knuckles turning stark white as the arena melted away, replaced by memories of Cameron and Rigel in the mountains flashing through her mind.

Elara leaned over and pressed a hand on top of Serena's, startling her out of the dark memory. When she met her aunt's eyes, there was something comforting in them, something that made her offer the queen a small smile of reassurance. She had been hard on her aunt when they first arrived. Hard on everyone, even herself. She didn't know who she was or where she was supposed to fit in anymore, yet as her anger slowed to a simmer, she realized she couldn't blame Elara or the guardians for that. It was all Rexton's fault. Every painful memory, every agonizing loss, the trail of blood was smeared across the canvas with his own fingers. Painting his masterpiece with the blood of the innocent.

The queen gave her hand another squeeze before shifting to sit upright, turning her eyes back to the competition. Just as Elara moved away from Serena, something flew across her line of vision, embedding in the queen's chair right between their heads, where Elara had leaned over only seconds ago. Serena blinked at the arrow lodged between them. People around them started shouting. Before she could think, Crystal yanked Serena out of her seat by the arm, forcing her to the ground and using her own body as a shield. The girl looked around, realizing Gerard Stirling had done the same to his wife, much to her horror.

"Form a shield wall around Her Majesty," Commander Stanton's voice boomed from nearby.

"Stay down," Crystal muttered, patting Serena on the shoulder as she rolled off her. Guards swarmed the queen's stand as bystanders ran screaming from the arena. Crystal stood, quickly informing Commander Stanton that she had seen the arrow come from one of the third-floor windows of the citadel. Serena rolled onto her side and stared at the arrow that protruded from her aunt's seat. Two inches over, and it could have killed either of them. She shivered; her throat went dry as she breathed heavily. For the first time since they arrived in Symptee, Serena realized that perhaps even the citadel was not fortified enough to keep Rexton from hunting down the last of the Garrick bloodline.

2

TRAPPED

Talitha sat in the corner of her cell farthest from the door, watching as the last rays of sun coming through the window lessened with each second. Her right ankle ached from the heavy shackle chaining her to the wall. She couldn't go anywhere, couldn't move to the other side of the dungeon and bask in what little sunlight there was. It had been 43 days, give or take, since she last felt the sun on her skin, and she had accepted that the next time would surely be for her execution—if she did not succumb to starvation first.

There was chatter down the dungeon corridor, and she knew the maids who brought the pathetic excuse for their daily provisions had arrived. They always stopped to flirt with the guards at the entrance, not giving a second thought to the starving mouths awaiting in each cell. It must have been nice to have the freedom to come and go as they pleased. She would have given her left foot for the chance. Being the king's servant had to be better than rotting in his dungeon.

As the slow patter of footsteps approached, Talitha sat up straight, her back resting against the stone wall. Her wounds had healed enough that every movement no longer sent a sharp burn through her. The physician had visited twice, first immediately after her whipping and then a week later to clean and rewrap the injury.

The maids and the guard made their way down the hall, stopping to unlock each door and place a small tray on the ground inside. The locks clicked loudly, the echo a solemn reminder that none of them would be leaving Graynor alive and well. Footsteps drew closer, and Talitha stared at the door to her cell. The gray wood was studded with black metal that had begun to rust. She prayed that it was the blonde maid's turn to deliver the measly crust of stale bread and cup of water that barely sustained her life. The young woman had twice snuck her a piece of fruit or cheese in her apron pocket. It was something a prisoner certainly couldn't count on. But that small gesture had given her a tiny morsel of hope. That hope made her salivate.

The footsteps paused in front of her door. The guard and the maid whispered softly. Talitha couldn't make out what they were saying. They were probably whispering sweet nothings while the other guards couldn't hear them. Not that it mattered to Talitha. All that mattered right now was gorging herself on whatever she could get her hands on.

The mechanism grated roughly as the guard turned the key in the lock. The unpleasant sound of metal scraping metal made her wince. The guard pushed open the door and said to the maid in a dangerously low voice, "Three minutes." Talitha narrowed her eyes at them. The maid wore a cloak with the hood up, her face concealed by shadows. She knew the guard's face. He was Emmaline's brother. She wondered if Emmaline had any idea who she was and where she actually lived.

The guard closed the door behind the maid, leaving the two of them alone. That's when Talitha realized something was off. She pulled her legs up to her torso. The woman walked toward her hesitantly. Her black cloak swept the floor, sending puffs of dust into the air. When she was close enough, the maid bent down and placed the tray on the ground in front of Talitha. But the prisoner suddenly wasn't interested in her pathetic dinner. Not when a ring with a shimmering ruby had caught her eye.

"Sabine?" she asked, squinting at the hooded figure. Her eyes shimmered with hope and confusion.

The woman lifted her hood and dropped it back. "In the flesh," Sabine whispered, giving her a wink.

Talitha stared, uncertain whether this secret visit was a good thing. The last time Sabine sucked her into one of her foolproof plans, it nearly got her killed. "What are you doing here?" Talitha asked, her voice laced with fear.

"I've come to see you, obviously," the princess replied, kneeling in front of her. Talitha's eyes widened as Sabine looked her over. "I haven't much time. How are your… injuries?" She reached for Talitha's shoulder, but the prisoner quickly lurched out of her grasp.

"They're healing, no thanks to you," she snapped. Talitha snatched the dry bread from the tray and ripped a hunk off with her teeth. Her stomach gurgled loudly as she chewed. The texture of the bread was as unsavory as the sound of her chewing it. Talitha recognized the sympathy in the princess's eyes and turned away. She didn't want her pity. She wanted to die.

She heard a rustling but refused to look at Sabine. As she had said, time was limited. Soon the princess would leave, and she would go back to being alone in the dark.

Then, a red apple appeared in front of her face.

"I'm so sorry for what happened. I never meant for you to be punished," Sabine said quietly. Her outstretched hand didn't waver as she waited for Talitha to take it.

After staring at it for a moment, she reluctantly took it. Hungry as she was, she did not scarf it down. Talitha held it in her grimy fingers and stared. The shiny, red surface brought back a flood of memories—moments with Anteros she wished she could forget. All the moments he had brought her food to build trust had been for nothing. In the end, she should have known she could not trust him. All men ever did was hurt her. In truth, the whipping had not hurt her spirit as much as losing his companionship. For weeks, she thought the sound of footsteps in the corridor would be Anteros coming to see her. To apologize. To feed her. To set her free. But he had abandoned her.

She often wondered if he even felt remorse for what he had done to her. Knowing who his father was, she had her doubts. After all, the apple rarely falls far from the tree.

With no one to talk to and no hope in sight, Talitha couldn't help allowing the darkness to take root in her mind. She felt worthless. No one was looking for her. No one cared where she was. No one cared that she was starving. No one would care when she finally succumbed. Death would be a sweet release from this pitiful existence.

The back of her eyes burned, and Talitha clamped them closed. Sabine exhaled and gently touched her arm. "He never wanted to hurt you," Sabine whispered. "Nor did I." Her voice broke toward the end, and Talitha turned to find tears slipping down the princess's cheeks. The princess reached into her pocket and pulled out its contents. She separated a folded piece of parchment from her handkerchief and held it out to Talitha.

"What's this for?" The parchment was rough against her agonizingly dry fingers as she unfolded it. Her eyes widened when a page covered in thick black ink came into view. All over the parchment were the words *I'm sorry*. Her chest ached as she read the words over and over. She didn't know the handwriting, but she did not need to. She knew who must have written it. "When did he—" Her words caught in her throat, and she sniffled.

"The night it happened... He was devastated," Sabine whispered. She clasped Talitha's hands around the apple. "You need to know... He did it to save you. And he hasn't been the same since."

There was a smear of dry blood on the corner of the parchment. Was it his? She didn't dare ask. "Why tell me now?" Talitha whispered back, staring down at their hands.

"We've been under close watch," Sabine murmured. "This was the soonest I dared try."

The guard knocked twice before pushing open the door, and they both whipped their heads around to look at him. "Time's up, milady," he said with a nod.

Sabine pat Talitha's hand twice before rising. She stared down at the girl whose life she had made far more difficult; her eyes were an infinite sea of melancholy. "I really am sorry, Talitha," she said before lifting her hood and exiting the cell.

The lock clicked loudly, and Talitha remained fixed in place, listening to the echo of footsteps retreating until she settled back into the eerie silence. She wished more than anything that they could have taken her with them.

Anteros clasped his hands behind his back as he walked down the hall by his father's side. The prince stared straight ahead as Antoine debriefed him on the convoy from Denorfia's arrival. They were expected to bring nearly a hundred cattle in anticipation of trade negotiations.

"Since disease wiped out half of our cattle, we have never needed a trade deal more," Antoine said. His face was stoic, unworried as they crossed under an archway into the sun. They traversed the stone pathway, heading toward a line of ornate carriages parked just within the main portcullis. "Be at your best, son, or you'll be eating nothing but soup this winter."

"I like steak far too much to ruin this for us, Father," Anteros replied, catching his father's reproachful glance.

Antoine paused and reached out to adjust the lapels on his son's navy jacket. "This visit is about more than mere cattle," the king said, his voice deep and low. "With Solaire's blessing, this could be the start of a key partnership with Denorfia. An arrangement that could help us eliminate those damned loyalists for good."

The prince lowered his gaze as his father released him. It wasn't the first time his father had mentioned forming an alliance with their northern neighbors. It wouldn't be the first time negotiations ended with Antoine fuming. That wasn't something he looked forward to seeing happen again. "May Solaire bless your endeavors with His favor," Anteros said, bowing his head briefly.

The king's mouth quirked up in approval as they approached a group near the carriages. Among the foreigners were a few of Antoine's high-ranked officials and some lower-level guards. The men greeted the convoy, helping remove luggage from the carriages.

"Gentlemen," Antoine boomed as they reached the visitors, "welcome to the great court of Graynor, home of the sovereign of Hyrosencia. I trust your journey was a pleasant one."

He reached out a hand to the closest of the men, a younger man with piercing eyes and short brown curls that had been bronzed by the sun. "Your Majesty, 'tis an honor to meet you at long last," the man said, taking Antoine's hand and returning a firm shake. "Ryker Umbryon, the Earl of Briar."

Anteros straightened, narrowing his eyes at the man whose full focus was on his father. Ryker Umbryon. He was young—younger than most envoys sent to negotiate with his father. His age likely fell between that of the king and his son. He had a short, neatly trimmed beard and a twinkle in his eyes, an expectation that this meeting could elevate him further.

The king turned and clapped Anteros on the shoulder. "Ryker, this is my son, Anteros."

The prince nodded his head and held out his hand. Their visitor shook it, while Antoine moved on to greet the other men who had traveled with him. "Your Highness," the earl said, nodding his head curtly. "We did not expect such a warm welcome."

A harsh breeze ruffled their hair and clothes, and Anteros drew his arm back to smooth his hair back from his eyes. "Well, my lord, we are nothing if not warm," the prince said with a smirk.

An easy smile made its way onto Ryker's face, and he turned his gaze upon the magnificent castle towering behind Anteros. "And are the women quite as welcoming in your court?"

Anteros cocked his head to the side, looking over the earl's pristine attire, black with gold threading interwoven along the hems. He certainly presented himself like a royal, though the earl would never sit upon any throne. "If they think you'll marry them," the prince replied.

"As fate would have it, I am in want of a new wife," Ryker said casually. He leaned closer, lowering his voice to add, "The last two did not keep for long." He winked, and Anteros's smile faltered, surprised by the man's candor.

The king's boisterous laughter drew their attention, and they turned to face him. "And here I am with the opposite predicament." Anteros winced at his father's words. He knew his father did not care for his mother, but it was brutal to hear him admit such a thing to strangers.

"Perhaps I shall have better luck looking among the women of Graynor then," the earl quipped. "I should give anything to sire an heir."

"You have yet to be blessed with a son?" the king asked, his tone indifferent. But there was something in the way his dark eyes cut toward Anteros. The wheels in the king's head were clearly turning at this piece of information, and his son did not like the chill that sent through his spine.

"Sadly, not, Your Majesty," Ryker said. His eyes drifted back to the castle, dancing between windows as though he were looking for someone. "Perhaps one day I shall be as blessed as you."

"Perhaps." Antoine grunted, patting Anteros on his cheek roughly. Then he clapped his hands together; the sound boomed across the stone path and reverberated off the brick wall that safeguarded Graynor. "Come, gentlemen. Join me for a drink. I wish to hear all about old Boreas and why he has refused yet another invitation."

"You waste no time getting down to business," the earl noted. His smile told Anteros that he was unsurprised, or rather impressed. "His Majesty sends his deepest regrets. He was quite uninterested in leaving his court for an extended time so soon after a long, grueling journey."

Antoine tensed, every muscle in his body tightening. Anteros saw the shift in his father, the way his pupils dilated, and his hands contracted into heavy fists. For a moment, the prince wondered if Antoine would dare lash out a foreign dignitary.

But Antoine released his tension with a heavy exhale. He cracked his knuckles—one, two, three—before replying, "That must have been quite the long journey for him. I hope Elara made the voyage worthwhile." He attempted an easy smile, but Anteros could still see the vein that stuck out on the side of his neck.

"I do not envy him for it," Ryker replied. He spoke with ease, seemingly unaware of how the guards unloading the carriage had slowed their pace. Everyone in the quad had tensed. "Boreas returned in a rather foul mood. He would have preferred Elara to marry another Denorfian, of course. He had proposed an arrangement, but she was quite set on her Islander."

Antoine scoffed. "She would have been wise to choose a Denorfian—but women are not known for their wisdom, especially not women who were never meant to wear a crown."

"I agree," Ryker said quickly. "Fortunately for us, her foolishness opened the door for this negotiation. In the field outside of the gates, my men guard my finest heifers and sheep—enough to feed and warm your entire court all winter."

"Magnificent," Antoine said, clutching the man's shoulder. "Come. You must be famished." He stepped forward, leading Ryker toward the castle's entrance.

The prince paused, taking in the kaleidoscope of fading colors on the horizon. The last of the sun bid him farewell, the pale orange sky causing a pang in his chest. He tried not to think of her, the girl in the dungeon he had foolishly come to care for. It had done neither of them any good. As he turned toward the castle and set off after his father and the Denorfian party, Anteros couldn't help his gaze wandering to the base of the castle. A row of small, barred windows lined the lower level of the castle, more for air flow than light. In one of those rooms sat Talitha Vise, watching as the light dimmed to nothing. Another day ending in an abyss of darkness, just as his every day began and ended.

He shook the vibrant flashes of red hair from his mind and quickened his pace. Catching up to his father and the earl, Anteros said, "If you think our lands are beautiful, just wait until you've tried the food. It's to die for."

3

CONSOLATION

The day after the tournament ended in disaster, Serena couldn't help but feel relief at the sight of her aunt in her usual chair, waiting to have morning tea. Elara peered up from the letter in her hands and a smile bloomed across her face. "Serena, it's good to see you. Did you sleep well?"

The girl shrugged. "As well as I could." She didn't have the heart to tell the queen that she had barely slept at all. When she finally drifted off, Serena dreamed of that arrow going through her aunt's head. The memory of that gruesome nightmare made her stomach churn.

Crystal and Xandra had spent the night camped out on Serena's bedroom floor, taking turns at watch to ensure the princess remained safe. By morning, the guardians could tell she had not slept well, so they changed her early lesson to archery instead of swordplay. Serena hadn't understood why she needed to learn archery—it wasn't like she planned to carry a bow like her guardian—but she was thankful for the less strenuous lesson when it ended.

Elara nodded and watched as Serena approached. Letting the letter flutter to the table, the queen stood abruptly to greet her niece. "I must apologize," Elara began. She paused and pressed her pink lips together.

Serena stopped in front of the table. Her brows furrowed as she stared at her aunt. "Why?" she asked quietly.

The queen sighed. "For years, our people were told that the citadel was safe. That Symptee was guarded. But within the past year, there have been multiple incidents. Acts with the intention of taking my life. Now I fear you are being targeted, as well."

Serena inhaled shakily; her heartbeat hammered in her chest. After all that she had been through, the citadel wasn't safe. No place could offer her the shelter and comfort of her old life. She ground her teeth, holding back the bitterness she felt. It wasn't Elara's fault—that she knew. They were both targets of Antoine Rexton. Their people had placed a crown and the heavy responsibility of saving them upon Elara's head when she was barely a woman. A young woman who had just lost her entire family and the only home she had ever known. The more Serena thought about it, the more she realized she had in common with her aunt. "You cannot blame yourself for the wrongs committed by Rexton. You're doing your best. We all are." She stepped toward her aunt and reached out to grab her hands.

Elara gasped, and it was like a dam broke forth. All the guilt she had been holding onto flooded out of her in shuddering sobs. The sound reminded Serena of Mary's wails the night that Cameron had left home. The reminder broke her heart over again. She reached around Elara's trembling frame and rested her hands on the queen's back, pulling her into a comforting embrace. The motion almost felt foreign—it had been so long since she had hugged anyone other than Will. But standing in the sitting room in their matching embroidered gowns, Serena felt closer than she ever had to her aunt. And she pitied the woman for the years of stress she had endured.

Serena stroked Elara's thick curls and patted her back gently. She was no stranger to these feelings. The overwhelming power of survivor's guilt. The chokehold that a dead body can have over a living one. The way longing for the life you had lost could make you feel so cold, so haunted by the people and places you had lost. Fighting the tension in her body, Serena cleared her throat and swallowed. "We're both alright," she tried to reassure Elara. Perhaps she was trying to reassure herself. Her eyes stung, but no tears fell. She had shed a lifetime's worth already.

When the queen finally grew still and quiet, she withdrew from the girl's embrace and wiped her hands over her damp face. "I am terribly sorry about this," Elara murmured. Her cheeks were flushed crimson. Serena wasn't sure if it was from the crying or embarrassment.

"You do not owe me an apology." Serena offered her aunt a gentle smile before taking her usual seat at the table. Turning her attention toward the table, Serena lit up when she realized what had been prepared. Her favorite delicacy since they had begun taking daily meals and tea together: petite vanilla cakes with sweet icing.

Elara sniffled loudly. "Divinity on high," she muttered in irritation. She swiped a monogrammed handkerchief off the table beside her floral-patterned teacup and dabbed at her face as she settled back into her chair. "Oh, please help yourself, Serena. I fear I have taken up too much of our time with tears today."

She didn't have to repeat herself. Serena swiped one of the bite-size pieces of cake off the tray and brought it straight to her mouth before Elara could finish her sentence. The queen watched her savor the first bite; Serena closed her eyes and sighed, wishing her mother was there to enjoy such a delicacy. "Mama would have loved this," she whispered. "If not the sweets, then at least the tea and the company."

The queen's hands tightened around her handkerchief. Serena noticed the way she tensed up anytime she mentioned her mother. Her adopted mother. She still didn't grasp the relationship that Mary and Elara had, how Elara was so deeply affected by the loss, but today she felt oddly grateful that someone else missed Mary Finch as much as she did.

"I am so relieved that you're here, dear girl," Elara barely managed to say. "I—I don't know what I would have done if—"

"Do not think it," Serena interrupted. She met her aunt's twin gaze and held it. After a moment of silence, the girl plucked a second piece of cake from the tray. She held it between two fingers over her place setting, staring down at the way her fingertips sank into the smooth white icing and fluffy sponge. Though she had been angry with Elara for keeping secrets, Serena found training to be cathartic. She fought through her rage, ever thankful that the guardians constantly redirected her hatred toward the man responsible for all their pain.

Through quiet morning teas, she found herself slowly opening her heart to her aunt. Serena needed someone to support her the way her mother, Mary, once had. And now she was old enough to offer that same support back. "I'm thankful you are still here, Aunt Elara." Her voice was higher than a whisper, yet still quiet, almost hesitant. As if it were hard for her to admit that stray arrow had unlocked a new fear. The fear of losing the last of her living kin and truly being the last Garrick.

While she didn't ever want the burden of the crown to fall on her own head, Serena felt a small comfort in knowing neither of them fought against Rexton alone anymore. Perhaps together, they might finally find an advantage against him. Perhaps together, they could make Hyrosencia their home once again.

The guardians settled onto the couches in the Guards' lounge after their afternoon training session was cut short by a rainstorm. Cole argued they could push the couches aside and make enough space for indoor training. Serena moaned, sprawling out on the rug in exhaustion.

"She's had enough training for one day," Xandra argued, scooching closer to him on the couch. She planted a quick kiss on his cheek, laughing at the way Crystal wrinkled her nose. But it was Cole's reaction that caught her attention. As two guards entered the doorway, he removed his arm from around her shoulders. He had been like that since they made it to Symptee—always quick to put distance between them around anyone he did not know. Six weeks at home, and even her father still wasn't aware of their relationship. Whatever their relationship was.

"Let her rest. We've had a productive week," Crystal agreed, settling on one edge of a chaise lounge. It was burgundy and quite faded, as though many tired men and women had used it to rest over the years.

Xandra pushed herself off the couch, lowering herself to the floor with her back against it instead. Serena's head was near her. The guardian reached over and started running her fingers through the girl's tangled tresses. It was something her mother had done back when she was a little girl. Now she found comfort in running her fingers through someone else's hair. "You must be excited," Xandra said to Serena.

The girl tilted her head slightly, glanced at the guardian upside down, and asked, "About what?"

The guardian chuckled. "About the Guards' Ball, of course. It will be your first ball, won't it?" Xandra sighed, remembering the ball the prior year. She had worn a beautiful orange gown that reminded her of bonfires in Envyre. She spent the entire night hoping Cole would notice her. He was the only man who didn't show her any attention whatsoever. He did, however, accept Elara's offer to join his sister's unit for their mission. That was the most unexpected part of an otherwise sparkling evening.

Serena propped herself up on an elbow. She kept her eyes down, tracing her fingers on the intricate patterns of the long-faded damask rug. "Well, yes, but... I'm more nervous than anything. Elara has commissioned this *elaborate* gown, and I don't know how I could possibly dance in it. I don't even know *how* to dance. Not like a noble."

Xandra reached for her hand and gave it a squeeze. "Oh, don't worry about *that*. Dancing is the fun part. We can teach you."

"When?" the girl asked. She turned her gaze up, her brows knitted in confusion. Xandra felt a pang of sympathy for the poor girl. She hardly got to have fun anymore. "We train twice a day. There's hardly a spare moment." The guardian cocked her head to one side. She was determined to find a way to help the lost princess enjoy her first ball.

"You have time now," Crystal noted. "Don't waste it."

Xandra glanced at her friend. They grinned at each other, hopping up from their seats. Each taking one of Serena's hands, they dragged her onto her feet. A ghost of a smile crossed her features as Xandra took one of her hands and placed it on her own shoulder. "I'll be the gentleman for this lesson," she said, winking. Serena giggled as Xandra noted that the man always takes the lead. As Crystal started humming, Xandra stepped forward.

"You're the prettiest man I have ever seen," Cole said. He shook his head. His casual grin sent her heart fluttering. Xandra wished he showed off that flirtatious smile more often.

They had hardly begun when two men shuffled into the room. A familiar voice declared, "I wager we should be offended by that."

Serena broke away from Xandra and exclaimed, "Rigel!" But when she whirred around and realized Will was with him, she froze. Serena hadn't seen him since the tournament. Hadn't spoken to him in even longer. Xandra held back her smile as she watched them slowly approach each other. A broad smile spread across their faces, and Will's dimples appeared. He lifted one arm and rubbed the back of his neck. He looked nervous.

"Hi," they said in tandem.

Ever since they reached Symptee, things had shifted between them. Xandra and Crystal had both noticed, talking about it in the privacy of their chambers. While Crystal did not care to entangle herself in anyone's romantic endeavors, Xandra couldn't help giving a little nudge where it was needed. These two were stubborn, but you'd have to be blind not to notice the way they looked at each other.

"Will! It's good to see you," Xandra said. The guardian stepped up to Serena's side and nudged her with an elbow. "We were just discussing the Guards' Ball. You'll be attending, won't you?"

He balked, clearly put on the spot. "I hadn't planned to. I thought it was just for the Guard." He glanced from Xandra to Serena and quickly back. She shook her head.

"Of course not! The entire citadel will be there," Rigel said, squeezing Will's shoulders from behind. "You must join us!"

"Must he?" Crystal asked, sitting back on her chaise with her brows raised.

Rigel made a sour expression and jogged in her direction. "Yes, he must. He's one of us now." Without asking, Rigel plopped down beside her. It was a tight squeeze for two, and he tossed an arm around Crystal's shoulders. "Admit it. It's nice having us all together again." She promptly shrugged his arm off and shoved him back. With nowhere to go, Rigel slid right off the end of the chaise, landing hard on the floor.

Everyone snickered. It was nice to see that Crystal and Rigel hadn't changed a bit, even after they had nearly lost him on their mission. Rigel's arm was healing nicely, and he had started training with Will to build his strength back up. Xandra smiled as she surveyed the room. It felt right having everyone back together after weeks of adjusting to their new normal. No more sleeping under the stars together, fighting enemy soldiers, and running for their lives from monsters in the mountains. Now they were safe. Free to work, train, and hang out in the lounge at their leisure.

"Is it just me, or were you two dancing when we walked in?" Rigel asked. He motioned with two fingers to Xandra and Serena. The latter blushed furiously, looking down at the rug in horror.

"Yes. I was trying to teach her before you interrupted us. This will be Serena's first ball. Her first formal event at the citadel," Xandra replied. "She wanted to learn how to dance."

Rigel groaned as he pushed himself off the floor. Brushing his hands off on the middle of his shirt, he stepped up to Serena and offered a hand. "I think I can help with that. May I?"

She glanced at Xandra as if looking for approval. When the guardian nodded, Serena placed her hand in his. She allowed him to place her hands the way Xandra had. As he lifted one of her hands in his, Xandra stepped back and noticed the way Will was watching them like a hawk. The warmth was gone from his eyes. His fists clenched at his sides as he turned away from them. Before he could retreat, Xandra cut him off. "And what about you, Will? Do you know how to dance?"

His eyes widened. "Not like that," he said, nodding toward Rigel and Serena. They moved about the open space in slow motion, counting out loud as Serena learned the steps.

"Then it's time to learn," Xandra said, holding out a hand to the sweaty blacksmith.

He was going to have to learn if he wanted to dance with Serena at the ball. Xandra grinned. She couldn't wait to watch these two willful kids stumble through their first dance. That just might be the highlight of this year's ball—besides finally getting to dance with Cole.

Twenty minutes later, their students were faring rather well. Xandra winked at Rigel and suggested, "Perhaps we should switch partners?"

Rigel grinned as he spun Serena once, letting go of her mid-spin. At the same moment, Xandra turned Will, and he collided into Serena. They grabbed hold of the other's arms to steady themselves. "I got you," he said softly. His dimples were on full display, and stars shimmered in Serena's emerald irises. It took all of Xandra's willpower to restrain herself from screeching in excitement.

As they bumbled through repositioning themselves, Xandra whipped around to face Cole. His eyes were locked on her, calm and calculating. He pushed himself off the couch and wrapped an arm around her waist, leaning closer to whisper, "You're a good teacher."

"That makes two of us," Xandra replied. His sapphire eyes bobbed between her expectant gaze and her lips. Taking that as her cue, Xandra pushed up on her toes to press her lips to his. Cole kissed her, but briefly, cautiously. When they parted, his eyes flicked toward the doorway.

"Get a room," Crystal grumbled. A messenger came through the door and made a beeline for her. Cole quickly released Xandra and stepped back. Crystal took three envelopes from the tray the messenger presented and thanked him. Then he disappeared just as quickly as he had come in.

"What do you think? Should we get a room?" Xandra asked coyly. Cole merely hummed in reply. She wished he'd take the initiative—sweep her off her feet and carry her to one of their rooms. Since their return, he had kept her at arm's length around others. He only seemed comfortable showing unrestricted affection around Crystal, Rigel, and Serena, and even then, it was rare. He avoided being alone with her. It was starting to make her feel undesirable. Like their fleeting moment at the hot springs was a flame doomed to die out.

Now Cole's focus was on the letters in Crystal's hands. She read the first and held it out for Rigel. While he skimmed over it, she used her dagger to cut open a sealed letter. Even from a few feet away, they could place the seal. Embedded in the deep green wax was a leaf with vines. The Windaef family seal.

"It seems Daephyra is looking for an update," Crystal said, worrying her bottom lip. "In person." Cole walked over to his sister and snatched the paper, skimming it quickly.

Serena and Will stopped dancing. The girl stepped beside Xandra. She had tensed at the sight of the letter.

Rigel huffed. "That old goat. Send her a letter saying you've saved a girl, and everyone survived. What more could she need to know?"

"Everything," Cole breathed. "When we came here, we agreed to keep her updated on the war. We've been away for over a year. Of course, she expects information." He exhaled, rereading the letter to himself.

"Well, we cannot just leave Serena. She needs us. There are spies in the citadel, and she needs to continue training," Crystal argued. She pushed off her seat and started pacing the open space between the entryway and the sitting area. "We made a vow to Elara."

"*You* made a vow to Elara. I only agreed to go on the rescue mission. Now that our mission is complete, they expect me to return home," Cole said abruptly.

Xandra felt as though her heart might shatter right there. He intended to return home. How could he after everything they had been through? She inhaled sharply; her amber eyes bore into him, willing him to look at her. To answer her unsaid questions. He didn't dare return her gaze.

"We've just returned. You're not planning to leave us so soon, are you?" Crystal crossed her arms, crumpling the last unopened letter in her fist. "You're the best with a sword. You must be the one to train her."

"Why must she continue training anyway?" Will interjected.

Everyone froze, their eyes slightly widened as they glanced between each other. Finally, Crystal closed her eyes and said, "As the daughter of a known loyalist—a knight no less—Rexton will never stop hunting her. That's why Elara insisted she continue training. Even the citadel has imperfections. We all saw that at the tournament."

Serena swallowed loudly. Xandra reached over and squeezed her hand. Serena squeezed back feebly before muttering, "I should head upstairs. Clean up before dinner."

No one moved to stop her, though Crystal huffed, "You cannot walk around the citadel by yourself." She moved toward the door as if she were going to escort Serena.

Will also stepped toward the doorway. "I should take my leave as well. I can escort her to her room if you'd like."

"Thanks, Will. We'll see you at dinner," Rigel said. Crystal growled under her breath but did not argue. Will wore a sword at his hip like the others, and they all knew he would protect Serena with his life, if it came to that. With the guardians' blessing, Serena and Will scurried through the doorway, leaving the four guardians alone.

"We have to be careful around him," Crystal said, rubbing her hands over her face. When she withdrew her hands, the bags under her eyes looked heavier. Her lips turned down in a scowl.

Xandra approached her friend. "We've both lost sleep with all the extra night watches. You should rest before dinner."

Her friend shook her head. "Someone needs to get up to Serena's room. Elara doesn't want her left alone, remember? And Will *isn't* a guard."

"I'll go. You rest. Then you can take the first watch tonight," Xandra reasoned.

Crystal reluctantly nodded. "All right. But this conversation is not over," she tossed back at her brother. With a quick wave of her hand, she headed for the doorway.

"It's over for me," Cole barked. He sat back on the couch and ran his hands over his face. Moving them up, he pushed his fingers through his locks. They brushed the top of his shoulders now. Xandra went over to sit beside him.

"I'll see you both at dinner," Rigel called on his way out.

Finally alone, Xandra turned toward Cole. She anticipated some kind of explanation, reassurance that he would go and come back. But he sat quietly, mulling over his father's letter without a word. "Will you always choose Daephyra over me?"

Cole inhaled sharply through his nose. "This isn't about us, Xan. It's about duty. And my duty is to appear when my queen summons me." He reached for her hands in her lap.

She looked over at him and struggled to decipher what he was thinking. Whether he was being honest with her and with himself. "And what if Daephyra asked you to stay in Montaris? Or return to Envyre?"

Cole tensed, breaking their eye contact. "She's the queen, Xan. It's not that simple."

Xandra shook her head. She understood him well enough to know that he was all duty and obligation, especially to Daephyra, High Queen of the Silveryl Elves. No woman, no human, would ever exceed his dedication to his sovereign. She felt like a fool for ever expecting him to choose her over his own kind. "When will you leave?"

"I'll need to meet with Elara first. Prepare supplies. Perhaps the day after tomorrow. I'll catch a ship heading to the port," he said.

She stood abruptly, ready to put distance between them. There was only so much she could give, only so long she could wait. If he wasn't committed to spending his life with her, then it was best Cole leave and not return to Symptee. Her chest constricted at the thought of never seeing him again, and she started toward the door.

"Xan, wait!" Cole hurried to grab her arm, whipping her around to face him. Her cheeks burned as he stared at her. Tears welled in her eyes, but she didn't try to brush them away. She wanted him to know he was hurting her. "Hey. Don't cry, sunshine. This is not goodbye. I will see you again. I promise."

"Why don't you want people to know about us?" she finally dared to ask. Her voice was a fractured whisper, her emotions seeping through the cracks. "Are you ashamed of me?"

He closed his eyes for a long pause. Too long. "Of course not," Cole said, reaching out to cup her face in his hands. "You know the way humans feel about our presence. I do not want you to be ostracized by your own people."

Tears slipped down her cheeks, and she looked down, too overwhelmed to meet his gaze. "I don't care what anyone else thinks. I only care what you think," she murmured.

He placed a kiss on her forehead and wrapped his arms tightly around her. His back was to the doorway, and for once, he didn't seem to care who might see them. "I have to go, but I promise it's not forever."

"Easy for you to say. You have much more life left than I do," she reminded him. The words were bitter on her tongue. They slipped from her lips like her dreams of waltzing with Cole at the Guards' Ball. And from the way his grip on her slackened, she knew her mortality was just another reason for Cole Windaef to pull away.

4

BITTERSWEET BIRTHDAY

After weeks of keeping her head down and her mouth shut around her father, Sabine Rexton had been shocked to hear her mother was planning an impressive ball for her sixteenth birthday—with her father's blessing. Most of the preparations had already been made before her mother casually brought up at breakfast that she had scheduled a dress fitting that afternoon. A gorgeous ball gown made of deep pink silk had been tailor-made for her big day. She was to be the center of attention, as she always wanted, and yet something felt off as Julian met her at the bottom of the stairs on the eve of her birthday. Her father had been in an unusually pleasant mood, having finalized a vital trade deal with the Denorfian envoys that week, and she could only hope he would remain that way through the evening.

The princess gaped as she entered the main hall, her eyes lighting up as she scanned the tables covered in over-the-top floral arrangements and burning candles. She couldn't help the broad grin that spread across her face for the first time in months. Everything was as she had always dreamed, and it was all for her. Maybe things were finally returning to normal after the tumultuous events of the summer.

"It's beautiful," Sabine breathed, her chest swelling with pride as she surveyed the guests. She had timed her entrance so that the room was nearly full when she arrived. Now all eyes were on them, and she couldn't help but recall the last time these people had all been together in this hall. The night of the Summer Solstice. The night that changed everything.

"Not nearly as beautiful as you," Julian said, lifting her hand to his face. He pecked her knuckles, his lips warm against her skin, and she smiled even bigger. Warmth bloomed

27

in her cheeks. She was tempted to push up on her toes and kiss his cheek. If they hadn't been surrounded by guests, she would have done that and more.

"There you are," her brother said. As they turned to look at him, Julian quickly dropped her hand. Anteros looked sharp as ever in his signature all-black ensemble. The candlelight flickered, making the gold embellishments on his jacket shine. He paused in front of them, his narrowed eyes fixed on Julian. "I was not aware you were her escort." His eyes cut from his friend back to her.

Sabine chuckled nervously, stepping toward Anteros and kissing him on the cheek. "Come now, brother. Surely you can play nice for one evening. It is my birthday, after all."

Julian took a deep breath and bowed his head in greeting. "Your Highness."

"You can cut the formalities, Julian. My father isn't here yet," the prince said, his voice clipped. Anteros ran one hand over his slicked-back hair. He had already lost interest in his friend. His eyes raked over the crowded hall for someone—but who, Sabine wasn't sure. He had kept to himself for the remainder of the summer—sulking when alone, following their father like a dog when necessary. Now, his hazel eyes raked over the womanly figures of court in a ravenous way that unsettled his sister. Almost like he was on the hunt.

"And did you escort anyone here this evening?" Sabine asked, stepping into her brother's line of sight.

Anteros huffed, shaking his head. "It doesn't matter who you bring, only who you leave with," he mused. His lips spread into a cheshire grin as he zeroed in on his latest prey—a blonde who was poured into a turquoise gown, leaving little to the imagination.

Sabine wrinkled her nose. Her brother had fallen back into his rakish ways, and things weren't the same between them. She noticed the way he never looked her in the eyes, if he could help it. Perhaps he couldn't bear another look of disappointment from her. Not since he told her to abandon any hope of saving Talitha earlier that summer. It still didn't sit right with her, going on with her life while the poor girl rotted in the dungeon below their feet. Her thoughts drifted back to her father's prisoner, as they often did when she now entered the main hall or the courtyard. These places she had once enjoyed were now tainted by the poison that was her father's cruelty. She knew it was only a matter of time before his wrath would strike again.

A horn sounded at the entrance, an ominous declaration that the monster they lived with had arrived at the ball. She wavered for a moment, biting her lip as she watched her parents waltz in together. Her mother had put so much work into planning this ball. She should have been beaming with pride, but the corners of her mouth were turned down, her jaw set as though they had just had an argument.

Without a word, Julian laced their pinkies together. Sabine looked down at their hands, carefully hidden by her voluminous skirt, and smiled gratefully at him.

Keeping his eyes locked on their parents, Anteros said in a low voice, "Let's get this over with." He held out one palm toward his sister, and she begrudgingly accepted it. The prince led his sister toward the main table at the front of the room. Their parents were busy mingling with a group of foreign guests in front of it.

"Ahh, there you are," Antoine declared, his booming voice sending a shiver through his daughter. He clapped a hard hand onto Sabine's shoulder. It was unlike him to be warm toward her, even in a public setting. Their relationship was strained at best.

"Good eve, Father," Sabine said, dipping into a deep curtsy.

"Father," Anteros echoed, briefly bowing his head.

"Everything looks wonderful, Mother. You've really outdone yourself." Sabine grasped her mother's hand and offered her a warm smile.

Chelsea downcast her eyes, squeezing her daughter's hand briefly. "You deserve a perfect night, my darling. And you look splendid."

"Indeed, she does," the gentleman beside her father said. Sabine glanced his way curiously. He had a neatly trimmed beard that matched his short, chestnut curls. His smile met his aquamarine eyes, and she thought him to be a kind-looking fellow. Handsome for his age. He must have been closer to 30 than 20 years of age. She had never seen him at court before and wondered what business he could have with her father today of all days.

The king gestured toward the man with one arm. "My dearest daughter, I'd like to introduce you to Ryker Umbryon, the Earl of Briar. He's come all the way from Denorfia on business, so I invited him to attend your party. I hope you don't mind."

Sabine's eyes widened. Her lips parted, but she could not find the words. Her father had never cared what she thought—what *anyone* thought. He was the King, and he did as he pleased. She swallowed and put on her best smile, hoping his guests hadn't noticed her surprise. "Oh, well, of course I do not mind. The more the merrier. You are the King after all." She chuckled nervously, and the others joined her.

Her father's laugh boomed over them all. "Yes, you are right about that. Such a good girl to remember your place." Antoine patted her roughly on the cheek, and she eased herself a step back from him. She hated when he put his hands on her. It was never gentle or loving.

Anteros slipped a hand around her waist and spun her around. When they stopped, he had placed himself between her and their father. She now stood closer to the earl and his entourage. "We're pleased you could join us, my lord," Anteros said, outstretching his hand.

The man shook her brother's hand firmly before his gaze drifted back to Sabine. "Please, call me Ryker. I'm sure we shall be seeing much of each other in the future." The princess swallowed. She was not sure how to take that. She did not usually spend time with the foreign envoys. They came and went so frequently.

The quartet started playing a new song, and Sabine immediately perked up. "Oh, I love this tune," she said excitedly, eager to ditch her parents and enjoy the night with her friends. "If you'll excuse—"

"Would you care to dance?" Ryker asked, extending his hand to her.

Sabine hesitated, looking from her brother to her parents. Her father's smile had faded; his jaw clenched. He folded his arms over his chest and cocked one eyebrow, silently daring her to embarrass him in front of an esteemed guest. She sighed and hesitantly accepted the man's hand. "Yes, thank you," she murmured. Anteros gave her a look of pity, and Sabine wished he would intervene. Instead, he lowered his eyes to the floor.

On the dance floor, they lined up with several other couples. Ryker gripped her hand, rubbing his thumb deep into her silk gloves. While the action might have been affectionate coming from Julian or her brother, it made Sabine vastly uncomfortable coming from this strange man she had only met moments ago.

"May I call you Sabine, or would you prefer Princess?" he asked. His mouth lifted in a slight grin as though he were teasing her. He laced their fingers together with one hand, grasping her waist with the other. Why did this have to be a waltz of all dances?

"I prefer Your Royal Highness," she said, matching his grin, "but Sabine will suffice." She put on her winning smile—the fake one reserved for the politics of Graynor Court. "How was your journey from Denorfia?"

Ryker twirled her around the dance floor with ease. It was obvious he must have spent a great deal of time dancing at his home court. "Very pleasant, thank you for asking," he said. "Sixteen. A lovely age. I remember that time fondly. I was but seventeen when I took my first bride."

Her eyes widened. "You married quite young." Sabine's statement tumbled out, sounding more surprised than she had intended. In truth, a part of her was relieved to hear that he was married. "And where is your wife? I should love to meet her."

Her dance partner's lips curled down. "Sadly, she died in childbirth many years ago." Ryker searched her face curiously—for what, she was unsure.

"I'm terribly sorry for your loss, my lord," she replied, biting her lip. Dancing was one thing; holding a conversation with someone she didn't know was far more difficult. The last thing she needed was to upset this man who was there to negotiate trade with her father. For once, she might have preferred to dance in silence.

"Ryker, please," he reminded her, giving her waist a small squeeze. "While I appreciate your condolences, they are not necessary. It has been many moons since her loss."

Sabine sank her teeth into her bottom lip. Losing formalities did not feel natural at that moment. This man had lived an entire chapter of adult life that she could not relate to. She didn't know what to say after hearing he had lost his wife. She knew her father was watching from the edge of the dance floor, his steel gaze fixed threateningly upon her. One wrong move, one impolite word, and the ball could come to a screeching end before she even began to enjoy it.

"Enough talk about me. It's your day. Tell me. What else do you like, besides dancing, Sabine?" His voice was deep yet soft. Cool like his eyes. He seemed nice enough, though she didn't grasp why he was so curious about her. His business was with her father.

"Oh, I enjoy matchmaking," she said, a flighty laugh escaping her. "It's quite fun to help the older ladies find a good match."

Ryker grinned, his cheeks rounding. "Matchmaking?" His eyes twinkled in the same way her brother's used to when he was up to some mischief. It made him look a bit younger. Perhaps it was just the beard that made him seem so much older? "How successful have you been at that?"

She grinned, lifting her chin as the conversation shifted to her favorite subject: gossip. "I'll have you know that I'm the best around."

His eyebrows lifted at that. She was used to people staring at her, as she had been a princess all her life, so she didn't usually mind the attention. But something about how closely he was inspecting her every pore made her skin start to itch. Then Ryker's gaze dropped lower. It was only for a moment, but the flash of hunger in his darkened gaze was unmistakable.

Sabine stopped suddenly. The music continued, but she was tired of being ogled by this stranger. "My apologies," she stammered, pressing a hand to her stomach. Her heart hammered against her chest cavity as she took a step back from Ryker. "I'm feeling a bit dizzy. Perhaps I should sit for a while."

The Denorfian frowned, his thick brows turning down as he stepped toward her. "Perhaps you should eat something."

"Sabine," a deep, worried voice said from behind her. She turned to find Julian quickly approaching, his pale hair and smooth face a welcome sight. "Are you unwell?"

She offered him a nervous smile as he touched the small of her back. "Dizzy. I should eat something before I take another turn on the dance floor," Sabine lied. She leaned her head gratefully against Julian's shoulder as he whisked her off to the main table where her family would sit for the feast.

"Sabine," her father's voice boomed as they approached. He stormed toward them, a vicious glint in his onyx eyes. Julian flinched. "It's impolite to leave a guest on the dance floor in the middle of a song. Return to the earl at once!"

She sighed, closing her eyes and pressing her fingers to one of her temples. It was too early in the evening for things to fall apart now. "I'm sorry, Father," she whispered. She couldn't look him in the eyes.

"It's quite alright, Your Majesty. Seems she was feeling dizzy," Ryker said from behind them. Sabine whipped her head around to find he had followed them across the room.

"Hopefully she will indulge me with an encore after dinner." He winked. It was so quick she almost missed it.

She bit her lip and turned back to face her father in hopes that his guest's understanding would transfer to him. Antoine's gaze shifted between his daughter and his guest. Slowly, the redness of his cheeks dissipated, and he nodded. "Of course she will," Antoine growled, eyes boring into his daughter.

She nodded back. "Yes, of course," she said. It was then that she realized Julian had released her and retreated from the conversation. She frowned when she spotted him talking to Anteros and two of their friends. He stole a quick glance at her, but his eyes didn't linger. It was obvious her father had scared Julian off for the evening. How disappointing.

Chelsea wrapped her bony fingers around her daughter's shoulder and led her to her seat. She sat to her mother's left while her brother sat to the king's right. Anteros was certainly playing the part of the perfect heir tonight. Not a hair was out of place on his head. Though his eyes roamed the hall in pursuit of beautiful ladies, he remained attentive to his father's every word. She didn't know how he managed it.

The feast was served, and everyone divulged in a delicious meal of Sabine's favorites—braised fish from the lake behind the castle, spiraled noodles with a crème sauce, and mixed vegetables. For dessert, the servants wheeled out a massive three-tier cake with berries and sweet cream.

As the servants cut and served the cake, Antoine tapped his knife on his water glass. A hush fell over the hall as all eyes turned toward the king. He stood and raised his gold chalice full of wine, marking the beginning of yet another speech.

"Welcome, welcome. Thank you all for being here today to celebrate this illustrious occasion," he said. Antoine lifted his chin, looking down his nose at those in attendance before turning to the side to face his wife and daughter. "It's not every day we celebrate our kingdom's only princess coming into her own as a woman."

Sabine narrowed her eyes for a second. His choice of words was curious. Him saying anything kind about her at all was a rarity. She stared into his eyes and what she saw shocked her to her core. Pride. Antoine Rexton was positively glowing with pride as he went on about his daughter's beauty and accomplishments. He even mentioned her aptitude for planning events like her mother. Sabine's smile stretched wide across her face. This was what she had always longed for: her father's love and affection. After weeks of being the perfect daughter, staying quiet and doing whatever he ordered, it seemed she had finally earned it. Tears rimmed her sapphire eyes, but she blinked them back.

Antoine scanned the crowd again before turning to face the other end of the table. Anteros peered behind his father at his sister and offered her a grim smile as their father continued, "And as the loveliest rose of Hyrosencia, my daughter has the most coveted hand in our court. Now that she is of marriageable age, it is no surprise that more than one gentleman has already approached me to ask for her hand."

Sabine froze, her wide eyes fixing on Anteros as her father's speech veered in an unexpected direction. Marriage? She was barely sixteen. There had been no discussion of her getting married. No indication of proposals. She clenched the edge of the table in her hands, leaning forward. She scanned the dark corridor, searching for the only boy she was remotely interested in considering. In the flickering candlelight, she spotted his blond hair. His lips were pressed into a tight line, his eyes trained on her. He looked as tense as she felt.

"I am most pleased to announce that negotiations are underway with the Denorfian envoys for my daughter's hand. I anticipate a most advantageous arrangement will be reached in the coming week," Antoine declared to everyone's shock.

Sabine sucked in a breath as fresh tears sprung to her eyes. *This is not happening*, she thought. Her father had mentioned the importance of making this trade for cattle, but to trade his own daughter? Chelsea reached over and squeezed her hand tight. "Did you know?" she hissed at her mother.

The sorrow in her mother's eyes answered her question. "I did not think he would tell you tonight," Chelsea whispered regretfully. Sabine snatched her hand away. Her stomach roiled at the feeling of betrayal simmering in her gut.

"After years gracing our glorious court, Sabine will soon grace the royal court of Denorfia with her radiant presence," Antoine continued, turning his gaze upon her again. He outstretched one hand to his daughter and commanded, "Rise, little flower, and greet the man who will soon be your betrothed."

Sabine swallowed hard. She stared at her father for a moment. Then hesitantly, she placed her fingers on his palm and stood. Her legs quivered beneath her gown. The heavy silk weighed her down. She wished she could sink down into it and let it swallow her whole. "Who?" she whispered; her voice nearly inaudible.

Antoine grinned as he whipped his head around, gesturing with his other hand. Earl Ryker Umbryon rose from his seat. When their eyes met, she wrung her hands in front of her waist and leaned closer to her father. "The earl? But I am a princess… Should I not marry a prince or a—"

Before Sabine could finish, her father's hand clenched around her throat, cutting her off. "Have I not taught you to be silent and obedient?" Antoine growled at her.

Tears slipped down her cheeks as he relinquished his hold. He lifted his chalice high and said, "To the union of Hyrosencia and our great northern neighbors." The rest of the room mimicked his motion before drinking from their glasses. The nobles wasted no time beginning to chatter about this announcement.

Sabine forgot how to breathe. She remained frozen in place. Shivers wracked her torso; her legs felt heavy. Her mother reached for her, wrapping gentle hands around her waist, but she couldn't feel it. Couldn't feel anything but the sheer horror that the life she had hardly begun was being taken from her.

Antoine settled back into his seat at the table. He dug into the piece of cake the servants had placed in front of him without giving his daughter a second glance.

Sabine noticed movement in her periphery and realized that the earl was coming her way. Snapping out of her trance, she turned to her mother and nearly shouted, "I need the lavatory."

Chelsea nodded. Sabine turned and rushed the opposite direction, clearing the head table and making her way toward the main exit. As she passed Julian's table, her chest constricted. She could barely hold in her sobs until she was out of the main hall. If this was how her father meant to celebrate her birthday, she wished he would go back to ignoring her existence.

When Anteros did not find Sabine in her bedroom, he had few ideas where she might be hiding. He stepped onto the garden path and peered out into the dark oasis. The night air was thick, but a pleasant breeze ruffled the tall plants. Anteros hated the courtyard with passion. He imagined his sister felt similarly, though he had not spoken to her much since the incident earlier that summer. He paused on the path, turning his head slightly. He thought he heard something, possibly a distant sniffle deep in the darkness.

The prince doubled back into the hallway and removed a torch from the wall. Raising his chin, Anteros stormed down the cobblestone path toward the fountain. The torch light barely illuminated a few feet ahead as he walked swiftly. As much as he did not want to go further, his sister was more important than the sinking feeling in his stomach.

As the fountain came into view, heavy breathing met his ears. Anteros walked around the right side of the fountain until he ran into an abandoned pair of gold-painted heels. "Sabine?" he called, trying to restrict his voice to the immediate area.

He lifted the torch higher and squinted into the darkness. Among the gentle ruffle of stems rubbing against stems, he heard it. The slightly less natural sound of silk and crinoline crumpling. He should have been ashamed that he knew the sound so definitively. But he wasn't.

"Sabine?" He bent to scoop up her shoes with his free hand. "Bine, come on. It's me."

"Leave me alone, Anteros," came a feeble reply.

Five more steps and there she was sitting on the edge of the fountain. The tear tracks on her cheeks shimmered in the torchlight, and he lowered his arm. When they were children, Anteros would always defend his sister. If someone made her cry, he was quick to exact his revenge. But now they were older, and the man responsible for her tears was untouchable.

"You don't mean that," he said quietly. The prince laid the burning torch on its side on the stone path and sat beside her.

Sabine breathed deeply. Her brother waited to see if she would push him away again, but she didn't. They knew all too well that on the days when their father was particularly cruel to them, it was always easier to cope together than alone. Anteros reached over silently and placed his hand atop hers. He could feel the faintest tremble in her fingers. As if her anger and sadness were so great her body could hardly manage it.

"Did you know?" Her voice came out as a whisper laced with accusation. She finally turned her tired face toward him. Her baby blues were full of fear. Like one more betrayal would shatter her completely.

The prince shook his head. For once, he was thankful his father had kept him out of that business. It was something he wouldn't have dared keep from his sister if he had known. He stared at their hands in the faint light and exhaled. "I'm sorry it was handled this way. You did not deserve to be left out of that decision," Anteros said.

Sabine scoffed. "I shouldn't be surprised. All these years, Father has loathed my presence. I knew eventually he'd send me away... But I never imagined it would be so soon." She sucked in her bottom lip as it began trembling.

Anteros wrapped his arms around her and pulled her into his chest. She shook violently, fighting back her sobs. "It's going to be all right, Bine," her brother whispered. One hand disappeared into her raven curls, cradling the back of her head.

The princess lifted her head abruptly. She glared at him through tear-filled eyes. "How can you say that? I am to marry a man I've barely met! A man who has already taken one wife, mind you. He's not even a prince—and he is twice my age. It is the greatest insult."

"I know. Believe me, I am insulted on your behalf," Anteros quipped.

They stared at each other for a moment before both broke into a half-hearted grin. "As you should be," the princess said decidedly. She swiped her fingers over her cheeks, wiping away the remnants of her outburst. A crisp breeze sent her curls up and over her shoulders, and Sabine closed her eyes. "What am I supposed to do now?"

"The night is not yet over," Anteros noted. He rose from the fountain and knelt on the ground in front of his sister. She frowned at him as he made quick work of slipping her shoes back onto her feet. "I think there's still cake and dancing to be had—if you're up for it." He stood, brushing the dirt from his knees before offering his hand.

"I meant about the betrothal." She eyed him suspiciously. Perhaps he deserved that now after weeks of keeping to himself. He didn't want to talk about the rage he was suppressing, didn't want her to tap into that and encourage him to do something foolish. He could make stupid decisions all on his own. But at least his stupid decisions had nothing to do with Talitha Vise anymore. They had nothing to do with anyone he cared about. It was best that way.

"You know there's no changing our father's mind once it's set," Anteros replied.

"Did Father send you to fetch me?" she finally asked, crossing her arms over her chest.

Anteros scoffed. "Of course not. I think Ryker considered going after you, but I stopped him. Figured you'd prefer a friend over a stranger."

She sneered. "Any chance my disappearance could make him rescind his offer?" Her eyes sparkled with faint hope before it fizzled out on its own. Dropping her chin, Sabine took her brother's hand and rose from her seat. Anteros could almost read her mind. Their father expected them to return. He expected her to smile and dance, to show the nobles that she's thrilled with her impending engagement. To convince the earl of it. That was her duty as princess.

Anteros scraped his teeth along his bottom lip. "The man seemed pretty pleased with the match."

Sabine scoffed as her brother picked up the dimming torch from the ground and led them back toward the castle. "He would be. He's only an earl in want of a wife. He'll never sit upon a throne. And now, neither will I."

"You never wanted to be a queen, did you?" her brother questioned.

Sabine was quiet at first. When they finally crossed under the archway leading back into the castle, she replied, "I never cared before, but we both know I would make a fine queen. The finest in any land. I already have the wardrobe fit for the role."

Anteros smirked, returning the torch to its place on the wall. "That you would. But you will also make a fine Countess one day."

The corridor leading back to the main hall was empty save for a few servants. When they caught Anteros's stern gaze, they quickly dropped their eyes and scurried off. Word had likely already spread throughout the castle about their father's unexpected announcement this evening. He wished he could spare his sister from the vicious gossip circuit, but there was nothing he could do to quell their tongues.

When they were nearly back to the main hall, Anteros paused and faced his sister. "Do you think you can hold it together for an hour?" She nodded quietly. "Try not to think about the earl. Have a drink and join me for a dance. You should have at least one good memory from your birthday."

Sabine inhaled, her spirit inflating with her lungs. She held her head high, her shoulders pushed back, as she tightened her grip on her brother's arm. If her father's goal had been to hurt her, she would not let him see it. Anteros patted her hand on his arm and smiled. Of all the people he knew, his sister was one of the strongest—not physically, but mentally. Their father had molded her into a formidable young woman, and she could not so easily be broken. Not even by their monstrous father.

5

CHANGE OF PLANS

Will wiped the sweat from his brow on his shirt sleeve and glanced up at the citadel. Though it was warm, the towering brick façade shielded them from the early morning sunlight. He couldn't help but wonder what Serena was doing. Was she eating breakfast? Or training with Crystal on the other side of the grounds?

He had been working hard at the forge in the city, mastering the art of sword making in the few weeks since his arrival. But that had meant less time at the citadel. Less chances to see Serena and their friends.

Running into them in the lounge the other evening had been a happy coincidence, though short-lived. Spinning her around that small space was the highlight of a rough week. He had missed Serena terribly; memories of her often flooded his mind while he was training. How could they not? The only reason he had ever wielded a sword was to protect her.

"Still there?" Rigel asked. He nudged his friend in the side. "Thinking of a certain lady again?" His cheshire grin was an unwelcome sight.

Will turned and flourished a thin blade in his hand. "Don't you have your own woman to pine over?"

The guardian's smile faded. They both knew his pining was useless. Crystal Windaef didn't show him any interest. She didn't show anyone any interest unless weapons were involved. "There will be many beautiful women at the ball next week. Perhaps I shall have a lady on my arm by the end of it!"

The young man from Durmak scoffed. "We'll see about that," Will said. He wasn't in the mood for their harmless teasing today. He wanted to get in an hour or two of practice

39

before his shift at the forge. Every minute mattered if he wanted to improve his sword skills.

He lifted the sword, feeling the flex of his muscles as he raised his arms. He'd grown stronger over the past few months. He could feel it in his biceps. Between the forge and training with Rigel, he felt stronger than ever. Like he could be useful against an enemy attacker. He dug his heels into the grass with one foot ahead of the other, ready for Rigel's first move.

Ever since the incident with the Mørkewulv, Rigel's dominant arm hadn't been the same. Though Crystal had managed to save the arm—and his life—healing was a process. A grueling process that often frustrated Rigel. Will knew that was why he preferred training alone. He didn't want his friends to see that his movements were slower, his shoulder still slightly sore as his muscles stitched themselves back together.

As Rigel lunged toward him, weapon raised, Will heard the wind carry his name across the courtyard, the familiar voice immediately grabbing his full attention. Whipping his head around to face the citadel, he found Serena running straight at them, her long hair blowing in the breeze as she neared. "Will!" she called again, greeting him with a broad smile. A smile only for him.

His blade slipped from his hand and landed in the grass while his attention shifted to her. Rigel muttered under his breath as Serena came closer. When she stepped up to them, she said, "Will, Rigel, it's so good to see you both!"

"What brings you out here at this time?" Rigel asked. He was wary of the others watching him practice. This much Will had figured out after a few interrupted sessions. That was why they had shifted their practice times. Serena practiced shortly after dawn, followed by tea with the queen mid-morning. That's when Crystal and Xandra usually tried to rest from their night watch and morning practice.

The girl lowered her gaze, her cheeks slightly flushed. "I might have told the maid to inform the queen I was not feeling well." She grinned, her green eyes glancing toward the boy from her hometown. "I was hoping to catch you out here. I've missed you." She glanced back toward Rigel and clarified, "*Both* of you."

The guardian grinned and made a grand bow. "Well, I am honored," Rigel teased, and she swatted at his arm.

Will chuckled. It was nice having her there. He could count the number of times he had seen Serena since they made it to Symptee on his fingers. Too few times, in his opinion, but they were both keeping extraordinarily busy. And when he did see her, he hardly knew what to say. After all they had been through together, he saw Serena differently now. She wasn't just his best friend's little sister, someone who needed to be protected. She was his friend. His closest friend. A person whose smile felt like home. And he could no longer picture the future without her.

He stepped closer to Serena and wrapped his arms around her waist. Lifting her off the ground, Will spun her around in a circle. Her vibrant laugh bubbled forth, warmth spread through his chest. This was what he'd been missing. *She* was what he'd been missing. Without her, all the work he was putting in felt futile.

"Looks like we have company." Rigel sighed. He looked down at the grass and kicked at the ground. Their private training session was over before it even began.

Will placed Serena's feet back on the ground, and they both turned to find three familiar faces approaching. Serena lit up immediately. "Rilura!" She stepped forward and bowed her head to the dwarf princess. "It is so good to see you."

Beams of light broke through the canopy of purple blooms above their heads, bathing Serena's face in a golden glow. As if Divinity had forged her from the light of his brightest stars. Will stared in awe. Had she always been this beautiful?

Of course, she had. Will had never thought she was bad looking. But for years, he trained himself not to look at Serena for too long. Not when Cameron Finch had always been there anytime he saw her. Will knew her brother would have pummeled him for even glancing her way. Their friendship had been strong enough to keep any thoughts of her at bay—until Cameron went away.

And now Cameron was dead. The person who connected them as children, gone from this world forever, and by Serena's own hands. Will still couldn't believe what he had witnessed on the mountain. His friend had always had an unhealthy obsession with the idea of being a soldier—a dream they never shared. Unfortunately, his allegiance had ended up polluting him against his own family. His own friend. What was left of him in the end was barely a shell of the boy they'd known in Durmak. Cameron had put his hands around Serena's neck, and Will knew that if she had not stabbed him, he would have done it himself.

Will tensed, pushing those dark thoughts back to the recesses of his mind. Thoughts of Cameron resurfaced daily, but no matter how much he asked Divinity *why*, he would never receive a satisfactory answer. Evil spreads like an overgrown vine, ensnaring minds and corrupting souls. That's what Rexton did. What he would continue doing until no good was left.

Or until someone fought back.

He listened quietly while Serena caught up with the dwarf princess. Apparently Rilura and Eldvar had been spending a great deal of time meeting with the highest officers in the Guard, going over the citadel's security and ways the dwarfs could further aid Symptee.

Rigel and Thomli caught up beside him. It was Thomli who finally pulled him from his trance. "And how are you faring at your apprenticeship?"

One corner of Will's mouth curled upward, and he rubbed the back of his neck. "Actually, my master said I had far surpassed apprentice level last week. Seems I've been promoted to partner."

"You finished your apprenticeship?" Serena nearly yelled, whipping around to look at him. Her wide eyes and broad smile made his cheeks warm. He wished he could make her that happy every day. "Will, that's amazing! I'm so happy for you."

Before he could think, she was in front of him, slipping her arms around his neck in a fond embrace. His heart hammered in his chest, and he prayed she wouldn't notice as he cautiously wrapped his arms around her waist. He rested his hands against her back and glanced at Rigel. The guardian was quiet; his stoic gaze neither reproachful nor encouraging. Will nuzzled his face in her loose hair and quietly inhaled. She smelled like flowers now. That was new. But the feminine scent suited her.

Serena pulled back from him and grabbed him by the cheeks. "I can't believe you didn't tell me the second you finished! This is huge. We must celebrate."

Will withdrew his arms and shrugged. "I meant to tell you, but the forge has been piled up. So many orders. New equipment, repairs for older weapons. I may have to start sleeping there."

That made Serena shrink back, the shimmer to her eyes fading. "Oh," she said quietly. "I didn't realize you would still be so busy." She worked her lip, visibly disappointed.

He cursed inwardly. "I didn't know either," Will mumbled, shoving his hands into his pants pockets. If he had known Symptee was in desperate need of two additional blacksmiths, he might have rethought his life plan. While it was nice to be needed, he preferred being needed by the girl he never had any time to visit anymore. He would have given anything for them to have an afternoon off from work, training, and tea parties so they could stroll the gardens and lounge under the wisteria in peace. "Perhaps I can work something out. Join you and Elara for tea one day," he said with a chuckle. That would never happen.

"Perhaps I'll have to skip morning tea more often so I can see you," she replied. Her fingers brushed his forearm, and Will's heart skipped a beat. Before he could respond, the sound of steel on steel rang out behind them, and Serena whipped her head around in search of the culprit.

On the lawn, Rilura and Thomli banged their axes together twice more in a show of camaraderie before beginning their duel.

"Dare not go easy on me," Rilura said, pointing her axe at her opponent as she slowly stepped backward.

"I would not dream of insulting you, Princess," Thomli replied, also stepping back. "Give me your best."

The Dwarven princess unleashed a ferocious battle cry, lifting her axe above her head. A thick braid slapped against her back as she charged. Will was convinced her steel gaze could have cut a man worse than any blade—and it was fixed on Thomli. He grinned as she gained speed. There was not a hint of fear in his eyes. He looked positively ecstatic that she was coming at him like a bear out for blood.

The harsh clatter of their battle axes meeting rang through the courtyard; the noise jarred everyone. Men on the citadel wall walked down to get a closer look. It wasn't every day they could watch dwarfs practice their battle skills. Rilura and Thomli took turns ducking their heads, swinging their arms around, and blocking blow for blow repeatedly. It was a heavy-footed dance. One Will would never dare partake in against a dwarf if he could help it.

He glanced to his side and noticed the way Serena watched the dwarf princess in awe. Her irises danced in tandem with each swift movement. They were a lighter shade in the direct sun, green as the grass beneath their feet. The color reminded him of springtime in Durmak. The crash of axes nearby made him jump slightly, but not Serena. She was unafraid. Her cheeks lifted as she urged on her friend. It was a wonder, seeing her smile like that while watching people duel. Will did not know where this new state of calm had come from. Serena had once felt such fear and dread at the prospect of fighting another person. But the mountains had changed her—had changed them both forever.

She reached out and grasped his forearm suddenly. "Did you see that?" He followed her pointer finger out to the match.

Rilura and Thomli were panting heavily. Their faces were close, their axes locked together near their throats. Rilura's wide jaw pulled taut in a grin as blood dripped from Thomli's chin. The princess had drawn first blood. Thomli sighed, slackening his grip on his battle axe. "Ye have bested me," he resigned, bowing his head. Rilura dropped her arms and held her chin high.

Some of the guards who had gathered to watch murmured about how odd it was that the dwarf princess was stronger than her personal guard. Will couldn't help but agree with the sentiment. Why would a woman need a guard if she could protect herself?

"A princess should not need a protector. She can shake mountains and defeat enemies all on her own," Rilura declared, leveling Serena with her gaze. Then she lifted her axe above her head and chanted something in the Dwarven language. Rigel and Serena applauded. Will wished Serena would realize that she was just as strong and capable as Rilura. She had already shaken the mountain and defeated men who tried to kill them. She was a marvel—beautiful, strong, yet still kind—and she had no idea that he watched her with awe in the same way she had watched the dwarfs compete.

Turning to Rigel, Serena declared, "It's my turn. What do you say?" The guardian swallowed thickly.

Will stepped between them and reached a hand out to Rigel for a weapon. "Let's see who's improved more," Will said. He hated the idea of Serena ever having to fight for her life again, but he knew she was strong. Stronger than she even realized. He wanted to show her that he was stronger now, too.

"Bold move, Burroughs," the guardian said, placing the hilt of a sword in Will's outstretched hand. When Will turned, Serena had pulled the blade from the sheath at her hip. It wasn't her father's sword. He wondered if she had returned the Heir's Blade to the queen. "It was nice knowing you," Rigel quipped, clapping him on the shoulder in passing.

Serena grinned as she paced out into the open space in the citadel's shadow. Turning swiftly, she asked, "If you're so busy at the forge, why continue training? We don't have to leave Symptee for anything."

"Actually, I most likely will," he retorted, getting into an offensive position.

His answer had done exactly as he anticipated. Serena lowered her elbows, allowing the blade to sag toward the ground, and Will took the opportunity to advance. He had learned to use any little distraction to his advantage.

But so had Serena.

She lifted her arms quickly, blocking his initial attack with ease. "You're leaving?" she snarled. Her nostrils flared as she glared past their entangled weapons at him. "We just got here."

"Every few months a group heads up to Silvermane to pick up supplies," Will said. He used his upper body strength to press her back a few steps before drawing his blade back. "Eventually they'll ask me to go."

Serena huffed indignantly. "You barely survived the crossing the first time," she argued. Without hesitation, she charged at him. Her blade cut through the space between them, but Will swiftly parried the attack. Their weapons clashed three times, eliciting cheers from Rigel and the dwarfs watching nearby.

"Atta girl, Serena. You've gotten faster," Rigel called out.

Will glared at his traitorous friend who was beaming at Serena. His grip tightened on the hilt of his weapon. He had improved, too. He wanted Serena to see that. The next time they were in danger, he wouldn't need her to save him. He'd protect her.

Where he lacked skill, he made up for it in strength. Will pushed her back again with sheer force. Her boots skidded, dragging in the dry soil as he pressed her further back. Serena gritted her teeth, unleashing a growl as she pushed back. When Will didn't let up, she narrowed her eyes at his posture. He noticed the way her gaze raked down his broad chest, his hands positioned on the hilt of his blade, and the position of his feet. When she looked up again, a faint smile greeted him, and he knew he was in trouble.

A breeze swept through their hair, the cool air a welcome reprieve from the heat. But Serena did not allow her friend to enjoy it. She turned her wrist in a circle, locking onto Will's blade and forcing it upward. As he focused on regaining control of his weapon, she dropped into a low squat. A quick swipe of her leg had Will tumbling to the ground.

He seethed as he landed hard on his hip. When had she learned to fight dirty? "I see you learned Cole's favorite move," he grumbled. His discarded weapon lay a few feet away in the grass, just out of reach.

Back on her feet, Serena stalked toward him like a lioness on the hunt. There was something predatory in her gaze that sent a chill through his spine. For a moment, he feared she might skewer him. "Do you yield?" He didn't grant her the satisfaction of quitting. She grinned. As she lifted her blade above him in a show of victory, Will rolled over twice. Grasping his blade by the hilt, he used one hand to quickly maneuver himself back onto his feet.

"That's it, Will! Never yield," Rigel called. Of course, he was playing both sides. That was typical. Both Serena and Will were determined to show each other up, and no one was getting in the way of their display. There could only be one victor in the end.

"You've got this, Serena," Rilura said, lifting her axe over her head in support.

Serena lowered her chin and raced forward. They parried blow after blow, wasting no time between swings. They panted, chests rising and falling quickly as they stared each other down. Hair clung to Serena's sweat-drenched forehead and neck. As she reached to wipe her face on her shirt sleeve, he rushed forward again. Any distraction was an advantage, according to the guardians, so he had learned to watch and wait for an opening. Before she could reach, Will swung his leg for the back of her knees, sending her crashing onto her back. "Blazing embers!" she cursed on impact. Her weapon bounced once before settling in the grass near Rigel.

Will stepped closer; his blade rested in one hand at his side while he stared down at her. Her chestnut hair fanned out around her head. The sun caught the lighter locks, framing her face. She looked angelic, like Divinity had sent a live star down to walk among them.

"With those skills, I'm sure Elara would gladly add you into Serena's guard rotation," Rigel said from beside them. Will's lips turned up, his dimples deepening. He had mentioned wanting to find other ways to help and make more money. At first, the idea of joining the Guard made Will uncomfortable, but when Rigel suggested that he could become one of Serena's personal guards, he quickly warmed up to the idea. He could endure a few guard shifts if it meant seeing her more frequently.

A swift slam to his right shin sent him careening to the ground. The impact knocked the air from his lungs. Before he could gather his senses, Serena slid one leg over him, sitting on his midsection and pressing a dagger to his throat. He hadn't noticed the weapon on her earlier.

Rigel and the dwarfs erupted into applause. Will stared up at the fierce warrior perched on top of him and swallowed thickly. They had never been this close before. Even though she had won this round, he didn't mind. Heat pooled in his abdomen at the feel of Serena's thighs pressed against each side of his body.

Leaning over him, her lips grazed the shell of his ear as she said, "You want to be a guard now? You'll have to do better than that."

Rigel piped up, "We could always enroll you at the Academy for a spell. Finesse those skills." Will couldn't see their friend, and he was glad. If he wasn't still pinned under Serena's dagger, he might have thrown a punch for even suggesting that. The last thing he wanted was to be miles away from Serena Finch right now.

She sat back on her heels and grinned, basking in her victory over the young man from her hometown. No one back home would have ever believed she could take him down. He should have felt shame for that, but he was much too distracted to care. Will placed his calloused palms against the sides of Serena's knees and gave her a light squeeze. "I'm quite fond of where I'm at now, but thanks," he replied to Rigel. He grinned, his eyes never leaving hers as he dared shift one hand higher on her leg, gently stroking his thumb across the top of her thigh. His touch elicited a small shiver, and something flashed in Serena's eyes. "Maybe you should be the one training me," he murmured.

Rigel chuckled as Serena dove off Will's lap, rolling away in the grass. They watched as she fumbled to retrieve her sword. She tried and failed to hide the way her cheeks turned deep crimson. From his words or his touch, Will wasn't sure, but he was damn proud to have elicited a reaction from her—especially right after she defeated him. Perhaps Rigel's observation in the mountains had been right after all.

Serena grumbled under her breath, loud enough for them to hear, "I don't need any more guardians. Clearly, I can fend for myself." With a huff, she turned her attention

toward the dwarfs and asked the princess if she'd like to go for a walk around the grounds. Serena couldn't even look Will in the eyes when she bid her friends goodbye. He watched her as she walked across the yard, and he hoped he would be lucky enough to see her again the next day.

The crisp night air blew in through the open balcony door. Elara shivered as she closed it and rushed to join her husband in bed. Gerard wrapped an arm around her and pulled her closer, pressing his lips to her temple as he tugged their blanket up higher.

"I missed you today," Elara said. She was incredibly pleased to end yet another day wrapped in his loving embrace. The queen reached up to caress his cheek and craned her neck to press her lips to his. His beard brushed against the corners of her mouth and chin. Since their wedding, Gerard had grown out a thick beard that he kept neatly trimmed. It made him look older, more rugged, even more attractive—or perhaps that was the raging pregnancy hormones.

"And I, you." Gerard drew her closer. His hands glided easily against her silk gown, sending a trail of heat through her body as he caressed her curves. Since they'd finally married, he could hardly keep his hands off her—and she didn't want him to.

Her husband's hand sunk deeper under their sheets. Warmth bloomed in her abdomen as he gently pressed one palm against her growing belly. She was a few months along now, and soon there would be no hiding her condition from the rest of her court. But for now, it was nice having only their innermost circle in on their miraculous news.

Gerard began humming a familiar tune. His thumb stroked back and forth against the swell of her belly. Eyes closed, he smiled contentedly. She wished she felt as peaceful as her husband looked.

"What song is that?" Elara asked. "I think I have heard you humming it before."

"They call it *The Islander's Way Home*. It's an old sea shanty from back home," Gerard said. His lips turned up as he recalled something—surely a memory from his childhood in the Eastern Isles. "My mother used to sing it to us when our father was away."

"Can you sing it for me?" the queen inquired curiously. She adored her husband's voice.

"I can try," Gerard said, clearing his throat quietly.
"When you're far from all you love,
Trust the stars to line your path.
Find the brightest star above,
And prepare to race dawn's wrath.
Waves wild but hands steady,
The star of the sea shines bright.
Make haste, ensure the sails are ready,
And follow the star of the sea's light."

"The star of the sea," Elara echoed thoughtfully. "That has a nice ring to it."

"It's how Islanders find their way back home," Gerard said, pressing his lips to her collarbone. "Reminds me of a lullaby. One day I hope to sing it to our little one."

She smiled, placing her hand atop his. "I look forward to that." Imagining her husband holding their baby filled her heart with joy. But where there was joyful anticipation, there was always an undercurrent of fear. Much could go wrong in the coming months, not all involving Antoine Rexton's hands.

"How was tea with Serena? Was she excited when you told her?" Gerard's voice was soothing yet eager. He could not wait to announce their news to the entire world.

His questions pulled Elara out of her daydreams. She had intended to tell Serena about her pregnancy over tea that morning, but her niece did not end up joining her. "I did not see her today. She told the maid she was feeling ill," Elara said, sinking deeper into her sheets. One of the other servants told her they spotted her out in the courtyard with two young men and their dwarven allies. "She lied to me. Someone said they saw her go right back out to train with the dwarfs and that boy from Durmak. I'm not sure how I should address that." She still could not believe Serena lied to get out of tea after all the progress they had made. If the girl had asked, Elara would have granted permission for a change in her daily routine. Not that she wanted Serena spending any extra time with her friend from back home.

Gerard's hand slid from her belly up her side. "Are you referring to the lying or the boy?" His tone was teasing as he worked his lips down the side of her neck.

Her cheeks heated. Sometimes, she hated how her husband could read her mind so easily. She scowled, pushing his hand away. "Both." There was no hint of amusement in her voice. Elara crossed her arms and contemplated what she should say to her niece the following day. Assuming Serena would show up.

Her husband chuckled, grabbing her by the hips and pulling her flush against him. "She's a teenager, darling," he reminded her, "and you aren't her mother. Give her a little freedom, or she will retaliate." He kissed her eagerly as though that would end their conversation.

The wind whistled and whipped against the glass panes on her balcony doors. Her thoughts drifted back to Graynor, to a time when she was not much younger than Serena. Structure and discipline were key for young royals, but even the crown prince and princess clawed at any semblance of independence they could. Her brother's greatest act of defiance was his unexpected elopement with a commoner. Elara couldn't have her niece following in her father's footsteps. Not with a war to fight.

She pulled away from Gerard; her brows furrowed. "Since when are you an expert on teenage girls?"

"Have you forgotten I have a sister?" he asked, cocking an eyebrow.

After a pause, laughter bubbled out of her, easing the tension in her shoulders.

Gerard grinned. His fingers brushed against her throat as he pulled one side of her nightdress off her shoulder. "We were her age once." He pressed a kiss to her bare shoulder. "I'm sure you remember how you felt at that age."

The queen groaned. "I remember the butterflies. But those feelings fade, and some men have nothing but ill intentions. She does not need to get swept up and have her heart broken—or worse, her *reputation.*"

Her husband paused, gazing down at her. "Would you have her be alone until the war ends? That hardly seems fair."

"The boy doesn't even know who she is—who she is destined to be," Elara prattled. "She is of noble blood. They could never marry." He seemed like a kind and sensible young man. Perhaps it was time that he learned the truth.

"The truth won't change anything if they already care about each other," her husband argued. "Look at us. We were never meant to fall in love, yet here we are. Married." He grinned, pecking his way up her jawline and cheek. "Love cannot be forced. It comes naturally. There's no stopping what's meant to be."

She felt that familiar flutter in her stomach and leaned in to press her lips to his. He laced his fingers in her thick curls and drew her closer, deepening the kiss. When Gerard kissed her like this, Elara knew what he wanted. But her mind was still elsewhere. Elara paused, pulling away from her husband. "That's what I'm afraid of."

"There are enough things to worry about as it is. Do not fret over the girl's heart. She's safe with her guardians. They will keep her from doing anything scandalous."

The queen knew her husband was right. "If she'd lie to *me*, she could lie to them. She's smart, incredibly stubborn."

"Must be a family trait," Gerard muttered, rolling his eyes. "She'll be fine. You don't have to worry about everyone all the time, love."

If only it were easy to stop. Perhaps a normal lady could find time to rest and forget her problems. "As queen, it is part of my role to worry." She was under immeasurable pressure, and it had only increased since Serena's arrival. The fate of Hyrosencia rested on the shoulders of an eighteen-year-old girl who wasn't raised as a royal or a warrior. She was once kind at her core; killing wasn't instinctual. Since leaving Durmak, her entire life had been twisted, molded into something new by her trauma. Now that she was in Symptee, there were many new things Serena had to adjust to—the citadel wall, the Guard, the busy schedule, the heavy ball gowns, the expectations. Elara had been in her niece's shoes many years ago—a crown thrust onto her head as her world crumbled to ruins. She could not allow Antoine to take anything else from them. To defeat the man who stole her family's throne, she needed Serena's absolute focus on their cause.

Gerard propped himself up on one elbow, staring her down. "Cast some of your burden on someone else. Worrying will not do you or the baby any good." His voice was deeper; his words more of an order than a suggestion. Ever since learning of her pregnancy, he was always concerned about the baby. Sometimes, too concerned. But she did not feel like arguing with him that night. They were finally wed, sleeping in the same bed chamber each night, and thrilled to be expanding their family. So, for tonight, she would ignore his demands and try to appease him.

Elara sighed. "You're right," she whispered. "I'm sorry, dear." She wrapped her arms around his neck and sank her fingers into his thick, dark hair. She hoped their child would inherit his raven locks and his positivity.

"That's more like it," her husband purred. Gerard's hands slid along her silk gown. They came to rest on her hips, drawing her closer again. This time Elara kissed him passionately, resolving to end their conversation and save the remainder of her worries for tomorrow.

6

DISILLUSIONED

Sabine plastered on her best smile for another uncomfortable dinner with her family and the Denorfian convoy. Her father had insisted she sit across from the earl and hold polite conversation. While she loved talking, conversation with Ryker left much to be desired. He prattled on about the abundant cattle he owned and the harsh winter up north.

"Should you not be returning to your estate before the bitter cold returns?" she asked abruptly.

Her bluntness made Ryker's eyebrows fly into his hairline. His surprise made her lips curl up on the sides. Perhaps it would be easy to convince him to revoke his offer. She was much younger than him and far from the silent, obedient type.

"We supplied a great portion of livestock to His Majesty for the winter. In return, he has generously offered for us to stay through the winter. The climate is far more temperate here, and the view is quite nice from Graynor," Ryker replied, staring her down.

Sabine swallowed hard. She detested the way her betrothed stared at her. Wished she could forget what that title meant for her future. Their future. Intertwined. She scrunched her nose. Her fork scraped against her dinner plate as she shuffled the food back and forth across it. She wasn't hungry. Not with lingering eyes watching her every move.

Anteros nudged her under the table with his foot, and she discreetly glanced sidelong at him. He cleared his throat, catching the eyes of half the table. "Will you not find yourself homesick if you're away for such a long time?" he asked their guest.

The earl smiled. "You are young. You have not lived until you have traveled." Ryker held his goblet out toward Anteros. "To your youth. May you see all the beauty this world has to offer before you saddle yourself a wife."

Sabine huffed, quickly covering her face with her napkin and pretending she had sneezed. "Excuse me."

Anteros grinned. She noticed. It was the first real smile she had seen on his face since the last time they had seen Talitha. She watched as her brother lifted his goblet and toasted the man she was set to marry, and in that moment, she envied him. He was their father's favorite. Even when Anteros screwed up, their father rarely treated him like dirt. He was the golden child, the heir to the throne. Their father's legacy. While she was expected to maintain her virtue, Anteros could have his choice of women—and he certainly did. Their father would proudly let him choose his own bride from a list of candidates one day. She would never have that luxury—or her father's love.

Her brother sipped his wine before returning the goblet to its place. "I may not leave Graynor often, but I can guarantee you've never seen anything as beautiful as our woods at first light," Anteros said proudly.

Their father clapped his hands, causing their mother to jolt nervously. "My son is right!" Antoine declared. "You must join us for the next hunt. Quail season begins when the first cold snap descends."

Ryker nodded. "It would be our pleasure," he said to the king.

Her father went back to indulging in his dinner, and the earl's gaze fell back on Sabine. She dropped her fork with a clatter on the porcelain plate and exhaled loudly. "My apologies," she muttered. The princess stared at the napkin she had wrung into a wrinkled ball in her lap. "I am not feeling well. May I be excused, Father?"

Antoine narrowed his eyes at his daughter, and she shrank under his scrutiny. Sabine did her best to make herself look sickly. She allowed her cheeks to droop, her back sagging tiredly against her chair. "Very well. Off with you," her father said, waving one hand nonchalantly.

His dismissal stung, though it was what she wanted in the moment. She stood suddenly; the chair legs vibrated against the floor as she moved. Barely glancing at her betrothed, she bowed her head and said, "Good eve, gentlemen."

Her heels clacked loudly as she made her escape from the dining room into the main corridor. With each step away from her oppressors, Sabine felt the color come back to her cheeks, and she smiled in relief. She would rather spend the evening in bed with a romance novel she'd swiped from her mother's room than another second under her fiancé's watch. She hummed to herself as she slowed her steps, admiring the towering paintings that lined the walls. Her father and Anteros were among the nameless portraits, of course. She paused, staring at the face of the man who shared her blood. Not that it mattered to him. She sneered at her father's portrait. She wasn't his daughter, only a bargaining chip, a tradable good whose value equated a field of livestock. Food that would likely be gone come the end of a bitter winter.

"Damned pigs," she muttered to herself.

As she turned toward the nearby stairwell, Ryker said, "I've never heard a lady speak so obscenely."

Sabine whirled around, finding him far too close for comfort. She hadn't even heard his footsteps approaching. "Heavens! I did not know you were there, my lord. Forgive me."

Ryker eased closer, lifting a hand to brush her raven curls over her shoulder. The way his fingertips brushed her collarbone made her face warm. He smiled faintly, leaning closer to whisper, "I expect you to be well-behaved, as your father promised."

Sabine glanced past him down the hall and found they were alone. She swallowed and leaned back as far as she could without stepping away. She knew he would only step closer if he wanted to. No servant or noble would stop him. None would risk incurring her father's wrath. She mustered her confidence and said, "I am always at my best, my lord." She bowed her head, hoping he would take the motion as a sign of dismissal, but he didn't budge.

Ryker reached out and grasped her chin, forcing her to look him in the eyes. "I wasn't referring to your words, love." He was handsome, but she couldn't get past the predatory way he looked at her. Like she was his next meal. He released her jaw and used both hands to straighten his suit jacket. "Next time you feel the need to leave dinner early, I'll take that as an invitation to join you for a stroll."

The lightest laugh escaped her mouth, and she quickly clamped her lips together. "I hardly think that would be proper," she began.

Her betrothed stepped closer, staring down his wide nose at her. Ryker lifted his hand again and pressed his thumb into her lips, shushing her. "I decide what's proper, love. You belong to me now, remember?"

Sabine's eyes widened as she stared up at him. The audacity of this foreigner to speak to her in such a way! "I beg your pardon?"

He loomed over her, his eyes darkening before he pressed his lips to hers roughly, his tongue forcing her lips to part. Ryker dug his fingers into her hip and back. She winced. Her hands pressed against his chest uselessly. She was far too weak to push him away. The back of her eyes stung as she squeezed them shut, willing her brother to come down the hall to rescue her.

No one came.

It wasn't anything like when Julian had kissed her the night of the Solstice Ball. When Julian kissed her, she wanted his hands on her. She didn't want him to stop. She would have gladly spent all night tangled in his embrace—reputation, be damned.

With Ryker, all she could do was ask the gods or whoever was out there to keep this man from forcing her into one of the nearby rooms.

To her relief, the earl eased his grip and pulled away. They both panted, hot breath mingling between them. Her legs trembled beneath her heavy skirts; the intensity of her fear kept her from running. "Good girl," Ryker whispered. His hot breath rolled across her face and made her blood run cold. He briefly dragged his thumb along her lips again. Then he turned and waltzed back down the corridor in the direction he had come from, leaving Sabine quaking with rage.

Sabine rapped her knuckles against her brother's door twice. After a moment, she tried the doorknob and found it was unlocked, as usual. She shuffled inside and closed the door behind her, saying, "Anteros, I need your help."

"What do you want, Sabine? I'm busy right now," Anteros huffed.

She turned, her forehead wrinkled in irritation, and realized her brother was, in fact, not alone. "Of course you are," she said, marching over to his private collection of alcohol. "I'm afraid that will have to wait." Sabine uncorked a bottle and filled one of the glasses to the brim.

The brunette in Anteros's bed scoffed. Sabine turned back toward the bed, relieved their clothes were still on. Mostly. Her brother's guest looked at her quizzically for a moment before shrugging. "Only one of us was invited in," the young lady said before pressing her lips to Anteros's neck. Sabine grimaced.

Her brother's eyes darkened as he glared at her. He was clearly in a foul mood. Sabine started chugging from her glass. When she lowered it, nearly empty, she found Anteros had turned back toward his lady friend and drawn her back. "We'll have to pick this up tomorrow," he said to the young woman. She fumed, of course, stumbling off the bed and cursing them both as she scooped her heels off the floor. She slammed the door closed on her way out.

"My day was finally getting better—not that you care." He seethed.

Sabine chuckled. "Honestly, brother. You can do far better than her."

Anteros growled, dismounting from his crumpled bed. He stalked toward her; the darkness in his gaze reminded her of their father. That look in his eyes sent a chill down her spine. She shuffled backward, bumping into the table. The glass bottles clinked together as the table teetered on its legs. Her brother's arms shot out to grab both sides, quickly stabilizing it. "Why are you here, Sabine? It's late."

"I know," she murmured, wringing her hands. For a moment, she questioned why she had thought he would help her. He hadn't been the same since the incident in the courtyard with Talitha. Neither of them had. But then she remembered the way the earl dared invade her personal space after dinner. If he was going to act with no propriety, she had to seek a way out of their engagement. "It's about the earl."

Her brother scoffed, shaking his head. He didn't meet her gaze. She knew he felt pity. He didn't have to look her in the eyes for her to see it. "Let me guess… You don't like him?" Sarcasm dripped from his words.

She recoiled at his disdain. "It's more than that," the princess argued, crossing her arms. The motion did nothing to make her feel better. She watched as Anteros picked up one of the bottles and started pouring his own drink. His hand was a little unsteady. He must have already indulged in a few glasses before she arrived. That was typical for him these days. She placed her glass beside his quietly, and he moved to fill hers. The princess cleared her throat and asked, "Did you not notice that he left the table shortly after I did?"

Anteros jerked his hand. The red wine sloshed all over the tabletop, missing her glass entirely. "I did," he said hesitantly. Placing the bottle back on the stand, he leaned over his collection. He braced one hand on the wall, his jaw ticking. "Did he go looking for you?"

When she didn't answer, her brother turned his head slightly. His hazel eyes softened, the green and gold flecks glistening like stars. Those flecks were filled with dread, a desperate plea for her to say no. Sabine nodded feebly, her own eyes taking on the appearance of rippling water. Anteros pushed off the wall and scooped his sister into his arms as she burst into tears. She pressed a cheek against his bare chest and listened to the hammering of his heart. He ran his hand over the back of her head and shushed her gently. The gesture was soothing, though foreign. The only person who normally hugged her was their mother. Perhaps she should have gone to speak with her instead.

"Did he touch you?" Anteros finally dared to ask. When Sabine looked up, her eyes wide with fear, he grabbed her by the cheeks. "I will kill him if he laid a hand on you."

"You can't," she whispered. She sniffled, and Anteros found a handkerchief for her. Blotting her face, she mustered her voice. "He didn't… He didn't hurt me, not in the way Talitha was harmed." Anteros tensed. She wasn't sure if it was Talitha's name or the insinuation that struck a chord. She added, "But he crossed the line."

Her brother turned away from her and started fumbling with the buttons on his shirt. "Tell me precisely what happened."

She exhaled deeply. Her hands trembled at her sides. She didn't know what had come over her. She wasn't the type to get emotional. She was the type to hold her head high, even when the world was stomping on her. Especially when her own father stomped. "I'm sorry. I shouldn't have barged in here." She should have run to her mother's room. Her mother was no stranger to living with a brutal man—a man who saw her more as property than a person. But it was farther from her own chambers. She had not wanted to risk running into Ryker again.

"No. You did the right thing, coming to me," the prince said abruptly. He turned back around and locked eyes with her. "You can always come to me, Bine."

Her heart swelled hearing that her brother wanted to protect her. That he still cared. She closed the distance between them and wrapped her arms around his midsection again. This time the cool silk of his dress shirt caressed her cheek. "Help me get out of this marriage, Anteros. Find a reason for Father to send him back to Denorfia. Please."

He grabbed her by the upper arms and pried her away from his torso. "Tell me what happened after dinner."

"He said I *belong* to him now," she said, voice tinged with disgust. Just thinking about it made her blood boil. "He said I had to behave. He put his hands on me, and… he kissed me."

Anteros cocked one eyebrow. "Is that all? I hate to break it to you, but I've done far worse to ladies who *weren't* my fiancée." He chuckled darkly. "You're so dramatic. You made me think he actually hurt you."

She stepped out of her shoes and chucked one at him. Her brother ducked. The embroidered heel slammed against the wall, and they both winced. "You weren't there. You didn't hear him. See the way he grabbed my face. He's possessive. He didn't treat me with any respect. It was abhorrent."

"You haven't exactly been open to getting to know the man," her brother argued. She fought the urge to slap the nonchalant grin off his face.

He took his drink from the table and shuffled toward the sitting area. Sabine frowned as she followed him. "And I don't plan on it after what he did tonight." She leaned against the arm of the emerald sofa and plucked the glass out of her brother's hand. Anteros protested as she took a long swig from his glass. "Will you help me or not?" she finally asked.

He raked his hands over his face. Resting his head on the back of the couch, Anteros exhaled. "I want you to be happy, Sabine. But I don't know that I can help you any more than I helped—" He paused, swallowing the girl in the dungeon's name. Sabine knew what he was thinking, but she didn't want to believe that was the truth. There had to be a way out.

"I will never be happy in this arrangement. He will treat me like one of his cattle. I'm sure of it," Sabine said decidedly. "I am not a mule to be bartered and bred. I am a princess!"

Anteros propped his elbows on his knees while contemplating their options. She knew there weren't many. But there had to be something. "Either we must find a reason Father would find Ryker unsuitable…"

"Which will not be easy, as he has already delivered the cattle," Sabine noted.

"Or you must make it to where Ryker no longer wants you," her brother finished. They locked eyes, and Sabine gasped at the realization.

She lifted the glass to her lips and downed the remaining contents. "You mean ruin myself?" Her voice came out in a whisper. She slid off the arm of the chair, flopping down in the open space beside Anteros on the couch. While she had no interest in marrying the earl, publicly ruining her reputation would make her a social pariah. Could make no man want to take her as a bride as long as she lived. "I cannot believe you would suggest—"

"Believe me, I do not wish to contemplate your *virtue*, sister," he rebutted. The prince pushed off the couch and began pacing the floor. "How else could you convince the earl to break off the agreement?"

Sabine pulled her feet up under her gown and hugged her legs to her chest. "I do not know. That's why I came to you. All I could think when he kissed me was that I needed to get as far away as possible."

Her brother stopped in his tracks. His eyes glazed over as a memory transported him elsewhere.

"Anteros? What are you thinking?" she asked. Hope swelled in her chest as she watched the wheels turn in his head.

"Anything we could try would be dangerous. We'd be taking a huge risk," her brother mumbled. He didn't sound as confident as he usually did. She didn't like his hesitation.

"I'll try anything if it gets me out of this engagement," Sabine proclaimed.

The prince hummed for a minute. "I don't even know if it would be possible. Would be easier to ruin you. You wouldn't even have to do anything. Gossip to the right friends, and let the rumors spread as they always do."

"If I am ruined, Father will have no use for me," she murmured. She lay back on the couch and stared at the high beams of the ceiling above them. "Do you think he would kill me? Or simply banish me from court?"

"He wouldn't kill you," Anteros said quickly. "He would find someone somewhere who would take you off his hands if Ryker did not want you. I have no doubt of that."

Her eyes welled with her rising anger. "I hate him. I would like nothing more than to get far away from him... yet Graynor is home. I never thought I might be sent away."

"I know," her brother replied quietly, taking a seat beside her. "Sometimes the easiest path is to comply, Sabine. Just do as he wishes. Perhaps you will find happiness in your new life in Denorfia."

"And never see you or Mother again." Her chest constricted at the harsh truth of her words. Losing them would be the worst part of leaving her home. They both stared at the beige stone walls that made up their shared prison. While she did not want to leave Graynor, the princess slowly realized that she might soon have no other choice.

"If I cannot break off this engagement, I should rather shed my title than what little freedom I have," Sabine declared. She shifted to sit upright and nodded to herself. Her freedom was everything. She would rather die than let any man who didn't value her take it from her.

"I should have known you wouldn't comply with Father's orders willingly." Anteros pinched the bridge of his nose. He closed his eyes as he added, "What will you do then?"

"I will leave before I'm forced to be a bride," she said. "I just need to figure out where I can run. It will have to be a good hideout. I'm sure Father's men will be sent after me."

Anteros straightened his back suddenly, dropping his hands into his lap. "I might know a place." He turned to look at his sister, really look at her, and she could not help the grin that spread across her face. She knew that look in his eyes. He had an idea. He wasn't sure yet if it was a good idea, a feasible idea, but Sabine was willing to try anything to make her great escape.

She pushed herself off the couch, feeling a wave of relief crash over her body. Her shoulders relaxed a bit, and she realized just how exhausted she was. "Can you look into it? See if it could work? Secrecy would be crucial."

Anteros pressed his fists to his mouth and hummed. "I can inquire. Would have to choose the messenger carefully. Can't have Father getting wind of your delusions." He zoned out staring at his bed as though he were entranced by a memory.

"Julian," she murmured. "We can trust Julian. If you tell him it's for me, I am certain he would help."

Her brother sneered. At least she knew he was still listening. "I'll see what I can do. For now, act normal and try to appease Father. And try not to go anywhere unchaperoned," he advised.

"Thank you," Sabine whispered. Her goodbye was interrupted by a drawn-out yawn, and she stretched her arms over her head. "I suppose we should both get some sleep." She padded across the room to pick up her discarded shoes, not bothering to slip them back on for her short walk next door.

As she reached her brother's door, Anteros stood and turned to face her. "Are you certain you want to do this? There would be no coming back to court."

Sabine lowered her gaze and considered the different places she could end up. Hiding in someone's barn, confined to a dismal room in a cheap inn. Wherever she ended up, she was certain she could make friends and find happiness there. "Anywhere is better than a gilded cage," she replied before opening the door and quietly slipping into the corridor. She could live with anything if it wasn't her father's choice for her.

7

ROYAL PAINS

The day of the Guards' Ball, Will donned a plain black suit he had borrowed from his master—now his business partner, Mister Warren Routledge. He was just about the same height as the older blacksmith, though the jacket strained against his broad chest and biceps. Looking in the ornate mirror hanging in the Guard's Wing hallway, Will felt out of place. This was the fanciest attire he had ever put on, and even then, he felt underdressed compared to all the men in their dress uniforms. He was thankful, however, that Rigel lent him a proper fitting dress shirt and vest to complete the ensemble. The royal blue paisley print stood out against his dark suit. He knew Serena loved that color.

Will unbuttoned and rebuttoned the top button on his suit jacket while waiting for Rigel to come out of the lavatory. After a few minutes, he tucked his hands into his pants pockets to keep himself from fidgeting. He watched as a sea of dark purple exited the Guards' Wing. The freshly shaven guards walked past him as though he were a ghost. Their chins high and their shoulders back, these men carried themselves with pride and grace—and Will envied their confidence. He turned his gaze back to the mirror and didn't recognize the young man standing before him. He wondered if there was any hope for him to earn his place among these well-respected men, or if he was merely getting a small taste of things that would always be just out of his reach. A new life filled with the finer things that he now knew Serena belonged in, but he wasn't sure if he did.

"Ready?" Rigel asked as he stepped into the corridor. Will glanced behind him in the mirror, meeting his friend's gaze. Rigel wore the same uniform the other members of the Garrick Guard wore—a dark purple jacket that buttoned to his chin with gold epaulets and black pants. The guardian insignia was proudly displayed on his right breast pocket.

59

Tree branches weaved out of gold thread stemmed off a silver sword facing downward. His friend was positively humming with anticipation, a bright smile playing on his lips.

"As ready as I'll ever be," Will said. He turned away from the mirror and fell in step beside Rigel, heading in the direction of the main hall. Glancing over at the guardian, Will asked cautiously, "So, Cole's really gone then?"

"I'm afraid so," Rigel replied. His lips pressed in a thin line as he stared forward. "Crys and Xandra are not happy about it, so try not to mention it."

Will nodded. If there was one thing he had learned on their hazardous journey over the mountains, it was that he did not want to be on a guardian's bad side, especially if that guardian was an Elven archer named Crystal Windaef.

They followed two uniformed gentlemen around a bend into a wider corridor filled with smiling guards chatting with ladies in exquisite gowns. Rigel greeted a young woman with straight shoulder-length black hair in a sleek black gown with a slit up to her knee. Beside her were several of the guards who had met them in Silvermane. Among them was Gideon Gilstrap, who greeted them with a dimpled smile and bouncing bronze curls. He clapped Will on the shoulder in greeting. "They haven't put you in a uniform yet?" the guard asked. His words were well-meaning, his tone as playful as his grin, though they still stung. Elara had made it clear he would have to earn a place in the guard like everyone else did. He didn't think any amount of training could bring him up to their caliber.

"I daresay I look better than you," Will teased in return.

The black-haired woman's eyes raked over him. "He's not wrong, Gid." Her violet eyes twinkled mischievously as she nudged the flustered guard. Will knew her face, but he couldn't remember from where. There was something graceful and dangerous about her that Will couldn't place. She chuckled as she walked ahead of them, slipping between uniformed men as easily as a snake in the grass. Will watched her black bob shift through the crowd, the distance between them increasing with each lithe step.

"She doesn't know what she's talking about," Gideon grumbled, running a hand over his hair. They followed the flow of eager guards down the corridor.

"Who was that? I recognized her from somewhere." Will tensed as they approached the end of the corridor, blurs of purple and black disappearing to the left into the main corridor.

Rigel and Gideon exchanged a glance before bursting into laughter. "That is Mad-Eye Milliorva—the sharpest woman to come out of Envyre," Gideon informed him.

"After Crystal Windaef, of course," Rigel amended. He lifted his chin, eyeing the crowd ahead of them. Will wondered if he was looking for one of their other friends—a tall, blonde friend. "You must recognize her from the tournament. Mads took first place in archery and dagger throwing this year, as expected."

"How many do you reckon she has under that dress?" Gideon asked. His grin widened, and Will felt his face heat as he recalled the way the black fabric clung to her curves. The memory of his fingers skirting over Serena's thighs flashed through his mind, and he shook the image from his head. He rubbed the back of his neck, his skin hot to the touch.

"Wouldn't you like to find out?" Rigel laughed, shoving his friend's arm. "At least two."

"But where?" Will's voice trailed off, his brows pinched in as he refocused, but Mad-Eye Milliorva had disappeared into the crowd.

"It's too bad she's still not quite up to par with a sword," Rigel prattled on. "Rotten luck as that's all most people care about."

Gideon shook his head. "You're far braver than I to say that aloud," the guard said, eyes wide.

They rounded the corner, entering a corridor double the width of the prior one. "Envyre must be in want of a new master since Cole left," Rigel said.

As the members of the Guard fanned out, many slowing their pace to chatter eagerly with their comrades, Will found himself scanning the shiny curls and pale shoulders of every lady in front of them in search of Serena. At the center of the corridor, well-dressed men and women made their way into the main hall. Rigel grabbed Will by the elbow and dragged him off to the side near the stairwell. "Crys said to wait for them here," the guardian said, clasping his hands behind his back. Gideon stepped to the side to wait with them.

Will nodded. He watched the bustle of striking guards flirting with beautiful women in various fashions that were wildly more colorful and opulent than anything he'd ever seen in Durmak. His chest swelled with longing at the flood of memories from home—late night bonfires, early morning walks in the woods, whispered secrets during school, the heat of the forge, the warmth of his family's home, the welcoming he always received when he entered the Finch home. In every memory, one face appeared, her carefree smile framed by soft waves and punctuated by a laugh as sweet as honey. He'd give anything to hear that laugh again. To bury his face in her neck and breathe in her scent. He imagined she would smell like rainwater, grass, and something floral. Like the forest in bloom at the start of spring.

Rigel elbowed Will in the ribs. He turned to scowl at his friend but found the guardian's gaze fixed on the top of the staircase. Will's gaze followed Rigel's until he spotted them. Serena descended the stairs slowly, flanked by Crystal and Xandra. Will sucked in a breath as his eyes trailed over Serena, unable to look away. Her deep blue gown was flecked with thousands of tiny silver embellishments. The neckline dipped in a low V that ended at shimmering symbols of the sun and two moons. The bodice was further accentuated with larger clusters of sparkling stars along her waistline, and a glittering sheer cape trailed off her shoulders, dragging the stairs behind her. She looked like the embodiment of the night sky. No, more than that. She looked like a goddess—

not that he believed in those. But if there ever were a celestial being to walk the earth, Will thought they would look just like this. Like *her*. He had never seen anyone outshine the stars until that moment. Now, he wondered if the stars could be jealous of the way a person dazzled as the light from the windows above reflected a kaleidoscope of rainbow refractions on the steps behind her.

She was dazzling. Every bit as beautiful and regal as a princess should be—because that's what she was. The thought sent his heart pounding. When Elara had summoned him the day before, he thought he was being assigned a temporary guard position. Never in his wildest dreams did he imagine the queen would inform him that Serena was her long-lost niece. That royal blood flowed through her veins. That her destiny was written in the stars, and that was why she was so vastly important. She *was* a princess. The lost Princess of Hyrosencia. And she was destined to save them all.

He had just begun to imagine a future where he dared to consider kissing her, to dream of starting a new life *together*. All those dreams came crashing down the moment Queen Elara said that Serena was destined for greatness. The queen had made it clear that there would never be a place for him by her side.

He stared up at her, the girl he had grown up playing with in the woods outside of Durmak, the girl who had always needed someone to protect her. She was destined to end the war? He still did not know how to wrap his mind around the revelation. She looked the same. Somehow more beautiful than the day before, yet the same bright smile greeted him when their eyes met. He had always loved the way her smile lit up a room. He had just begun hoping perhaps their futures could be entwined. That perhaps she did see him as more than just a friend. Now she was untouchable. Unattainable. How was he supposed to walk away from her now?

"Pick your jaw up off the floor," Rigel muttered before stepping toward the base of the stairs. He extended a hand toward Serena, and she took it, clearing the final step to join them on the corridor floor. "You look positively enchanting." Rigel pecked the top of her knuckles before releasing her hand.

Will felt his face warm and shifted his gaze toward the other guardians. Crystal wore a jade green gown with no lace or embellishments. The simple scoop neck and thick straps accentuated her muscular arms and tone figure. Like Mad-Eye's, Crystal's gown was also thinner, less cumbersome than Serena's. She looked beautiful and strong. But still ready for a fight.

Xandra wore a gown the color of an amaranth plant, the deep reddish-pink satin vibrant against her warm skin. Wispy sleeves covered her shoulders, and her natural curls were pinned up. Her skirt was fuller than her friend's, and Will recalled Rigel and Gideon's prior conversation about hidden weapons under gowns. Knowing the guardians, he was certain they all had weapons on them. He paused, his eyes flicking back over to Serena.

Could she have a dagger sheathed under her gown as well? What he would have given to find out.

"Will, I'm so glad Rigel convinced you to come." Her voice snapped him out of a dangerous daydream, and he refocused on her face. Her eyes were lined with black coal, and her eyelids shimmered in the sunlight. He didn't understand why she needed additional embellishment when she was already beautiful.

"And miss the chance to see you like this?" He grinned, holding out his arm the way he had seen others do it. Serena's cheeks tinged the most beautiful shade of pink he had ever seen as she looped her arm through his.

She squeezed his arm as her eyes drifted toward the open doors to the main hall. The faint sounds of string instruments carried out into the corridor, beckoning guests to enter. Serena leaned her face closer to him and whispered, "You clean up nicely, as well."

"Everyone here looks nice. But you… You look—" He paused. His gaze was drawn back down to the dark fabric that hugged her torso in ways he could only dream, the stars along her waist taunting him. He swallowed nervously. "Breathtaking."

Serena grinned, squeezing his arm tighter as he led them toward the ballroom. Her eyes scanned the room eagerly, following streaks up the marbled columns and tracing the intricate stitching on the suits and swaying skirts that passed by. As her gaze skimmed the mass of unfamiliar faces, Will assumed she was searching for her aunt. The thought was strange, that royal blood ran through Serena's veins. Will glanced back at the girl on his arm and realized she did not know that he was aware of the truth. That she had been hiding it from him for who knew how long. He wanted to know why she hadn't trusted him with that information after everything they had been through together.

Before he could work up the nerve to ask, Crystal sauntered by them, one hand draped delicately on Gideon's arm, though she was certainly the one taking the lead. "Follow us. We'll introduce you to some friends." Xandra and Rigel followed close behind them, their beaming faces coaxing the two to join them.

Serena practically skipped, her grip on Will's arm tightening as they followed the guardians. Toward the center of the ballroom was a cluster of attractive young people in fancy garb—among them, the woman in the slinky black gown. Mad-Eye, as the guys had put it. Gideon and Rigel made a beeline for her, and Will avoided her gaze as they introduced Serena to her. This time they introduced the woman as Madeline.

"Finch? You must be the girl we've heard so much about. The knight's daughter who made the crossing!" Madeline said, her voice a low drawl. She eyed Serena over as she shook her hand. The muscles in her arm contracted as she worked their hands up and down. She must have spent a great deal of time training. "Not an easy task. I'm dying to hear all about it."

"Let her breathe, Mads," Xandra said gently. As Madeline withdrew her hand, Xandra swooped in, draping her arm around Serena's back. "This is all so new to her. Especially the dress."

"She wears it well," a deep voice said. A man with dark hair and bright blue eyes stepped out from behind Madeline, an easy grin on his clean-shaven face as his eyes raked over Serena. Will tensed, wishing Serena were still on his arm; his biceps flexed involuntarily as the man stepped closer and outstretched a hand to her. She glanced toward the guardians hesitantly before placing her fingertips on his palm. He brought her hand to his lips and placed a chaste kiss atop her knuckles. Will's stomach roiled. If he was going to have to watch other men put their mouths on her hand all night, he was sure he would be sick.

"Kieran," Crystal said, her voice clipped and curt. Serena quickly withdrew her arm; she fidgeted nervously, her eyes fixed on the floor.

"Crystalira." He didn't bother looking at her, though his eyes did dart from Serena to their other friends. "Xandra, darling, you are looking stunning as usual. How has no one made you a bride yet?" He extended his hand again and repeated the same motion with her. Her smile didn't meet her eyes then, his words obviously a sharp-edged sword to her heart after Cole's abrupt departure.

Xandra pulled her hand back, putting on her sweetest smile. She made a small clicking sound, weighing her response. "I've been too busy working for Her Majesty. And what about you? Still cannot find a woman to keep you in line?"

Kieran glanced back at Serena, who was not paying him any attention. She had stepped to the side for Rigel to introduce her to another young man Will recognized from the tournament. "Who says I haven't?" Kieran quipped. His lips curled upward, his eyes still fixed on Serena's profile. Will didn't like the way he was looking at her. Like she was prey. There was something smarmy about this Kieran fellow, and he wanted to keep Serena far away from him.

Suddenly, a hush fell over the ballroom; the final strokes of string instruments sharp before fading to nothing as all eyes turned toward the entrance. A uniformed guard announced the arrival of Queen Elara Garrick and her husband. Will watched as they swept through the doorway arm-in-arm. The crowd parted as they made their way up the center of the room, chins high as they nodded at their guests. When they reached the front of the room, Lord Stirling swiveled his wife around to face the members of the Garrick Guard and the nobility; her massive gold skirt swept across the floor as she turned, a dazzling smile stretched through her cheeks. The queen looked far happier than the last time Will saw her. Why wouldn't she be happy on the arm of a handsome nobleman who loved her? Will couldn't help but wonder if this was what Serena's future would look like: greeting the people in a bejeweled crown and ornate gown, on the arm of some nobleman or prince whose suit fit far better than his borrowed one.

The ballroom was buzzing with anticipation as everyone stepped toward the regal couple at the front of the room, filling in every empty space before their monarch. Will didn't move with the crowd. His legs remained fixed in place; his gaze locked on the queen from afar. Fingers brushed against his arm, and he glanced over to find Serena had snuck back to his side. When their eyes met, he watched as relief washed over her features, the uncertainty in her eyes replaced by a gentle smile. She leaned closer, her breath tickling his neck where the suit jacket gave way to bare skin. "Nervous?" Her whisper sent a wave of goosebumps up his spine.

Will swallowed and stood straighter, his eyes darting back to Elara. She addressed the room, first thanking her Guard for their noble service. "No, of course not," he mumbled in reply. He hated that she could see right through him. Prayed to Divinity that nobody else could.

The queen called forward those who had competed in the Guardian Tournament a week prior. Madeline, Kieran, and ten others sauntered to stand before Elara. They watched quietly as the queen recognized their valiant efforts. Madeline was honored as the top archer of this year. A woman scoffed to their right—he had to assume it was Crystal.

Fingers laced around the crook of his elbow. He could feel the vibration of a silent chuckle through Serena's hand. "Seems Crystal has a rival."

"Good to know I'm not the only human she loathes," Will replied, perhaps louder than he had intended. Serena squeezed her hand on his arm and shushed him. The grin on her face made his heart jump. She was so close, her warm hand pressing into his suit jacket as though he was her anchor. And he wanted to be. Desperately. With his free hand, he reached up and pressed his hand over hers. The jacket pulled taut over his chest and biceps, and he squeezed his eyes closed, praying the buttons held on.

The competitors disbursed from in front of Elara, taking a place among the crowd as she called up Guardian Unit 13. From beside them, Crystal stepped forward. The sound of her heels clacking against the floor parted the crowd. Rigel and Xandra followed her down the make-shift aisle to stand before the queen.

"She doesn't loathe you," Serena finally murmured. Her fingers stroked higher on his arm, tracing up the curve of his bicep. He never knew the faintest touch could send his pulse pounding. He couldn't form a coherent response as he watched Elara present something small to each of the guardians.

As their friends turned to rejoin them, Serena slipped her fingers back down into the crook of his arm and bit her lip, murmuring, "I hope she doesn't summon us. I already feel out of place as it is." She exhaled deeply, as if she had been holding her breath.

Will tore his gaze from the queen to a younger but incredibly similar face. The resemblance was undeniable. He didn't know how he had not figured it out the moment he first laid eyes on Elara. "You don't look out of place." Everything about her suited the space. She was as beautiful as the ballroom and the people surrounding them. He was the only one who was truly out of place there. He tore his gaze away, unable to look Serena in the eyes any longer as the truth swirled back into the forefront of his mind.

She hummed, the surprised noise sending heat to his stomach. "You don't think this dress is too much?" She reached down and held out the star-speckled skirt, releasing it to flutter back to her side.

His lips curled at the teasing tone of her question. Almost like she could not believe he had meant his comment as a compliment. "Not at all. It looks like it was made for you," he replied. She might have been a princess, but she was still the same girl he had grown up with. Vibrant, energetic, with a smile that could break through any man's armor. The gown matched the twinkle in her eyes perfectly. It was good to see some color back in her cheeks after the abysmal journey they had been on.

The crowd began to applaud, wrenching them out of their intimate conversation. Turning back toward the queen, they found that she had finished honoring the guardians. The musicians resumed playing, and servants worked their way between guests, offering glasses of wine on outstretched trays. Serena reached out and took one, giving the servant a nod of thanks. Will shook his head, deciding it was best not to indulge in the queen's presence.

"Can you believe that?" Rigel asked as he moseyed up to them, his own glass in hand.

"What?" Serena asked. Her brows pinched in as her gaze swept between him and her aunt.

"The queen's pregnancy," Xandra chimed in. She bumped Serena's hip playfully before taking a swill from her glass. "Suppose it shouldn't come as a surprise since she was wed two months ago."

"Elara is pregnant?" Will coughed out, wishing he had anything to drink at that moment. If the queen was with child, could it be possible that the prophecy their people clung to wasn't about Serena? Could it be about another Garrick heir?

"Ah, yes, I knew about that. She mentioned it at tea last week," Serena said. The words rolled off her tongue. As if the queen telling her such an important detail was a common occurrence.

"Why would she tell you before the rest of her court?" Will asked. The question was intentional, a desperate call for her to admit the truth to him. He watched her closely. She froze with her glass pressed to her bottom lip, not moving to tilt it up. His question had caught her off-guard. Rightfully so. He had many more unanswered questions, and he hoped she would start providing answers.

Serena cleared her throat as she lowered her glass. One finger traced the gold rim as she weighed her answer. "Oh, well, you know she was close to my mother," she prattled, "and my father was a loyal knight. I suppose that's why she's taken me under her wing. She sees me sort of like…"

"Family?" Will asked. Her doe eyes met his, and they stared at each other for a moment, the insinuation hanging in the air. She studied his face, the panicked look in her eyes telling him she was suspicious, afraid that he might know the truth. That he knew who she was, and she had not been the one to tell him.

"This is it. The perfect tune," Xandra said. She swiped Serena's nearly-empty glass out of her hands and shoved her at Will. He reached out and grabbed her by the upper arms before she could take them both out. "Time to show off your moves," the guardian added. She linked arms with Rigel, broad smiles on their faces as they marched for the center of the room.

Will stared at Serena, her eyes wide with worry. Their faces were so close he could have kissed her. All he had to do was lean in. He wanted to, desperately. But Elara's words rang in his ears, and he straightened his arms, putting space between them. He cleared his throat as she regained her footing, avoiding his gaze. Will hesitantly held out his hand palm up to Serena. "Shall we?"

Serena was quiet as she nodded, placing her fingers on his palm, her eyes on the back of Rigel's head as he led Xandra to the dance floor. Will dared glance around the room as they approached where a dozen other couples were lining up. Crinkling crinoline shuffled against the floor as the women moved. Sunlight coming from the high windows reflected off the studded jackets and shiny shoes of every stuffy noble and stoic warrior in attendance. His eyes raked over the medallions and embroidered patches on each purple jacket and wondered how each had acquired their accolades. What would it take to earn Elara's respect and affirmation?

They came to stand beside Rigel and Xandra, and Will dropped his hand to his side. Serena swallowed, blinking at him. She had lost her air of confidence from earlier; he hated to see her falter and draw into herself. She was the most beautiful and important girl in the room—even if he was the only person who saw her that way.

Before he could say anything, the other couples stepped toward each other, clasping hands and readying themselves for a waltz. Will stepped forward and grabbed Serena's waist before she realized what was happening. As she stumbled into him, he grinned, mumbling an apology near her ear. A timid smile appeared as she took his other hand. "Let's show them us country folk know what we're doing," he added with a wink.

He led her around the ballroom as if they were the only ones there, the hundreds of staring strangers fading into the background as they focused on each other. Serena smiled brighter than the sun, her lips parted as she giggled faintly. It was a smile that could shine through the darkness of any room. One that could inspire a peaceful man to become a soldier to preserve it. Perhaps the way her smile could disarm a man might prove even more lethal than her ability to wield a blade.

When the dance came to an end, his hand lingered on her waist for a moment, their eyes fixed on each other, and he wished the song had not ended so soon. There was so much left unsaid between them.

"What a lovely dancer you are, dear," the queen said. Her voice tore a rift between them, their hands and bodies flying apart on instinct. Will turned and bowed low to Elara, careful to keep his gaze from meeting hers.

Serena smiled, offering a half-hearted curtsy in reply to her aunt. "Thank you, Your Majesty." She gestured to Xandra, who stood just to the queen's right, and added, "Once again, we have the guardians to thank for their expertise."

"I owe them my gratitude once more," the queen replied, nodding briefly to Xandra and Rigel. Turning back toward Serena, she curled delicate fingers over the girl's shoulder and said, "Perhaps you should like to show off your skills with *another* partner? Have you had the pleasure of making Lord Kieran Brooks's acquaintance yet? He has just won the Guardian Tournament."

It was then that Will looked up and realized the queen had not approached them alone. Behind her stood two dark-skinned women he did not know, along with the tournament winner. His brow furrowed when he met the new guardian's sneer. The man stepped up to Elara's side and smiled as he said, "We have indeed had the pleasure. I should be more than happy to show her what dancing with a nobleman is like. Much smoother than with a *commoner*." Will clenched his fists at his sides, his jaw aching as he bit his tongue. He would have liked to show the arrogant jerk what a commoner was capable of with his fist.

A body shifted to stand between them, and Will found himself staring at the back of Serena's head. Her curls were shiny and smooth, not one hair out of place on her head. He fought the urge to reach out and run his fingers through the strands.

"I quite enjoyed dancing with someone who is at my own skill level," she informed them, the strength in her voice making Will's muscles relax. She was defending him. While her words warmed his heart, he hated that she always felt the need to protect him. It should have been his job to protect her, not the other way around. When had she become such a spitfire?

The toe of Elara's heel tapped the floor impatiently, a small twist in her smile momentarily revealing her displeasure at Serena's comment. "It's your first formal event, dear. I am only suggesting you dance with a variety of gentlemen, as is customary." There was a bite to her last few words, an unspoken threat that made Will take a step back from them. If Elara wanted her to dance with someone else, it was best he not stand in her way.

Serena nodded. "Well, if it's customary." Kieran extended a hand to her, and Will turned in search of the guardians, desperate to distract himself with familiar company while the pompous noble took Serena for a turn.

But before taking Kieran's hand, Serena glanced over her shoulder at Will, raking her teeth over her bottom lip. Of course she was worried about leaving him on his own. He didn't belong there. They both knew it. He offered her a slight smile and gestured an upturned palm toward the other man. "Go on. Show him that commoners can dance just as well," he said gently. She looked disappointed as he turned and headed toward where the other guardians were gathered.

The sweep of string music increased in tempo, drowning out the hum of chatter through the ballroom. Will kept his back to the dancers, trying and failing to focus on the story his friends were rehashing with old friends from the Academy. He swiped a chalice of wine off a passing servant's tray and downed the contents swiftly. Wiping the edge of his mouth with the back of his hand, Will exhaled, the agitated puff earning him a piteous look from Rigel.

"It's just one dance," his friend said, swiping the empty cup from his hands and placing it on another servant's tray. He glanced behind Will and nudged him with an elbow. "Besides, she doesn't look like she's enjoying it near as much as dancing with you."

Will whirled around to face the dance floor, unsure what he was hoping to see. He didn't want Serena to be miserable. Perhaps agitated, or mildly inconvenienced. But not *miserable*. It was her first ball, after all. He wanted her to enjoy it. But even more than that, he wanted her to enjoy it *with him*. His gaze flew to her like a moth to the flame. He knew he wasn't the only one looking, not when she dazzled like the celestial heavens, beckoning all to feel the peace of eternal rest in her calming presence.

His breath caught as he watched Kieran effortlessly twirl her with one hand. Their entangled hands made his gut clench. Serena couldn't help but crack a shy smile. Of course she was having fun, even on the arm of that pompous noble. Will shook his head, turning away again. Watching her dance with another man made him feel things he had never felt before. A simmering anger and a smoldering sadness that he had no business feeling when she didn't belong to him, not in the slightest, though he was beginning to realize how desperate he was to change that.

His gaze roamed over the guests until it landed on Madeline Milliorva, her cat-like smirk commanding the full attention of Gideon Gilstrap and Heath Grange. She was stunning, too; there was no denying that. But looking at her did not elicit the same desire that Serena did. There was so much history between him and Serena Finch—a shared childhood, a shared homesickness for the place they both once called home. Though he missed Durmak and his family constantly, he knew that wherever he went would feel like *home* as long as Serena was near.

As the music faded out, the longest song ever written finally came to an end, Will marched for the dance floor, determined to swoop in and save Serena from having to dance with Kieran. The queen had also been waiting nearby, immediately approaching with yet another man in uniform. His footsteps faltered as he watched Serena greet yet another noble, reluctantly placing her hand atop his and allowing him to kiss her knuckles. The audacity of a man to put his lips on a woman he had just met. Will couldn't stand to watch her dance with someone else, so he turned and stormed for the entrance.

He was halfway down the main corridor, heading back toward the Guards' Wing, when he heard the clacking of heels behind him. "Will!" Serena called out. The pace of her footsteps increased as he came to an abrupt stop, scrubbing a hand over his face. "Where are you going?"

As fingers brushed his arm, he opened his eyes and smiled grimly, not sure what to say to her. "I need some fresh air," he replied with a huff. "You should go back. The queen will be looking for you."

"She knows where I am. She watched me leave," the girl replied. She stuck her bottom lip out, her arms crossed tightly against her chest.

Will blinked hard, forcing his gaze away from her body. "You can't walk away from her, Serena. She's the queen. If she wants you to dance with every stuffy noble in that room—"

"Then she will be sorely disappointed," Serena interrupted. She side-stepped, trying to catch his eye. "What's wrong, Will? You can tell me anything."

Her fingers warmed his forearm, her thumb stroking across the dark fabric in a comforting way. He reluctantly obliged, meeting her concerned gaze. "The way you tell me everything?"

She jolted slightly before recovering, nodding silently in reply. "Yes," she breathed. She leaned closer as if willing him to tell her a secret. As if daring him to finally kiss her.

Will studied her lips before meeting her emerald eyes. Dropping his voice to a whisper, he replied, "Your aunt doesn't want me spending time with you anymore."

Serena frowned, her gaze dropping to the place where her fingers curled around his arm. She pressed her lips together, obviously troubled by the truth in his statement. Will waited. It only took a few seconds for the realization to dawn on her, and she raised wide eyes to stare at him in horror. "When did you—? Who—who told you?"

"*She* did," he replied through gritted teeth. The truth hung between them like a heavy fog, weighing them down, leaving them both struggling to fill their lungs. The pain, the questions, the feeling that his body had been lit on fire—by his burning anger or his unfulfilled desire, he wasn't sure—all of it flooded his senses as she stared at him. The distance he felt extending like a chasm between them made him feel ill. "A better question is… Why didn't *you* tell me? We've known each other our entire lives. Why didn't you trust me with this?"

Her bottom lip began quivering as she clamped her lips together, no response offered. She shook her head slightly, gripping his arm tighter as though their proximity could fix whatever had been fractured by this revelation. "They said I couldn't tell anyone," Serena finally stuttered, her voice barely a whisper. A tear slipped down her cheek as she searched his hardened face, but he offered no glimpse of his smile. "I wanted to tell you, Will. Please believe me. I wanted to tell you the day the guardians told me. Crystal ordered me not to."

His chest constricted, and his legs screamed for him to run. How long had she kept it a secret from him? Since the mountains? Since before they crossed the border into Norlee? "How long have you known?" Will knew it wasn't fair to blame her for this. Not entirely. She had been just as in the dark about her identity for most of her life. The truth must have been a shock. Flashes of bloody memories ricocheted before his eyes, and Cameron's face, full of anger and distrust, made his heart stop. Had she known then how important she was? That she had a divine purpose to live for?

"They told me a few days before we left Jordis for Silvermane," she said quietly. Her eyes glossed over as she stared at the center of his chest, recalling some memory he had been prohibited from sharing.

Will gently pulled his arm out of her grasp and shoved his hands into his pants pockets. Her empty hands fell limp at her side. "The day Cole forced me to train with him… That's when they told you?" His words barely sounded like a question. He knew that must have been it. That had been one of the only times he didn't have eyes on her during the crossing. She had been withdrawn after that day. He had written her mood off as grief. Now he realized she had been mourning more than just her brother. "Why then? Why not before we crossed the border? Or when we reached Symptee?"

She wrung the speckled fabric of her skirt between her hands, her chest rising and falling quickly. "After everything that happened on the mountain, I was so angry that Rigel had thrown himself between me and the Mørkewulv. I didn't understand why he would risk his life for me. The queen had asked them to wait, but Rigel insisted they tell me the truth. I deserved that much."

He exhaled in frustration. "You did." Instinctively, he pulled one hand from his pocket and swiped his thumb over the tear track on her cheek. He took a deep breath, releasing some of the tension from his shoulders as he lingered, cupping her cheek in the palm of his hand. He wanted to wrap his arms around her and hold her like he had under the willow tree. Before either of them knew that she was the heir to the throne that Antoine Rexton had stolen. That she was destined to fight him for it one day. Will pulled his hand back and cleared his throat. "I don't fit in this world of fine wine, fancy clothes, and noble blood," he admitted with a shrug. "But you do. You were meant for this place, this extravagant life. You were never meant for life on a farm. You're destined for greatness."

"I don't belong here any more than you do," she snapped, narrowing her eyes. "I will never wear a crown. I will wield a sword and fight beside our friends. I may have accepted my destiny, but I'm the same girl you grew up with. I love the forest and picking wildflowers and the feel of grass between my toes, and I don't need sparkling gowns or a crown. I need family, and I don't mean Elara. I mean *you*."

His heart could have burst from pounding so hard against his rib cage. Her eyes sparkled with unhindered adoration and desperation. He suspected Rigel had been right all along—damn him—but this was not the time or place for expressing how he felt about her. Not with the queen and half her court in the ballroom just down the hall. Not with the queen's warning echoing in his ears.

"This isn't Durmak, Serena. And we can't go back now. Things have changed, and it's best we both get used to it," he said. The finality of his words caused an avalanche between them, and they both stepped back from each other. *This is for the best*, he lied to himself. His feet dragged and his heart felt unbearably heavy as he walked away from her, quickly rounding the corner into another hall and leaving her alone in the main corridor.

8

TAINTED

Serena seethed as she downed the contents of the first glass she could get her hands on. When her gaze found Elara staring back, she gritted her teeth, glaring at the queen with every ounce of hostility she could muster. The queen's matching eyes widened in realization, and she leaned over to whisper something to the dark-skinned woman beside her—though she could not remember which sister it was. When the woman's smile faltered, their eyes meeting briefly, Serena whipped around and trotted toward the guardians, their platinum and red hair standing out among the crowd.

Their eyes lit up when she joined them; their prior conversation trailing off. Rigel glanced behind her and asked, "Where has Will gone?"

She tensed, clenching her fists as she crossed her arms. She wanted them to know every muscle in her body was calling for her to scream, run, and hit something—or someone. What should have been a fun night with her friends had been ruined, tainted by Elara's desperate attempt to control everything. "He wasn't feeling up for playing pretend," she replied, shooting a hostile glance over her shoulder. "We can thank Elara for that."

The guardians balked. Xandra hushed her gently, afraid someone else might overhear the disdain dripping from each word. "What happened?" Xandra whispered. Her fingers curled around the girl's shoulders protectively, but Serena shrugged it off.

Her arms felt cold, though it was only August. She had been looking forward to dancing with Will for weeks. The feel of his hand holding hers felt natural, his warmth a welcome comfort. But one dance with Will was all she would have to remember the night by. One brief, perfect slow dance and the look of hurt on his face when he told her he knew who she really was—and he didn't feel like he belonged there with her. She would

73

never forget the betrayal in his eyes, the way the warmth had diminished from their honey hue.

"He knows," she murmured, burying her face in her hands. The stinging behind her eyes only fueled her rage. She swallowed hard, pushing back the urge to cry and the even greater urge to scream. "He knows, and he's upset that I didn't tell him myself." Her arms slumped down to hang limply at her sides. "How could she do this? He's my friend. It should have come from me."

The guardians grimaced—the humans more noticeably than their Elven ally. Rigel's fingers brushed the inside of her bare wrist as he leaned down until they were at eye level. "Will cares for you. I don't think there's anything you could do to change that. He'll come around, just like you did. Give him a few days."

Xandra nodded vigorously. Her gaze drifted to the dance floor, where Kieran and a few others were dancing. "Don't fret. The ball has barely begun. Perhaps he'll return later."

"You didn't see the look on his face," Serena muttered, snatching a tall glass off another tray. She eyed the bubbling yellow liquid suspiciously, sniffing the rim of the glass before beginning to down its contents.

Crystal snatched the glass from her hands and scowled in the way mothers do when their children are misbehaving. It was so comical Serena had to choke back a laugh. "No more moping, and no more drinks for you. You never know who is watching." She whispered the latter part, her cold gaze sweeping around the room as if she were looking for someone.

"You're no fun," Serena grumbled. As the strings tapered off, she realized that no less than three young men were staring at her, two starting in their direction. "Oh, no," she groaned, grabbing Rigel by the hand. "I am not getting roped into dancing with an endless line of strangers." He lurched as she started for the dance floor, plowing her way through numerous nobles and disappointed guards.

The guardian jogged to catch up, adjusting the death grip she had on his hand. As they reached the other couples, he lifted Serena's hand and spun her around, catching her off-guard. Her lips parted in surprise as Rigel pulled her back toward him, settling his hand at her waist as the music picked up tempo. "You can't ignore everyone all night, you know," he murmured.

Serena leaned a bit closer and lowered her voice. "I'm not ignoring everyone. I'm dancing with *you*," she argued, her lashes fluttering in feigned innocence.

Rigel chuckled, a deep rumble that she could feel through the hand placed on his shoulder. Now that she was inches from his face, Serena noticed the faint freckles across the bridge of his nose, so light they were nearly invisible on his slightly sun-burned skin. He was a few inches taller than her, about as tall as Will, but he carried himself with more confidence. There was no hesitation in his hands as he guided her through their dance.

He was a perfect gentleman, his firm hand warming the skin between her waist and hip. Unlike Kieran, his hand never shifted. His cheeks were smooth for once, having had time for a close shave before the big event. He was handsome in his guard uniform—what man wasn't? But staring at the insignia on his jacket, she couldn't help imagining Will wearing it.

"Still thinking about Will?" Rigel's voice brought her back to the present.

She inhaled abruptly, feeling as though she had been holding her breath, and nodded. "Is it that obvious?" She tilted her chin up, meeting her friend's gentle smile with her own feeble attempt.

One side of his mouth quirked upward in a knowing grin. "You're both quite easy to read, but that's not a bad thing." When her gaze returned to his jacket, Rigel gave her hand a light squeeze and added, "He will come around. He cares far too much to give up on you now. Especially after he's seen you in this dress—"

"Oh, hush," she muttered, her brow knitted together. Heat spread through her cheeks, settling uncomfortably in her ears and the back of her neck. She thanked the stars they were hidden by her curls.

"My apologies," he said, no hint of remorse in his words. She hated when he teased her about Will. The lull of the orchestra rose to a crescendo, and Rigel smiled wider, slowing their pace. His hand slipped off her waist, and with a turn of his wrist, she was twirling again, her skirt fanning out and sweeping the floor. "The truth doesn't have to change everything, you know. You can be who you are destined to be and stay true to who you are."

"I don't see how," she said, voice full of regret. A few months ago, she might have found their proximity and her admission terribly embarrassing, but there was something oddly comfortable about talking with Rigel. Perhaps because he had not known Serena Finch before she was forced to leave her old life behind. Before the blood and secrets and feeling of betrayal coiled in her stomach where her ignorance had once been, feeding her self-doubt and letting her fears fester in the heaviness of her heart.

The song tapering off into silence, and half of the room erupted into applause. Rigel released her hand and bowed his head to her. The gesture made her wildly uncomfortable, only reminding her that she was above his station. The notion felt silly given her upbringing and his years of training. Blood was only something to be spilled. Though it was still a secret kept from most of the Garrick Guard, she still felt eyes on her everywhere she went. She was sure people were speculating about her resemblance to Elara, figuring out that she must be more than a former knight's daughter.

As they turned to go in search of their friends, one of the Cinderfell sisters stepped in front of Serena. Her head was wrapped in a vibrant silk scarf, covering any hair she might have had. The fabric was a swirl of dark blue, deep crimson, and rich purple—an unusual combination. "Serena, you are looking well," the woman said, dipping her chin in acknowledgement. "I was hoping I could speak with you tonight, if you can spare a moment."

Serena narrowed her eyes, curious what an herbalist or oracle might have to say to her. Probably a message from Elara about propriety and decorum. She glanced at Rigel, who saluted with two fingers and went ahead to join their friends. Realizing someone had walked up behind her, Serena blurted out, "Shall we take a walk?" The woman simply nodded.

When they entered the main corridor, the music trailed off to a distant hum. Away from the prying eyes of nobles and guards alike, Serena rolled her shoulders and sighed, feeling some of the tension ease from her body. The sequined cape cascading down her back and over her shoulders itched, and she fought the urge to reach underneath it and claw at her skin. "I hate to sound rude, but… Please remind me. Are you the herbalist or the oracle?"

The woman's chocolate skin made her teeth seem unnaturally white, and Serena wondered how she had managed to keep them so clean. "Idonea, the oracle, at your service."

Goosebumps started at Serena's neck and spread out in waves down her back and arms. She folded them in front of her body and chewed on her lower lip. They had met a few times at tea with Elara, but nothing had been mentioned of the prophecy. Nothing ever was. Not since her first meeting with the queen. "What did you wish to speak about?" She stared into the inky eyes that held all the secrets of the stars and shivered.

"No need to worry," Idonea said, patting Serena's upper arm. The woman walked toward the staircase; her keen gaze scrutinized the hall for listening ears. "I wondered how you are settling in. Things have been hectic since your arrival."

Serena frowned, feeling a deep crease appear down the center of her forehead like a great wide reminder of all the things she was ignorant of growing up in Durmak. "I would feel far better if Elara stopped trying to control every aspect of my life," she said quietly, no shame in her tone. Three parents dead, one hiding under Rexton's nose, and yet Elara wanted to treat her like a little girl in need of parenting. Never had Serena been coddled the way she was in Symptee, and she loathed it. She had crossed the mountains, killed soldiers, and saved herself from the edge of the abyss. The last thing she needed was a new mother. What she craved was a little respect, especially if she was to lead the rebellion against Rexton one day.

"She means well," the oracle said. Idonea may have believed what she was saying, but her smile faltered. "Your destiny is not an easy one to accept, especially since you were raised in hiding."

"And why is that?" Serena asked, tossing her arms out in indignation. "If my parents knew the truth, why was I left in the dark?"

"You were never in the dark, Serena," the oracle insisted. Her stern gaze was punctuated by a raised eyebrow. Serena braced herself for more riddled words with confusing or indecipherable meaning. "Darkness cannot conquer darkness. Rather, it is light the world needs. *Your light.* Mary raised you to be kind, caring, and willing to help others. To value nature and every life you encounter. That's why you only kill when necessary. Your compassion is what will help you adapt to become a merciful leader. It's how you'll inspire men to our cause."

A couple stumbled into the corridor giggling, and Serena bit back the response on the tip of her tongue. She wanted Idonea to know she didn't feel *compassionate* most days. Not anymore. She pictured her brother Cameron hovering over her, remembered the heavy imprint of his fingers digging into her neck, her airway closing, and her stomach roiled like the angry pit of a volcano ready to burst. She remembered her mother and younger brothers laying in pools of their own blood, her unending sorrow dripping from her eyes like raindrops off a willow after a storm. She watched as the couple made their way down the corridor, heading in the opposite direction. When she was certain they were out of earshot, she whispered, "No one in their right mind would follow me into a fight."

Idonea smiled knowingly. The look on her face made Serena's pulse race—and not in a good way. It wasn't fair for this woman to receive divine visions and only share the most nonsensical riddles. "I have seen many things, some easier to decipher than others. But of your fate I have always been quite certain," the oracle said. She was utterly calm, as if it were some ordinary task to read fortunes in the stars. Why couldn't she tell Serena something useful? The girl still wasn't sure if she even believed such a thing was possible. That Divinity could *gift* people. That He had chosen the Garrick family to rule and chosen *her* specifically to take back their territory. Her life certainly would have been easier if there were less believers in Hyrosencia. Alas, her destiny was universally known; her safety prayed for all these years. And now that she was here, her destiny prattled off as fact, she had never felt more *unsafe* in her life.

Her chest felt heavy; she struggled to inhale, feeling as though there was no oxygen in the drafty corridor. "I'm not feeling very well," Serena said breathlessly, pressing a hand to her midsection. "Was that all you wanted to tell me?"

Idonea looked her over, keeping her concern veiled beneath a passive gaze. Her lips remained relaxed, neither smiling nor frowning. Only the slight crease in her forehead gave an indication of her worry. "Should I send for a physician? Or my sister?"

"No," Serena said abruptly. Taking a deep breath in, she shook her head and offered the oracle a weak smile. "No, it's just nerves. It's… been a very busy day. I think I'd feel better if I retired early." Idonea nodded, squeezing her hand sympathetically. "Would you mind… letting Crystal know I've retired to my chambers? But not right away. I don't wish to ruin anyone's night. I'll be fine for a few hours. I'll lock the door and read until the night guard comes." She knew she was rambling, but she hated the idea of the guardians having to leave their celebration early because she did not feel up to dancing with anyone else.

The oracle gave her a pitying look and nodded. There was hesitance in her gaze, as if she were considering telling Serena something. "I can understand the need for privacy. The citadel can be a vast but suffocating place sometimes. Go. I will pass on your message."

Serena breathed a sigh of relief and smiled. It was a relief to hear that the oracle agreed to her plan. Especially when they both knew Elara would argue about her being left alone. "Thank you," the girl said, shaking Idonea's hand eagerly. "I think a bit of alone time is just what I need right now."

Idonea returned her smile, but it was grim. Forced. Serena wondered why the oracle looked so sad. As she turned to head up the stairwell, the woman's hand shot out, catching her forearm, and she said hesitantly, not meeting her eyes, "There are many battles to be faced… But you can survive anything as long as you keep fighting." She released the girl's arm and turned on her heels. Serena watched as the oracle sauntered back through the doorway into the main hall and disappeared.

Serena turned and took the stairs as quickly as she could manage. She draped her itchy cloak over one arm and clenched her billowing skirt in two fists, freeing her feet to race up the steps. The upstairs corridor was empty, to be expected as all the nobles and members of the Guard were still enjoying the ball on the main floor. When Serena reached her door, she dug a small brass key out of a deep hidden pocket at her waistline. She unlocked the door, stepped inside, and locked it behind herself. Leaning her back against the door, Serena closed her eyes and let out a heavy sigh, feeling some of her tension ease in the quiet sanctuary.

The sound of shoes shuffling against the floor snapped her attention back to her bedchamber. Every hair on her body was immediately on edge as she realized she was not alone. Someone had already been in her room, even though the door had been locked. Serena pushed off the door and took two steps around the corner, locking eyes with the intruder.

Captain Richard Bramley straightened, a lazy grin curling on his smug face as he placed a book back on her nightstand. He was still wearing his full uniform, his captain's insignia visible on the sleeve of his purple Guard uniform. She had seen him at the ball earlier that evening. Elara and Commander Stanton seemed to favor him—to trust him. Perhaps he had been assigned to her guard? To keep a watchful eye on her chambers?

"Captain," Serena said slowly, dragging out his title. "Did—did Elara ask you to take the night watch?" *No, that's not it*, she thought. They would have told her of a change to her usual guards.

Bramley stared, taking tentative steps toward her. The space was wide, and he stood close to the center, beside her bed. Serena glanced sideways at the door, debating whether she could outrun the man. "I wouldn't do that, if I were you, Princess."

Serena froze, the air knocked from her lungs. He knew. She didn't recall him being in the room with the few people who knew the truth. But Elara had told Will the truth without conferring with her. Could she have entrusted this secret to the captain as well?

He rounded the corner of her bed, and she stumbled back, tripped over her cape, and slammed into an armoire. She grimaced, yelping in distress, and Bramley took the opportunity to advance on her, giving her no time to think. His arms rose, reaching out for her neck, and a fuzzy memory flashed through her mind. Her arms shot up to block her face and neck. A strong grip tightened around each of her forearms, wrenching her away from the furniture. He yanked her sideways, tossing her to the ground in front of her bed. "So *this* is Hyrosencia's lost heir?" he asked, his voice laced with spite as he looked down upon her. "Pathetic."

She rolled onto her rear and glared at him from the damask rug that had done nothing to cushion her tumble. Her wrists and knees ached from the brunt of the impact, but this was no time to focus on pain. Not when Bramley was grinning, his darkened gaze indicating exactly his intentions. "Why are you doing this?" She pulled her legs in under her body, wobbling beneath the layers of her gown. Bramley had chosen the perfect moment to strike. The plentiful layers of tulle and silk could lead to her ultimate demise. She reached for the bed, using it as leverage to pull back onto her feet as Bramley lurched forward again. His knee struck her in the side. She gasped, overwhelmed by the impact as he pinned her body against the side of her bed. Staring into his smug face, a new fear swelled in her chest, and she realized there were other foul things he could do before killing her. If he managed to knock her unconscious, she would be dead long before anyone knew anything was wrong.

Bramley reached for her again, but she lashed out, clawing at his jacket and slashing the side of his face. He grabbed her by the wrists and gripped tight. She winced in pain as he leaned closer, his nose skimming her ear. "You'll pay for that," he hissed.

"Over my dead body," she retorted. Taking a huge risk, she threw her head forward with as much force as she could muster. The force of the impact made them both groan as Bramley staggered back.

Blood trickled from Bramley's nose over the curve of his lips, filling the crevices between his teeth, and dribbled off his chin onto his uniform. "That's exactly my intention," he sneered, roughly wiping his mouth on his sleeve. Crimson liquid seeped into the purple material, leaving a dark stain. Serena pressed a hand to her thigh, feeling the dagger strapped to her leg. It was still there, buried under layers of her gown. She cursed the tailor who had made her leg completely inaccessible.

"Why are you doing this?" she asked again. Hope surged through her veins as she imagined one of the guardians banging on her door, irritated that she had left the ball with no escort. She didn't need their ire; she was angry enough at herself. Leaving alone had been foolish. Now she had to fight for her life… again.

With Bramley between her and the only exit, she knew she needed to draw attention to her plight. Her eyes flicked toward the balcony; the door was propped open to allow fresh air to circulate. If she could make it out there and yell, the guards and guests below would hear her. Someone would come. She just had to stay alive until then.

She took off for the door right as Bramley surged toward the bed. His fingers collided in the empty space, narrowly missing his target as she surged toward the glass. Just as Serena's fingers curled over the edge of the door, there was a sharp yank that sent her reeling, and her feet went out from under her body. She yelped as she cascaded to the floor. The glass edge of the door sliced into her palm as she grasped it on her way down. A breeze blew in through the opening, and Serena gasped. One half of her glittering cape had been torn off her gown, leaving the shredded remnants of the right side of the bodice hanging down, her chest barely covered.

Bramley yanked her cape again, and Serena grimaced, losing her grip on the door as he dragged her backward. "I thought this would be more challenging." He chuckled darkly. "Seventeen years I've waited for this moment, and this is the best you can fight? You're nothing but a frail little bird."

Serena ground her teeth as she rolled over, leaning on her arms and knees. Facing him again, she realized he had her cape wrapped around his fist, turning it into a leash of sorts. She wouldn't be getting far with his grip on it. She shoved the piece still attached to her gown underneath her arm, deterring her attacker from turning it into a noose. "I'm not as frail as you think." Wrapped in too many layers, she stomped down hard on the wad of skirts as she pushed herself up onto her feet. The fabric pulled tight under her heels until it released with a sharp ripping sound. Cool air caressed her left leg, and she twisted the cape around her arm, yanking Bramley toward her with all her strength.

He stepped forward on one foot and stopped, a pleased glint in his eyes. "It's charming that you think you have a chance, Princess." Bramley reached toward his hip and unsheathed a long dagger. The flash of cold metal in his pale irises sent a chill through Serena. She was running out of time.

"Seventeen years, and you never thought to switch sides? To help the people you've lived among for so long?" She couldn't understand how anyone could be so heartless.

Bramley grinned. She might have found him handsome had he not smiled in such a sinister way. Perhaps it was the cold, calculated look in his eyes. He had ill intentions, and there would be no talking him out of it. "If there were any hope that these people would win the fight against Rexton, perhaps. But as it stands, you are mere moments from your final breath, taking the last of Hyrosencia's hope with you to the stars—if you believe that rubbish."

If he wanted a fight, that's what she'd give him. She would never let another man try to squeeze the life out of her without putting all her strength and skills into the fight. She knew herself capable of spilling blood—she had done so more than once already. When it came down to kill or be killed, her instincts took over, even when the enemy had the face of a once-beloved brother. But this man, Captain Richard Bramley of the Garrick Guard, was not family. He was a spy, sent by Antoine Rexton to bring an end to the Garrick line. He had likely orchestrated all the attempted assassinations within the citadel, and for that, she would feel no guilt when she drove her dagger through his chest. "You've been here all this time, and you never managed to kill Elara. What makes you think you can kill me?"

The man snarled, yanking the cape, but Serena held her footing. She eyed the dagger in his hand and knew she had to disarm him. Cole had worked with her in hand-to-hand combat after she recovered from the last incident. While Rigel sang her praises, she hadn't felt confident in her movements and choices during the face-off with Cameron. Each move she had made was driven by adrenaline and desperation to survive.

This time, she felt more clear-headed. Bramley's moves were pathetically easy to predict. He lifted the dagger over his shoulder and stepped toward her, a cocky grin spread over his mouth. The bastard thought he had already won. That she was as good as dead. He swung his arm down, and Serena caught his arm in both hands. They struggled; Bramley gritted his teeth as he bore down. Their arms wobbled, muscles tired from overexertion. Feeling the tremble of Bramley's muscles straining, Serena forced his arm to the side. She looped the weapon around the bundle of fabric tying them together and yanked his arm up, forcing his weapon to sever the cape in half. Bramley's eyes widened as his chest heaved. One corner of his mouth ticked up, and she wasted no time twisting his arm and kicking him square in the chest. The dagger clattered to the floor as he slammed back into a bedpost, the wind knocked from his chest.

Scooping the dagger off the floor, Serena turned and raced for the balcony again, wrenching the door open and screaming, "Help! Somebody help me!" She pressed her hands into the brick banister and peered over the edge. Several men in purple uniforms and women in brightly colored gowns peered up at her, and she waved her arms over her head. "Help!" People yelled, and men scrambled to run inside. She could only hope they would manage to knock down her door before Bramley overpowered her.

She turned just in time to see Bramley flying toward her, but the impact of his shoulder in her chest knocked the weapon out of her clutch. Serena gasped, grabbing two fists full of Bramley's jacket to keep herself from falling backward over the banister.

Her assailant chuckled darkly as his arms snaked up. With one hand, he grabbed her wrist and yanked it free of his attire. With the other, he pressed down on her chest, fingers splayed out on the bare flesh just below her throat. His touch seared her skin; her heart pounded furiously against his palm. "Tell me... Can you fly, little sparrow?" His eyes glistened as he pressed down. The ache in her sternum forced her to lean her torso back over the edge of the banister. Her head hung over the edge with only two stories of thin air between her and an excruciating demise. That's when she realized there might be a worse way to die than at the end of a blade. He intended to throw her over and let the sparrow die screaming.

"It's Finch, actually," she spat. Serena wrapped her legs around his waist, anchoring her body to his. "Last I checked, it's weasels that cannot fly." If she was going over the edge, she would take him with her. Realization dawned on Bramley's face, and one hand dropped from her forearm to her leg, attempting to pry her off him. As he managed to loosen one of her legs from him, laughter bubbled out of her mouth. "It's a pity you won't get to see it," she said, shaking her head.

"Your death?" he mused.

"No." She grunted as she pawed at the thigh wrapped around Bramley for her dagger. "Your king's." An overwhelming sense of déjà vu made her chest swell, and she hesitated when her fingers brushed the leather scabbard strapped high on her thigh.

Bramley cackled as he released her other arm, his fingers digging into her skin as they slid up her neck. Not again. She refused to die with hands wrapped around her neck. She sunk her fingernails into the sensitive flesh at his neck, leaving a bloody trail in her wake. He winced, stood straighter, and cursed as he yanked at her bloodied hands.

No longer leaning halfway over the balcony, she unclenched her legs from around him and slammed both heels onto his feet. The impact sent her assailant reeling, and they both tumbled to the floor. Serena hoped the pain would give her a head start for the door, but Bramley gnashed his teeth, grabbing her by the ankle as she tried to get back on her feet. "You're not going anywhere." Angry red streaks were prominent on his neck, but not nearly as aggressive at his wide, wild eyes. If a man's hatred could light a fire, Richard Bramley would have already burned her alive.

The stone dug into Serena's back as she rolled over to face her assailant. Clenched in his fist was the dagger she had dropped moments ago. Her heart hammered as she threw her forearms up to shield her face and chest. A sharp sting tore through her forearm as he slashed into her. Hot blood dribbled down to her elbow, splattering the stone beside her and dripping onto her mangled gown. Her injured arm trembled as she used both hands to latch onto Bramley's wrist, holding him at bay. "You're shaking. Tired so soon?"

She scoffed as she jammed her knee into his chest, knocking the air out of his lungs. Bramley staggered back. "You wish." When Serena got back onto her feet, she quickly unsheathed her dagger. Her hesitance to pull it out sooner had nearly gotten her killed; she would never make that mistake again. She had been ripped open from her wrist to her elbow, yet she could hardly feel it, save for a warm ache. Something pulsed through her veins, a tingle reminiscent of Crystal's healing magic spreading through her injury. Her head pounded as though she had been punched. She wasn't sure what was happening, but she knew something was wrong.

"Ah, there it is," Bramley said with a faint laugh. "You should start feeling the effects any second." He sneered as he paced the balcony in front of her, rolling the hilt of the dagger between his fingers.

Divinity on high. The blade was poisoned.

Serena's vision blurred along the outer edges, and she knew she had minutes before she would fall unconscious, or worse, drop dead. She rushed at her attacker, letting out a shrill battle cry. Bramley slashed out again, making a shallow cut over her ribcage but failing to block her elbow from slamming hard into his right cheek. He had underestimated her, and it would be his undoing.

The blue sky faded into a lovely orange as the sun kissed the earth. Serena clenched her jaw as she swung her leg and kicked Bramley in the gut. He stumbled back into the banister with a crash, the brick beginning to crumble from the impact. She did not give him any time to recover, kicking him again while it was clear he was still out of breath. "You're dead, sparrow," he sputtered. Blood trickled from the corner of his mouth, and she grinned.

Serena kneed him in the abdomen, feeling a wave of warmth sweep over her face and neck. Was it the fight or the poison setting her veins on fire? She didn't have time to worry about it. Stepping closer to Bramley, Serena took a steadying breath and said, "You won't live to see that." Then she stooped, grasped him behind each knee, and lifted until his torso dangled over the edge. Fragments of brick façade crumbled beneath his weight. "Who else is in the citadel?" she screamed at him. "Who are Rexton's spies? Tell me, and I will spare you."

Bramley chuckled, his darkened gaze full of resolve. "After tonight, they'll all know who you are." He struggled in her grasp, no fear in his face. Only contempt. He grabbed a fistful of the sheared cape attached to one of her shoulders. "And how *weak* you are."

Serena released him then, stepping back to reassess her options. But as Bramley threw himself at her once again, all strategy became null. She crouched, jumping and kicking with all her strength. This time, the balcony did not cradle Bramley in its embrace. This time, three large bricks broke free of the banister and tumbled off the balcony, taking Richard Bramley with them. Serena gasped, rushing forward in time to see the man splat against the ground below. Chaos ensued as men and women shrieked, pointing and racing for the citadel doors. Crimson quickly pooled out from his body, and her stomach turned.

Serena stumbled back, suddenly feeling weak in the knees. There were other traitors within the citadel. She was certain of it. But she had to find help. She fumbled with the lock on her door just as she heard her name being yelled down the hall. With difficulty, she shoved the massive door open and staggered into the corridor, where she came face to face with her guardians.

Evidence of the altercation was splayed down the front of her gown, the crimson smears covering many of the sequin embellishments, leaving a gruesome trail down the center that had maid servants in the hall gasping in horror. There was no mistake, there had been an intense fight—and she had managed to win it on her own. But at what cost?

The echoes of screams and running footsteps trailed up the stairwell, and Serena sucked in an unsteady breath. She had killed Captain Richard Bramley, and there were no witnesses. Only a torn ball gown and a dead man splayed out in the citadel courtyard. She lurched forward, the word *poison* frozen on the tip of her tongue as Rigel caught her mid-fall, and everything faded to black.

9

GAMES OF DECEPTION

Anteros tossed two cards onto the tabletop, and his friends groaned. Julian slammed a fist on the edge of the table; their glasses teetered back and forth with the sudden motion. "Turn out your pockets," he demanded, pointing an accusatory finger at Anteros. Pale locks framed his face as his wild eyes scowled at the prince.

"You dare accuse me of cheating?" Anteros asked, one brow quirked up. It wasn't the first time Julian had accused him of such a thing. But he had never needed to cheat a day in his life. Not when his friends had always been piss-poor at cards. And when it came to playing Prophecy, Anteros was the luckiest man alive.

Julian grumbled, swiping his glass from the table and chugging its contents. The lounge was quiet except for their occasional outbursts—to be expected when the four young men met to gamble after the rest of the castle had grown eerily still.

"He always wins half the rounds," Calix reminded their friend. "Been that way ever since we learned to play." He wasn't wrong. Anteros always made sure he won the first game so he could have the first choice of the prizes his friends had brought. He threw the others a bone now and then to keep things interesting. He wanted them to continue their monthly tradition, especially when it meant he could take home some new piece of treasure or exotic beast at no cost to the crown.

James chuckled, brushing thick honey-blond bangs out of his eyes. "Go on then. Pick your prize," he said, motioning to the small black table covered in extravagant goods perched between two empty sofas. Atop it sat their buy-ins, a variety of unusual and rare items only a fortune could procure.

Anteros's eyes sparkled as he leaned back in his chair, lifting his legs and propping his feet up on the table's ledge. He could just make out the scruffy ash-covered feathers of a small bird in the brass cage on the table. James had brought the poor creature from his father's collection, likely hoping they wouldn't realize what an incredible prize it was before he could choose it for himself.

"The bird. Does it have a name?" The prince lifted his chin, admiring the sleeping creature over Calix's shoulder.

James swallowed. "That ruddy beast? Well, I think it's a him. My father calls him Phinnian."

"Phinnian the phoenix. Plucky," Anteros said, bemused. His lips curled in a triumphant grin as Calix whirled around to stare at the filthy bird. He had access to messenger hawks, but they were not always compliant with him, preferring to serve only one master.

"You pinched a phoenix? Your father's going to kill you," Calix said to James, his eyes blown wide. Their friend slapped a hand over his face in shame. He was notoriously a fool, and this was no exception.

The prince nodded his head at his friends, his selection evident. Then it was time for the next round. James quickly shuffled and dealt the cards. Anteros picked up his hand and frowned at the court jester, the most useless and loathsome card to be attained. With this in his hand, he would not have to throw his friends a bone.

Nestled beside the jester were a queen and a milkmaid. While the queen was much more valuable in the point system, the milkmaid also had worth when paired with any of the male suitor cards below a noble rank. Not including the jester, of course. As it was, his hand was a wash. He had one chance to discard and redraw one of his cards, but only if the entire group agreed. And he knew better than to let on that his hand was horrid.

His thumb traced the top edge of the milkmaid card, his gaze entranced by the simple woman's ginger locks. A deep, consuming yearning settled heavily in his chest. He missed Talitha terribly. At this time of night, he always considered donning a cloak and making his way down to the dungeon. But then he reminded himself that she was surely sleeping. That visiting her would do more harm than good. He had done all he could to try to shed the memory of her from his heart and his head, taking other young ladies to his bed and training harder than ever. Yet none of it filled the hole that the whip had torn in his own heart earlier that summer. The taste of her lips had begun to fade from his memory. The flavor of crisp, red apples was all that remained in his bleary daydreams of those brief blissful moments in time. He could hardly bear to look at them at the breakfast table now, much less partake in their sweetness. Somehow the fruit had lost its flavor, replaced by something bitterly nostalgic.

It was hard to get through a day without thinking of her—impossible when Sabine or some other fool brought her up. To his friends, she had been Lady Adelaide, a brief tryst that ended when she returned to Denorfia. They could never know the truth about her, that she was a commoner from the south imprisoned and accused of high treason against his father. That he had come to care about her despite that. Or perhaps, because of it.

"How's Sabine been handling the news?" Calix asked, plucking one of the cards from his hand. He held it up, captured between two fingers, and studied his friends' expressions. No one reacted.

"Any word on the date, Anteros?" James added, finally plucking a card from his own hand.

The prince looked up from his cards then. Julian pulled out a pipe, cursing under his breath as he struggled to light it. Anteros almost felt bad for him. *Almost.* Except the girl his friend was flustered over was his sister. The princess doomed to an arranged marriage to a Denorfian. "Uh, no, not yet," Anteros muttered, plucking a card from his hand. His friends did a terrible job hiding their relief that he was willing to discard and redraw this round.

"Hopefully not anytime soon," Calix said, his gaze darting between Anteros and Julian. A heavy tension had filled the air like smog, the room suddenly feeling stale and suffocating.

"Things have been *tense* around here lately," James noted. "We've been talking of heading back to Jessiraé next week."

Julian leaned back in his chair and puffed out a ring of smoke leisurely. He stared out the tall window at the moon half shrouded by shadows. "I'm in," he said, but his voice lacked his usual confidence. Without looking down at the cards in his hands, Julian plucked one and tossed it onto the table face up. A princess. To discard a royal was a bold move. Anteros did not miss the irony. Neither did their other friends by the wide-eyed looks they exchanged.

"What about you, Ant? Think the king would set you free for a week?" Calix prodded, flicking the card in his hands onto the table. A knight. Not a bad card, though it was strongest when paired with the king.

The moon mocked Anteros as he stared at the pale face that watched his discretions in the dead of night. She knew with which bodies he slithered into bed on lonely nights and what truths he only dared whisper to himself as the ruby liquid in his glass finally lulled him into an unrestful slumber. Worse still, she knew where his heart lay buried deep in a dungeon. "Not with the envoys here," Anteros replied sullenly. With a flick of his wrist, the jester landed atop the table, and his friends sighed in relief knowing the card was out of play for this round.

"That's too bad," James muttered. A fourth card dropped on top of the pile, covering the jester's taunting smile with a harlot. Just about as useless as the jester.

The prince could only dream of having a week away from his father's smothering presence. He only knew true freedom in the shadows of the night, in the rare hours his father was silent. In the morning, the monarch's anger blossomed with the blood-kissed sunrise; Anteros's hopes fled to the back of his mind at the first sign of his father stepping into the room. There was no hope for happiness in the daylight, only blind obedience he would try to drown in spirits when the world swallowed the sun.

They took turns drawing a new card from the remaining deck at the center of the table. He could tell from the crinkle in Calix's nose that he had not drawn anything worth celebration. James likely also had a dud as a prominent wrinkle appeared on his forehead just below his bushy hair. Julian remained unreadable; his expression indifferent as he waited. Anteros eyed the prince card in his hand before narrowing his eyes suspiciously at Julian.

Calix was the first to admit defeat, placing all three cards face up to show them his pitiful hand. Then James followed, tossing his down and declaring that he had matched the Viscount and Viscountess. Not a great hand, but at least he earned a few points for it.

Finally, Anteros flourished one hand in surrender, tossing down the prince and milkmaid cards. He could have put down the prince and queen, arguing they were from rival kingdoms instead of relatives, but he did not have the energy to argue the case. James and Calix snickered, thrilled that his loss was guaranteed this round. They all turned to Julian, who stared blankly at Anteros. The longer he stared, the more uneasy the prince felt. Like perhaps Julian knew exactly what he had done—with his cards and his unconventional romance.

"You can't win them all," the blond finally declared, laying down his cards. A king, a seer, and the sun. The golden trio. Julian would have won no matter what cards the others had.

"Prophecy," they all breathed. Though it was the name of the game, it was incredibly rare for someone to end up with the perfect hand.

James slammed his palm on the table and groaned. Anteros rolled his eyes. As the absolute worst at strategy, James should have been used to losing on game night by now.

"On that note, I will claim my prize and take my leave," Julian said, pushing back his chair and rising to his full height.

Anteros stood as well, following him over to the table. As his friend admired the other glittering options, the prince admired his scruffy new pet, poking a finger into the cage and allowing the infinitesimal bird to peck at his flesh. "I think I shall retire early as well," Anteros said.

An icy glare cut through the warmth of the room. Julian picked up a necklace made of rubies and pretended to inspect it, his gaze never leaving Anteros. "That's not like you," he muttered. "Got a girl waiting?" He cocked an eyebrow as he pocketed the sparkling piece.

Anteros scoffed. "Not tonight."

Their friends grumbled behind them, reluctantly stacking the deck of cards and returning their glasses to the servants' cart in the corner of the room. Julian bid them farewell with a slight wave and made a beeline for the door. As Anteros watched him traipse away, a brilliant idea struck him. He hoisted Phinnian the phoenix's cage by its handle and barked good night at the others as he rushed after Julian, meeting him a few feet down the hall.

"Come with me," Anteros said, making his voice as commanding as he could muster. He shouldered past Julian and continued down the hall toward his chambers.

Julian huffed as he trudged a few feet behind him. "What do you want, Rexton?"

The prince paused. His friends were going to Jessiraé soon. He had not thought through his plan yet, but he knew he could not allow this opportunity to be wasted. Anteros held up the cage and stared at the phoenix. Close up, he could see tufts of red and yellow feathers beneath the ashen remains. This creature and their trip could be the keys to pulling off the impossible. "I need your help with something *delicate*."

"Why *me*?" Julian pressed, stepping closer. "Calix would be far easier to recruit."

"Because Sabine trusts *you*," Anteros snapped, his deep voice low and brisk.

The hall was eerily quiet. Then the soft squeak of shoes against the tile echoed, growing closer until Julian came to a halt at Anteros's side. Without turning to look at him, he asked, his voice resigned, "Where to?"

"My chambers," Anteros replied, lowering the phoenix's cage to his side and continuing on his way. Julian followed closely, his brooding presence looming behind his friend's shoulder. Almost in the same manner that Anteros shadowed his father. The thought unnerved him, and he clenched his fingers tighter on the cage handle.

Anteros pushed open his door and motioned for the blond to go ahead. Julian narrowed his eyes as he crossed the threshold, and Anteros turned the lock behind himself. "If she's with child, it's not mine," Julian said suddenly, raising both hands in surrender. The way his eyes had softened in trepidation almost made the prince feel guilty for dragging him into this.

But his words made Anteros want to throw a punch. He gritted his teeth, his chest heaving in aggravation. "How dare you even suggest such a thing?" Anteros paced through his chambers over to the bar, placed the phoenix's cage on the floor, and started pouring. He didn't care what he grabbed; he just needed something strong in his system to have this conversation with his least friendly acquaintance. When he was done, the prince turned and joined Julian in the sitting area, offering him one of two glasses that were filled to the brim. The liquid was brown, pungent, and burned the back of their throats as they both took a long swill.

Clearing his throat, Julian asked, "What does she need?" Sadness and frustration tinged his quiet question. It was obvious that he cared for Sabine, as much as Anteros hated anyone thinking about his sister in that way. Of all the men at court, she could do far worse than Julian.

Anteros leaned his elbows on his knees and pressed his glass to his temple. He couldn't believe he was about to involve someone else in such a traitorous conversation. "Sabine wants me to help her get out of her betrothal." Julian swallowed loudly, waiting for him to get to the point. "I told her I had only two ideas, as we all know my father will not change his mind on his own." Julian grunted in agreement. "The first is for her to ruin herself, *publicly*, but we all know the risks involved. Of course, she fears the permanent damage to her reputation."

Anteros glanced over the table and found Julian stiff. Every muscle in his body was drawn tight, green veins protruding in his pale neck and bare forearms. "We both know you'd never ask me to touch her. What's the other option?"

"If I cannot convince my father that the earl is unfit, she wants to run, to leave Graynor behind," Anteros concluded. He chugged the remainder of his glass's contents, wincing at the intensity of the burn in his throat and chest, before plunking the empty vessel on the nearest table.

"You want me to take her back to my father's estate?" Julian guessed, cocking one eyebrow.

"No. That would be far too obvious," the prince said decidedly. "We would have to send her somewhere my father would never expect her to willingly live."

Realization dawned in Julian's pale blue eyes. "Jessiraé." Anteros nodded. "It's mostly brothels and poor families. I cannot imagine she'd enjoy it." He leaned forward, taking a similar stance to Anteros while humming thoughtfully. "Did you have a place in mind?"

The prince glowered at the dark wall behind his four-poster bed. He struggled to name the place in relation to his sister. "The Untamed Mare." Bile rose in the back of his throat, and he forced it back down.

Julian puffed out a chuckle, the irony not lost on him. "If she were found there, that would certainly diminish her reputation. Your father would never have her back at court."

"That may be the only way to save her from being sold to the earl," Anteros snipped. He rose to his feet, running his hands over his hair and resting them on the back of his neck.

His friend stood as well, sauntering over to the open area where there used to be a window. Fractured bits of glass remained around the frame, but Anteros had never requested it be repaired. Julian stared over the balcony at the half-shrouded moon and sighed. "You are aware this conversation alone could earn us an execution?"

Anteros nodded his head, but his friend did not turn toward him. "You are welcome to leave anytime. I cannot force you to help."

The young man whipped around, the severity of his features bathed in the subtle glow of the moon and stars. "You're damn right you can't. I'm only helping you because it's for *her*." Anteros looked down and found Julian had jabbed a bony finger in the center of his chest.

"You actually care about her," Anteros said quietly. Julian took another sip from his glass, and the prince felt a pang of regret for being hard on his friend. He had been a hypocrite for getting angry about Sabine and Julian's flirtations when he had been enjoying the same flutter of new feelings with Talitha just two months ago. Some things, some *feelings*, cannot be helped. But perhaps with careful planning and trustworthy allies, there was hope. Something none of them dared hold onto as long as his father was pulling the strings in Graynor.

"What do you need me to do?" Julian finally asked. His grip was tight on the glass. Anteros expected it to shatter in his grip at any moment.

The prince sauntered over to his desk and leaned over it. Rummaging through half-read invitations and love letters from silly girls, he pulled a blank piece of parchment and smoothed it out over the top of the desk. He dipped a feather in an inkwell before scribbling a short letter in script. "Give this to Madam Rosmerta at the Untamed Mare. *Discreetly.* Ask her to have a reply readied before your return." As he finished the letter, Anteros folded it thrice and moved on to melting wax over a candle. He poured a bit over the fold and pressed his ring into the wax, leaving an imprint of the Rexton family crest. A bear with a crown hovering over it. If only his father knew what treasonous words lay beneath his own seal. Anteros grinned. Reaching into the top drawer, he pulled out a burlap bag that fit perfectly in the palm of his hand and added, "Offer this as down payment—if she agrees—and tell her there is plenty more to come."

He tossed the bag, and Julian jerked to the side to catch it one-handed, sloshing part of his drink onto the floor. He grimaced, looking down at his shoes. "And if she doesn't agree?"

Anteros pressed his lips together in a fine line. This had to work. He had no other ideas. If the brothel would not hide Sabine, there was nowhere she could hide from their father. If the brothel would not take her, she would have to wed Earl Ryker Umbryon. Either way, he feared his time living under the same roof as his sister was rapidly coming to an end.

10

HEAVY HEADS

Feeling a warm pressure on the top of her hand, Serena's lashes fluttered, her mind still groggy from sleep. She was in bed in the Infirmary, she assumed, though it was her first time in this wing of the citadel. Will sat beside the bed, one hand resting atop hers; his chin leaning on his other fist. He frowned, his bloodshot eyes focused on their hands as his thumb stroked back and forth across her skin. He didn't notice her blinking at him.

Her lips parted, only a whisper escaping her dry mouth. "Will." She cleared her parched throat, desperate for a drink of water.

His eyes shot to her face as he stumbled onto his feet, leaning over the bedside to caress her cheek. "You're awake," he said, closing his eyes and sighing. "I was worried sick." She attempted to smile, her heart fluttering at the thought of him worrying about her health.

"We all were," another voice said. Serena turned her head and found Rigel leaning against the wall. "But I knew you'd pull through. You always do, somehow."

He pushed off the wall and stepped up to her bedside table, picking up a silver pitcher and pouring water into an empty glass. She watched as the clear liquid trickled into the glass, the way the bubbles fizzled into nothing as soon as Rigel stopped pouring. The hollow feeling deep in her belly threatened to drag her back to Death's gates. She greedily accepted the glass from Rigel, chugging the contents without a word of thanks. When she had depleted its contents, she breathed heavily, tired eyes resting on the empty vessel.

"How long was I out?" she asked, strength returning to her voice.

Rigel reached out and poured more water into the cup nestled in her hands. "Just one night," he said calmly, as though losing one night to injuries were a trivial thing. "Luckily, between Crystal and Ismenia, you were in good hands."

Serena glanced about, finally registering that Crystal and Xandra were not there. In fact, there wasn't another soul outside the three of them in the entire Infirmary. Not even a physician. "And where are they now?"

"Ismenia went to rest. She was here all night and said you seemed stable," the guardian replied, setting the pitcher back on the bedside table. "Crystal and Xandra were summoned to the council meeting."

"The council has convened?" Serena asked, propelling the blanket off her lap. As she planted her bare feet on the floor, cold air swept over her legs, and she realized she no longer wore the heavy ballgown that had been ripped to shreds during the attack. Now, all she wore was a cream chemise that went to her knees, her collarbone and arms bare.

Will turned swiftly and cleared his throat, acting as though he had not seen anything. Rigel did not flinch, nor did he turn away. He kept his eyes fixed on hers as she sheepishly drew the blanket back up to her chest. "I should be there," she stuttered, searching the sides of the bed for any sign of clean clothes and shoes.

There were none.

"No," Rigel said sternly, holding out one palm to block her only exit. "You should be in bed. You're in no state to address the council right now."

Serena flexed her jaw and huffed loudly. She knew Elara well enough to know this meeting would be about the attack. About the safety of the citadel. About keeping Serena safe at all costs. Even if it meant keeping her under lock and key until she was ready to lead the rebellion. Her fingers curled into quaking fists, and she chucked the blanket aside. Sliding off the bed, her feet plopped on the cold floor, taking up the small space between Rigel and the cot. "I think I can decide that for myself." She pressed her hands against his arms and maneuvered her body past him. She walked slowly at first, trying to hide the wobble in her knees. Exhaustion threatened to take her legs out from under her, but she refused to return to bed. Not when important conversations were taking place.

"Serena!" Rigel followed on her heels, quickly wrapping a blanket over her shoulders. "You can't just waltz around the citadel like this. Ismenia will have my head—if Elara doesn't first!"

Another set of frantic steps sounded behind them, and Serena glanced back to find Will behind Rigel, his eyes wide. "Perhaps you should listen to Rige," he pleaded, eyes flicking to meet hers before casting them back to the floor.

She remembered Richard Bramley's hands on her, pushing her to the floor. Her hesitation to use the blade strapped to her thigh for that very purpose. Sinking her fingernails into his flesh. His knife slashing through hers. Their desperate push and pull on the balcony that ultimately ended in his traitor's demise. She would never forget the relief she felt as he tumbled over the edge, no longer able to put his hands on her. Her vision had been clouded by a fog, no doubt the product of some poison on his blade. She still didn't know how she'd managed to survive that, but having a healer in their midst, nothing surprised her. If Bramley had not fallen, she knew she would not have survived. And she felt not a shred of guilt for pushing him.

Serena stopped abruptly, and both men nearly collided into her. She turned to face them, one hand gripping the blanket at the center of her chest. "That man who tried to kill me—he was one of Elara's Captains. Was he not?"

Rigel swallowed hard and nodded.

"Then her council has been compromised, for Divinity-knows how long, and I guarantee he was not working alone," Serena hissed. She rubbed her hand over her face and realized the slice down her forearm had closed. A faint scar remained, slight soreness as well. But it was Crystal's handiwork, she was certain. That was the only way such a wound could heal overnight. The guardian must have been exhausted from constantly healing her human companions.

"Elara knows that much," Rigel said, rubbing the back of his neck.

"I will not allow that council to have any say in my safety again. They have proven themselves incapable of protecting anyone, and I intend to tell them just that."

Rigel jogged until he was in front of her, forcing her to stop again. He held up two palms in surrender as he pleaded, "At least stop by Ismenia's chambers first. Please. She's right down the hall. Perhaps she can lend you a gown and some shoes. Anything to make you more presentable."

Serena exhaled, wiggling her bare toes against the cobblestone. Rigel was right. She hated to admit it. But she couldn't possibly convince Elara and her council that she was fine if she barged into their meeting half-dressed. "Fine."

Relief washed over Rigel's tired features, and she felt a pang in her heart, remorse for causing him such distress. He turned to lead the way, pausing to address two guards at the Infirmary doors. She waited a moment, whispering to herself, "I don't even know what to say to them. I… I wanted so badly to believe I was safe here. But now I know. I'll always be in danger, even within these walls." She exhaled, yet the tension didn't leave her aching shoulders. The truth cleaved her to the bone. They would never be safe, not while war loomed and Rexton remained in power. One side or the other had to fall.

She couldn't let it be theirs.

Gentle fingers caressed the back of her hand, and she turned her palm, allowing Will to take her fingers in his. Heat pricked the corners of her eyes at the small but needed comfort, especially after their argument the day prior. Part of her had been surprised to see him when she opened her eyes, but part of her wasn't. Through everything that had happened, he had stayed by her side, reminding her of her strength and her worth when she felt her lowest. She closed her eyes and squeezed his hand, an unspoken thanks for his presence.

Will leaned closer and murmured, "I'm sorry I walked away from you yesterday. If I had known—"

"Don't," she whispered back, turning to face him. The skin under his eyes was red. Her chest constricted as she inhaled sharply. "This wasn't your fault. I chose to go upstairs after the oracle said—" She stopped, turning over Idonea's words in her head. How they made sense now.

Will reached out to tuck a lock of hair behind her ear. "What did she say to you?"

Serena clenched the blanket so tightly her knuckles turned stark white. Idonea had to have known the attack was coming. She must have known what awaited her. Yet her words had hardly been a warning. "She told me that if I kept fighting, I would survive." The words felt like a different kind of poison on her lips—a taunt, if anything. Once again, someone knew more than she did about her own fate, and it filled her with slow, simmering rage ready to burst forth.

"I'm glad you did," Will said, startling her from her thoughts. He squeezed her hand and offered her a faint smile, no dimples to be seen. "Next time, you won't be alone."

"The next time I have to fight like that, it won't be inside this fortress. It will be on my terms."

His brows raised at the harshness of her tone. She released her grip on his hand and started toward the hall, where Rigel and two guards were ready to escort her. She eyed the men wearily, wondering whether these men could also be spies for Antoine Rexton. And she knew in her heart that the only people she could trust were those who had made the crossing by her side.

Guards pulled the doors open just as raised voices began yelling over each other. Rilura banged her fist on the table.

"Your Majesty. With all due respect, this is unnecessary," Crystal said, her voice strong and stubborn as ever.

"Clearly, she can handle herself," Rilura argued. Red patches bloomed across her pale cheeks and down her neck as she leaned over the table, a thick finger pointed at Elara.

"Are you referring to me?" Serena stepped through the doorway, and all eyes turned on her.

Ismenia had done her best to make her look presentable in the five minutes Serena was willing to spare. Her hair had been plaited, the ends bound in a cream ribbon. The blush gown covered much of the bruising that remained from her fight, though she knew the fingermarks at the base of her throat remained prominent. She held her chin high, having nothing to be ashamed about. Her bruises were a badge of honor. The man who had dared to touch the Garrick heir had met his fate at her own hands.

Elara's eyes widened as her gaze skimmed the girl's wounds. Her back straightened. "Serena, what are you—"

"My apologies for being late," Serena interrupted. She stepped up to the table, filling an open space between Crystal and Rilura. "I was surprised to hear you called a council meeting while I was *resting*." They moved over to make room for Rigel to join them at the table as the guards closed the doors. Glancing over her shoulder, she realized Will had not followed them. She wished he had.

The queen swallowed audibly, her chest heaving as she took a deep breath. Her hand pressed to her distended belly, her bump barely visible above where her skirt jutted out from her waist. "We were uncertain when you would wake, dear," Elara said, a hesitance to her voice. "You should have stayed in bed." She cut an agitated glance at Rigel, who bowed his head in submission to the queen.

Serena gritted her teeth. "I am quite capable of deciding when to get out of bed, Your Majesty," she barked. "I can assure you I am well enough."

"Those bruises show otherwise," Elara snapped back, gesturing toward Serena's neck. The girl pouted, gently laying one hand over the marks. "It's clear that you are not safe here, so we are trying to find a solution." Elara plopped back in her chair, rubbing her temples.

Serena skimmed over the items on the tabletop: a huge map hand-painted on canvas, a handful of letters with broken seals—none recognizable to Serena—and a list of names so covered in circles and slashes it was illegible. "And what has been suggested?"

"Nothing reasonable," Rilura grumbled, crossing her toned arms over her chest.

A muscle ticked in Elara's neck, and she stood again, rearing for an argument to ensue. Before she could reply, Crystal interrupted, clarifying, "Her Majesty thinks we should take you to Envyre."

"Which is preposterous with the protection of the mountains to the west," Rilura said, her deep voice resonating through the room. "Your city is safe because the dwarfs have made it so."

Serena tensed as several people sprang into protest. She held her breath, turning over the idea of being sent away in her head. They had only just reached Symptee a few weeks prior, and now Elara wanted to send her away?

Crystal reached out and smoothed a hand over Serena's back, offering a solemn smile. "It would not be the worst place to finish your training," the elf whispered.

A wave of intense memories surged through Serena's head then. Soldiers in the valley. A man swinging at Will. Crimson spewing from a fatal wound she had inflicted. Snowfall in the mountains. Her brother Cameron poised to execute Rigel. His hands clamped around her neck, her airway constricted. The bloodied blade she had dropped in the snow. The Mørkewulv that nearly ripped Rigel's arm off—the same monster that could have ripped her in two had he not gotten in the way. So many times, they could have lost someone. They nearly did.

"No," Serena proclaimed loudly.

The chatter died down immediately; all eyes turned on her. She leaned her hands on the edge of the table, her full focus on the queen. "We barely made it here alive. Some of us are still recovering from injuries. Leaving the city now would be a mistake."

Elara exhaled, her brow relaxing as she stared at her niece. They both knew she was right. The group had stumbled into Symptee beaten and bruised. Crystal and the Infirmary continued to work on Rigel's patched up shoulder for weeks after their arrival, a task that drained the healer though she never complained. Serena herself had been covered in scars and bruises, refusing Crystal's aid because their friend needed her more.

"I know why you wish to stay, but that does not overshadow the fact that the citadel has been compromised. Your safety is the most important thing right now," Elara said. Her voice was quiet, not as confident as before. She spoke warily, as though trying to appeal to Serena with her gentle, motherly tone.

It didn't work.

"But you live here. And you will continue to live here, yes?" Serena asked. All others in the room fell away as she stared at her aunt.

Elara brushed her hands over her lap and nodded. "I have lived here for 17 years, and Antoine has yet to kill me—try as he might. I am no threat to his reign, and he knows it."

Rigel glanced sidelong at Serena, unable to muster a smile.

"If you are worried about those still recovering, they are more than welcome to remain here," Elara began.

"I can assure you I am well recovered, Your Majesty," Rigel interjected. Crystal and Serena gave him a disapproving look. "I am healed enough to travel."

Serena cocked her head to the side, eyeing his arm wearily. He still had not regained his full range of motion and speed. She knew that much from watching him practice with Will. "Even so, I do not wish to leave," she said decidedly, grabbing a chair from behind her. She whirled around and plopped down as though her seat might anchor her to the citadel. If only Elara saw it that way. "I can handle a fight. I'm not afraid of Rexton or his spies."

"And when a servant manages to poison your dinner? What then?"

"Do you not employ food tasters for that very reason?" Serena huffed. "Running away will make both of us look weak."

"Then don't look at it as running away," Elara snapped, an edge creeping back into her voice. "This is not your decision, Serena. I am Queen, and I have already decided. You're going to Envyre."

Serena's fingernails dug into her arms. Her face flashed hot—so hot she was certain her anger was seeping from her pores, permeating the space with stifling heat. "Perhaps it's time you relinquish that title to the true heir of Hyrosencia."

Stunned gasps echoed through the small chamber, followed by whispered scolding from half the people around the table. Turning toward the others in the room, Serena realized she had crossed the line. Commander Stanton and Lord Stirling were quick to defend Elara while Rilura and the three guardians stared back in shocked silence. None dared speak against the queen.

Yet again, she would have to fight alone.

Metal banged against wood; a sharp vibration rang in their ears as something heavy skittered across the table, coming to rest in front of Serena. Everyone turned to see Elara's crown planted in the center of the pile of papers. Wisps of her hair fell recklessly from its pins, adding emphasis to the crazed look in her eyes. "Take it then." Her chest heaved as she sat back in her tufted chair.

Staring at the amethyst gemstones in the gold crown, Serena realized her error. She had told Elara she never wanted the burden of the crown—and she still didn't. Seeing it inches before her, a shimmering prize up for the taking, did not make her desire it any more. She didn't even want to touch it for fear of the power it held.

A ghostly whisper echoed in her mind: *Patience, child.* Her stomach seized at the memory of Mary Finch's calming voice. Her mother had always strived to instill patience and respect in her children. Mary would be mortified by the way Serena spoke to the queen—even more upset by the fact that she was disrespecting her own kin in such a way.

Pressing her hands into the armrests, Serena pushed herself up onto her feet. Time froze as the small gathering awaited her next move. Slowly, she leaned over the edge of the table and wrapped her fingers around the cold metal. To take this crown would be treasonous. Anarchy would surely ensue as most of the refugees had no idea who she was, and she did not want them to find out. Not yet.

Shifting the crown delicately between her hands, Serena walked behind the guardians toward the head of the table. Rigel's eyes widened as she passed, but he did not move to stop her. As she reached her aunt's side, Gerard stepped closer, as though he worried she might hurt Elara. Serena held up her hands and said, "I'm returning what isn't mine." He swallowed thickly, remaining by the queen's side. Elara stared as Serena lifted the crown and placed it back onto her head, carefully tucking the stray strands behind her aunt's ears. Then she dropped onto a knee before her. "I beg your forgiveness, my Queen."

Elara closed her eyes then as the weight of her title returned to her head. Serena stared at the woman's face, tracing the lines at the corners of her eyes and the way her mouth drooped into a frown. Elara was tired, no doubt. None of this was easy for either of them. It never would be.

"There must be a way we can compromise on this," Serena said, her own exhaustion seeping into her voice. Her legs shook, still weak from her fight with Richard Bramley, and she grabbed the table to steady herself.

"Why must you fight everything I say?" Elara asked. Her eyes opened, and Serena realized her aunt was holding back tears. "I am acting in your best interest. I don't want something terrible to happen to you. Not because of a prophecy, but because you are the last of my family, Serena."

"What you think is best does not always match what I think," the girl said softly. Squatting before the queen, Serena reached for her aunt's hand and breathed out. "I do not wish to fight with you. I have been fighting for my life every second since I left Durmak."

"I know. I never wanted that for you," Elara whispered, inhaling sharply. Tears filled the queen's tired eyes, making her irises an even brighter green, and Serena looked down at their hands.

"I am tired of running and hiding. Nowhere is safe. Not for me. We both know that," Serena said. She cleared her throat, fighting the lump rising in the back of it. "If I must fight, I wish to fight on my own terms. I want to push back against Rexton before his army descends on our doorstep. I don't want to be cornered. I want to take control of my life—my destiny. I beg you, please allow me that."

Elara nodded slowly, swiping a tear from her lash line before it could escape down her cheek. She sniffled, squeezing her niece's fingers tight before lifting her chin to address her plea. "In what way could you push back without risking your life?" Her question was laced with terror and dread, but she waited patiently for an answer.

"She is meant to lead the rebellion, Your Majesty. We have always known that," Idonea said gently.

"Once we leave the citadel, there will always be a risk," Crystal added.

Serena lowered her chin, considering what she could do to further their cause. For years, they had been making weapons, searching for allies, and waiting for the true heir— for her. Now she was here, training every day. What more did they need to win? "How are our numbers?"

"Finch's last correspondence stated they were at least three hundred strong in the north," Commander Stanton chimed in.

Serena's heart stammered at the mention of her father. She knew he was alive—Elara had confirmed so much when she first arrived. But they seldom received word from him. Sir John Finch was busy recruiting weary Hyrosencians to their cause. They knew building an army in the shadows of Rexton's domain would be no easy task. Every man who had once been loyal to the Garricks now cowered in fear of the king. But some were ready to risk their lives for a small chance at a better life, free from tyranny and fear. She missed her father terribly every day, though she knew he was tasked with preparing for her arrival—the inevitable fulfillment of her destiny when she would lead a rebellion into battle against Rexton. The thought of finally reuniting with him before marching into battle made her insides twist in displeasure.

"Three hundred?" Rigel asked skeptically. He scratched at the stubble on his chin. "How in the stars have they stayed hidden?"

"Many have committed while remaining in their homes, awaiting further orders. Others are living underground, meeting in secret," Stanton said. "Weapons are the greatest issue. There are only so many smiths, and Rexton keeps eyes on them. It's been difficult for them to procure armor and weapons without drawing suspicion."

"That hardly matters. Three hundred will not be enough to breach Graynor," Elara said. Her shoulders slumped as she scanned the room. Their numbers paled in comparison to the army Rexton had built up with stolen sons and Garrick family traitors over the past 17 years.

"We will need allies to win," Serena said decidedly. She rose to her feet and winced at the soreness of her body. Perhaps she did need more time to rest. But if Elara wished for her to leave, she would make sure the next journey would be worth the effort.

"Ye will have my sword and any pledged to serve their king," Rilura declared.

"That would double our numbers at most," Stanton said. His lips pulled into a straight line as he massaged his beard, his thoughts drifting.

Serena nodded to the dwarf princess. "We appreciate your aid."

Crystal stepped closer to the table and asked, "You have many guards here. How many from Symptee would be able to make the journey?"

Stanton opened his mouth to answer, but Rilura interrupted. "Ye know well the journey through the mount is strenuous. It would leave your men weary, vulnerable. Rexton would see them coming."

"Then we find another route," Serena said, jabbing her finger into the map on the table. "We made it into the valley before. It was risky, but it's a safer place to cross."

Rigel shook his head. "Rexton controls the valley, remember? They've set up walls, border patrols. It's why we were forced to take you north into the mountains."

Elara sighed; the heavy puff of air seemed to hold the weight of the world. Her husband loomed over her right side, planting a supportive hand on her shoulder. "These are things for the Council to discuss. The focus of this conversation is Serena and her safety."

"I don't want to hide anymore," Serena said quietly, defeat edging into her voice.

"Perhaps you can find a way to use your journey to our advantage. Challenge the students in Envyre, test them, recruit those who are ready to join your unit," Gerard suggested.

Crystal nodded. "There are nearly a hundred at the Academy between Hyrosencians and Silveryl Elves. Some are too young for battle, but many are of age and skilled enough."

"It won't be hiding. You'll be able to train, recruit numbers, and better prepare in safety," Elara said. Her red-rimmed eyes pleaded with Serena to accept this. To go quietly and make the best of it.

Serena leaned over the table, gripped the edges for support, and skimmed the dark outlines in the lower southeast corner of the map. Ord Metsiilva—the realm of the Silveryl Elves. She traced her fingers over the black strokes of another foreign city's name, hanging just on the edge of the sea, followed by a larger city farther south. Three cities tucked away in an enchanted forest, safe-guarded by a sizable community of healers and warriors. "Perhaps this will be for the best," she murmured thoughtfully. If she was to leave the City of Mercy, she would make sure the journey would be worth it. The elves had aided the Hyrosencian refugees by allowing their orphaned children to live and train in Envyre. Surely there was more they could offer. Weapons, warriors, intel. Serena was determined to sink her teeth into every morsel of information the elves were willing to serve on a platter. Perhaps the elves would be the key to breaking Rexton's chains and setting their people free at last.

11

HOMECOMING

Gravel crunched under Alarcole Windaef's boots as he made his way down the dirt road toward Montaris, the capital city of Ord Metsiilva and home of Daephyra, High Queen of the Silveryl Elves. He could already see the immense stone towers peeking through the thick foliage up ahead, a looming reminder of the stern regime that would greet him the moment he reached the city's threshold.

Cole slowed his pace unintentionally. The palace had once made him feel at ease. It had been like a second home to his family. He had walked the revered halls of Montaris Palace many times over the past century, finding an odd sense of comfort in the towering ivory walls—the way they mirrored his strength and unwelcoming demeanor. Now, the sight of the palace getting closer with each step filled him with dread, and not simply because he would be subjected to an onslaught of questions as soon as he arrived.

For three years, he had been away from his homeland, working beside his sister and her friends to rescue the hidden heir of Hyrosencia. With careful encouragement, Daephyra had appointed Cole to travel to Symptee as an ambassador so she could have her own eyes and ears within Elara's court. They never intended for him to be gone so long. He loved his people and his home, and he had missed the tranquility of the flourishing forest terribly. But somehow, the humans had weaseled their way into his cold heart. Not just Xandra, but Rigel, that stubborn human princess, and the hopeless farm boy, too. Now he felt an unfamiliar ache in his chest, as though he had left something vital behind. How he would do anything to feel whole again.

The gravel under his feet gave way to a smooth stone path, and the city sprang to life before his eyes. Armed guards stood watch around the perimeter gate, as well as in watch towers hidden among the trees. He had passed at least four posts on the walk from Sarkli.

The guards paid him no mind, as his platinum hair and pointed ears made his origins clear.

Cole crossed through the open gate, nodding to the guards as he passed. Sweeping footsteps and the gentle hum of conversation filled the street. Well-kept shops with carved wooden signs lined both sides of the main road, and elves donning vibrant swaths of rich fabrics bustled back and forth between them. He stood out—as he always did, though he never cared—for wearing a simple black tunic over the more vibrant wares favored in the capital. Some watched curiously as he started down the road, keeping to the right to avoid those riding horses toward the city's entrance. He recognized many of the light eyes and cheery faces that waved in passing, though he was in no mood to stop and socialize. He was there at the Queen's order; she would surely hear word of his arrival before he even reached the palace doors, if she had not already, so it was best not to delay.

After a brief walk down several bustling roads, Cole quickly ascended the grand staircase that led up to the Elf Queen's front door. At the entrance, a familiar face grinned and reached for his hand. "Alarcole, 'tis been a long while, my friend!"

"That it has," Cole replied, taking his old friend Deldrach Erlamin's hand and clapping him on the back with his other. They had been bunkmates during their tenure at the Envyre Academy, back before the human war changed things. "Tell me, how has life been at court? Anything I should know?"

Deldrach smoothed a hand over his obsidian hair, which was tied back in his signature high ponytail. It was good to see some things never changed. "Three years is a long time, my friend. So much has happened, I hardly know where to start," Deldrach admitted, squinting as he looked over the city. His gray eyes lit up when he recalled something interesting. "Ralnor bound himself to Helartha Iliynore, if you can believe it!"

Cole scoffed at the useless gossip, having never expected their rowdiest friend to settle down in this century. Then again, his friends would be shocked to learn of his own affections that developed for a certain human woman while he was away. But when he pictured Xandra's cheery smile and bouncy curls, he couldn't help the slight smirk that overtook his sharp features. He shook the memory of her lips away and refocused on his friend, who had led him inside the palace. They walked side by side down the main corridor while Deldrach continued to list various unimportant happenings.

"How is your sister, by the way? Still under the employ of the human queen?" his friend asked casually. Deldrach kept his gaze straight forward, his face revealing no hint of emotion behind his questions.

Cole's lips wrinkled as he thought about his friend's longtime interest in his sister. "Crystal is… Crystal. She is the head of a guardian unit for Elara Garrick. I implored her to return home with me, but she refused to leave behind the girl we rescued." He dragged a hand over his face and exhaled. Daephyra and their father would both be displeased that she ignored their summons.

"She always did have a stubborn streak, that girl," Deldrach replied with a smirk. "Might be what I like most about her."

Cole paused and narrowed his eyes, scrutinizing the man who had once been his closest friend. Deldrach was once a notorious flirt with more confidence than he should have had. After their graduation from the Academy, he was offered a position in the Queen's service, thanks in part to their fathers' connections. "I still cannot understand why you have such interest in my sister of all people? Some days I think she loathes *all* men."

Deldrach chuckled and shrugged. "What can I say? I've always had a soft spot for blondie. She is as strong as she is stunning."

Cole withheld the urge to gag. "Anything else I need to know? Obviously, you haven't bound yourself to anyone yet." He snickered at his friend's sour expression.

"Yes, one more thing. An elder passed on not too long ago—Thallan Dasatra," Deldrach said, not bothering to appear sad about it. Thallan had been the second eldest of the Silveryl Elves, second only to the queen herself. For him to choose to cross over now, Cole had to wonder what prompted it. The old elf could have easily stuck around another hundred years if he had wanted.

As they rounded a corner, nearing the main doors to the throne room, Deldrach added, "Your father is being considered to take his place on the High Council, last I heard."

Cole nodded. That was no surprise given his father had devoted his life to the Queen's regime, spending much of the past sixty years by Daephyra's side. "I assume he is with Her Majesty?" he dared ask, staring at the gold double doors embossed with a swirling leaf pattern, the ornate vines stretching up the sides and over the top of each. Each leaf had a slight variation that represented a different noble family of their clan.

Deldrach nodded once before addressing the two guards posted on either side of the entrance. They knocked twice before opening the doors for them, loudly announcing their names as they passed through the doorway. Cole held his chin high and met the ice blue gaze of his queen. His stomach sank. There was no turning back now.

"It seems the long-lost son of the Windaef house has graced us with his return at long last," Daephyra declared, her icy irises boring into him. The way she never broke eye contact was unnerving. She looked as youthful and ethereal as the day he left a few years prior. No human would ever guess she was over six hundred years old. The eternal youth of the elves was something other races could only dream of.

"Alarcole!" His father's voice boomed through the chamber, as devoid of warmth as Cole remembered. Cassius Windaef took four steps down from the dais and paused. There was a question in his deep blue eyes, a fear Cole knew his father would never want the queen to witness. His voice remained cold and proud as he asked, "Where is Crystalira?"

Cole froze a few feet away from the dais, taking the moment of eerie silence to bow low before the queen. When he straightened, both Daephyra and Cassius were staring at him, awaiting his reply. He took a slow inhale, glancing sidelong at his friend, before saying, "Crystal was unable to leave her position at Elara's court at the time we received your letter. She is the lead guardian for someone of crucial importance."

Cassius's eyebrows lowered; the raging storm in his deep blue gaze fixated on his son. "Crucial?" The venom in his father's tone could have sliced the marble throne in half. "No one is more important than our queen!"

"That's not what I meant—"

"That's enough," Daephyra's icy voice cut through the room, sending a chill down Cole's spine. Cole pressed a fist into his chest as he bowed in reverence. "Deldrach, you may return to your post. Have the Council summoned. We have much to discuss with Alarcole Windaef."

Deldrach turned and marched for the doors without delay. As Cole lifted his chin, he found one silver brow raised as the queen inspected him from head to feet. She drummed her long fingernails against the curved armrests of her throne. The doors behind him closed firmly. The sharp echo pierced through the massive chamber, making Cole flinch, and he knew he had a long, unpleasant afternoon ahead.

When they emerged from the Queen's meeting hall four hours later, Cole's head pounded. The weight of his exhaustion from the long journey home had finally set in. He answered their questions, giving as many details as he felt necessary to appease Daephyra. Her face remained stoic throughout the Council's questioning. Aside from a snide comment about his sister's inability to join him, she contemplated his answers in unusual silence, as had his father. Now, as Cassius led his son out into the streets of Montaris, Cole could feel the tension in his father's clenched fists and knew he was to receive a greater scolding in the privacy of their home.

Not far from the main palace, Cassius walked up the stone path to a brown brick cottage. It was the same modest home where their father had brought Crystal after the southern invasion killed their mother. Despite the years he had been away, the house appeared brighter than he remembered. The porch had clearly been rebuilt and the front door painted a fresh shade of deep green with an ivy pattern climbing up one side. Cassius opened the front door and gestured for his son to enter first.

The second the door closed behind them, Cassius growled, "How dare you disregard a summons from your queen so callously?" He stepped forward, his nose nearly pressing into his son's forehead as he lifted his chin in defiance.

"I left the day after I received your letter. I did as I was asked," Cole argued, crossing his arms to force more space between them. He was no stranger to his father's harsh words and aggression, though he had not lived under his father's roof in half a century. He was increasingly thankful that he had been able to attend and then work at the Envyre Academy.

Cassius breathed out through his nose. "That summons ordered you both to return, yet I see only one of my children before me."

Cole rolled his eyes and turned partly away from his father, knowing he would never win an argument. His gaze raked over the small sitting space, the cozy fireplace full of ashes and the carved wood chairs with cushioned seats. It was all the same, just like his father. "Crystal is grown now. She makes her own decisions. She took an oath and would not break it. That sort of dedication is something she learned from *you*, if I am not mistaken." He did not miss the way Cassius faltered at his statement, his fists relaxing at his sides.

Exhausted, Cole turned to retreat to the empty bed chamber when his father's whisper made him pause. "Why has Crystalira not written me? Is she unwell? Surely, she must miss her home."

Without turning around, he sighed and said, "She is well enough." His mind drifted back to a time when she rescued a fallen baby bird behind their home. The poor creature had broken its wing in its first flight attempt. That was the first time Crystal used her healing powers after their mother's death. He could still picture the slight smile on her face as she climbed the tree and returned it to its nest. He never told her he had watched from the window. But that hadn't been the last time he witnessed her determination to save the weak and injured. "You know Crys… If someone needs help or protection, she cannot abandon them."

"I know why she does it," Cassius said solemnly, the confidence returned to his quiet voice. "It's just a shame that she should rather waste this time among people who will be dead in half a century."

"Their lives may be shorter, but that does not mean they don't matter," Cole snapped, whirling around to face his father. "They are good people. Kind, selfless, hard-working people, not unlike most of our kind."

Cassius narrowed his eyes and stepped forward, squinting into the shadowed hall. "You sound like her," he said, a note of suspicion in his voice. "Perhaps you have been away from home for too long. Finding you a position in the Queen's service would do you some good."

"And if that's not what I want?" The words came out harsher than Cole had intended, slicing through the tension between them like a knife. The back of his neck burned with shame, though he had every right to oppose his father's plan. He lowered his eyes to the frayed jade rug under his feet.

Stunned, Cassius stared at him for a minute that felt more like an hour. Finally, he dared to ask, "Did you wish to return to Envyre instead? Your old position has been filled."

Cole shook his head. "I'm not sure what I want." He turned his head and came face to face with an old family portrait. He remembered the day their mother made them sit for hours for the artist. Lyrissana smiled brightly at her son, her light brown hair pinned back from her face and loose over her shoulders. She was a head shorter than their father, who beamed down at his wife with an affection Cole had not seen in all the years since her passing. Staring at the happy version of his father, Cole couldn't help noticing how much he favored the man. They had the same platinum hair and sharp cheekbones; the only distinction was that the children at their feet had their mother's eyes. Cole had been an adolescent at the time, and from the look on his face, he clearly wanted to be anywhere else. Crystal was still a small child with eyes full of wonder and a smile as beautiful as their mother's. The portrait was a painful reminder of what they had all lost.

His father took a deep breath. "You should get some rest, son," Cassius began. Cole could tell his father had more to say by the way he paused. There was a hesitance to his next words. "I have missed you—both of you—a great deal. It's good to have you back where you belong." Something stirred in Cole's chest, and he clenched his jaw.

When his son did not reply, Cassius added, "Tell me, Alarcole... What must I do to bring your sister home?"

His gaze shot back to his father, his blood boiling at the stupidity of his father's question. "Your letter was cold. You should have said how you feel. That you missed her," Cole said. Cassius withdrew his gaze, and his son wondered if the man actually felt shame for the way he had addressed his own children. "You spent years forcing what you wanted onto both of us when what Crys really needed growing up was your affection. That's why she went to the Academy! She couldn't take living in this house anymore. Perhaps if you had shown her you cared, she would be more inclined to come home." He knew his words were harsh, but Cole feared that was the only way to get through to the stubborn elf. Cassius was far too much like his daughter in that regard.

Cole did not wait for a response. He turned and continued down the hall to the last room on the left. He closed the door with a quiet click, tossed his bag in the empty chair by the window, and sank onto the bed, not bothering to pull back the blankets before he drifted off into dreams of a fortress far away and the people he had left behind there.

12

TOO LITTLE TIME

When Serena's strength had returned enough to travel, Crystal and Xandra escorted her down to the main hall to bid Elara farewell. Behind them, two guards followed, carrying three small bags packed with clothes and weapons. Though Serena had ultimately agreed to the plan to go to Ord Metsiilva, she felt like she was being exiled from the place that was meant to be her haven and home. Her eyes skimmed every step until they reached the main floor, continuing along the stone tiles, brick walls, and tapestries that hung in the halls. In the little time she had been there, she had hardly taken the time to appreciate the citadel's beauty—not that it mattered. But she could not help but wonder when, or if, she would ever return there.

At the main hall, guards came and went, depositing bags and supplies in the back corner of the room. Serena walked straight up to Elara and bowed her head, finding no point in faking a curtsy when she was back to wearing travel attire. Her aunt stepped forward and wrapped her arms around her middle, squeezing so tightly that Serena could feel her aunt's bump press against her stomach. "I hate to see you go so soon," she whispered into Serena's hair. Though her voice was strong, her hands trembled against Serena's back.

The girl bit the inside of her lip, fighting back the lump rising in her own throat. "You said this is for the best, remember?" Serena teased, pulling away.

Elara's eyes glistened as she pat her niece on the cheek. "I did… but that does not make saying goodbye any easier. Not when we've had so little time together."

Serena nodded, glancing about the room while Elara went on about the small ship she had commissioned to take them down to the port city of Lei'wana. Crystal and Xandra stood a few feet away, questioning the guards as they brought supplies in. Near the back of the room stood Kieran Brooks, Maddie Milliorva, Heath Grange, and Wesley Ironside. They had been selected to join Serena's unit based on their tournament performances—though they did not seem pleased to be returning to Ord Metsiilva. Kieran caught her eye and grinned, his chiseled face sending heat into her cheeks. She whipped around and locked in on Rigel and Gideon coming through the doors.

"Rigel!" Serena lifted one hand over her head and waved. She didn't miss Elara sighing loudly as she skipped off to greet her friends. Her mind was clearly elsewhere; her gaze drawn behind them to the doorway as she bit into her thumb nail. "Have you seen Will this morning? I was hoping to say goodbye before we leave."

Her friend smirked as though he knew something she didn't, which irked her. She crossed her arms over her chest and asked, "Is he still at the forge? They have been so busy, I haven't seen him in over a week."

A firm hand squeezed her shoulder, and Rigel leaned closer to reassure her. "He isn't at the forge today. He'll be by soon. He wouldn't miss this. You know that." Serena begrudgingly nodded, continuing to glance over his shoulder until Rigel whirled her around and steered her across the room by the shoulders.

Wesley's catlike eyes scanned the room, lingering when they fell on the approaching stranger. Rigel whispered from behind Serena, "He can be intense, but he's harmless. He'll be a good addition to the team." She swallowed down her nerves and nodded, breaking eye contact with the man.

Crystal summoned everyone to gather round and announced to the newest members that Serena would be taking command of their recruiting mission in Ord Metsiilva. Several faces dropped in surprise, considering there were two tournament winners in their unit. Serena's true title was still unknown to them, though she would not be surprised if they had their suspicions. The servants were notorious gossips, and the death of Richard Bramley—and the extent of her own injuries—were impossible to hide.

Maddie stepped forward, her cropped hair swaying around her shoulders as she narrowed her eyes at Serena. "What makes *you* qualified to lead *us*? We've spent our lives readying ourselves for battle."

"This was my choice," Elara proclaimed, stepping into the open space between Serena and the other guardians. The new recruits clamped their mouths closed. "Her father was a respected member of the Garrick Guard. She was trained by your peers, and I daresay she has fought in more life-or-death battles than any of you. Learning to work as a team and use each other's strengths will be good for all of you. This war will not be won by an individual." Serena met her gaze and bowed her head slightly. The new guardians mumbled their agreement.

Crystal pat Serena on the back of her shoulder supportively. "She's quick on her feet, and quite good at one-on-one combat. And she knows Hyrosencia better than any of us, having lived there her entire life. Give her a chance."

"Would it not be to our benefit for Crystal to lead the negotiation given her heritage?" Maddie asked.

"As I elected to fight for a human queen, I suspect I am not in Daephyra's favor," Crystal said with a shrug. "But I will accompany you nevertheless. Nothing could stop me."

"It was Serena's idea to approach Queen Daephyra and request warriors for the coming battle. If anyone can convince her, it's Serena," Rigel said.

Of the warriors gathered before her, Kieran was the first to step forward, a curious smile curled on his lips. "I, for one, am looking forward to seeing you in action." He extended his hand toward Serena, and she hesitantly took it. He placed a chaste kiss upon her knuckles before relinquishing her hand.

"That's enough kissing up," snapped Crystal, grabbing Kieran roughly by the shoulders and hauling him away from Serena. "Come help with the bags." The dark-haired man gave her a wink on his way to help the others bring their cargo out to the dock.

Feeling a blush creep into her cheeks, Serena glanced back at the doors. Guards exited the room weighed down with bags, but there was still no sign of Will. Her heart ached at the thought of leaving without saying goodbye.

She turned to face Elara one last time. The queen's eyes filled with tears as she coiled her arms around Serena's back and squeezed. Elara's lips brushed the shell of her ear as she asked quietly, "Do you have your ring?" Serena nodded, pulling back to look her aunt in the eyes. "Good. Keep it safe. Try to check in one night a week, if you can."

"How does Thursday sound?" Serena said jokingly.

Elara squeezed tighter for a moment before releasing her. "I will clear my schedule." Noticing the way Serena continued to watch the guards trickle out the doors, the queen pressed her palm against the girl's cheek. "Go. Your friend will meet you at the dock."

She frowned. "You mean Will?" Elara nodded. Serena tensed, turning fully to face her aunt. There was an edge to her voice as she asked, "Did you tell him not to come here?"

"He came to me yesterday. That boy has every intention of being there when the ship leaves. It would be a fool's errand to try and stop him," Elara said, crossing her arms over her chest. Serena breathed a sigh of relief, trusting her aunt spoke the truth. "You had best join the others now. You have a long journey ahead."

Serena nodded, giving her a final hug. "Until we are united," she whispered. The heaviness in her chest threatened to burst forth, and she struggled to hold back her tears.

The queen's chest constricted, and it took a moment for her to repeat the bittersweet goodbye to her niece.

When they broke apart, Serena turned, slung her knapsack over her shoulder, and made her way for the exit. Toward the back of the room, she noticed Xandra bidding her father farewell; tears streamed down their cheeks as they hugged each other tight. Her chest tightened, and her mind drifted to thoughts of her own father. She wondered where John Finch was and if he knew how far she was from home. She couldn't help but wonder whether Divinity would string their fates together again before the war ended.

She didn't wait for Xandra, not wanting to interrupt the heartfelt goodbye with her father. Entering the main corridor, Serena spotted Rigel and Gideon following a trail of guards and jogged to catch up to them. They both seemed eager enough to be heading back to Ord Metsiilva after a few years away. Gideon particularly missed how much more potent Elven wine was.

Guards allowed them to exit the citadel wall through a small side gate past the garden. Serena inhaled the floral smell, relishing the way it reminded her of her aunt and her sparring lessons at the same time. She would miss the shade and the smell of the fragrant blooms in the garden—the wisteria petals most of all.

A short walk down a cobblestone path brought them close to the river. The air thickened from the spray of flowing water nearby, making the path slick. When they reached the harbor, Serena was surprised to find the dwarfs had ventured out to see them off. Rilura embraced her, briefly lifting the girl's feet off the ground.

"Never forget who you are," the Dwarven princess said, tapping a thick finger to the center of the girl's chest. "You are destined for greatness. Wield Sannarvin with pride."

Serena nodded; her fingers instinctually wrapped around the hilt of the blade strapped to her hip. It somehow felt heavier than it had in the mountains. "I will. Thank you."

Rigel clasped arms with Thomli in a fond farewell. "I shall miss watching the princess destroy you in dueling," the guardian teased.

"It's too bad you cannot join us," Serena said, lowering her chin dejectedly.

Rilura huffed a laugh. "While I shall miss our talks, I am all too aware that the Elf Queen would not welcome dwarfs in her kingdom." She leaned forward to add in a whisper, "She is far less welcoming than we are."

Crystal snorted as she approached them. "You would be correct. Daephyra is anything but *kind*." She pat Rilura on the arm and lowered her head in respect. The archer wasn't one for showing affection, but the Dwarven princess accepted her gesture with a matching nod of her head.

Serena tensed as she glanced back down the path. The top floor of the citadel peeked out over the inner wall, and she thought she could make out a few bodies on the upper balconies. Perhaps one was Elara. She lifted one hand and waved, though she knew they were too far away to see the motion. As she dropped her arm, her eyes searched the path one last time. Only a pair of uniformed guards headed toward the harbor.

"We should board," Crystal said. She wrapped an arm around Serena's shoulders and turned her toward the small ship.

"A moment more," Rilura interjected. They paused, turning back toward their ally. The dwarf reached into a large sack tied to her belt and produced a horn with a thick brown leather strap attached. "Though we cannot join ye for this quest, our vow to Elara remains. My father has pledged to join ye in battle. When the time has come, blow this horn, and the dwarfs will come."

The horn was gruff against her palms as she took it. Serena flipped it over, inspecting the instrument before putting the strap over her head and tucking it behind one arm. "Thank you," she said again, taking hold of Rilura's arm and squeezing it. "Until we are united, stay safe, my friend."

The dwarf nodded. "Till we meet again." When they released arms, Rilura bowed low to Serena, and the girl returned the gesture. It still felt foreign to have anyone bow to her, and she hoped to never grow used to it. When Rilura stood upright, she smiled before turning toward the citadel, waving an arm over her shoulder for Thomli to follow.

As Serena scaled the wooden ramp leading up to the ship's deck, freshwater spray peppered her cheeks. The current lapped against the side of the small ship as crew members readied white sails for their journey. She had barely reached the deck when a familiar face emerged from the hallway to her right. "Will," she breathed out in surprise.

Two dimples greeted her as he approached. Crystal turned and winked at her before disappearing down the same dark hallway. Serena glanced around the deck and found everyone else was too busy to pay any attention to them. She worried her lower lip as Will paused in front of her, the tension yet to dissipate since their conversation at the Guards' Ball.

"I was starting to think you weren't coming to say goodbye," she mumbled at last, staring at the strings tying his shirt together.

"Goodbye?" The question in his voice drew her gaze up to meet his. "You didn't actually think I was staying behind, did you?"

Her lips parted in surprise as she recalled her aunt's words. She had known he intended to meet her at the harbor, but no one had indicated he would be joining them on their travels to Ord Metsiilva. He was a blacksmith. What use could he possibly be on a diplomatic mission?

Will's face fell as he registered her silence. "Oh… Did you not want me to go?"

"No, I do," she said hastily, reaching for his arm. The gentle touch warmed her cold fingers. "I am only surprised. I thought you were still angry with me. And with how busy the forge has been—"

"I could never stay angry at you." His arm slipped out of her grasp as he stepped closer; fierce eyes locked on hers. "And the forge will be fine without me."

"Are you sure?" she whispered, her voice betraying her nerves. Calloused fingers caressed her face, and fire bloomed within her cheeks. Will was coming with them. He was so close, yet she wanted his hands wrapped around her the way they were when he comforted her weeks before.

"I only came to Symptee because of you, and if you're leaving, nothing in the heavens or the nine realms could keep me from joining you. If you will have me." His gaze seared into her soul, branding his promise on her heart, and she knew then that he would always be by her side.

Her arms slid around his muscular frame as she pulled him closer and nestled her cheek against his chest. Where she was going would be dangerous, and many lives would be lost in the battle for their homeland. "I thought you did not wish to be a soldier," she murmured. "You don't have to put yourself in danger for me." Tears pricked her eyes. This was her last chance to convince him to stay behind where he would be safe.

Will's hands slid to her forearms and pulled her away so he could look at her. The sadness in his eyes told her she had been right. He did not want to fight, to take the life of another person. He was a good man; he could live a long life if he remained in Symptee. He reached for her face again and shook his head solemnly. "You never wanted to be a soldier either, if I recall correctly. You wanted to be a teacher, a baker... a mother... I know you never dreamed of this."

Her chest ached for the life she once pictured. The simple life they both once imagined for themselves back in Durmak. Until the war was over and Rexton's ashes were blown into oblivion by Divinity, that dream could never be.

Steeling herself, she straightened her back and said, "You're right, Will. But Divinity has foretold that I must."

"Then allow me to fight beside you," he pleaded. Fear flashed in his eyes, so briefly it was gone in a blink. Will offered a grim smile, his dimples nowhere to be seen, and she returned it, only able to nod dejectedly. There would be no convincing him to stay behind. And despite the dangers ahead, she was relieved to know this wasn't goodbye.

A throat cleared behind them, and Serena whipped around to find Kieran watching them. His hands were folded behind his back, and the smug grin on his face told her he enjoyed interrupting their private conversation. "The others are gathered in the captain's quarters. They're asking for you." He stared directly at her, making it clear that Will was not included in this invitation.

Will tossed an arm over her shoulders and leaned down to whisper, "It's not too late to leave that guy behind." Serena snorted and shoved him playfully, unable to contain her smile. While she did not intend to leave the latest winner of the tournament behind, she quite enjoyed watching Will and Kieran size each other up. Having a rival would make Will train even harder while they were in Ord Metsiilva. Then perhaps she would not have to worry about him come the next fight.

13

PROMISES

The Rexton family was finishing breakfast when their patriarch cleared his throat, calling all eyes at the table to him. His gaze was settled on Anteros, who gently set down his fork and awaited what his father had to say. Whatever it was, he already knew it would not be good.

"Today you will be joining me for a special task," the king informed him. He lifted his glass and took a long swill.

Anteros bit back the urge to sneer. He plastered a winning smile on, as he had been for months, and feigned enthusiasm. "What shall it be today? Meeting with the generals? Another beheading?"

The corner of his father's mouth turned upward. "Anything is possible." The sinister look on his face sent chills through Anteros. Goosebumps spread over his arms in a tidal wave. He swallowed thickly, cutting his eyes to look at his sister. Sabine's baby blues were wide, but she kept her mouth shut. Smart choice, for once.

The slow, grating scrape of forks against porcelain resumed. Chelsea kept her head down. She sported a fresh bruise on her left cheekbone—likely the product of her husband's drunken wrath. She had done her best to cover it with powder, but the swelling was unmistakable. They all saw it, but no one would dare mention it aloud. Anteros clenched his fist tight around his fork, feeling the metal ridges dig into his palm. He needed to punch something—someone in particular—but he would never risk bringing down Antoine's wrath upon someone he loved. Not again.

"Your Majesty, if I may," Ryker said. The earl sat beside Anteros, directly across from Sabine. The prince glanced at their guest and noticed the way he flashed a cocky grin at the princess. When the earl looked back at the king, he continued, "I should like your permission to take Sabine horseback riding this morning."

"By all means," Antoine said, holding out his glass in a sign of approval. "Enjoy the ride."

Sabine coughed, her fork clattering against the edge of her plate and ricocheting onto the floor. Embarrassment was obvious in her pink cheeks. She didn't dare look at Ryker or her brother.

"I think that sounds lovely," Chelsea finally said. She placed her fork down quietly beside her plate and blotted her cloth napkin to her lips. "I have not been riding in ages. Would you mind if I join you?" She smiled sweetly at Ryker.

Anteros turned his body to watch the earl's reaction. Ryker's smile faltered for a moment; his gaze cut to Sabine before returning to her mother. "Not at all, milady. Of course you are welcome to join us," he replied, giving her a half-hearted smile.

Anteros watched the tension ease from his sister's shoulders as she silently mouthed her thanks to their mother. Fortunately, their father did not interfere. He was studying his children intently, his eyes narrowed so slightly Anteros wondered if he could read their minds.

"It seems your friend in the dungeon has recovered from her recent punishment."

"Talitha?" Sabine asked loudly. For a moment, she forgot to conceal the relief on her face. When she realized her error, her cheeks reddened, and she hid them behind her napkin.

Anteros forgot how to breathe for a moment. It was the first his father had mentioned Talitha since the whipping in the courtyard. The prince had done his best to hide his feelings deep beneath the mask of a dutiful crown prince—that and many glasses of wine. Catching his father's eye, Anteros clenched his jaw and gently laid his fork on his plate. "A traitor to the crown is no friend of mine," he said, as though he were reciting something from memory.

His father eyed him suspiciously for a moment before taking a bite from a bright red apple. Anteros couldn't look at him then. He had thought his father might have finally forgotten about Talitha. Unfortunately, once someone had garnered his attention, Antoine Rexton would never forget them—not until they were cold in the ground.

Ryker's voice cut through the silence. "I'm curious. What crime did the lady commit?"

A harsh laugh cut through the dining room, and his children sank lower in their chairs. "She is no lady," Antoine said. He took a sip from his chalice before continuing. "Why don't you tell him, son?"

The prince clenched his fists in his lap. "She's just a girl from the south. She knew a family of wanted traitors, two of whom are still in hiding. But we never managed to gain any valuable information from her."

"You mean *you* couldn't," Antoine corrected. His son tensed as the king told Ryker, "I should have known better than to put my son in charge of an interrogation. He's much too *soft*."

"Yes, I was wildly unsuccessful in my task." The prince gritted his teeth, afraid he would pay for his sarcasm later.

"And what are your plans for the girl?" Ryker asked.

Avoiding his father, Anteros chanced a look at Ryker instead. The earl drank from his glass as though the topic of the conversation wasn't unusual over a formal breakfast.

"I have no plans for someone so meaningless. She can starve to death for all I care," the king said, waving one hand nonchalantly.

"That seems a waste," Ryker said, sinking his fork into a piece of meat.

The crunch of his father's teeth sinking back into the apple made Anteros cringe. He needed to get out of there. Quickly. He couldn't take much more talk of Talitha and her pathetic living conditions. She did not deserve such mistreatment. No one did.

Anteros pushed his chair back and cleared his throat. "I must apologize. I'm meant to spar with James this morning. May I be excused?" He bowed low for his father, waiting to be dismissed.

The king hummed for a moment before turning his attention to Ryker. "What more would you suggest I do with a traitor?" Anteros turned to find his father leaning in on his elbows. He was curious, not angry, and his son knew that was dangerous.

A smirk formed on Ryker's face, as though he had told a riddle only he knew the answer to. "If I may," he began. Antoine lowered his chin in approval. "In Denorfia, those convicted of nonviolent crimes must work off their debts. In the fields or—if they aren't thieves—in the homes of nobles."

Sabine's eyes widened in horror. "You mean as slaves?" Ryker seemed to like the way her full attention was on him—even if she looked mortified. Her voice trembled a bit as she continued, "That's barbaric. We don't—"

Her father's deep voice interrupted her. She nearly leapt out of her chair in surprise. "Why don't you and your mother go ready yourselves for your ride? The earl can meet you in the stables in half an hour."

Sabine chewed her lower lip and nodded. Two chairs scraped against the floor as the ladies rose from their seats. Chelsea and Sabine curtsied to Antoine, wishing him well

before exiting the dining hall. Their absence made Anteros' heart race. With his father's curt dismissal of the ladies, he knew nothing good could come from discussing slavery with the earl.

The prince strode slowly down the winding steps, his heart hammering in his chest. He had not seen Talitha in over two months. Despite his best efforts to forget about her, the flash of ginger hair and broken sobs were always on his mind, like a scar carved into his soul.

As Anteros stepped onto the dungeon floor, three guards fell in line to greet him. Anteros surveyed the men as they bowed low at the waist. "Keys," the prince demanded, holding out one hand. One of the guards scrambled to detach a key ring from his belt and hold it out. The prince tried his best to remain aloof as he took the keys from the uniformed man.

"Your father said you weren't permitted anymore," one of the guards said. His voice was laced with hesitation. Fear. And Anteros knew how to exploit a man's fear. He had learned from the most ruthless man in Hyrosencia, after all.

Anteros whipped around, nostrils flaring, and shoved the guard up against the nearest wall. "Do you think I would be stupid enough to go against my father's orders?" He seethed, fists bunching the man's crimson jacket. The man trembled slightly, eyes wide with fear as he shook his head vigorously. The prince released him roughly, smoothing his hand over his raven locks as he inhaled. "Do not question the crown again, or you'll lose your head."

All three men fell back into line and bowed. An influx of apologies echoed after him as he turned and stormed off. The torch light barely illuminated the dark space. His eyes strained to see the other end of the hall. His dress shoes squeaked against the damp tile as he made his way down the corridor toward an all-too-familiar cell. When he reached it, he paused, struck by the sickening fear that she might be angry at him. That she might scream or lash out or cry. Or even worse, declare that she hated him.

But it was time to face her, no matter how she felt. He owed her that much.

Looking through the bars on the door, Anteros narrowed his eyes and struggled to focus on the figure huddled in a dark corner. The sun had descended, and no lanterns were lit within the cell. He hoped his untimely visit would not frighten her if she were asleep.

The lock clicked in the door. Anteros winced at the sound before slowly pushing the door open a crack. Before entering, he paused, removing a torch from its mount on the wall. Inside the cell, he squinted, tired eyes trying to focus on Talitha's crumpled frame in the darkness. She leaned against the wall, her ankles shackled in heavy steel. His chest constricted as he lifted his eyes to meet hers. They were wide, fearful like an animal caught by a predator in the woods. Nothing like how she used to look at him.

The longer they stared at each other, the more terrified Anteros was to speak. He turned and sauntered over to the wall, where he lit the untouched torch. How long had she been sitting in total darkness?

Chains rattled behind him, and he whipped around to find her sitting straighter, her knees tucked into her chest. She wore the same cream frock from the last time he had seen her. It was tattered and bloodied, hanging limply off one side to expose her thin neck and freckled shoulder. He dragged his eyes away from her bare skin, cursing himself for looking. He wondered if she ever got cold at night. With autumn approaching, he would have to smuggle a warmer dress and cloak down to her soon.

"Why are you here, Your Highness?" Her whispered question was hesitant; her voice quivering slightly.

"Please don't call me that." He approached her slowly, laying the lit torch a few feet in front of her so he could better see her face. She was gaunt; a shell of the girl he used to know. "I came to see an old friend, if I may?" He waited a moment for her answer.

Talitha studied his face in the harsh light for a moment. "I don't think your father wants us to be friends." She turned her face, failing to hide the tears that rimmed her bloodshot eyes.

Anteros took a slow, deep breath. "I don't care what he wants anymore. I wanted to see you, so I came here." He lowered himself to sit on the floor. The few feet he left between them felt like miles. Carefully, he pulled the contents of his pocket out and began unwrapping the cloth napkin from a baguette he had swiped from the kitchen. Fresh, not stale like most prisoners' meals. "Hungry?"

Untrusting eyes swept over his face, going straight to the offering in his hands. He couldn't blame her for her reluctance, but he hoped she wouldn't pass up the opportunity to eat more. With a timid nod, Talitha reached across the space between them and accepted it.

The wall was rough against his back. He could only imagine how hers felt. He glanced over to find her staring at the opposite wall. The piece of bread laid on her skirt uneaten. "Talitha, I never wanted—I did not intend—" He paused, growling under his breath in aggravation. Apologizing to others was not his strong suit—much less to someone he cared for. Would an apology even matter after so long had passed?

"I know," she whispered. Her head rested on the wall as she took a steadying breath. "Sabine came by. She gave me your letter."

"What?"

She finally turned to face him and must have noticed his puzzled brow. A look of hurt flashed across her features. "Oh," she muttered. She fished a folded parchment out of a crack between the bricks behind them. Her hands shook as she unfolded it, her eyes darting back and forth with the words on the page. "Did you not write this for me?"

Anteros leaned closer and grasped the edge of the letter, turning it more toward himself. His heartbeat quickened when he realized what Sabine had given her. "I did… but I had no idea Sabine gave it to you." As he released the paper, his fingers brushed against her arm, and they both lurched in surprise. "I'm sorry," he said, quickly shifting away from her. All he could do was bury his face in his sweaty palms as a rush of emotions hit him. "I'm so sorry for what I did to you, Red. Words cannot express how truly sorry I am. You didn't deserve that. No one does. And I should have tried harder to stop it. To stop him."

"You couldn't have stopped him, Anteros." She turned tear-streaked cheeks to face him. "Your father is dangerous and cruel, and he would have done the same to you—or worse."

He shook his head. "I couldn't stand there and watch him kill you. And he would have."

"Perhaps that would have been for the best," she murmured. Her grimy fingers picked at the bread in her lap as silent tears rolled down her rosy cheeks.

"Red," he pleaded, his voice catching in his throat. His father's cruelty weighed heavily on his mind and his heart. He would have given anything to free Talitha Vise from it.

"Why did you come back after so long?" She sniffled loudly before finally crunching into the small baguette. The moan that followed was the most beautiful sound Anteros had ever heard. He nearly forgot to answer her question until he noticed her staring.

He exhaled slowly. "At first, it was because Father said Sabine and I weren't allowed down here anymore." Talitha cocked her head to the side slightly, awaiting more. "I tried to forget you like he wanted, but turns out, you're unforgettable."

She gaped at his admission. Her cracked lips parted, and he stared at them. Filthy, starved, miserable—Anteros realized it didn't matter. No other girl at court would ever satisfy him because none of them were *her*.

Anteros pushed himself onto his feet and started toward the door. "I should go." He might care for her, but that did not mean she would ever trust him again. And he did not deserve her trust. He had lifted a hand against her, marring her beautiful skin and leaving them both with long-lasting scars. She was better off without him complicating her sad life any further.

Chains clattered as Talitha drew her legs underneath herself and attempted to stand. "Wait. Will I see you again?"

Pain gripped his chest; he stood frozen in the middle of her cell. Anteros wanted nothing more than to return to the way things had been, but that was impossible. "I don't know if that's wise." Not because he didn't care but because he *did*. So much that he knew the truth would put her at risk. He continued to the door and wrenched it open.

"Do you remember your promise to me—that day at the games?" There was something different in this question—a hopefulness he wanted desperately to hold onto.

Of course, he remembered. He promised her that day would not be the last she would see of the sun. He turned around and nodded quietly. Talitha nodded back. "Please, Anteros… Don't let that terrible day in the garden be the last time I see the outside of this cell."

The prince studied her pale face until he could no longer bear to look into her sad gray eyes. How she had maintained a sliver of hope after everything, he could not fathom. "It won't be." His whisper hung between them like a promise, and he knew Talitha would cling to it with every fiber of her being. Because even starving, she was stronger than anyone else he knew.

14

ROCKING THE BOAT

When their ship docked at the port town of Lei'wana, everyone trudged back up to the deck. While some were quick to disembark, Serena and Will lingered behind. Resting her hands on the damp wooden railing, Serena peered out over the Lestera Sea for the first time. She had never seen so much water at once. Will's arm brushed against hers as he settled beside her to take in the view. The way the sun reflected off the gentle waves was stunning. Serena closed her eyes, basking in the sunlight as the breeze peppered her face with saltwater spray. Something about the sea was calming.

"I've never seen anything so beautiful," she said with a faint smile.

"Neither have I."

When she turned back to Will, his eyes weren't on the horizon; they were fixed on her. His dimples deepened with his smile, making her heart leap. His hair ruffled in the breeze, and she thought about reaching out to run her fingers through it. Will leaned over on his forearms as if he wanted her to do that and more.

Suddenly her cheeks were on fire. Serena turned away from him, scanning the deck for the others. The crew had just placed a gangway, and most of the guardians charged off the ship as though they couldn't bear to be on board for another second. "Let's head to the tavern. I'm starved," Rigel said before disappearing after them.

Kieran lingered, calling to Serena, "Are you ready, Captain?" He grinned, clearly joking, though the nickname didn't sit right with her.

"We'll be down in a minute," Will called back. Kieran narrowed his eyes between them before sauntering down the ramp. Once he was out of sight, Will exhaled and mumbled, "Still don't like that guy."

An amused laugh came from behind them. "You aren't the only one, Burroughs," Crystal said. Serena didn't miss the way Crystal wedged herself in the space between them, resting a hand on Serena's shoulder. "If you think this is beautiful, just wait until you see Ord Metsiilva. It's breathtaking."

Donning their knapsacks, Serena and Will followed Crystal off the ship. Boards creaked under their feet as they traversed the dock, heading toward the bustling town. Several merchants had stands set up along the edge of the wharf. The air reeked of the fresh fish they were trying to sell. Serena wrinkled her nose, inhaling through her mouth in hopes of avoiding the smell.

Eyes followed as they passed the fishermen, leaving behind the saturated pier for cobblestone roads. Further from the dock, the musty smell was less prominent. The scent of fresh baked bread wafted out of one shop as they passed the open doorway. Will and Serena slowed their pace.

"Come on. There's bread and hot food just around the corner," Crystal called. Turning to keep an eye on them, she walked backwards slowly until they caught up.

"How long are we to stay in town?" Will asked. He glanced in the window of one shop before getting distracted by a smith across the road.

Crystal shrugged. "No more than a day. Let those with seasickness recover."

Serena kicked a loose rock, sending it skipping down the road. "I was hoping to see more of the town. Who knows if we'll ever come back here?"

The guardian stopped in front of a two-story brick structure with a simple sign above the door that read The Siren's Call. Before Serena could ask if sirens were real, Crystal turned to face her. "I can show you around after we eat if you like. You'll soon see that Lei'wana is a bit of a melting pot—Eastern Islanders, Hyrosencia refugees, foreigners who have traveled from far overseas to trade. Even some elves make their way here to trade wares—though Daephyra does not approve." Serena's cheeks ached from smiling. She thought a place where so many different cultures came together sounded fascinating. Then Crystal leaned closer, lowering her voice to add, "There are also seedy men lurking about. Promise me you will never wander these streets alone." Serena nodded slowly, wondering what darkness lurked in the shadows of Lei'wana.

Will stepped closer to them. "I won't let anything happen to her." His promise pulled at Serena's heartstrings, but Crystal rolled her eyes, yanking the door to the tavern open and motioning for them to go first.

Once they'd had their fill of baked fish and bread, the guardians booked four rooms to be shared among their group that night. Madeline and Heath, who had both had a particularly unpleasant time on the voyage down the river, each took a key and slunk upstairs to rest. The rest fanned out in the streets in small groups, each with their sights set on different wares. Kieran and Gideon were on the lookout for spirits, while Rigel joined Xandra on the hunt for a special gift.

Like a curious child, Serena dragged Crystal and Will into nearly every shop they came across. Fine linens, embroidered cloaks, and waterproof boots were among the wares to catch her eye. In another shop, they perused belts, bracers, and other leather wares. Serena tried to secretly watch Will to see what caught his eye, but he kept glancing up and grinning at her.

The sun had begun to set when they heard a scuffle in an alley. Crystal tried to steer them in the opposite direction, but Serena argued that one of their friends could be in trouble. The guardian laughed loudly. "No one from Envyre would struggle against a couple pirates. Trust me, this is not our fight."

Still, Serena worried for whoever was distressed. As they walked back toward the tavern, she thought about the man who had captured her in Cinders. She wondered where she would have ended up had Will not come along to rescue her when he did.

Then a man approached them. His eyes were wide and fearful as he pleaded in a thick foreign accent, "Have you seen a young woman with long black hair? About your age." He gestured at Serena. "She's my sister, Lucianna. I told her not to go off alone, but she didn't listen to me."

Crystal shook her head and apologized, trying to put distance between them and the stranger. Serena glanced back at him over her shoulder as he rushed toward the next set of people walking in the road. "Please! Help me find her," he pleaded. Her chest constricted as the distance between them stretched. Would nobody help him?

She stopped suddenly. "The alley. We must go back."

Crystal crossed her arms over her chest. "It's my job to keep you safe. Charging into an unnecessary fight would be reckless." As if that were the end of the conversation, she placed her hands on Serena's shoulders and tried to steer her forward.

"She's right. This isn't our fight," Will added. "I'm sure someone else will help him."

Serena pulled out of her grasp. "I'm not asking permission," she snapped. Her hand was already on the hilt of Sannarvin; her instinct to help flaring. "How am I to save Hyrosencia if I avoid every fight we come across?"

Crystal and Will both growled under their breath. She knew they weren't in favor of intentionally looking for a fight, but if someone were in trouble—someone weak and defenseless as she once was—she couldn't ignore it.

She stared at Crystal knowing she was the one who needed convincing. "What would have happened to me if no one had saved me in Cinders?" Her words seemed to hit a nerve as Crystal's brows furrowed.

The guardian could no longer look her in the eyes. Glancing down the road, she replied, "We never would have let that man get far. We were right behind you."

"That's not what I asked," Serena said sharply. "I asked *what if no one saved me?*"

The elf ran her teeth over her bottom lip. "You may have ended up in a brothel… or you may have been put on a ship. Sent somewhere far away. There's no way to know for certain."

Serena's heart pounded harder. "Then you know why I cannot walk away from this."

Crystal nodded, unsheathing the dagger that was strapped to her thigh. "Will, head to the tavern. See if you can find Rigel and Xandra. Tell them I have a feeling our search will end at the docks."

Will hesitated. Gently grasping Serena's forearm, he turned her to face him. "Perhaps you should let the guardians handle it. They know what they're doing."

She had to hold back the urge to shove him away. Yanking her arm out of his grasp, she shook her head in disappointment. "And you think I don't?"

"No, that's not what I—"

Crystal chuckled, stepping out of the path of Serena's ire. "Wait here. I'll find the others. Do *not* run off without us." Serena nodded without turning to look at her friend. She stared at the ground and listened to the gentle squeak of Crystal's boots until the sound trailed off in the distance.

"Serena?" Will's voice was deep and quiet, almost soothing. "I know you can fight. I know that." He reached for her arm.

She jabbed her pointer finger into hard pectorals. "I don't need you to protect me, Will. I can fend for myself. If you're too scared to fight, *you* can stay behind."

"I'm not scared to fight." Will stepped closer—almost too close for comfort. His brows furrowed; his face more serious than she had ever seen him before. Hands slid against the sides of her face, forcing her to look at him. He might claim to not be afraid to fight, but his eyes said otherwise. His voice strained when he admitted, "I'm scared you're going to get hurt again."

All she could do was blink at him. His face was so close. His eyes held a vulnerability that made her heart ache. Of course, he was worried about her safety. He had always been like this. Caring, concerned, ready to help. But after everything they had been through that summer, everything they had seen, every near-death experience, could she blame him for that fear? Only a week prior, she was in the infirmary with cuts and bruises from a nearly successful assassination attempt. Just as he was her anchor to their home and childhood, she was also his.

She reached up to brush her fingers over his hands. "I don't want that either," she whispered. "But I can't ignore someone in need. Not when that girl could have easily been me if you hadn't intervened." Wrapping her fingers around his hands, she slowly peeled them away from her face. Her cheeks went cold in their absence.

Will nodded. "Then I am going with you."

"Thatta boy, Will! They don't stand a chance against us," Rigel declared. He jogged over and tossed an arm around each of them.

Behind him were Crystal, Xandra, Kieran, and Gideon, all with their weapons at the ready. "Where to, Commander?" Kieran asked Serena with a grin.

Crystal studied the blade in her hand, awaiting Serena's reply. "We should quickly sweep the streets in pairs," the princess began. The guardian did not look up, but the slight inclination of her head told Serena to go on. "If we don't find the culprits, then we should go to the docks. It's possible the kidnappers will look to take her elsewhere."

"Are you certain the missing girl was kidnapped? She could be a runaway," Gideon pointed out.

"No. There was a scuffle in an alley, and her brother was panicked," Serena said.

"Then we're running out of time," Xandra concluded, charging forward into the street.

Serena nodded and did the same. Everyone fanned out, checking dark alleys and asking skittish people questions as they scurried home. There was a reason the people, particularly the women, were afraid, and Serena was determined to uncover it.

Following a fruitless search of the streets and a local brothel, the guardians led their smaller groups until they all reconvened on the edge of town. The sun was low, bathing the sea gold as it descended. Three ships were docked at the port—one of which they had traveled on mere hours before. Led by Serena and Crystal, the group approached a large vessel made of rich red oak. Over their heads soared black canvas sails that were frayed along the edges.

Two by two, they marched up the gangway. As they stepped onto the deck, gruff faces punctuated by twisted sneers greeted them. Despite the unwanted intrusion, most of the crew members continued readying the vessel, ignoring their presence. "In a hurry," Crystal said aloud. "Where are you boys off to this fine evening?"

Three older men approached them. Their tattered clothing and unshaven faces matched the hostility in their sunken faces. The roundest of the men stepped close to Crystal; his hand flexed on the hilt of the sword at his hip. "To what do we owe the pleasure of this intrusion? 'Tis not often that we have guests on the *De Lunae*." The men behind him snickered; the menacing sound sent a shiver down Serena's spine.

Crystal scoffed, twirling a small dagger between her fingers with ease. If this man was supposed to intimidate her, he was failing miserably. Chin held high, the elf sheathed her dagger. Serena tried not to chuckle knowing these men posed no threat to her friend. "We are not here for a visit. We are looking for the captain of this vessel."

The pirates' leader cocked one brow curiously. "Who be asking?"

"We are members of the Garrick Guard from Symptee," Rigel answered quickly. Serena wondered if he was trying to take the pirate's attention from Crystal.

It didn't work. The stout man leaned closer to the elf and extended a greasy hand. "Captain Maars Zuck, at your service." Crystal ignored the hand between them, her eyes never leaving his. After a moment, the captain dropped his hand and narrowed his eyes in irritation. "And what brings ye aboard my humble vessel?"

As his gaze dropped to inspect Crystal's figure, Serena clenched her fists and stepped forward. "We're looking for a missing girl. Dark hair. Around my age."

Crystal cut a warning glance toward Serena. She understood why the guardian was trying to keep the captain's attention on her, but that did not change the fact that Serena was now in charge. Coming to the dock and boarding the *De Lunae* had been her idea. It was time for her to take full control of the situation.

Zuck stepped toward her, his men stepping past Crystal to get a better look at the rest of their party. "Only girl I've seen by that description is you, lass. And you are a pretty one." The pirates snickered as they inched closer. More of Zuck's men had turned their attention toward their unwelcome guests. The men were sizing them up, and the guardians knew it. The air was thick with anticipation as hands found their weapons, readying for an impending fight.

Serena swallowed, gathering her courage as two men crept closer. Will and Rigel stepped toward her without hesitation. The pirates cackled at their concern, but Serena paid them no mind. She focused on the captain as she stammered, "I'm afraid we'll have to search your vessel, just to be sure. She could have stowed away when no one was looking."

With a flick of his wrist, Zuck's men unsheathed their swords, and Serena's party immediately followed. She ground her teeth together, eyes flicking between the two men closest to her, but Rigel and Will were already flanking her, ready to take them on.

"And what gives you the authority to do that? This city, this port does not belong to the Garrick Queen, nor will it ever." Zuck grinned confidently; his gap-filled smile made her skin crawl.

Suppressing a shiver, Serena held her head high as she replied, "I am the one destined to liberate the people of Hyrosencia from evil. *All of them.* And I will cut down anyone who stands in my way."

Zuck's pupils flared as shocked whispers filled the deck. "*You* are the *star-chosen savior?* Well, that does change things." His lips pulled to one side as though this was a game and he now had an advantage. Serena's breath hitched as she wondered why the pirate was so pleased by this discovery.

Kieran and Gideon whispered behind her. Though she could not see Crystal, she was certain the guardian was cursing under her breath. But there was no reason to hide the truth from any of them. After all, they were about to fight to the death.

Metal rang out as the first of Zuck's men slashed out at Rigel, who skillfully blocked the strike. And like a bell signaling townspeople to come together, everyone on the deck collided all at once. Swords clanged in an unhinged cacophony. Men grunted and groaned as blades sliced through the thick air and thicker skin. The guardian unit was outnumbered nearly two to one, but where the guardians lacked numbers, they were clearly better trained. Crystal and Rigel had each managed to overpower a man in a matter of minutes. Kieran was close behind, his blade slashing through the arm of an assailant and splattering blood across the deck. Serena held her own against one man who obviously had not been in as many sword fights as his comrades. She almost felt bad when she finally managed to slice through his torso. As he flopped onto the deck with a wet squelch, she was relieved to find Will holding his own against one of the younger pirates in the crew.

"You claim to be the lost Garrick princess?" Zuck slurred as he stepped into her peripheral. The tip of his blade dragged against the wooden planks near his feet, leaving a pale, thin line across the dark wood.

"I claim it because it is so," she countered, taking a defensive stance.

"You have no idea the price on your head." His chuckle gave her goosebumps. Standing over a head taller than her, Captain Zuck would be the largest opponent she had ever faced. Yet his size did not intimidate her, even as he surged forth with surprising speed. They parried back and forth, both panting as they assessed each other for weaknesses. Zuck seemed almost impressed with her skills. "Trained by a master, I see."

Their blades interlocked, and Zuck pressed in with his upper body strength, forcing her to take a step back. "And you learned through experience?" she retorted. Thinking on her feet, she found her balance and used one leg to kick the pirate. The blow knocked the wind out of the rotund rogue.

As he stumbled backward, Serena scanned behind him for her friends. Crystal sliced through another pirate and pushed the limp body at Zuck as he slammed into the banister. The captain shoved his fallen comrade aside with a vicious sneer. "Think you're clever, eh?"

Wiping her bloody sword off with a handkerchief, Crystal grinned. "Of course she is. She learned from the best, Captain." She glanced about the deck and beamed. Her eyes positively twinkled with pride.

Without looking, Serena knew the others must have been overpowering the pirates. She also knew that taking down their captain was the quickest way to end this fight. "Where is the girl, Captain?"

He snickered, holding his arms out at his sides. "What girl?"

"I know she's here. I *will* find her," Serena insisted, readying herself to attack the man.

Crystal held her blade out in front of Serena's path. "Together," the elf said firmly. Serena nodded, and they both started toward their target.

Zuck was cornered against the banister. His beady eyes swept over the blood-smeared deck where his crew's bodies continued to pile up. "You think ye can take me down? You've no idea who you're dealing with," he hollered. When he held up his blade, his arm trembled slightly. He knew he would soon be joining the others who had responded with violence and hostility. "So, this be how Elara plays it, eh?"

Serena tensed at the mention of her aunt. "This is not about her," she snapped, lifting Sannarvin over her shoulder. They began to parry again. This time Zuck's movements were more erratic as he swung back and forth, blocking maneuvers from each of his opponents with haste. Sweat pooled on his forehead. As his speed decreased, Serena knew his stamina was failing him. Making eye contact with Crystal, they nodded to each other. As Crystal blocked Zuck, locking his sword behind hers, Serena stormed at them. Plunging the Heir's Blade underneath their arms, she drove the blade up into his abdomen. When she turned her eyes to face the man she had just stabbed, Cameron stared back at her.

15

STARS ABOVE

A shriek rang out across the deck. Serena yanked her blade from Zuck's body, and he flopped to the deck like a dead fish. She scanned the deck for the culprit and found that her friends were staring at her, concern etched in their features. Will strode toward her, asking, "Serena, are you hurt?"

She shook her head slowly, turning back to inspect Zuck's body. Blood oozed between his fingers as he pressed against the wound she had inflicted. It was a futile effort in the end, as his eyes glazed over a moment later. "No. I'm fine," Serena said.

Crystal wiped her blade and sheathed it before tenderly taking Sannarvin out of Serena's hands. She wiped the blade off with careful reverence before offering it back to the girl. "You did well tonight," the guardian said, finally catching her eye.

"Let's find that girl. I'm ready to get off this bloody ship," Serena said. She shoved her blade into its sheath and headed for stairs that she assumed would lead to the brig. Two sets of boots scuffed the floor, following close behind her. She didn't turn back to see who. When they reached the lower level of the ship, they found two small cells sitting empty. Serena kicked the iron bars, her boot doing nothing to stifle the pain that shot through her foot from the impact. "Blazing embers!" The agony plaguing her heart came through in her outcry, making it plain that her misfortunes were far worse than a small self-inflicted injury.

A firm hand clasped her shoulder as she clenched the bars in a death-grip. "Take it easy. We don't need you breaking your foot," Rigel said. His smirk told her he was trying to lighten the mood. He didn't know what was bothering her, but that never stopped him from trying to make her feel better.

His voice was like a salve for her aching heart; his warm teasing reminded her of the way her father once teased her and her younger brothers. She exhaled, trying to let go of the anger bubbling in her chest, but Cameron's face was burned into the inside of her eyelids. Dark, lifeless eyes stared back at her until her eyes snapped open. Serena shook her head and muttered, "Why would they fight us if they weren't hiding anyone down here?"

"Who says they aren't hiding anything?"

Serena whipped around to find Kieran near the top of the steps. His shoulder leaned casually against the wall. His white shirt and exposed chest were flecked with bright crimson. "Have you found something elsewhere?"

He grinned as he pushed off the wall and ambled down a few steps. "I have my suspicions. It's not my first time on a ship like this," Kieran said nonchalantly. Sauntering past Rigel, he grasped one of the metal bars and yanked the door open. He nodded for Serena to enter, but she hesitated. "Come on. Trust me, Princess." She grimaced at the hand he extended toward her.

"Don't ever call me that again," she snarled, folding her arms over her chest. Kieran balked at her irritation. His hand dropped back to his side as he scrutinized her. She knew what he was thinking: *This is the lost heir? We're doomed.*

Rigel shoved his way past Kieran into the cell. He pressed his hand against the wall on the right but failed to find a hidden door there. That's when Kieran clomped into the cell and started tapping his boot against the floor planks. He turned his head to one side, listening carefully. Serena didn't understand what he was listening for. She leaned against the cell bars and watched as he finally squatted down to feel along the floor. Deft fingers skimmed across the wet boards until he found a crack just big enough to fit three fingers inside. With a slight jerk of his hand, three large boards lifted at once.

Serena and Rigel stepped closer, peering down into the secret compartment. In the dim light brought in by the fast-fading sunset, she could barely make out eyes blinking back through the darkness. But not one set. Four.

"Divinity on high. We have to get them out," Serena ordered.

Rigel and Kieran bent forward to offer their hands, but the cowering bodies did not move toward them. Realizing her error, she sent the men to search the crew's quarters and requested that Crystal and Xandra join her instead.

"Lucianna?" Serena spoke softly, inching a bit closer to the opening in the floor. Two faces were becoming clearer as her eyes adjusted. A pair of blue eyes lit up at the name, and Serena smiled in relief. "Is that you? Your brother sent us. He was so worried about you."

The young woman shuffled around until she managed to get on her knees. As her head peeked out of the alcove, Serena finally got a good look at her. She was beautiful. Long hair fell over her shoulders, and plump lips sat between round cheeks. It was no wonder the pirates had snatched her off the street. Serena extended a hand and asked, "Won't you come out? The bad men are gone now. I promise. Slayed two myself."

Lucianna took her hand, and Serena helped her climb out of the hole. Once the girl was free, the next girl stood, ready to embrace her freedom.

Crystal and Xandra came downstairs with blankets and canteens in hand. Just as Serena helped the third woman climb up, Xandra gasped. "She's Silveryl," she murmured, going straight for the young woman with brown skin and pointed ears.

Crystal whipped around from inspecting the second woman for injuries. She squinted to focus on the elf's face in the dim light. "Ausha?" The elf's eyes lit up at the name.

"You know my sister?" the girl asked. She turned and reached out to help Serena and Xandra pull the last woman out of the pit.

The archer stared when she laid eyes on the woman. "Ausha! I cannot believe it's you." Crystal pulled her into a tight hug. Serena had never seen her greet another so warmly. Perhaps it was because this girl was an elf. Pulling back, Crystal noticed the dried blood on her friend's forehead and frowned. "What happened to you?"

"I came with Iriela to sell wine at the market. We were packing up in the evening when those bastards attacked us. I was knocked unconscious in the scuffle," Ausha answered, running fingers through her blood-tangled hair with difficulty.

Xandra hugged the woman before turning her to face Serena. "This is Ausha Wyntaburn. She trained at the Academy with us. Ausha, this is Serena." They shook hands briefly.

They helped the four women up the stairs onto the deck, where the others had gathered miscellaneous things they had found on the ship, including three more pirates. Rigel said they'd called for a parlay, laying down their arms and begging for mercy.

Serena pointed her sword at the scruffiest prisoner's nose. "Was taking these women a mercy?" He cowered at the edge of her blade, awaiting judgement. She wanted to end him—and his comrades—for daring to touch those women. For what they had done and the worse things they intended to do once they left Lei'wana. How many women had they taken over the years? Where were the ones no one had protected?

Warmth bloomed on her lower back as Will stepped closer. He stooped to whisper for only her ears, "Let the guardians handle them." She couldn't look at him then. Couldn't bear to allow this kind and selfless man to see the hate in her eyes. Hate that could drive an ordinary woman to slay an unarmed man. Would that make her a monster, even if the world would be better for it?

Before she could make her decision, Ausha surged at the man kneeling on the end of the row, driving a dagger deep into the man's chest. Glassy eyes stared at his attacker as his heart rate slowed to a stop. "No, it wasn't," Ausha answered for him. Blood sprayed her clothes and face as she yanked the blade free. Backlit by the moonlight, there was something primal and truly terrifying about this elf. That was enough to make Serena stay out of the woman's way as she moved down the line.

"Papa's wine!" Iriela declared. Her feet were heavy as she ran across the deck to Gideon, who had found the captain's liquor stash, among other oddities. Clutching a beautiful green glass bottle in her hands, Iriela inspected the script on the label. It was smudged—from the scuffle or the pirates' poor storage, no one knew. The girl frowned, inspecting the bottle in Gideon's hands. "I was hoping to sell more before returning home, but now I cannot read the labels."

Gideon grinned. "Lucky for you, I've been dying to get my hands on some genuine Silveryl wine." He lifted the bottle over his head and called out to the group, "There's a dozen of these. Who wants one?"

"They're seven shillings each," Iriela informed him, holding out her palm. Gideon chuckled, reaching into the pouch at his waist. He handed over a gold coin and said, "I'll take two then."

"Let's finish up here and move down to the beach," Rigel suggested. He paid the little salesperson her fee and picked up a bottle. Then he approached Serena and Will, tossed an arm around each of them, and said, "You've done well. Think you two can get a bonfire started?"

Will's dimples appeared, sending Serena's heart fluttering. "I think we can handle that," he replied.

"What about the other two girls? We need to take them home," Serena argued.

"We'll make sure they get home safe," Xandra assured her.

Kieran was eyeing the beach over the railing when Crystal snapped him out of his thoughts. "Go with Xandra. Make sure she gets back to the beach safely." He rolled his eyes but obliged.

Will and Serena followed them down the gangway, and the two groups parted at the edge of the dock. Iriela had joined Serena and Will while Ausha stayed behind to help the others dispose of the rest of the pirates' bodies. A short time later, two large fires lit the night—one a pyre for bodies and the other a bonfire for the living to enjoy. Iriela splashed her face in the shallow water. Serena was glad to see the harrowing experience had not scarred the young lady who couldn't have been older than she was.

Will popped the cork off a bottle of Elven wine. He offered the bottle to Serena first, and she hesitantly took it. The deep burgundy liquid was sweeter than any fruit she had ever tasted and went down much smoother than the moonshine the boys made back home. She took a second swill before handing the bottle back to Will. Their fingers brushed as he wrapped his hand around the bottle's neck and smiled at her. This was what it should have been like for the two of them. Drinking and smiling at a bonfire in Durmak with their siblings and friends. A few sips of moonshine, and perhaps they'd have snuck off into the woods like Cameron used to.

But if they had all stayed home, someone would have always been there to keep them apart.

As the rest of the group slowly made their way back together, more bottles were opened, and all but Crystal enjoyed the potent concoction. Ausha went a few feet away to wash her hair in the sea, but the archer kept an eye on everyone from her seat in the sand. Serena couldn't tell if the elf was concerned for her friend or lost in other thoughts.

Serena sat beside her friend and ran her fingers through the cool beige sand. It was coarse yet soft against her calloused palm. "What's wrong?"

"I hate sand." Crystal barely glanced at her. Serena inclined her head and raised her eyebrows. The guardian sighed, pressing her hands between her knees. She stared out across the sea as if lost in thought. "You made a good call today. If it had been me, I might not have gone after those men… and then two of my own people would be gone."

"Don't beat yourself up over that, Crys. You were right to be cautious."

"I was not expecting to see anyone from home today," Crystal said quietly. She watched Iriela dance around the bonfire, weaving between the other guardians. Though she was petite, Serena now knew the young elf was actually twice her age. "Ausha mentioned my father."

Serena nodded. Crystal had never really been open about her family. All she knew was that her mother had died when she was much younger. "Is he ill?"

The elf scoffed, grinning a bit. "Elves do not get sick like humans do." She looked down at her lap peppered with sand and attempted to brush it off with the back of her hand. "No, he is well. He is up for a place on the Elder Council."

"Is that a bad thing?"

"No. He's earned that." Crystal paused. "She said he often speaks about us. Like he misses us. Not sure I believe that. My father's never been very *warm*."

"I'm sure he does miss you," Serena rebutted. "How long have you been away?"

Crystal twisted her lips, watching as Ausha wrung out her saturated locks. "Over two years. He was displeased that I chose to go to Symptee with the others instead of returning home."

"I'm sure he isn't upset about that anymore. You're his only daughter, right?" Serena tried to offer a reassuring smile, but the truth was she didn't know the man. If he was anywhere near as grumpy as Cole when they first met, she could be wrong.

"Yes," the guardian muttered. Turning to face Serena, she nudged the girl toward the bonfire with one hand. "It's nothing for you to worry over. Go enjoy yourself."

As she stood up, Serena shook off her clothes, sprinkling Crystal with even more sand. The guardian growled and rolled her eyes as Serena giggled and ran to rejoin the group. A crisp wind whipped her hair behind her shoulders, the cool rush burning her cheeks. She smiled, remembering the way the trees around Durmak would change colors. Rich reds, oranges, and yellows filled the air before fluttering to the ground. She wondered if they would get to see the changing of seasons in Ord Metsiilva.

Fabric brushed her shoulders, caressing her back as warmth settled over her. But when she turned, she was surprised by the face behind her. Kieran curled one arm over the top of her shoulder confidently. "You looked cold." Serena turned to face the bonfire and lightly shrugged her shoulders. Kieran got the hint, dropping his arm to his side. He shifted to stand more in her view. "Is what you told the captain true? Are you the Garrick princess?"

"I am no princess." Serena glanced over his shoulder and made eye contact with Will, who had tensed mid-conversation with Rigel. He suddenly looked angry. Frustrated. She wondered if he might be angry with her for dragging them into battle against pirates. Shifting her gaze back to Kieran, she added, "Elara will remain queen until the day she joins the stars."

"And after?"

"Then, it will go to her heir." She turned away from him in hopes of escaping further conversation about her family affairs—and suddenly in desperate need of more wine. But she had only gotten two steps away when a hand grabbed her by the arm, pulling her back. "Let go," she snarled.

A dark figure shot past her right. Before she could register what was happening, Kieran landed roughly in the sand, a red welp visible on his left eye. "Don't touch her," Will shouted.

Kieran ground his teeth as he stumbled onto his feet, sending sand flying in all directions. "You dare lay a hand on a Lord? I should put you on the flat of your back."

"I'd like to see you try," Will said.

Kieran's hand went to the blade sheathed at this side. Serena stepped between them, hoping to diffuse the tension before a fight escalated. When she touched Will's arm, his skin radiated heat. "Take it easy, boys. This is just a misunderstanding," she said gently.

Will stared down the guardian, who did not move to release his weapon at her words. Kieran's eyes darkened as he glared back. "He attacked me unprovoked," Kieran said. His jaw tightened as he waited for someone to take his side.

"You grabbed her, and she told you to let go. I was merely helping you follow orders," Will argued.

The other guardians started toward the commotion, and Serena looked to them to diffuse the situation. Rigel and Gideon approached from behind Kieran. "We've all been drinking. Let's take a walk and clear your head," Gideon said, putting an arm around his friend.

The enraged nobleman glared at Will as they led him down the beach, away from the bonfire. Serena watched as they left, still breathing heavily. "Did he hurt you?" Xandra asked.

"Of course not," she snapped, turning to face Will. "What were you thinking? You can't just go around punching people."

Will smiled in disbelief, shaking his head. "He was making you uncomfortable, and he wasn't taking a hint."

Crystal nodded her head at the other guardians, and they slowly stepped away toward the sea, allowing Serena to address the incident on her own.

"I'm not a child. I don't need you to protect me anymore. That's not why you're here."

"That's where you're wrong." Will ground his teeth. He ran his fingers through his hair, leaving it even more tousled in his wake. "That guy was being a prick. You can't expect me to watch him invade your space and do nothing."

"Yes, I can! He wasn't trying to kill me." Serena sighed, rubbing her temples. "This isn't like you, Will. I've never seen you like that. Did you drink too much?"

He rubbed the back of his neck, avoiding her scrutiny. "I'm not drunk. I'm just... tired."

"It's been a long day. Perhaps we should return to the inn," she suggested.

"No, please," he pleaded, stepping toward her. "This is the first time in so long that something has reminded me of home. I don't want to go back yet."

Her chest swelled with nostalgia for their home. He was right. This bonfire was the closest thing they'd had to a normal night in Durmak in ages. And having Will there is what eased her constant homesickness. "Then we'll stay—if you can behave yourself." Her teasing smile broke the tension between them, and Will exhaled in relief.

They stood side by side staring at the fire, neither daring to move or say a word for several minutes. Heat permeated the space, and Serena realized she was still wearing Kieran's cloak. In the heat of the moment, she had not realized it was still there. She gently brushed the dark fabric off her shoulders, allowing it to cascade to rest on the sand.

"When I saw him grab you, I thought about Cam, how things escalated so quickly in the mountains," Will said, his deep voice full of emotion. "In the mountains, I was a coward. I thought there was no way he would ever hurt you, and I was wrong. Then at the citadel, I wasn't there when you needed me. Again. So, when Kieran grabbed you, something snapped in me... I'm sorry I acted rashly."

His admission stunned her. Warmth spread through her ears and down her neck as she considered his actions. Though she did not want him to feel obligated to protect her, she never imagined that he might feel guilty for the times he couldn't. "I thought about Cameron tonight as well. On the ship," she confessed. It was painful to admit, but she knew only Will would ever understand the guilt she lived with. "When I killed the captain, it was like killing him all over again." Her eyes welled with tears, and she shook her head, swiping them away with her fingers. She didn't want to mourn him, didn't want to be sad that her elder brother was dead. She closed her eyes and found it impossible not to think about his final moments—how in those final moments he had chosen to attack her.

"You cannot let that haunt you for the rest of your life, Serena. He was hurting you," Will said, stepping closer. "He was one of Rexton's soldiers, lost to the dark in a way we couldn't have imagined. I should have protected you."

"You aren't a killer, Will. And I don't want you to become one," she whispered, staring into the flickering flames of their bonfire. "Not even for me."

"I injured a man tonight. Perhaps he will survive, perhaps he will succumb. I wasn't brave enough to stick around and see." He exhaled, his words hanging heavy between them. "This is the path I've chosen—to follow you—and I will fight any man that lifts a hand against you."

"Slaying an enemy may be justified, but Cameron was not just another soldier. He was my brother. I will not soon forget his face."

"I wish you could find a way to forgive yourself. It's not good to dwell on the dead. There are people here who care about you. It's best to focus on the people you still have instead."

"I'm trying." She paused, steadying her breath. "You said I would never be alone, yet I have felt utterly alone ever since we reached Symptee."

"But you've been with people every day. You train with the guardians—"

"The guardians don't understand my pain. Neither did Elara. I didn't realize it at first. But I needed this—*you*—more than anything. Because you understand what I lost."

Will's shoulders slumped as he looked down at the sand beneath his boots. "I'm sorry I wasn't around more. I wanted to see you, more than anyone. But the apprenticeship kept me so busy, I could barely keep up."

Serena crossed her arms and asked, "Was it worth it?"

"No. I missed you far too much," he admitted.

Her cheeks burned at his admission. She turned toward him and found him staring. "You did?"

"Of course I did," he said, running a hand through his hair. "I asked Rigel about you every time I saw him. All I wanted was to know you were well."

"Most days I'm not. I'm just pretending to be." She bit down on her bottom lip, worried she was saying too much.

"But you will be. One day. I truly believe that. If anyone deserves happiness, it's you."

"I don't know about that," she mumbled, clenching her jaw. The autumn breeze whipped her hair over her shoulder. Serena shivered at its gentle caress. She closed her eyes and remembered how warm Will was when he held her under the willow tree in Jordis. How safe she had felt. She'd been desperate to feel that way again ever since they reached Symptee.

"Yes, you do. I knew you before all this. I know who you really are. You're the first person to offer a stranger help. You put your whole heart into everything you do, care deeply about every person you meet. You're crazy to think anyone could see you as anything but perfect."

Serena looked up, her lips parted as she studied his face. He was the same boy she'd had a crush on in Durmak, yet he was much changed. His face, now peppered with dark stubble, had lost some of its boyish charm, replaced with a man whose eyes studied her with newfound appreciation. The heat from his gaze sent another wave of chills down her spine. "I'm far from perfect, and you know that. I can see it in the way you look at me sometimes—with such sadness in your eyes. I'm not the girl you grew up with. That girl is gone."

The corners of his mouth turned down as he stepped toward her. He closed the gap between them, pausing right in front of her. The fire reflecting off his irises reminded her of fresh honey—warm, sweet, yet smoldering as his eyes bore into hers. "I'm not sad that you've changed. I've changed, too. I'm sad because you can't see the good in yourself anymore. And you are so much more than good, Serena." The pads of his fingers gently caressed her cheek. "You are exceptional. There are as many reasons to love you as there are stars above us. I hope one day you'll believe that."

"What?" Serena asked, her voice barely a whisper. *Love?* Her eyes widened as his lips curled, revealing the dimpled grin that always set her heart aflutter.

Will nodded his head slowly as he reached for her hand. "I love you. Every version there has been and everything you will be in the future. No matter how you change or how far we go from home, I will always choose you." His smile sent butterflies through her stomach. "I'm sorry it took me this long to admit it."

Serena sucked in her breath, a knot forming in her throat as her breathing intensified. He loved her. Despite all she'd done and all she was expected to do, he still saw someone good and kind. Someone worthy of his affection. His love. Even when she didn't feel that she deserved it.

She propelled her body at him. Wrapping her arms around his neck, she laced her fingers through the dark hair at the nape of his neck and pressed her lips to his. Strong arms wrapped around her waist, pulling her flush with his chest as he deepened their embrace. His lips were soft yet needy, kissing her with a fervor that heated her entire body. She would have gladly drowned in the taste of his lips, rich and sweet as the Elven wine they had shared. Coarse stubble scraped her chin, and she didn't care. Her lips moved against his with equal need. She wanted every piece of him—his calloused hands, warm eyes, stubble-flecked chin, dimples, and everything between. He was hers, and she was his, and for the first time in a very long time, everything felt simple. In his arms, everything felt right because the safest place is in the arms of the person you love most.

They drew apart, resting their foreheads against each other as they caught their breath. "I love you, too," Serena whispered. She smiled as tears streaked her cheeks—not of sorrow, but of joy and hope. Of a selfless love that was mending her broken spirit in ways he could never fathom. She had lost so much in so little time, but she knew they could survive anything so long as they had each other.

A slow applause broke out behind them, and they turned to find the guardians hooting in celebration. Serena's cheeks turned bright red as she pulled away from Will, unaware they had an audience. Rigel and Xandra ran over to embrace them. Xandra lifted Serena off her feet and spun her around, while Rigel tackled Will, their tumble sending a burst of white sand into the air. Their excitement was palpable, and it made Serena that much more certain that they belonged together.

She noticed that Kieran and Gideon weren't among the others. A wave of relief crashed over Will's features when he realized the same. They must have returned to the inn. That was probably for the best.

As she turned to face Crystal, the archer tried to suppress her own grin. "You look happy," the elf noted. Serena nodded, beaming as she pulled her friend into a hug. Rigid at first, Crystal slowly relaxed into it, patting the girl on her back before pulling away.

Will turned and asked, "So, you're not going to kill me?" Serena laughed uneasily knowing the guardian had done her best to keep them apart.

Crystal shook her head and shoved his shoulder. "Not as long as you treat her well, Burroughs."

Wrapping an arm around his girl, Will pecked her on the temple. When he looked at her, he looked as though he had found the world's greatest treasure. Serena leaned into his warmth, certain that his love was worth more than gold.

16

WHAT HAPPENS AT
MORNING TEA

Elara swirled her spoon in her tea for far longer than necessary. The conversation had lulled after Rilura's detailed recollection of her general being mauled to death by a Mørkewulv, the story leaving the queen's stomach in knots. Rubbing one hand against her swollen midsection, she glanced across the table at the Cinderfell sisters for a change of topic.

Ismenia turned toward the Dwarven princess. "What a harrowing ordeal! We are so relieved you were able to survive those beasts. It was a blessing we did not encounter them on our own crossing."

An untouched teacup sat in front of Rilura. The queen felt foolish, realizing that dwarfs must not partake in morning tea. She should have offered an alternative option for their meeting.

"A blessing, indeed." Rilura smiled bitterly. One hand curled around the delicate cup before her, covering the entire floral pattern with her large fingers.

The queen cleared her throat and finally placed her spoon down on her saucer with a definitive clink. "Would you care for something other than tea, Your Highness? I fear I must apologize for not being more familiar with your people's customs."

Rilura quickly lifted the cup to her bare lips and slurped a sip. "The tea is lovely, Your Majesty. Do not worry for my sake. I am not fussy as some ladies." She offered the queen a kind smile, and Elara couldn't help but wonder if the princess was considered beautiful among her rugged kinfolk. Her eyes were pale and bright, and her smile was pleasant. Her long black hair was freshly washed and plaited, falling nearly to her rear. It caught the

141

light coming in through the window behind her. If she had worn a gown, she would almost fit in among the women of the citadel. Almost.

"I, for one, prefer black tea," Idonea said. "Save the sugar for Elara." The queen didn't miss her friend's grin.

"Sugar is a rarity for my people," Rilura said. She reached for a square sponge cake on the platter between them, forgoing the dainty serving utensils. Plucking a cake between two fingers, she brought it straight to her mouth and then licked her fingers clean. "As are babies." She nodded toward the queen.

Elara met her statement with a quizzical brow. "I am surprised to hear that as I remember seeing great numbers upon my crossing. Though I do recall seeing mostly men. I assumed the women and children were housed elsewhere."

Hanging her head, the Dwarven princess was quiet for a moment. The humans waited patiently for her to go on. Finally, she looked up, resting her gaze on Elara's belly, and said, "There have always been far more men among my peoples. It is why the women are highly encouraged to wed. If we do not, one day the Steelcast clan will cease to exist."

"Though women are far from scarce here, we, too, are encouraged to wed for the sake of bearing children," Ismenia said gently. "Do your people often arrange marriages?"

"On occasion, but both parties must consent. Not even my father can force someone into a lifelong bond, much as he longs to live to meet a grandchild." Rilura's cheeks flushed at the thought of her having a child one day. Elara couldn't help but smile at the woman's shyness.

"Have you any suitors currently?" Elara inquired. Ismenia leaned forward eagerly while Idonea sipped her tea in silence. Rilura couldn't look the queen in the eye then, making it even more obvious that she must be interested in someone. The queen reached for her hand and gave it a gentle pat. "I must apologize for prying. We are quite used to oversharing during tea, but you are not obliged to share anything. You are a guest, after all."

"But we can promise that nothing you say at tea will leave this room," Ismenia added.

Rilura lifted her chin and nodded. "Several suitors have shown interest. There is but one I have an interest in. I worry my father may not approve of the match."

"Do you love this man?" Ismenia asked. She rested her cheek on her hands. The herbalist had always been a romantic. Elara wondered if she was still being courted by one of her guards or if the early sparks had already faded.

Rilura coughed into her fist, eyes blown wide in surprise. "Ah, I do not think… We have yet to enter any arrangement. He is strong and kind, protective while still allowing me to protect myself. He is a good man. A loyal friend."

"Friends can make the best lovers," Ismenia said. The women at the table all gasped at her shocking admission before bursting into a fit of giggles.

"She is not entirely wrong," Elara said. She grinned, recalling the early days of getting to know Gerard. They had spent many hours walking, conversing, and enjoying music together before their relationship became physical. And when it did, it was unlike any of her prior experiences. When she wed Caspian, they had not known each other. He was kind and respectful, but there was rarely any passion because they never truly fell in love with each other. With Gerard, it was hard to cage the inferno of desire lit within both of their hearts. Each kiss and caress in secret only made their stolen moments that much more intimate.

"When did you know you were in love with Lord Stirling?" Rilura asked.

Elara cleared her throat lightly, feeling heat rise in her cheeks as all eyes fell on her. In truth, she wasn't even sure exactly when. Gerard confessed his love for her first, a few weeks after they began secretly courting. He wasted no time telling her that he wanted to make her his wife if his cousin approved of his request. She couldn't bring herself to say it back until they received word that Prince Kailan had given his blessing.

"It happened so quickly, I could not say when. All I know is that the moment I let him in, I knew I would be a fool to ever let him go," Elara replied. "I knew he was the one because I never feel safer anywhere else than I do in his arms. And I never feel happier than when he smiles at me."

Even Idonea could not help but smile at the queen's admission.

"While I do not require a man to feel safe, I most certainly feel safe in Thomli's presence. He brings my spirit a sense of peace, and he allows me to be exactly who I am—as much a Steelcast warrior as a woman and a princess."

"Sounds like you're on your way to some big feelings there," Ismenia noted. Her nose wrinkled in sheer joy. "Perhaps you should talk to him? Did he accompany you to the citadel?"

Rilura nodded. "Aye. Perhaps it is time. I've fought monstrous beasts. How hard could it be to speak of feelings with a man?"

"It may not be easy, but it will be worth it. That I can promise," Elara said. The queen smiled, though what Rilura had said replayed in the back of her mind. *I do not require a man to feel safe.* What a luxury it was for any woman to feel such a way. She certainly had not felt safe since Antoine killed her father, forcing her to flee her home.

"Does something troubles ye, Your Majesty?" When Elara looked up, there were worry lines visible on Rilura's wide forehead.

"Please, you must call me Elara, as we are now confidants."

"If that is your wish. But you must address me as Rilura in turn."

Elara nodded. She had grown tired of donning her practiced smile. As she relaxed her face, blowing out a weary breath, she wondered if her mother had always felt the same pressure to put on an effortless smile as though nothing were wrong. "It has been many years since I've felt safe without the presence of guards or a husband. I must confess I envy your strength and confidence, Rilura."

The dwarf blinked at her in confusion. "Why should a queen ever envy myself?"

"I'm afraid. I'm afraid of so many things, and that does not make me feel regal in the slightest," Elara admitted. She lifted her teacup to her lips with a trembling hand. Taking a slow sip and trying to steady her heart, the queen pondered whether anything could be done to lessen her constant anxiety.

"Oh, dear… You should have told us sooner," Ismenia said, her voice a calming whisper.

"You feel unsafe because Rexton has tried to assassinate you?" Rilura asked, folding her hands together on top of the table.

Elara nodded. "His attempts on my life have been much too close for comfort. And I fear eventually he shall set his army upon us. What will become of us then if the citadel is breached?"

The queen could see the wheels turning in the dwarf's head, and she wasn't sure she would like any solution her companions offered. Finally, Rilura pressed her hands into the table and pushed herself onto her feet. "If you worry about being attacked, then you should learn how to defend yourself. Be it with a sword or a bow, it would be good for you to be prepared. All of you." She gestured toward the Cinderfells.

"You think we should learn to fight?" Idonea asked, no hint of surprise in her tone.

Ismenia's eyebrows had disappeared behind the curls on her forehead. "But Elara is with child."

"And why should that stop her? When a Dwarven warrior becomes with child, that does not stop her from training. The love of her child gives her added strength. And should her people go to war, so shall she," Rilura said proudly.

"I began training shortly after I arrived at the citadel. No one could say I was any good at it, polite as they were at the time," Elara said, recalling how different the early years at the citadel were. Everything was new and different and intimidating, yet she did not feel completely unsafe. She never intended to march into any battles, but she was confident that she could protect herself if the need arose. "When I became with child, my advisors agreed it was unnecessary as we all knew Serena was alive. She was the one destined to fight, so I laid down my weapons and did not look back."

Rilura cocked her head slightly. Her eyes began inspecting the queen's figure, squinting as she took in her narrow upper body and thin arms. "You lack muscle, but that is easy enough to improve. I could practice with you, if you'd like."

Elara hummed, biting into her bottom lip. More than once over the years, she had considered asking Commander Stirling or another trusted member of the Guard to train with her. But after losing her first pregnancy and her first husband in quick succession, she found it easiest to throw her mind into the political aspects of being a queen displaced from her own kingdom. After over a decade, she wondered if it was too late to start over again. If she were too old, too inactive, too pregnant for such an arduous task.

"I am not asking ye to lead your people into battle," Rilura clarified. "I only suggest you learn how to protect yourself. Only then do I think your anxieties will lessen."

"What do you think, Ismenia? Would I be a fool to lift a sword?"

Ismenia leaned back in her chair and blew out a breath. "Gerard will not like it. Not in your present condition." Her eyes dipped to the queen's swollen belly. She was likely halfway into her pregnancy, and she would only grow rounder with each passing day.

"What do you think, little one?" Elara rubbed her stomach, relishing in the feeling of flutters within her. "Perhaps we could have tea out in the gardens next time?"

She met the dwarf's gaze, and they both smiled knowing the meaning behind moving their tea. Though Gerard's constant concern echoed in her ears, Elara pushed the intrusive thoughts aside. This was something she needed to do for her own peace of mind, and if it would not bring her husband peace, perhaps it was best to keep whatever happened at morning tea a secret between friends.

17

SHACKLED

Sabine Rexton learned how to fake pleasantries before she could walk. If there was one thing she was skilled at, it was charming people with whom she did not wish to spend time. Her fiancé, Ryker Umbryon, was no exception.

Taking her brother's advice, she exchanged daily pleasantries with the man and acted as though she had accepted her fate. Ryker seemed pleased with her growing interest. She asked more about his upbringing and delicately inquired about his previous wives, learning both had died due to complications from childbirth. Sabine's compassion when he spoke of his first wife was genuine. He seemed to have truly loved her, and she wondered if he might ever feel so strongly about another woman again.

Having a son was incredibly important to Ryker as he had a title to pass on. Sabine never missed his comments on that subject. Each was a reminder that he was expecting that from *her*. Chelsea would try to cut the tension by reminding Ryker how young they both were—that there was plenty of time for that. But Sabine knew she could not hold the earl's advances off forever. With winter around the corner, she wondered just how long he would be willing to wait to wed her.

One morning, when her mother was not feeling well, Ryker took the opportunity to steal a moment alone with her—much to Sabine's dismay. Anteros was busy preparing for the hunt, leaving them unchaperoned for an impromptu stroll on the grounds. When he offered his arm, Sabine wrapped her hand around the crook of his elbow and looked up at him wearily. By all accounts, Ryker was not bad looking. Had there not been such a large age difference, she might have found herself more comfortable with their arrangement.

She turned back toward the hall, shaking the thought from her mind. "Are you looking forward to joining the men for the hunt?"

Ryker smiled. "I have heard great things from your father, though I think I shall miss your company greatly."

Her cheeks blazed. She knew he felt some kind of ownership over her, but she couldn't imagine that he had grown attached to her in such a short amount of time. Ryker looked at her expectantly, and she cleared her throat, struggling for a proper response. "That's very kind of you," Sabine said, biting her lip. "I hope you will have a successful venture. It would bring me great joy if someone outshone my brother on this endeavor."

Her fiancé paused, turning to face her. A hand caressed the side of her chin, fingers entwining with the hair behind her ears as Ryker whispered, "And what would you offer me if I succeeded?"

The princess swallowed, thankful the castle halls were bustling with servants that morning. Ryker's gaze dropped to her lips, and she knew what he was asking for. What she didn't understand was why he was waiting for her permission when he had already stolen a kiss once before. "What is it you want?" she asked, her tone more playful than even she expected.

The earl leaned closer. Hot breath tickled her face as she awaited his answer. "Your mother has begged me to wait until your eighteenth birthday to marry you." The admission made her eyes widen. She knew he must not be pleased with her mother's request. His thumb stroked her cheek softly. "I am trying to be a patient man, Sabine, but I do not wish to return home without you. I want your consent for a spring wedding."

She stared at him for a moment. Her brow furrowed as she considered the change in his demeanor over the past few weeks. Since their encounter in the hall after dinner, Sabine had never expected the man to ask her permission for anything. "If that is what you want, why not ask my father? He would grant your request." Her hands quivered, and she squeezed them together.

"I realize I made a poor impression when we first met," Ryker said. "I know I can be *abrasive*, but I do not want you to be afraid of me." His deep voice sent a shiver up her spine, and her gaze dropped to his jacket—jade green, as many of the men wore on the hunt to blend in with the woods. Perhaps that was what he was doing now, disguising his true nature in hopes of winning her over to his side.

It was almost working.

But two could play this game.

Sabine smiled slightly. "I'm not *afraid* of you." Her voice wavered.

Ryker grinned. "I'm not a foolish man, Sabine. I know why your mother has been watching us like a hawk." She tried to avoid his gaze, but he lifted her chin gently, forcing her to look at him. "I will not hurt you. You have my word."

A breeze blew through the open windows into the hall, and she shivered. Truth was the greatest and rarest of all whisperings at court, and she could not tell whether Ryker Umbryon was being honest. She'd never know unless she married him.

"I should join the hunting party," Ryker finally said, taking her hand and kissing it. "Please consider what I've asked while we're gone."

Sabine nodded, muddled feelings of confusion and relief stirring in her heart. Somehow, she felt she knew him far less after their latest conversation, and that made her feel unsettled. Could Ryker Umbryon be a kind man? Could her own fear have affected her judgment of him? Perhaps there was a chance she could come to care for him in time, given this was the real Ryker—but she still had her doubts.

A rough clink jolted Talitha from her slumber that evening. As the door to her cell swung open, she sat upright, leaning her head back against the wall. The last streams of daylight illuminated half the room. It must have been dinnertime.

Not that most would call the pathetic excuse for daily rations a proper dinner.

A cloaked figure approached, and Talitha realized it wasn't one of the usual kitchen girls.

"I hope you've brought poison this time," Talitha said.

Sabine dropped the hood of her cloak, revealing tired eyes and bare lips turned in a frown. "I've got something better." Arms emerged from under her cloak, revealing a canteen and a small brown sack.

Talitha leaned back against the wall and closed her eyes. "If that's wine, no thank you."

Sabine scoffed, walking over to Talitha and squatting beside her. "I'm not completely daft. I've brought the essentials." The princess shook the canteen in Talitha's face until she finally accepted it.

"What brings you this time?" The girl drank greedily from the canteen as though her thirst might never be quenched. Sabine's heart ached, seeing her friend in such a poor state. Before she met Talitha, she gave little thought to the people her father hurt—there were far too many to allow herself to linger on those thoughts for long. After all, how could anyone possibly help an enemy of the king?

But now, staring at this starving girl who was not much older than her, the princess hung her head in shame for ever having played games with her life.

Talitha blinked at her expectantly as she wiped water from her chin.

"I am betrothed."

The girl's brows raised. "Aren't you too young to get married?" She pulled open the small canvas bag and was pleased to find a mix of nuts and cheese inside.

Sabine flopped onto the floor with an agitated huff. "Tell that to my father. He's traded my virtue… FOR CATTLE!"

Her impassioned shriek ricocheted off the walls, the harsh truth slapping her in the face.

Talitha winced and stuffed a handful of nuts into her mouth. The sound of her chewing was amplified in the enclosed space. Sabine closed her eyes and clenched her teeth. Water dripped from a leak in the ceiling across the room. Plop. Plop. Plop. It was a wonder Talitha had not lost her mind in such a place.

"Tell me about your betrothed. What's his name?" Talitha finally asked, much to Sabine's surprise. There was no pity in her voice, merely curiosity. As though the princess's struggles were the most entertaining thing to happen to her in months.

Then Sabine realized it was.

She exhaled, realizing how foolish it was to look for sympathy from a prisoner. "His name is Ryker Umbryon. He's an earl from Denorfia."

Talitha popped another handful into her mouth. There was no crunch when she chewed this time, much to Sabine's relief. "What do you think of him? Do you like him?"

The princess wrinkled her nose, recalling that Ryker had seemingly changed personalities in the past few days. She honestly wasn't sure whether she could trust him, and that was reason enough to keep him at arm's length for now. "He is *different*. Certainly not what I pictured for myself. But we needed his cattle to survive the winter, and I became part of the bargain."

"You do not sound pleased. Is he old? Unpleasant?" Talitha uncorked the canteen using her teeth, then guzzled more water. Sabine watched it trickle out of the side of her mouth onto her disgusting old gown.

"He is more than a decade our senior, but I suppose it could be worse. He could have been an old man." Sabine shrugged. "I am not so certain he is nice or trustworthy. I fear his personality will change entirely once we've left Graynor. I dread the day."

"You're leaving? When?" The storm clouds in Talitha's eyes told the princess that she was displeased to hear that. Then Sabine remembered that she brought her friend extra rations. That would stop once she went to Denorfia. Then what would become of Talitha?

"I'm not certain when. The wedding will be here, though no date has been set. My mother has begged them to wait until I am eighteen—or at least, closer to it—but Ryker would like to marry in the spring and take me back to his estate." She ran her dirty fingers through her falling updo and longed to submerge herself in a warm bath.

Talitha nodded. "At least you will get out of this horrid place."

Sabine frowned, looking away from her friend. While she was scared for the future, she knew it would be a blessing to leave in a carriage, live at a wealthy estate, and be taken care of for the remainder of her life. If only her friend could be afforded the same luxury. She sat up straight, an idea coming to her out of nowhere. "What if you could come with me?"

"What?" Talitha whispered. Arms crossed tight over her chest, pushing away any hope she might have had seconds before.

"Ryker spoke with my father about selling prisoners to be servants, and he seemed to like the idea," Sabine said. She shifted onto her knees and grabbed Talitha's hands in excitement. "What if I can convince Ryker to ask for you as part of the deal?"

"No," Talitha said firmly. She snatched her hands away from the princess in horror. "I don't want to go to Denorfia. I don't want to become your slave, Sabine. I want to go home, or I want to die in peace."

Sabine's heart sank. Though the idea might have saved Talitha from starving to death in a dungeon, she had no idea whether Ryker would even agree to it. Whether her father would let Talitha go. Or whether Ryker was good to his servants. "You're right. I'm sorry," she stammered.

The prisoner did not reply, instead turning her face away.

The princess pushed herself up onto her feet and brushed her hands against her skirts. "Suppose I should let you get some sleep," she murmured, starting toward the unlocked door. If Talitha was not willing to become a servant to escape Antoine Rexton, then Sabine was not sure how else they would free her. But she hoped her brother would have a better idea when he returned from the hunt.

18

ON THE HUNT

Antoine Rexton led the hunting pack toward the edge of the woods. Hunting fowl was his preferred sport when the sweltering heat of summer finally simmered down. It was early in the new season; the wind was refreshing, but the leaves had yet to fall from the trees. Anteros hoped the men would be able to flush out a decent variety of birds—his father's mood for the rest of the week would be determined by the success of this hunt.

"What is your favorite animal to hunt, Your Majesty?" Ryker Umbryon asked. One of his servants walked beside him, his prized canine practically dragging him toward the brush.

The king stopped abruptly, and the two dozen men behind him came to a halt. "I enjoy the thrill of the boar in the spring, but there is something about smaller prey—doves and quail and the like—that is extra satisfying to chase."

Anteros adjusted the strap on his crossbow over his shoulder. "Birds are smaller targets, and they tend to fly off at the smallest sound. That's why they're a more satisfying kill."

"You like a challenge," Ryker said, dipping his chin in humble acknowledgement toward the king. "I, too, enjoy such every now and then. We make sport of taming wild horses in the northeast."

The king's brows raised. "A difficult task. I am impressed."

Ryker beamed, clearly pleased with the praise. "When I return to my estate in the spring, I hope to have new captures to tame."

Anteros grimaced as he stalked past his father toward the edge of the woods. He had had enough talk of weddings and diplomatic hogwash. If he had to participate in the hunt to remain in his father's good graces, then he wanted to shoot something—and soon.

He hoisted the cross bow onto his shoulder and exhaled slowly. In the brush, quail would be found nesting among tall grass and weeds. Further in the forest, doves and other small creatures could be flushed out of their nests in the trees. He scanned the terrain, ultimately deciding that a closer target would suffice.

"I intend to present my wife with her own prized mare as a wedding gift," Ryker drawled on from behind him. The prince shook his head, imagining his sister riding off into the sunset on said horse, leaving the earl in a cloud of dust.

Antoine snickered. "My daughter might enjoy that. She is much like her mother in that regard. But we all know such a gift is more to your own benefit, for riding only has one great purpose when it comes to women—as I'm sure you're aware." Ryker and the other men chuckled darkly.

Anteros clenched his jaw, zeroing in on a black head plume peeking out between the brown grass. The corner of his lips quirked as he squeezed one eye closed and lined up his first arrow.

"Speaking of women who enjoy riding… I sent word to Boreas. I think he will be pleased with your proposal," Ryker informed the king. Anteros perked up, trying to listen while taking aim at the proud male quail. It fluffed its feathers with its back toward the hunters. Easy prey.

"It seems only fitting that we formally unite our realms in a royal union," Antoine replied. "I look forward to his reply."

The prince lowered his weapon in surprise. "You wrote to ask Boreas' permission for Sabine's marriage?" For a second, he hesitated, glancing away from his mark. His father was not known for asking anyone else for permission. Or forgiveness. He did whatever he wanted with no care for how it affected the rest of his court—or his own family.

"Don't be daft," the king snapped, the sharpness to his tone making Anteros grit his teeth. Obviously, he'd put his foot in his mouth, but he couldn't imagine what else his father could have been referencing. The king cleared his throat and continued speaking as his son took aim again. "The ink has dried on your sister's engagement terms… I've written him about his youngest daughter Myra on your behalf."

Anteros loosed the arrow in his hand, missing his target by several feet. The men behind him chuckled as he cursed under his breath. The prince whipped around to face his father's smug smile. "You cannot be serious," Anteros said.

Ryker tried to hide the smirk on his face. "Come now, Anteros. Princess Myra is the jewel of the Denorfian court." Anteros held himself back from punching his sister's fiancé in the face. Of course, the envoy must have been there to negotiate more than a simple cattle deal. He'd be leaving with a princess as his wife and two kings who owe him a debt for negotiating their children's engagement.

Antoine placed a hand on Ryker's shoulder and encouraged him to go ahead and take his best shot. "Surely it cannot be worse than my son's display." His father's eyes twinkled with malice, and a sinking feeling settled in the pit of Anteros' stomach.

Anteros marched closer to his father as the other men followed Ryker ahead on the trail. Leaning close and lowering his voice, the prince whispered through clenched teeth, "This is a punishment, isn't it?"

An eyebrow quirked up at his insolence. "And what reason would I have for punishing you, son?" A twisted smirk remained on his lips as he used one hand to disarm his son. "Luckily for you, your engagement will not meet the same end as your sister's."

"What do you mean?" Anteros glared at his father, trying not to show the fear that pulsed through his chest. He couldn't imagine what nefarious plans his father had in mind—for either of them.

"You will be formally engaged, but you will not have to marry her." Antoine lifted the bow to his shoulder and scoped out his own prey from behind the hunting group. Anteros turned to see where he was aiming and was shocked to see he was pointing it at the back of a Denorfian envoy's head. "Myra is presently the most eligible royal in the Five Realms. There were stirrings that she met Prince Maximus of the Isles at Elara's wedding, and the two hit it off. By offering your hand to King Boreas, even with your age difference, he would be a fool not to choose you. The match would place one of his children upon the throne in Hyrosencia. That's all the old goat has ever wanted."

"But once you negotiate a marriage treaty, how will I get out of it? That could start a war with Denorfia," Anteros argued. His chest constricted as he watched his father's cruel smirk broaden. Did his father *want* to start a war?

Antoine finally shifted the bow in his hands toward the forest to the right of the hunting party. "Once Maximus has taken a wife, we shall invite the princess to Graynor so you can get to know each other. If you dislike her, you make her miserable and then send her home. She is her father's precious little jewel. If she begs him not to return, Boreas will oblige. And he will pay handsomely for breaking our accord." His father loosed an arrow, and it planted in the chest of a small bird. Anteros sucked in a breath as the creature plunged to the ground. "Then you will be free to choose your future queen from a list of other *suitable* maidens."

His plan was wicked. Calculated and cruel as ever. Anteros shouldn't have been surprised—but somehow, he was. For his father's plan could certainly go wrong, especially if he went too far in trying to scare off the Denorfian princess when the time came. Antoine had never shown love or respect to either of his children, so his son couldn't fathom how the man could bank so much on the Denorfian king's love of his youngest daughter.

"Stunned silent? A refreshing change from you," Antoine said, lowering the weapon to his side. "Now, fetch my kill."

His father's sinister sneer brought Anteros back to the garden incident. Black spots threatened the corners of his vision as he stumbled back a few paces. His breath came in short, heavy bursts as sweat pooled on his brow. He would always be trapped within his father's cruel game. There would always be new victims, fresh kills to set his father's twisted heart aflame. The king would never change.

Anteros turned and jogged for the tree that the bird had fallen from. As he zeroed in on the poor creature, he heard a ruffling in the grass to his left. "Your sister said you were a fine shot," Ryker said on approach.

The prince closed his eyes, blocking out the sight of the dove. Its pure white feathers were now smeared with crimson liquid. Hunting had once been one of his few pleasures in life. Now, he could hardly stand the sight of blood. "This kill is my father's, actually." He blew out a breath before meeting Ryker's gaze.

"That does not surprise me. Surely, he has taught you everything he knows?" Ryker's question was innocent enough, but Anteros was not in the mood for pleasantries. In truth, he wanted to turn around and return home. Return to his bedchamber, his solitude, his bottles meant to drown out the noise of court and the blood on his hands that he could never seem to wash away.

He stooped to lift the bird by the neck. "He has tried," Anteros replied. Rough feathers brushed his palm as he glanced back at his father. Straightening his stance, he turned to look his sister's fiancé in the eyes and asked, "What was the real reason for your visit to Graynor? A cattle sale or marriage negotiations?"

Ryker blew air out of his nose as if the question amused him. "At the time your father wrote to Boreas looking for cattle to trade, that was the intention behind the journey. But your father is a brilliant man. He does not miss an opportunity when it's right in front of him." Anteros pursed his lips, finding the answer unsatisfactory.

The earl surveyed the trees and ground for prey. Spotting a plump quail nesting among the vegetation, Ryker lined up his shot. "Are you displeased with the lady's age or the fact that you were left out of the discussion?" Before Anteros could answer, he fired off a shot; the arrow pierced straight through the chest of the small bird. As Ryker lowered the weapon with a confident grin on his face, he placed a hand on the prince's shoulder and said, "I can assure you that Myra is quite a beauty. I'd have taken her for my own if her father had agreed."

Anteros yanked free of the man's grasp, eyes narrowed in disapproval. "How unfortunate for you. Instead, you are stuck with my sister."

"Your sister is no downgrade," Ryker replied quickly. The mischievous glint to his eyes made Anteros' muscles clench—and the earl did not stop there. "No, younger ladies are always easier to integrate into an established home. They're always nervous at first… eager to please."

"Sabine is not like other ladies. She will not be easily subdued," the prince noted. He could only imagine the arguments that would ensue between this experienced earl and his untamable sister.

Ryker smirked. "Even wild mares have a breaking point."

Anteros whipped around and grabbed the earl's jade jacket in both fists. Pushing him backwards through the tall grass, the prince slammed his back into the nearest tree. Through clenched teeth, Anteros said, his voice dangerously low, "My sister is not a horse. If I ever find out you've hurt her, no alliance, no border, no gods will keep me from coming for you. Do you understand?"

There was shouting behind them—his father, Anteros was certain. But he stared down the earl, making sure his anger seeped from his hands and his glare into the man's own body. Decorum be damned; he'd had enough of men treating women like animals.

Finally, Ryker took the boy's hands and removed them from his shirt. Dusting himself off, he shook his head. "Inherited your father's anger, I see. Noted."

The prince reeled back as though he had been punched.

"Fret not, young Prince. I do not see dearest Sabine being any trouble," Ryker said, straightening his jacket. "She will learn her place soon enough—as all wives do."

As Ryker walked toward his kill, he lifted a hand toward the rest of their party, signaling all was well. Anteros remained in place, staring at the dead eyes of the bird he had discarded in the heat of the moment. Bile rose in the back of his throat as he questioned whether his sister might be leaving behind the Great Bear of Graynor to be ripped to shreds by a wretched wolf in Denorfia instead.

19

A COLD GREETING

Elves parted down the center of the busy street, watching from the shade of carts and shop doorways as Serena and their party made their way toward the palace at the center of Montaris. Some elves whispered and pointed as the mostly human group passed. Serena marveled at their chiseled features—high cheekbones, sharp jawlines, untrusting gazes. Though they came in many heights and skin variations, they all bore the signature features of eternal youth—just as Crystal and Cole did.

Some recognized Crystal, Ausha, and Iriela, offering them a reluctant wave or smile. Serena couldn't help but wonder whether Crystal was pleased to be back home after such a long time. The city was beautiful, but the archer's face remained impassive. That is, until they came upon a crossroad lined with brown cottages lining both sides. Crystal's gaze snagged on one in particular, her pace slowing slightly as they passed the intersection. Serena wondered if the house with the dark green door was her family's home.

Iriela waved at them before racing down the road. Home must have been but a breath away. Serena was relieved to know they had saved the girl and brought her home safely.

"Not what I was expecting," Will said, catching Serena's hand in his. He raised it to press a kiss on her knuckles, and her toes curled at the contact.

Since leaving Lei'wana, they hadn't had a moment alone, merely moments where Will swept her up for quick, butterfly-inducing kisses—teasing audience be damned. He couldn't seem to get enough of kissing her. It always set her cheeks aflame when he wrapped his arms around her waist, not a care in the world who was watching. She wished they could stay like that, safely wrapped up in each other with no war to worry over.

But that was the whole point of coming to Montaris. They needed to recruit numbers. They needed the elves on their side.

159

Now that they were in Montaris, Serena was dying for some time away from the guardians, even if it was simply dinner for two in a tavern. Surprisingly, she missed her bed in Symptee. Or maybe she just missed having a little privacy. She'd have paid handsomely to not have to cram into a bedchamber with Crystal, Xandra, and Madeline again.

When they reached the palace, Crystal and Ausha led them up the grandiose steps past guards swathed in colorful tunics of greens and blues, leather bracings, and lightweight golden armor. Serena studied their serious faces, as sharp and menacing as the swords at their hips. They nodded as Crystal and Ausha passed, but none moved to acknowledge the humans following them. Serena remembered the story Crystal had told her about the Elf Queen loathing humans and swallowed thickly.

At the top of the steps, two elves stood guard before a large open doorway. Upon seeing them, one narrowed his eyes while the other nearly ran at them, a vibrant smile stretching his cheeks as his long raven ponytail whipped behind him. "Crystalira!"

Crystal gasped as he wrapped his arms around her waist and lifted her feet off the ground with alarming speed, drawing a laugh out of Xandra and Ausha.

"Return to your post, Erlamin," the second guard, a burly man with a gruff mustache, snipped.

The elf put her down and swatted a hand at his colleague. "If you had not seen your lady in two years, you would break protocol as well." He slid one hand into the hair behind her ear and pulled her into a searing kiss.

Serena's eyes widened. From the looks on Xandra and Rigel's faces, they were equally as shocked by the gesture. Crystal had never mentioned leaving a lover behind in Montaris.

Crystal pried herself out of his grip, the deep crimson of her cheeks spreading down her pale neck and chest. "Deldrach, it has been a long while," she said, pausing to clear her throat. "I did not expect to see you on guard detail."

Deldrach slung an arm over her shoulders, his smile radiant and bright white against his olive skin. "I've nothing better to do while I wait around for my bride."

Bride? Was he referring to Crystal?

From the adoration in his eyes—and the uncomfortable smile Crystal was feigning—Serena could only assume he meant her.

Deldrach was tall and handsome, and Serena found herself at a loss for words as she stared at him. When he finally surveyed the rest of their group, his smile faded, and he leaned over to whisper something indiscernible in Crystal's ear.

She shook her head. "We've come on behalf of Elara to see Daephyra."

"She won't like it," Deldrach said, dragging his arm off her shoulders.

Crystal rested a hand delicately on Deldrach's bare arm. "I know she won't. But we've come all this way. We have to try. Please."

He nodded, then turned toward his comrade. "I will escort them in." The other elf scowled, waiting a moment before stepping aside to allow them entry.

Inside the palace, the hall dripped with fanciful architecture. Marble floors and towering pillars accentuated the ornate wooden furniture carved in swirling patterns. It was far more regal than the citadel. This palace dripped with gold-painted accents; even the servants walking the halls wore luxurious fabrics in rich shades, entirely different from the human court.

Reaching a massive set of gold doors, Deldrach told them to wait quietly. Then he disappeared through the doorway, leaving them waiting for the longest half hour of their lives. When he finally returned, he looked paler, his confidence stripped bare, as he addressed Crystal directly. "Daephyra will see the Silveryls alone. The others must leave."

"Leave? We have spent two days on our feet. Surely she cannot turn us out without an audience," Serena said rashly. All of the nearby guards' hands shot to their weapons. Will's arm snaked around her waist, pulling her back a step.

Crystal held out her hand, palm facing Serena, abruptly silencing her ward. "We will see her first. Perhaps once Ausha tells her of your heroic rescue, she will be open to inviting you for a meeting." Turning to face the other guardians, she added, "Head down to the inn and see about lodging for the night. Then fill your bellies. I will fill you in later."

Serena watched as two guards escorted Crystal and Ausha into the queen's hall. The doors slammed quickly behind them, locking out the rest of the group. As Deldrach escorted them back to the palace entrance, she hung her head in disappointment. She had been so certain she would be able to win Daephyra over to their side with some emotional appeal. Perhaps she knew elves even less than she thought.

When Crystal met the unforgiving glare of her sovereign, she knew the task they had

set out to accomplish was futile. Daephyra's displeasure was apparent. Though her face held not a single wrinkle, her extra-long fingernails dug into tight fists, and her lips puckered in discontent.

"So, Crystalira Windaef has finally returned to her queen's court. And not nearly so promptly as your brother," the queen said. Her voice was as icy as her silver locks and gray eyes.

Not many things scared Crystal, but the way the queen was scrutinizing her made her stomach twist—in fear or shame, she was not certain. She bowed as low as she could manage before speaking. "Your Majesty, I am deeply regretful that my work has kept me away for so long. I have missed the pleasures of my home court greatly."

"Have you?" Daephyra asked, her voice dripping with disdain.

"Of course." They both knew that she was lying. There was a reason she preferred to keep human company. She had not missed this court, nor the cruelty of her own queen.

"And Ausha Wynterburn, what brings you before your Queen on this day?"

Daephyra's shift in focus told Crystal that she was not in the queen's favor, as she had anticipated. In all the years she had known her, Daephyra had never changed. She always looked down upon humans. Allowing them to train in Envyre had been the most shocking decision in her hundreds of years as ruler—and Crystal suspected she had agreed to it merely out of boredom.

"I was in Lei'wana selling my father's wares at the market with my sister, Iriela, when pirates attacked us," Ausha said boldly. She wasted no time with pleasantries—something Crystal appreciated about her. "If it weren't for Crystal and her human companions, we would be halfway across the Lestera by now, sold off like cattle to the highest bidder."

Daephyra scrutinized the proud elf for a moment. "Perhaps we should send *you* back to Envyre." Ausha lowered her head. Then the queen's gaze cut back to the archer. "And why would a group of humans stop to save two of my subjects?"

Eyes as cold as steel bore down on her. Her hatred for humans knew no bounds, and Crystal knew she would have to choose her answers carefully. "The human princess, Serena—who I'm sure my brother has told you all about—heard of pirates snatching a young woman off the street. She insisted we investigate. It was pure happenstance that we discovered two Silveryl among their captives."

The queen's berry lips twisted in a sneer. "I see. So it was other humans she sought to save."

"At first, yes, but Serena would have pursued the men, even if the initial account had been about Ausha and Iriela. She would not discriminate," Crystal began.

Daephyra stood suddenly, flinging her body weight down the steps of the dais with the grace and precision of a leopardess. Pointing a sharp finger at the archer's face, the queen said, her voice shrill, "All humans know how to do is discriminate. They cannot help but see the differences between themselves and between us. They covet that which they do not possess, and they destroy that which they cannot retain."

Crystal lowered her head in submission. "I mean you no great offense, Your Majesty, but I have spent years among them. Humans, they are not all like that. Not anymore."

The queen's pale skin shimmered under the candlelight as she circled the two elves before her. Her heels clacked loudly, the sound ringing in their ears as it echoed throughout the vast chamber. "You sympathize with these humans," she said, her voice twisting and hissing in utter disgust.

"How could I not, Your Majesty?" Crystal raised her chin proudly. "We were once in their position. Hunted by enemies who sought our land, our magic."

"Is that why you have brought them here? To the sacred forest of our people? They seek magic to use in their mindless war," Daephyra said. She grinned in a most satisfied way, no doubt feeling self-assured that the humans sought to take what was theirs once again.

"No," Ausha said rashly. Her eyes widened as she added, "Your Majesty. These people, they merely seek your aid so they can end this wretched conflict."

"And what aid might I have to offer these simpletons who will be dead in less than a century, hmm? Their war could drag on for as long, as it would only be a blip in time for us," the queen said.

Crystal exhaled, the heaviness in her chest remaining firmly in place. "With additional warriors, they could defeat Antoine Rexton and return to their kingdom."

"You dare ask me to send my infantry to fight in a human war?" Daephyra's nostrils flared, and Crystal swore the queen's body lifted several inches in the air as rage ripped through her slight frame. "I should throw you in the dungeon and leave you to rot."

The archer's heart beat out of control. She knew Daephyra was unlikely to agree, but she had not considered how she would react to one of her own people making such a request. "I beg your forgiveness, Your Majesty. It was not my suggestion, but that of the Garrick princess. She is the one destined to end their war, but she knows she cannot do it alone."

Daephyra sunk her clawed hands into Crystal's shoulders, her nails biting through the fabric of her shirt and sinking into her flesh. Her gray eyes flashed red for a moment as she hissed, "The audacity of a human child knows no bounds. She who has not faced battle—she who has never proven herself a worthy leader—wishes to command *my* armies." A menacing cackle ripped free from the queen's throat. She relinquished her grip, and Crystal stepped back to catch her balance. She inhaled sharply at the pain that radiated through her shoulders like a dozen needles. Daephyra's gaze flashed silver once again.

"Serena has fought in her share of small skirmishes. She has killed time and again to protect herself and her friends, including myself and my brother. Cole trained her well. She knows how to fight, and I daresay she is more than capable of leading a charge," Crystal said.

Daephyra turned away from them and walked back up the steps slowly, her hips swaying with each stride. Only the echo of her delicate footsteps cut through the deafening silence that followed. Crystal prayed she would not end up spending the next century in a cell below the palace. When the queen reached the top of the dais, she perched on the edge of her marble throne. She tapped her red-tinged fingernails against the armrests of her throne, pleased to see Crystal squirming uncomfortably where she stood.

"Tell your dear princess that it would be unwise to ask for my aid again before she has a true victory to her name." With that, the queen flicked her wrist, and the guards threw open the hall doors.

The elves bowed, holding their positions for a full minute before turning for the door. Ausha shrugged as they made their way out of the hall. She leaned over to whisper, "That was brazen of you."

Crystal gave her a withering look as they exited the chamber, and the heavy gold doors closed behind them. "She would not even grant Serena an audience. I had to at least try."

Ausha nudged her with an elbow. "Cheer up. We'll take her to the Academy. The fighters there are yet to pledge oaths to either queen. They are free to do as they please. Perhaps we can start to build Serena's army from there?"

The guardian nodded. Though it was not what they had been hoping for, at least it would soften the blow when Crystal delivered the news later. Her stomach was in knots as they passed the entrance, brushing off Deldrach for another time. She had too much on her mind to address *that* problem at the moment.

Before returning to her friends, she had to pay her father a visit.

20

COMPLICATED

When Cole answered the door to his father's home, the last person he expected to see was his sister. She smiled and asked, "Hello, brother. Is Father home?"

"Crystal? What the blazes are you doing here?" He stepped back enough for her to pass through the doorway into their sitting area.

Her gaze swept over the carved furniture and the faded jade rug, uneasiness apparent in the wrinkle above her brows as she glanced down the hall. "There was another assassination attempt," she said. "Elara wanted us to take Serena far away, somewhere safe. Where's more safe than Ord Metsiilva?"

Cole stepped out onto the porch and glanced around, but there was no sign of Serena or the other guardians. A flash of dark skin in his left periphery caught his attention. Standing on the porch two doors down, Ausha noticed him and lifted a hand in greeting. Cole's heart sank, but he lifted two fingers in a half-hearted hello before stepping inside and closing the door. "Where are the others then?" Cole leaned his back against the door, crossing his arms.

"You know Daephyra. She would not entertain an audience with humans, even a princess from a longstanding bloodline. So I had to fill her in myself." Crystal rolled her eyes and flopped onto one of the more comfortable chairs in the sitting area. "I sent the others on to get rooms and lunch at the inn, but we'll have to leave in the morning."

"So soon?"

She shrugged again. "The queen will be of no help to Serena's cause, but we may yet have luck adding to our forces in Envyre. Most students have yet to take vows for either queen."

"Poaching elves from the Academy will not earn you Daephyra's favor," Cole pointed out. His fingers tapped an agitated rhythm against his biceps, his body itching to get to the inn. To the only person he cared to see more than his sister. "Did Xandra come with you?"

Crystal smirked, stretching her arms out in front of her like a tired housecat. "Of course." A few dots of blood stood out on the upper sleeves of her blouse. Still bright red in color, a fresh wound, and her brother wondered what had happened. It wasn't like his sister to be injured—much less to leave a small wound unhealed. "And Rigel, too—not that you asked."

He exhaled in frustration. Whatever it was, she was clearly fine. Turning toward the door, he muttered, "Father went into town to meet someone. He should be back soon if you want to wait for him."

As he turned the doorknob, Crystal leaned forward in her seat. Her pale hair fell in a curtain over her shoulder. "And where are you going?"

"Where do you think? The inn."

She huffed, plopping back in her seat. Soft light from the open window hit her face, and she closed her eyes, basking in the warmth. "Would have been nice if you'd stuck around to soften the tongue-lashing I'm to get from him."

Though he had a feeling their father would be relieved more than anything when he came home, he could never be certain how the man would react—or overreact—when it came to his own children. Things had always been complicated between the three of them. "He was furious you did not return with me, but he will be relieved to see you. He said as much. Perhaps it will not be as bad as you expect."

Cole studied her pale face as it twisted in a grimace. She pinched the bridge of her nose. "Since when are you an optimist?" she muttered, the exhaustion evident in her voice alone. There were bags under her eyes as though she had not been sleeping well, which caused her brother to linger in the doorway. He rarely saw her in such a state. What could have transpired after he left Symptee?

Perhaps leaving them behind had been a huge mistake.

Crystal opened her eyes just in time to see Cole nod his head in farewell and close the door, effectively ending their reunion and trapping her alone in their childhood home. Then he turned and rushed down the porch steps into the street knowing the person he was dying to see was mere blocks away.

Focused on the massive building with white columns and a towering ceiling up ahead, Cole cut through the open-air market with purposeful strides. His fists clenched at his sides, he wove through the stalls in a trance, nearly walking right past some familiar faces.

"Cole!" The deep voice drew him out of his spiraling thoughts, and he turned to find Rigel and Serena waving from one stall over. "What luck to run into you here," Rigel added.

Taking a deep breath, he redirected his steps, pivoting to greet his friend with a firm handshake. Rigel chuckled and batted his hand away, pulling him in for a hug instead. Eyes flicking side to side, he noticed some of the elves in the market were watching, whispering. Their attention was unnerving.

"Cole?"

His eyes widened at the angelic voice that had been haunting his dreams, and he wrestled himself free from his friend to turn and face her. At the sight of her bouncy curls and sunset eyes, the tightness in his chest eased up. "Xandra," he murmured. One corner of his mouth turned up as long strides closed the distance between them, but before he could wrap his arms around her, she stopped him. Her elbows locked as she pressed firmly against his chest, keeping him at arm's length. It wasn't close enough. His hands came up to caress her arms. "It's good to see you."

Xandra furrowed her brow as she considered the unexpected affection. "You as well." She lowered her arms, shaking off his touch in the process. As she glanced behind Cole, he realized she, too, must have noticed the way the elves were staring at them. It wasn't every day that a group of humans armed with weapons waltzed into the capital city of Montaris.

He raked both hands through his hair, gripping the back of his neck where the strands ended. "I wrote you a few days ago. I wish I had known you were coming," he said, keeping his voice low. He had just sent that letter to Symptee two days prior. Now, he prayed to the gods that the letter would be lost, destroyed, never to be read by another soul. He cleared his throat. "I could have had lodging prepared in advance."

Will stepped up to Serena's side and lazily draped an arm over her shoulders. She smiled at him as he pecked her on the temple. "Hey, stranger," the blacksmith greeted him, not bothering to look away from the girl.

Just when I thought they left the oaf behind.

"I see you finally grew a pair, farm boy," Cole replied.

Will bristled. "See you haven't changed." Serena grabbed the hand hanging off her shoulder and shushed him.

Xandra slapped the back of her hand against Cole's chest, and he seized her by the wrist. Pulling her a step closer, he leaned down and whispered, "I need to speak with you. *Privately.*" The way she licked her bottom lip made his mouth water. He hadn't realized just how hollow he had felt since leaving her behind—and now he knew that only her lips could satisfy the hunger raging within him.

The caramel color of her cheeks deepened as she stared at him. "Where?" Her breath tickled his collarbone before she shrank back from him, his hand falling away.

A pair of elves cut through the small space in the aisle between them, severing the intensity of their stare down. Cole shook his head, suddenly at a loss as to a proper answer. He couldn't very well take her home—not when his father would return there any minute—and going to her room at the inn would be the greatest scandal in Montaris in over a century. "It's best we are careful in the capital. Crystal said Daephyra was quite perturbed by the humans coming here to ask for aid," he said.

"You've seen Crystal?" Rigel asked. His brows furrowed in disbelief. "Where is she?"

"She's home, awaiting our father," the elf answered. His friend nodded solemnly, the understanding clear in his downcast gaze. "She didn't go into detail, but I'm sure she will fill you in later. She mentioned moving on to Envyre tomorrow."

"Tomorrow? But we've just gotten here," Serena piped up.

Her newfound confidence almost surprised the elf. But confidence was a dangerous thing. Too much of it unwarranted often led humans to an early grave. "Daephyra does not take well to humans in her city," was all Cole replied.

"On that note, perhaps we should join the others at the inn," Xandra said, wrapping an arm around Serena. The girl's bottom lip jutted out as she peered back at the rest of the market, clearly disappointed to cut her exploration short.

"That would be wise," Cassius Windaef said from behind them.

Cole whirled around, eyes wide as he took in his father's sneer. Cassius folded his arms across the front of his emerald green tunic. Ignoring his son, he stared at Xandra for a moment before sweeping over the others. "Rigel," he said, giving a curt nod. "I thought you were now employed by Elara Garrick."

"Yes, Mister Windaef." He rubbed the back of his neck sheepishly. "That's why we've come back. We brought Serena, the lost heir to the Garrick throne, to speak with Daephyra."

"Do not speak so plainly of Her Majesty, High Queen of the Silveryl Clan. Her name demands respect," Cassius snapped. The savage glint in his eyes had Rigel bowing his head in shame, his cheeks turning as red as his hair.

Cole moaned. "He meant no disrespect, Father. Her Majesty is not present."

Cassius clenched his jaw and raised a finger, effectively silencing his son. "That is beside the point. When you come into someone's home, you show the head of the house respect—be it a queen or a parent." He leveled his son with a judgmental look, his chin lowered and brows raised.

"Yes, of course, Father." His lips pulled into a straight line as he waited for his father to leave them, but Cassius remained. Cole suspected that his father meant to scare the humans out of the market with his stern expression.

"My sincerest apologies," Rigel said, bowing to the elder elf. After a beat of silence, he added, "I hope you have a pleasant visit with Crystal, sir."

The elder elf's face scrunched up in confusion. "Crystalira is here? Why did you not say anything sooner?"

Cole scoffed. "You did not ask."

"We mustn't keep her waiting," Cassius said, turning on his heels without a word of goodbye to the humans. When Cole did not move to join him, he peered over his shoulder and added, "Come, Alarcole."

He locked eyes with Xandra, the weight of his father's expectations heavy on his shoulders. The spark in her eyes simmered like a dying fire as she grimaced before turning toward the others. She nodded her head in the direction of the inn. Serena and Will walked hand in hand behind her.

"Alarcole," his father repeated; a cold needling sensation trickled down his son's spine.

With a resigned sigh, he waved farewell to Rigel and followed his father out of the market in the direction of their house. Cassius took long strides, trying to maintain an air of dignity while clearly wanting to move faster. Cole nearly had to jog to keep up with him.

When they finally bounded up the porch steps, Cassius threw open the front door without a moment's hesitation. Three steps into the house, he froze. Cole pushed in behind him and realized they had caught Crystal napping on the couch. Their father exhaled roughly, stalking closer to the couch where she snored lightly. Her hair cascaded off the side, the edges sweeping the floor. He ran a hand over the top of her head, and her eyelids fluttered open.

"Father?" she asked sluggishly. Blinking herself out of a daze, she sat abruptly, running her hands over unkempt hair. "My apologies. It's been a long day."

Cassius straightened his spine, his lips twisting in discontent as he stared down at her. "I thought I raised you better than this. How indecent to fall asleep while waiting for someone." He made an irritated clicking noise with his tongue as he moved to his favorite chair and took a seat.

"It was not intentional," Crystal hissed. She rubbed her fingers in small circles on her temples. "My ward tends to find danger, so I've not had a decent night's sleep in months."

Their father nodded. "This is your home. You are welcome to stay here for as long as you wish. Your chambers remain untouched."

Cole went into the kitchen to pour himself a glass of water, pretending he was not hanging on their every word. He knew in a matter of seconds their father could start harping on her about her long absence, and Crystal had a hard time accepting his criticism of her choices.

"I cannot stay. My friends are waiting for me to join them at the inn," he heard her reply. The hesitance in her answer made her brother wince. He knew she would want to join the others at the inn, and that would greatly offend their father. They were eerily similar when it came to their pride.

Cassius raised his voice to announce that her answer was unacceptable. "This is your home. I will not have my daughter stay at the inn with travelers, those with no kin, and humans. What would people say?"

"I don't care what people think, Father. I am on an assignment, and I cannot be away from Serena and the other guardians for long. We must escort her to Envyre tomorrow," she informed him.

As Cole walked through the doorway back into the sitting area, he found them both on their feet. Crystal's arms were crossed, her brows pinched in frustration.

Their father looked much worse. His face was deep crimson, his arms raised as he spoke animatedly. "How can you only spare a brief moment for your father? I have not seen you in over two years."

Cole met his sister's gaze, and she clenched her jaw, unwilling to ask him to come to her rescue. With a nod, he headed down the hall, pausing to glance at the old family portrait once again. He wished there was a way to repair the broken pieces of his family somehow, to mend the bonds they had once had when their mother was still alive. When their family was whole.

His sister's voice carried down the hall, cracking before she could finish her response. "Why would I want to spend another moment under the same roof as you? Nothing I do has ever been good enough for you."

Cole shook his head, continuing down the hall to his room. Once inside, he closed the door gently behind him, the sounds of their voices finally muffled by the wooden planks between them. But the tightness in his chest took hours to disperse, even after he heard the front door slam.

21

INSTINCTS

Wearing pants was a rare and freeing occurrence for Queen Elara Garrick. Even when she went horseback riding in her youth, her maids had been trained to include a detachable skirt with a slit over her riding attire. It simply was not lady-like otherwise.

Two of Elara's maids trailed after her, tripping over themselves on the lawn as they followed behind her with an overskirt that might have doubled as a ship's sails. Today she had refused to wear it, citing the stifling heat outside, but they insisted on bringing it anyway. Even one of the guards tried to help by picking up the material off the ground, much to Elara's amusement.

The queen strode with unabashed confidence toward the wisteria tree she loved so much. Waiting in the shade were Rilura and her two dearest friends, both of whom were dressed down for their unorthodox morning tea arrangements.

"Elara, you are positively glowing," Ismenia said, joy beaming from her face and voice. The queen did not feel like she was glowing. This pregnancy had not been easy on her physically between the nausea and the appalling visions that intermittently plagued her dreams.

"And growing, with all due respect," Idonea added. She gestured to the queen's round belly, which was emphasized by the flowy cream blouse she had crammed into that morning. "Are you quite certain you're not further along?"

Ismenia made an indignant sound and smacked her sister with a folded hand fan. "Sister!"

Elara chuckled, turning to her maids and asking them to fetch them some cold refreshments. Reluctantly, they looked between each other and the skirt in their hands before abandoning it on the ground like a picnic blanket. The queen smiled triumphantly as the unwanted ears disappeared into the citadel.

The wisteria tree's canopy provided ample coverage from the sun and the prying eyes of those inside. It was Elara's hope that her shaded refuge would keep others from uncovering the truth behind taking her morning tea outdoors—especially her husband.

Rilura unsheathed a broad sword from her hip, looking over the queen curiously. It looked comically out of place in her large hands, yet Elara was relieved to see it. She could not imagine going up against a dwarf's axe. "Have you no sword?"

Elara's brows raised. "Ah, yes, I do." She turned to one of the guards poised along the edge of the wisteria branches and held out a hand. "Sir Caleb, if you would."

The middle-aged blond reached for his belt and produced one of the two swords that were strapped to his side. As he held the hilt out to the queen, he hesitated. "Are you sure you can handle this in your condition, Your Majesty?"

Elara held her hand higher. "It's in your best interest if you do not question your sovereign," she hissed, snatching the hilt from him. The knight bowed before shuffling back a few steps.

When she turned, Rilura's face lit up. "You wield the Blade of Everlasting Devotion."

"What a title," Idonea said. She had quietly made herself comfortable on top of the queen's discarded overskirt, her legs tucked neatly to one side as she reclined on her arms.

Ismenia stood next to her, arms crossed as she glowered at the oracle in disapproval. "Elara might have wanted to wear that when we return inside."

The queen shook her head. "Absolutely not." She chuckled, lowering her weapon to her side. "Please get comfortable. This is sure to be the most ridiculous thing you'll see all week." Ismenia reluctantly sat beside her sister on the blanket of satin.

"Do not jest about weaponry, Your Majesty. Holding a Dwarven blade be no small task," the Steelcast princess said. Taking a few steps away from the tree's trunk, Rilura flourished the sword in her hand and motioned for Elara to follow.

Elara took a beginner's fighting stance and gripped the hilt of her blade in both palms. In truth, she felt small holding the gifted blade, but she would never disrespect such a momentous gift in front of the Steelcast princess. A slow, steady breath helped to calm her nerves, but not for long. She tried to remember what Alexander had taught her in the months following her relocation to Symptee. She remembered how to take a defensive stance, properly hold her weapon, and observe her opponent for signs of attack. She had been so young then, full of fear and anger after Antoine betrayed her family. Though she tried to channel that anger into training, it only did so much good. She lacked upper body strength, and she could never seem to react fast enough to her tutor's movements.

It was ultimately the greatest relief when Prince Caspian agreed to marry her, not because she thought Denorfia would help her take back her kingdom, but because she could put down her sword and entrust her husband to protect her.

With Gerard, it was different.

She felt safe with him, but he did not make the citadel feel any safer. Theirs had been a marriage of love, not convenience, and therefore, she did not expect anything from him except tenderness and devotion. She would never ask him to take up a sword and lead an army, much less stand between her and any enemies that found their way into their home.

No, she longed to keep him safe just as desperately as she longed to protect their unborn child. Knowing Antoine Rexton, there were sure to be more spies and more assassination attempts, and she could no longer sit around and wait for his next move. The next time someone dared threaten her, she would point this blade at their throat.

"You said you trained once," Rilura began, inspecting the queen's rudimentary stance. "How much do you recall?"

Her palms had already become sticky with sweat, and they had yet to make the first move. "Come closer and find out," she replied, the confidence in her voice surprising herself. For a brief second, she questioned her own sanity as she watched the dwarf pace across from her.

Rilura did not hesitate at her challenge, lifting her blade over one shoulder and charging at the queen with a warrior's cry that was sure to draw attention. Elara lifted her blade to counter the dwarf's first swing, but she was nearly knocked backward by the sheer power Rilura possessed. "Nice counter," the dwarf said through clenched teeth.

They ripped their blades apart hastily, stepping back from each other. Rilura stalked in a circle around the queen, much to the chagrin of Elara's guards. The men had all turned toward them, fear and horror punctuated on their crooked brows. "If any harm comes to Her Majesty…"

"I shall run myself through with my own blade," Rilura replied, rolling her eyes at their overprotectiveness. Turning back to the queen, she added, "Perhaps after some practice, ye can cut back your number of guards." The men behind her made disgruntled noises.

"Oh, no, I could never replace them," Elara said, more for her guards than anyone else. "I simply want to be prepared for the worst case. If the citadel were ever breached."

Rilura raised her blade again and shook her head. "They would have to get past the dwarfs first." Though that should have brought Elara some inkling of comfort, it didn't. For she knew the depths Antoine Rexton could go to when he wanted something.

Steel glinted in Rilura's blue eyes, and she paced the ground with surprisingly light steps for a dwarf. Elara gripped her sword tighter. The hilt was rough against her delicate hands as she adjusted her fingers. Observing her opponent, the queen couldn't have felt smaller. Though she was taller than Rilura, it was not by much, and what the dwarf lacked in height, she made up for in muscles—something Elara lacked entirely.

But if she was meant to carry a child, then surely, she could carry a sword. They had to weigh about the same.

As the dwarf charged toward her, the queen instinctively blocked her again. This time, she braced one leg further back, helping her to maintain balance and control as Rilura bore down on her blade. "You have the instincts, but do you have the strength?" the dwarf teased, pushing harder.

Elara gritted her teeth. She had spent the past seventeen years being strong for everyone else when she felt utterly broken inside. Her strength may not have been in her arms, but it was ingrained in her heart. That's why she knew she could protect herself and her child if she must. A mother does not sit by and wait for a hero; she stands and fights for her family.

"Though my body may be weak, I will not surrender," the queen said. Summoning all her might, Elara dug her heels into the grass and pushed back. Their blades hardly moved. Rilura did not yield, which did not shock the queen in the slightest. The dwarf was a proud warrior, and she wanted to see Elara become the same.

Just as they pushed away from each other, Ismenia called out, "Be careful, Elara. Make sure you're breathing steadily."

Elara inhaled, filling her lungs with fresh air. The scent of the wisteria petals was refreshing; the gentle smell helped her to focus. Taking the initiative to swing her blade down at the dwarf, she pleaded with Divinity to give her strength. Any boost would do. Rilura turned, narrowly avoiding the blade as it swooped down through the air behind her. "Blazing embers!" she shouted, stumbling forward with the weight of her blade when it did not connect with her target.

With an aggravated huff, she paced backwards, putting distance between herself and the dwarf so she could recover before Rilura's next move. Her chest heaved, her blouse suddenly feeling too snug. Feeling a sudden flutter of movement, Elara instinctively pressed one hand to her stomach.

Rilura unleashed a guttural growl, a warning for the queen to focus before she charged at her friend again. Elara gathered the hilt of her blade in both hands, turning to avoid Rilura before blocking her blade low to the ground.

That's when her husband's deep voice full of fear broke her concentration. "Elara! What in the raging seas are you doing?"

She stepped back on one foot, spinning around to face him. "Gerard," she breathed. The sight of him and shock of being caught knocked the breath out of her lungs. He stood under the wisteria's canopy, a purple curtain of petals behind him, his cheeks visibly red beneath his beard. But his gaze was not on his wife. His ire was fixed on Rilura.

"We were just having a bit of fun, dear," she began, stepping between the two of them.

Her husband scoffed. Stomping toward her, he removed the Blade of Everlasting Devotion from her hands and narrowed his eyes at it. "You call putting your life in danger *fun?*"

"It was just a bit of practice, my love. She would never have harmed me," the queen argued, but her husband was not listening.

Stepping around her, he pointed at Rilura and asked, "How dare you lift a sword against the queen? You are here as an ambassador."

Multiple guards pushed through the wisteria branches to see what the commotion was about. Elara pressed a hand to her belly, lowering her gaze. Now there would be no keeping this a secret. Soon, the entire citadel would know she had dressed like a traveler and dared try her hand with a sword—behind her husband's back.

"It was at your wife's request, my lord," Rilura replied, sheathing her weapon at her hip. She did not seem phased by the man's intensity.

"This is treason. Bring the dwarf to the dungeon," Gerard demanded, pointing at Rilura.

"No," Elara said loudly, holding an arm out toward her men. "That will not be necessary."

Gerard turned to face his wife, his brows lowered in a scowl. "She came at you with a weapon."

She stepped closer to her husband. Pushing up on her toes, her nose barely brushed his chin. She wished he wasn't so tall in that moment. "Need I remind you that you are *not* king. You have no authority over my men," Elara said. She scowled, returning his sour expression like a mirror.

Gerard tilted his chin down slightly. "Need I remind you that I am your husband—and this is my child." He pressed a palm to her abdomen, his gaze softening slightly. "This is not safe for either of you. Go inside."

One brow ticked up in defiance before Elara swept his hand off her stomach. "You cannot order me to go anywhere. I am the Queen of Hyrosencia."

"And you will be the queen of nothing if you and your only heir perish from overexertion," he replied. Her husband rubbed one hand over his face and shook his head before turning toward her friends. "I cannot believe the two of you condoned this. You should have come to me."

Idonea shrugged, sipping her lemonade nonchalantly, but Ismenia's face drooped, unable to look them in the eyes. "Her Majesty said she could handle this," the herbalist said, her confidence wavering.

"Do not scold my friends, Gerard. You know as well as anyone here that I will do whatever I wish. I know my own limits," the queen argued.

Her husband held out a hand, the motion stunning her silent. "That's enough, Elara. I will not continue to argue over this. It is not good for the baby."

Her cheeks burned at his dismissal. Anger—burning and unforgiving—bubbled within her chest. "Yes, *darling*," she spat, venom dripping from her every word. "Of course, you mean best. As such, you should doubtless sleep elsewhere tonight. I'm afraid I'm too overheated to share my bed."

Gerard stared, his mouth agape, as she motioned for her friends to follow her inside. Elara did not look back as she walked past him, nor when they disappeared into the citadel halls. It took everything within her to quiet the simmering rage in her heart. She wanted to scream from a balcony, to punch something, to do and say a number of things that were far from lady-like.

But all she could do was fold her hands over her bump and bite her lip.

She was not just a wife. She was a queen chosen by Divinity to rule a kingdom. Though she only held control over a few small cities safely outside of Antoine Rexton's reach, Elara was determined not to allow him to take anything else from her or her people. And if that stubborn determination upset her husband, so be it. A queen never shies away from a fight.

22

EXPECTATIONS

When Crystal entered the inn, she made a beeline for the attached tavern. Spotting the bright red hair of her comrade Rigel, she moved swiftly to sit on the barstool beside him. Of course it was empty, as no elf in their right mind would be caught sitting beside a human in public in Montaris.

Luckily, she was already at odds with Queen Daephyra and her father, so she didn't care.

Lifting two fingers to flag down the barkeep, Crystal said, "I need a pint."

Rigel turned and winced. "That bad, huh?"

She simply shook her head as the barkeep placed a glass in front of her. Liquid sloshed over the edge as she lifted the full glass to her mouth, coating her fingers in sticky ale. *Bottoms up*, she thought, chugging in hopes the alcohol would drown out the ringing in her head.

When she slammed the glass back onto the bar, Rigel stared, his brows disappearing under the hair hanging down over his forehead. "I don't think I've ever seen you do that."

She lifted two fingers, flagging down the barkeep again. "I'll have another, please." A shiny gold coin dropped onto the shiny surface of the bar, circling on the rim a few times before laying still. The barkeep pocketed the piece and refilled her glass.

"Crystal, you're back!" Xandra said from the tavern's entrance. She jogged over to them and claimed the seat beside her friend.

Now sandwiched between her closest human friends, the archer was all too aware of the eyes on their backs. "I am back," she said calmly. Lifting the glass, she took a long, slow pull of the ale. Fruity and potent, the bitter aftertaste only made her want to drink more, but she put down the glass, knowing she was in for a line of questioning she did not wish to answer.

"Rough time with your father?" Xandra asked, wrinkling her nose. She lifted a hand to flag down the barkeep, and the female elf ignored her in favor of a male elf at the end of the bar.

Crystal slid her glass over to her friend and nodded for her to take it. When the barkeep returned, she leveled her with a gaze, ordering another pint for herself. That was when she noticed that Rigel had a near-empty glass in front of him. She shouldn't have been surprised that he'd managed to weasel his way into being served, despite the Silveryl Clan's distrust of humans. Rigel was the most likeable, charming human she'd ever met.

"We ran into him and Cole in the market earlier," Rigel informed her.

She winced, unable to imagine her father being friendly with them, even though he had met them in Envyre several years prior. "I fear I owe you all an apology… and a drink. His manners are reserved solely for the palace, I'm afraid," Crystal said.

"You don't have to apologize for him," Xandra interjected, patting the top of her friend's hand.

Rigel scoffed. "Yeah, it's not your fault your Pops has a stick up his—"

"Rigel!" The elf's voice echoed through the tavern as she slapped a hand over his mouth. He waggled his brows, his shoulders shaking with laughter. Xandra chuckled, too. When Crystal removed her hand, her lips curled in an unwelcome grin. Laughter slowly bubbled up from her chest until it morphed into an uncontrolled cackle. "Stars alight, he really does." She snickered.

As they recovered from their laughter and wiped the tears from their eyes, the elf's expression quickly sobered. Turning in her seat, she scanned the tavern, frowning. "Where's Serena?" Xandra tried and failed to hide her grin, making her friend groan in disgust.

"Give her a break, Crys. She's got the weight of a whole kingdom on her shoulders. She deserves to live a little," Rigel argued. He took a swig from his own pint.

"They're at the market, not upstairs," Xandra added. "Will is head over heels for that girl. He will keep her safe."

"Safe," the elf scoffed. Her friend spoke as though the blacksmith was known for saving lives. Crystal grimaced at her ale, debating whether to retire to bed or finish it.

Xandra nudged her arm, breaking her from her trance. "Speaking of head over heels…"

The elf's heart sank as she realized exactly where their conversation was headed. Perhaps it was a good time to retire. The stress of the day had drained all her energy. She moved to stand up, but each of her friends put a hand on her shoulders, holding her down on the barstool.

"Not so fast," Rigel said. "You've got some explaining to do."

"Deldrach is handsome," Xandra commented, giving her a wink. "I can't believe you never mentioned him! How could you not tell me? Am I nothing to you?" She placed a hand over her heart and sighed dramatically, but Crystal could tell from her voice that she was hurt by the discovery.

Despite their interrogation, Crystal felt relief at her friends finally knowing the truth. They were the only two people who made her feel secure enough to talk about Deldrach and how complicated the situation was.

The ale didn't hurt either.

"There is not much to tell," she began. "He has always liked me. He visited Cole at the Academy a few times after completing their training, and we got to talking. I did not hate him. He was kind, not pushy... until graduation."

"Graduation?" Rigel asked without looking at her. He stared at his pint, his usual carefree smile gone.

She nodded, biting her lip. "When Cole and I went home to visit our father... Deldrach and his family came over. Apparently, he had been singing my praises for months." She paused, wringing her hands together in her lap. The memory of that dinner was like a ghost haunting her; she could never escape the shock and fear she felt when Deldrach Erlamin pulled out a ring and put her on the spot. "I did not expect him to propose marriage so abruptly. Our fathers were thrilled. Mine pulled a special bottle of wine out before I could even manage to give an answer."

"Did you love him?" Xandra asked. It was plain in her eyes that she knew the answer already. Crystal loved her friends, but she had never been one to have romantic feelings for anyone. Not even when the whole of the Academy was a prison full of raging hormonal youths.

"I don't think I've ever felt quite what you have," she whispered. Reaching into her blouse, she pulled a thin gold chain out, revealing a gold band with a leaf pattern. "But in the moment—in front of my father, who smiled for the first time in decades—I said yes. And then I left to join you in Symptee the next day."

Xandra gasped. "You did not!"

Her cheeks burned as she hung her head in shame. "I did." She knew it was bad, leaving Deldrach abruptly after his proposal, but she could not bear what would have come next had she stayed. Her father would have pestered her to start wedding planning immediately, and her chances of ever joining either queen's service would have died that very summer, replaced by brightly colored gowns and insufferable comments about future children.

Crystal shuddered. If there was one thing she was certain of, it was that she had no interest in ever bringing a child into this world.

Rigel glanced sidelong at the elf, the usual twinkle in his eyes dimmed. Her heart ached knowing she was the cause of it. He cleared his throat and asked, "What are you going to do now? Obviously, he's been waiting for you to come back."

Rigel had made it obvious that he was fond of her, the starry look in his eyes reminding her of the way Deldrach looked at her when their courtship began, sweet and innocent and puppy-like. Caring. Downright *infatuated*. A wave of guilt turned her stomach, and she pushed her glass away, standing from her barstool.

"I did not come back for him," she answered firmly. "We're here for Serena, so I'd best find her and let her know the change of plans."

Rigel nodded, tapping his fingers on his glass as he thought over her answer. Avoidance was the coward's way—a side she had never once shown her friends—but the golden noose hanging around her neck was tighter with each passing second. This mess was her burden to bear, and she had no intention of marrying or breaking Deldrach's heart quite yet.

Cassius Windaef was in a foul mood when Cole emerged from his chambers the following morning. Perched at the breakfast table with a stack of unopened letters and an untouched plate, the bags under his eyes and the deep crease in his forehead told Cole that the man had hardly slept. He swiped a grapefruit from the bowl at the center of the table, intending to continue straight out the front door, when his father looked up. He had not seen the man this torn up since the wound of losing Lyrissana Windaef had been fresh for all of them.

"Where are you off to?" Cassius had tried to sound nonchalant, but there was always an ulterior motive behind such a question.

Cole paused, turning toward his father out of respect. "To the inn. Crystal said they would leave for Envyre today. I thought I might—"

His father zeroed in on the knapsack slung over his shoulder and worked his jaw. "Were you planning to leave without a word of goodbye?" The malice in his voice made Cole's heart pound harder in his chest. He knew another fight was impending—a fight he did not wish to have. There was no way to make his father understand why he had to go with them.

"I thought I might accompany them to Envyre seeing as the majority are humans. It might bring comfort to the Silveryl who are weary of them," Cole lied, starting to peel his fruit as his father eyed him scrupulously.

Cassius hummed as he pushed back his chair, pressing his fingertips into the pine table on each side of his plate. "And why should your presence matter when Envyre is already overrun by human refugees?"

"I don't know," he grumbled, shoving a piece of grapefruit into his mouth. A sweet taste exploded on his tongue, quickly turning bitter as he chewed it. Normally, he enjoyed the fruit, but at present, it was perhaps too tart for this situation. His father's expression was sour enough without the added flavor. Cole swallowed the bitter fruit, no longer wanting the rest of it. "Even so, I should like to check in with my old students."

"Here I was hoping you might convince Crystalira to stay longer," Cassius said, disappointment carrying in his deep voice.

Cole winced. He had hoped his father would not bring that up. His sister was already irritated that he had left the group behind to return home. She would never take kindly to the request to stay home—especially coming from her own kin. And he didn't blame her after the parts he overheard of their argument the night prior. "She is an adult now. We both know she is going to do whatever she wants, and that's not staying in Montaris."

"She sounded like she was leaving because Daephyra wanted those humans gone. Perhaps if you escorted them to Envyre, she might stay a few days more?" His question was laced with anguish for they both knew even that would be a tough sell. "I cannot leave off where we did last night—not if she will be gone another year or longer."

Sometimes it was difficult to look his father in the eyes because it felt too much like looking at his future in a mirror. Cole adjusted the strap on his shoulder and stared at his boots instead. The brown leather was worn along the edges from many miles traveled, but they were sturdy, the seams still holding together, much like his father. "I wish you could have put aside your pride yesterday and spoken to her differently."

Cassius flinched; a vein pulsed in the side of his neck as his fingers curled into fists. "*My* pride? She is the one who showed me disrespect in my house."

Cole blew out an exasperated breath. "She has never intentionally disrespected you. She only wants for you to see her—the person *she* wants to be. Someone who can protect others—and herself."

"Fighting for humans in their petty squabbles is a fool's choice," his father argued, knocking his chair off its legs. He stormed closer to Cole until he was inches from his face. "All I want is for her to be safe. To stay where she belongs."

"Have you forgotten what she witnessed when neither of us was here to protect them?" Cole exploded, shoving his father back.

Cassius bumped into the table; dishes skittered noisily on the tabletop as he found his balance. "I will never forget! That was the day I lost them both!" He breathed heavily, wiping a hand through the sweat on his brow.

They stared at each other for a moment, the air in the room feeling charged. Cole waited for the lightning to strike him down, but his father didn't move, didn't speak. Just stared. Finally, Cole said, his voice deep, confident, and full of sadness, "Crystal feels safest with a weapon in her hands, and all you've ever tried to do is take that from her. That's why she cannot stay."

Not waiting for his father to argue any further, Cole chucked the half-eaten grapefruit on the table. He was almost to the front door when his father's voice made him pause. "If you are going to leave, at least speak your own truth to my face. You are not leaving for Crystalira. You're leaving for the other girl—the human from the market."

"They do not need me to train Serena. The others are perfectly capable—"

"Not the princess. The one from the Academy. Your sister's… friend," Cassius said, his voice level and certain, though there was a hint of revulsion behind his statement. "Of all the people you could care for, why a human girl?"

"Xandra is not just some human girl. She's an incredible woman. She's sunshine incarnate. She is joy and hope and all things good about humans—all the things I never could find in another soul in Montaris." Saying those words aloud for the first time, Cole sighed in relief. Xandra was the missing piece he had spent decades believing didn't exist. Now that he had tasted her lips, he couldn't imagine letting that go forever. No edict, no time apart, and no distance could change that.

His father's eyes widened; he froze in the doorway between the dining room and the sitting area, his lips parted as he struggled to respond. Cole knew what was going through his father's mind. If their people—Queen Daephyra, in particular—uncovered the truth, he would never be welcomed in Montaris again. "You know the edict," his father whispered. "You would forsake your own people for this girl?"

"Yes!" Cole screamed, exasperated. He ran a hand over his face knowing these may be his final words to his father, and they needed to matter. He needed Cassius to truly hear him for once. To understand why he chose Xandra. "I was like a dying plant banished to the shadows of this gods-forsaken forest. I did not know how lost I was until I left this place behind. The more time I spent near her, the more alive I felt."

"You would turn your back on your own kin for a fleeting infatuation?" Cassius asked.

"It's not fleeting. I tried not to choose her, but her soul calls to mine in a way I can hardly describe," Cole said. Closing his eyes, he pictured her bright smile, remembering the feel of her skin against his fingertips as he kissed her in the hot springs. If he had but a moment left to live, he needed to spend it entwined with her. "Xandra is the sunlight that sustains my life. Her smile is the very water that nourishes my spirit. It would be death to turn away from her now. She is the only woman I have ever wanted in this way— and the only one I ever will."

Cole turned away from his father and grasped the doorknob. In a moment of agonizing silence, he thought his father had given up. He was nearly out the door when his father sighed and said, his voice quiet but firm, "You will suffer for your choice."

"I will take every foul word and look with a smile if it means I have her." His heart raced, his grip tightening on the doorknob.

"That's not what I mean, son," his father said solemnly. Cole fell silent, daring to glance over his shoulder. The pained expression on his father's face was the same look he always had when he remembered his late wife, Lyrisanna. "I loved as fiercely as you once. But when they go first—and she most certainly will—you will be left alone for much longer than any human spouse. Is her love worth the centuries of pain it will cause?"

"I would suffer infinitely if it meant I had held her for as many days as I possibly could." There was a foreboding silence as his father processed his answer, and Cole watched as Cassius's astonished expression morphed into something different. A deep-rooted understanding of the love his son felt.

Cole took a deep breath and ran a hand through his hair, the scraping of his fingers against his scalp oddly calming him. There were so many things he wanted to say, so many questions he had wanted to ask his father but never dared. Now, only one question mattered. "If you could go back, knowing you would lose Mum so early, would you choose someone else?"

Cassius stared out the sitting room window. "No."

Cole nodded and muttered, "I always said I wouldn't lose myself the way you did after Mum passed. But now I see so much of her in Xandra—the joy she has for life. Her laugh is like medicine. No one else will ever compare. I would hope that you of all people could understand how it feels to find someone like that."

Cole turned to exit their home, and Cassius reached out a hand. "Alarcole! Wait."

Flinching, he released the doorknob. "I know you cannot support my decision. I never expected you to," he told his father with a shrug. "I know I shall be exiled. That Daephyra would never see me return to Montaris in her lifetime… But staying here, letting her go, would be far too painful."

"I know that feeling well," Cassius said with an exasperated sigh. "Wait here." His father turned and walked toward his bedchamber silently, leaving Cole standing alone in their entryway.

When he returned, Cassius held a small red velvet ring box cupped in his hand. "This was your mother's. Do with it what you wish."

Cole blinked incredulously, staring at his father's outstretched hand. "Is that—"

"Yes," Cassius cut him off abruptly. "Lyrissana would have wanted you to have it. She—your mother loved you very much. Both of you. I hope your sister will not mind."

Cole lifted the clasp on the box and opened it. He had not laid eyes on the beautiful gold band with a single jade stone fixed in the center since they laid his mother to rest many moons ago. His eyes stung as he fought back the swell of emotions it brought on. Blinking tears back, Cole cleared his throat and snapped the lid closed. "I will make sure Crystal is willing to allow me this. I suspect she will not mind."

Cassius nodded. "I suppose you should go after her then." He stepped forward and wrapped his arms around his son's back, much to Cole's surprise. "Promise you will write to me?"

Cole clapped his father on the shoulder and nodded. "Of course."

As they pulled apart, he realized a stream of silent tears had streaked his father's pale cheeks. Cassius looked away from his son as though he were embarrassed by the show of emotion. Cole clenched the ring box tighter in his fist, drinking in the silent gesture of acceptance he'd received from his father.

When they had both composed themselves, Cole finally turned the doorknob, pausing to take a final glance back at his father. "Thank you," he said proudly. They nodded their farewells with bittersweet smiles on their cheeks before Cole closed the door behind him, ready to track down the people his heart belonged with.

23

THE SAME CRUEL FATE

On her way to visit her mother, Sabine ran into Anteros and his friends in the first-floor hallway, likely on their way to the training hall now that the hunt was behind them. She nodded at her brother, but her eyes snagged on the blond boy standing to his right. It had been a few weeks since she had seen Julian at court. She'd heard from her brother that he joined James and Calix on another rowdy romp in Jessiraé. The idea of him being entertained by courtesans made her stomach turn, and she could not look him in the eye.

"Where are you off to?" Anteros asked her. When she looked up, there was sympathy in his eyes. She wanted none of it.

Sabine fluffed her blush pink skirt to distract herself from staring at Julian. "To see our mother. And you?" The nonchalance to her tone told them she did not care. In truth, she was more interested in speaking with her brother's sullen friend.

"Training," her brother replied, glancing between her and Julian. "It's been a while since we've all been together. Why don't you come by, cheer me on to victory?" An impish grin appeared on her brother's face, and for a moment, she considered it. It was nice to see him smile, even if it did not linger.

"Who says you will win?" Julian asked, drawing all eyes to him. He was staring right at her, the purple rings under his eyes telling her he had not slept well. But why?

"I always win, especially against you," Anteros countered. He shoved Julian playfully, interrupting the heated staring contest between his friend and his sister.

"Perhaps I will come along if only to see Julian knock you on your rear." She chuckled, lifting her skirt to follow them in the direction she had just come from.

Then she heard her betrothed call out her name. "Sabine, darling, I was sorry to miss you at breakfast." As he closed the distance to them, she winced, dreading another awkward encounter with her betrothed. "Must have needed the extra sleep after such a physical excursion." She wrinkled her nose at his choice of wording.

Ryker nodded his head at Anteros. "Have you told your sister of my hunting prowess?"

Sabine could see the way her brother struggled not to roll his eyes at the earl, and she had to hold back the urge to giggle. Then she remembered their last conversation, and her smile melted away again. "I'm afraid I have heard nothing of your prowess, good sir," she teased, adopting a playful tone to mask her discomfort.

Her fiancé grinned, coming to stand beside her. One hand curled around her waist, and Sabine feigned a sheepish smile for the sake of their audience. That was when she caught Julian glowering at them. Her cheeks burned as she tried to discreetly weasel her way out of Ryker's grasp, but he drew her back as if she weighed nothing. "I bested all the hunters—with the exception of your father, of course." He beamed—positively thrilled to brag to her about this accomplishment. His arrogance rivaled that of her brother's.

All she could think at that moment was that she was just another fowl waiting to be shot.

A prize to be put on display in his home.

Sabine shuddered. "Sounds like it was a productive day," she said unenthusiastically. "I look forward to quail at our luncheon."

"There are plentiful fowl in the meadow on my estate. You can request quail anytime once you join me there," Ryker said. He leaned his face closer to her ear and whispered, "Might you have a token for me besting your brother at the hunt? You said it would please you."

Sabine paled, her stomach sinking until her legs felt unsteady. "Oh, I was just on my way to meet my mother. I haven't had the time to prepare anything."

Ryker grinned as she looked up at him, his face dangerously close. "I'm sure you can think of something, darling." His gaze dropped to her lips, his thumb stroking her cheek. She had barely nodded her head once before he stooped down to steal his prize. The stubble on his chin burned her skin as he languidly pressed his mouth to hers. He wasn't a terrible kisser; this was certainly an improvement on their first. Yet she could not stop her mind from drifting back to the Solstice Ball when she'd snuck away with Julian. He had been so tender, yet there was obvious desire behind his restraint. Ryker could learn a thing or two from him.

When her betrothed released her, Sabine stepped back and sucked in a deep breath. Feigning a shy smile, she patted her hands on her skirt, feeling ruffled in an unsightly way. Anteros cleared his throat, and her eyes shot back to the group of young men who had just witnessed Ryker's display of *affection*, if one could call it such a thing. Julian was no longer at Anteros' side.

She glanced down the hall in time to see him round a corner and disappear. Clenching her fists in her gown, Sabine exhaled slowly before turning back to Ryker. His head was cocked to the side as he observed the change in her mood. Before he could say anything else, she blurted out, "My mother's expecting me for tea. I bid you all a pleasant day."

Her feet could not carry her away from him quickly enough. Walking as fast as her heels and propriety would allow, Sabine was too paranoid to look back, afraid she might find her betrothed in pursuit. It wasn't until she closed the sitting room door behind herself and rested her back against it that she finally breathed easy.

"Heavens, child, have you been running?" her mother asked. Metal scraped against the floor as her mother stood abruptly from her seat at the table on the far side of her private sitting room.

Sabine opened her eyes and shook her head. "You taught me never to run," the princess said, rubbing her palms against her crinkled skirt. As she walked over to the table, a delectable scent filled her nostrils, and she smiled. Her mother had ordered her favorites: petite sandwiches and macarons. "What's the occasion?"

Chelsea's mouth pulled in a tight line as she gestured for her daughter to take a seat beside her. Once seated, the maid who stood quiet as a statue in the corner approached, lifting the kettle to fill their cups with piping hot tea. Stepping back, the woman looked at them expectantly before Chelsea dismissed her to the kitchen.

This was not good.

Sabine slumped in her seat, covering her tired eyes with a hand. "What has he done now?" She dreaded the answer, knowing it was likely to involve her impending marriage.

"Your betrothed has made an unusual request of your father," Chelsea said slowly, as though she was unsure how to broach the subject.

Sabine's heart skipped thinking Ryker must have requested they set an earlier date for their wedding, despite the fact that he said he would wait for her consent. "A spring wedding?" she asked, her whispered words filled with dread. Plucking a macaron from the tray, she popped the entire morsel into her mouth, struggling to chew it for the flavor had lost its appeal in the moment.

Her mother's brow furrowed in shock. "Heavens, no. Why would you think that?"

Sabine paused, realizing she might have been wrong. Swallowing the bitter bite, she sputtered, "The earl might have asked my blessing for such before he left for the hunt."

"And did you give it?" her mother asked, her voice an octave higher.

Sabine shook her head. "I said I would consider his request. I never gave an answer."

Chelsea breathed a sigh of relief. "Good. I have fought hard to make him wait until your next birthday. You are so very young."

Tears welled in the princess's eyes as she stared at the empty plate in front of her, the weight of her situation pressing her back into her chair and her heart into ashen remains. "What difference will six months make? He will only be agitated if he is made to wait longer."

Chelsea leapt out of her chair and wrapped her arms around her daughter. "Are you truly so afraid of Ryker Umbryon's temper?" Sabine's wet cheeks pressed into the lace of her mother's bodice as she sniffled helplessly. She did not know whether fear was the right word to describe the dread she felt. Ryker was putting on a show, and the only other man she knew who could put on a mask when he wanted something was her father.

And she knew what monster hid beneath *his* mask.

"Not every man is like your father," Chelsea finally said.

The way her mother's fingers combed through her curls calmed her, and Sabine closed her eyes, feeling her breathing steady. She loathed crying. It made her feel weak. Pathetic. Inadequate.

She lifted her head and wiped her tears away with the palm of her hand. Sabine Rexton was not a weak young lady; she had been raised to be a force of nature with confidence flowing through her veins, spite in her glittering skirts, and influence in the clack of her high heels.

Her mother caressed her cheeks and pecked her on the forehead, her deep blue eyes full of pride at her daughter's strength. "You are so much more than your beauty, Sabine. Your wit and strength never cease to amaze me. Should the earl not appreciate every part of you, then he is a fool. Never forget that. To forget your worth is to give your husband all the power."

"I would never," Sabine replied, the smallest smirk forming on her lips.

Her mother patted her cheek sympathetically before returning to her own chair. Sabine watched the woman's mask slip as she took a miniature pair of tongs and carefully selected a finger sandwich before bringing it to her plate. The latest proof of her father's cruelty had finally healed up; her mother's eyes were back to being a matching set, one no longer swollen and bogged down by an obscene amount of powder. Though her age had begun to show in the fine lines beside her eyes and the corners of her mouth, Chelsea Rexton was still quite beautiful. Her dark red hair had yet to lose its lush color, something Sabine sometimes envied. She would have preferred not to resemble her father in the slightest.

"Did you truly love him once?" Sabine asked.

A pregnant pause followed, interrupted only by the sound of Chelsea gently laying down the tongs on the tray before her. Her mother locked eyes with her, not shying away from her unexpected question. "Yes," she answered, her voice softer than usual. "He chose me out of all the young ladies in his father's court. Swept me right off my feet. I admired his ambition, and he was easy on the eyes." She smiled wistfully at a memory, some version of Antoine that her daughter would never know. "Antoine was so gentle in the early days. He used to whisper sweet nothings to me about making me his bride. It was all very romantic at the time." She flourished her fingers in the air and sighed.

"What changed?" Sabine immediately noticed the slight change in the reminiscent look in her mother's eyes. Chelsea's muscles had tensed, the lines near her eyes becoming more pronounced. Like she was fighting back the urge to cry.

Chelsea feigned a smile that did not reach her eyes. "His father discovered our affair and ordered us to separate. The king sent Antoine off to battle a neighboring kingdom as a reminder of his place. It was there he bonded with many of his officers and hatched the plan to betray the Garricks when he came here to wed Elara."

That's right. Her father was supposed to marry the Garrick princess. She had learned that in her lessons, but somehow had not dwelled on their engagement. How it had been arranged, despite Antoine's love for another. If it was ever love on his part.

And now he had done the same to his own daughter.

Her mother cleared her throat before taking a sip of tea. "He came back changed. Anger does that to men. If they let it fester… it ruins the best parts of their hearts." She picked up her sandwich and inspected it before taking a small nibble.

"Why did you come to Graynor then?"

"Because love makes people do stupid things," her mother said firmly. There was no nostalgia in her voice anymore. No, these were the words of a scorned woman who had loved a man and lived to regret it.

Sabine wondered if all women were doomed to a miserable fate, whether they married for love or for political motivations. If such were true, wouldn't it be better to be disappointed by a stranger rather than someone you've given your heart?

Her mother noticed the way she was staring dejectedly at the treat tray and reached for her hand. "I do not tell you this to make you fear falling in love, my dear," Chelsea said, squeezing her hand. "Not every man leans into hatred. There are good men out there. And if you never grow to love your husband… that does not mean you will never know love. It just means your time hasn't come yet."

Sabine wrinkled her nose, believing her mother was spouting nonsense to make her feel better. She did not want to know what her mother could mean by that. Pulling her hand away, the princess pretended to take a macaron, placing it on her plate as she avoided her mother's sympathetic gaze.

"I hope you find happiness wherever you end up, my dear. Be it with your husband or in the faces of your beautiful children. You deserve to find some sort of happiness," her mother concluded.

Sabine nodded. "We all do."

Yet somehow it still felt far out of reach.

When morning tea had concluded, there was one thing the princess was certain of: she would never allow herself to fall victim to the same cruel fate as her mother.

24

LEGACIES

Anteros was not amused when Ryker Umbryon asked to join them at training. After the earl's grotesque display of affection with Sabine in the hallway, the prince knew Julian would be in a particularly foul mood, and he did not want to be caught on the other side of his friend's blade when he was fuming.

When they entered the room, Ryker scanned the walls, taking in the various weapons lining them. "Quite the arsenal," he commented, though his deep voice hardly sounded impressed.

"Do you have an arsenal at your estate, my lord?" James asked. Without waiting for an answer, he walked over to the far wall where Julian was inspecting the fencing swords. Anteros, Ryker, and Calix followed.

"I have accumulated an array of swords and bows over the years—several of which I inherited from my father. Sadly, managing the estate has kept me quite busy. It has been a pleasure to get away," Ryker answered. There was a mischievous glint in his eye that told Anteros this man enjoyed any sort of physical challenge and likely had not had anyone to spar with in a long while.

"Kissing a beautiful woman always lifts my spirits," Calix said. Julian quickly shoved his cackling friend away.

"You are right about that," the earl replied, exchanging a grin with Calix.

The prince marched up to his friends, leaned around them, and plucked his favorite sword off the wall. Admiring his reflection in the cool metal, Anteros asked their guest, "Have you experience in swordplay?"

"What nobleman doesn't?" Ryker replied, amusement clear in his grin. He reached for one of the sabres to his right. Julian scoffed, making the earl pause.

Calix and James exchanged grins. "His Majesty does not permit Anteros to practice with sabres anymore. Says men should practice with a real blade."

Ryker's brows disappeared under his light brown curls, and he nodded in understanding. "Very well. I suppose I must oblige by His Majesty's rules then." He returned the sabre to the wall, then stepped up beside Julian to inspect the swords.

As Ryker moved to make his selection, Julian cut him off, snatching the sword out of his reach. The boy grinned smugly. "Have you ever seen real combat, my lord?"

A deep chuckle escaped the earl. "Alas, Denorfia has not had need for my skills as we are a more *peaceful* land. The Treaty of the Five Realms ensured peace for decades. That is, until Antoine took the throne here. My liege has always preferred to settle disputes through diplomacy rather than violent means." Ryker took a different blade from the wall and tested its balance on his pointer finger. Pleased with it, he gripped the hilt in his fist and said, "I am up for a challenge should you be interested."

Anteros turned and found the earl's words had been a direct challenge to Julian. The men glared at each other. Hatred seeped from Julian's pores, making the air feel charged. "Do not let my age fool you. I have bested many grown men in this very square." Julian gestured toward the sparring square near the room's center.

Ryker studied him with fascination. He approached the boy, circling him like a vulture, inspecting his physique. "May the best man win," he finally said, extending a hand to Julian. Begrudgingly, the boy took it, shaking once before withdrawing to the square.

The prince and his other two friends moved to the bench beside the training area to observe their fight. Though Anteros was not involved, he could not help but feel responsible for both parties. Julian was his friend—one who had just done him a huge favor. One who was seething at the sight of Sabine's newly betrothed. Meanwhile, Ryker was a foreign dignitary, and his father would beat him senseless if the man were somehow injured or embarrassed enough to withdraw his aid before the worst of winter was upon them.

There was no way for this fight to end well.

Anteros watched with bated breath as Julian and Ryker rushed toward each other, their blades clamoring loudly as they parried. He should have stopped them before they began. Flashbacks echoed through his mind with each sharp sound—his father's speed and power, being knocked to the ground, being sliced as a reminder of his weakness. Anteros ran two fingers over the small scar on his collarbone. His jaw ached from clenching his teeth, and he blew out his breath.

Focusing on Julian, he realized his friend's confidence had returned—or perhaps Ryker's lack of practice was feeding into his friend's arrogance. Calix and James whooped in support of their friend, but the prince remained quiet. Unable to keep his legs still any longer, Anteros rose from the bench and went to stand behind it, clenching the metal back in his hands.

Since their father's visit to the training facility that summer, the boys had all been training harder and longer than before, and it showed in Julian's impeccable technique. Guards who were lifting weights or sharpening their swords paused to watch him knowing Antoine had told the boys they must draw blood to end a proper duel.

Perhaps he should have mentioned that to Ryker sooner.

The earl's hair clung to his forehead, sticky with sweat. He was only a decade older than them, but the bulk of his everyday attire weighed him down considerably. Ryker dressed for the cold in the north. In Graynor, such thick fabrics and heavy layers were unnecessary, having little purpose besides slowing down the wearer.

Yet a smile reappeared on the earl's face, unnerving Anteros.

"I'm afraid we've not been properly introduced. Of what importance are you at Graynor?" Ryker asked his opponent as they pressed their blades against each other in a futile standoff.

"My father is Duke Lucien Malloy." Julien grunted as he shoved Ryker several steps back. His breath came in heavy pulls.

Ryker chuckled, using his sleeve to wipe his brow. "Ahh, yes, I have had the pleasure. When I expressed interest in finding a wife, your father was all too eager to offer your sister as an option."

Every muscle in Julian's jaw went taut; a deep green vein pulsed in the side of his pale neck. "Which sister?" It was bad enough that Julian was obviously struggling against his jealousy over Ryker kissing Sabine. Now that the earl had brought his kin into the conversation, Anteros did not know what Julian would do.

"He only mentioned the one. Lucille, was it?" The smugness in his voice told Anteros this was a jab meant to ruffle Julian's feathers—and it was working.

Julian flew forward, swinging wildly at his target. The earl twisted out of his way, coming up behind him and holding his sword to the boy's throat. Ryker grinned, drawing Julian closer to whisper in his ear, "No hard feelings, Malloy. Sometimes it's best to just lay down our arms and admit defeat."

But Ryker did not know Julian. Did not know that Julian would never quit.

Anteros rounded the bench right as Julian's head slammed back into Ryker's face. The earl's blade nicked Julian's throat, but just barely. Not enough to kill him. Still, blood dribbled from the scrape, seeping into his cream tunic as he turned to admire his handy work. Ryker's nose was gushing—clearly broken by Julian's thick skull.

The prince cursed as he swiped a towel from the end of the bench and rushed for them. Holding it up to Ryker's nose, he glared at his friend knowing somehow the blame would fall on his shoulders for allowing this to occur. "That was uncalled for, Julian. What are you trying to do, kill him?"

His friend ran a hand over his head, slicking back his sweaty blond locks with a smear of blood. "First blood wins, remember?" He grinned.

"And who's to say you drew blood first? Look at yourself," Anteros snapped, gesturing toward his friend's crimson-stained tunic.

Ryker cursed under his breath, taking the bloody rag from Anteros. "I was not privy to that rule." He leveled the prince with an agitated look before ambling over to the bench and taking a seat. He pinched the bridge of his nose and held it up as though this weren't his first nosebleed.

Perhaps the earl had a habit of pushing buttons?

Anteros followed like a younger sibling poised to beg on his knees for forgiveness for a crime he had no part in. "My sincerest apologies, my lord. I never thought he would—"

"I wondered how cunning you were taught to be in a fight," Ryker said with a smirk. He locked eyes with Julian and nodded. Lowering the rag, the bleeding seemed to have stopped. "Boreas would be impressed with you boys."

"You haven't seen Anteros in action yet," James said, nudging the prince.

Anteros cringed, hardly thinking it was right to face a man who had just had his face bashed in. "I think the earl has had enough action for today," he argued.

"You may be correct," Ryker replied. He discarded the soiled rag on the ground and leaned forward on his knees. Deep red streaked his chin, imbedding in the spaces between his teeth. Sabine should be relieved Julian had not knocked out his front teeth. "But I should like to stay and watch you practice. I'm sure Boreas would be pleased to hear you can protect his daughter."

Anteros' stomach flipped.

"So, the rumors are true?" James asked, his question edged with delight. "You're to wed the Denorfian princess?"

His spine went rigid at the thought of meeting this foreign woman at the end of an aisle. "No time soon," Anteros muttered. He shuffled over to where he'd discarded his chosen weapon in his haste to aid the earl.

"There is no time such as the present. She's young, beautiful, ripe for producing heirs," Ryker said with a grin.

"Then why don't you marry her?" Anteros snapped. He froze, his back still to Ryker, as his mind caught up to his mouth. Eyes wide, he surveyed the doorway, catching the eyes of a few men who had just entered. The room had gone eerily quiet. Julian stepped into his periphery, giving him a piteous look.

Finally, Ryker and Calix chuckled uneasily, breaking through the tension. "I can understand your hesitation," the earl said in earnest. "My first marriage was arranged by my father, who—bless his soul in the beyond—suffered from an awful affliction before his untimely death. I hardly knew Annaliese, but she was a sweet girl, much like Myra."

"How is it you have been married twice and yet have no heirs?" Julian asked. He wiped his blade with a towel, not bothering to look up at the earl.

"Annaliese died during childbirth. The babe—a boy—was stillborn. It was a very difficult time," Ryker admitted, dropping his chin onto his interlaced fingers. "I was still in mourning when my father grew ill. On his deathbed, he stressed how important it was that our legacy live on, which is why I ultimately remarried."

"And your second wife?" James asked. One brow quirked up in interest. Anteros had never seen his friends care so much about the subject of marriage.

"After her third miscarriage, we had both given up on the prospect of welcoming a child. Then, poor Ramona was exposed to the plague when visiting her sister. She never returned."

"How long has it been since she passed?" Calix asked.

Ryker grimaced, wringing his hands. "Three years this winter."

"No wonder you are in want of another wife," James jeered. But his lighthearted jest was lost on the others.

A faint smile appeared on the earl's face when he finally lifted his head. "I dreamed of my father telling me our legacy must live on. Mere days later, Boreas reached out to see if I should be willing to meet with Rexton to negotiate a cattle sale. It was divine providence."

"Fathers usually care more about their legacies than their sons, especially at our age," Calix said in a self-assured tone. "I, for one, am in no rush to wed."

"Only to bed," James interjected. He shoved his friend's shoulder roughly as they cackled. Even Ryker seemed amused by the vulgar sentiment.

Anteros once would have laughed at it, too. He had had his share of fun over the past year, both at court and at less savory establishments, but he had come to realize no number of beautiful women could fill the void in his heart.

Only one girl had ever come close. And she nearly died for it.

"Enough talk." Anteros pointed his blade at James. "You. To the square."

James swallowed before reluctantly shuffling over, taking the freshly polished blade from Julian on his way. Ryker perked up. He leaned his back against the metal bench, irises blown wide like a cat chasing its prey. There was a hunger for blood in his deep brown eyes that made Anteros nervous—though he knew his skills were superior to his friend's.

"Think you might last more than three moves today, James?" Calix jeered.

Their friend gritted his teeth and brushed his fingers through his bushy curls, making sure they were out of his eyes. He zeroed in on his opponent as though they were enemies on opposing sides of a war he would die trying to win. Anteros had never seen such focus in his friend's green eyes before, and he wondered what had changed during their trip to Jessiraé.

Then he remembered the phoenix.

"You never told me how your father took it when he discovered Phinnian was gone," Anteros said, a delighted grin stretching his cheeks wide. By the look on James' face, he had struck a nerve. Good. He always fought better when he was fired up.

"Not well," James declared. He lifted his weapon over his left shoulder and narrowed his eyes at the blade that would soon come at him with relentless power.

"Phinnian?" Ryker asked, clearly curious.

"He filched his father's phoenix a few weeks back," Calix said gleefully. "Anteros won him in a game of Prophecy."

"A phoenix is quite the prize." Ryker's brows raised. "You shall have to invite me next time you play. I quite enjoy a high stakes card game."

"It's by far the greatest prize any of us has scrounged up," Anteros said with pride. He loved that even Ryker was impressed to hear he owned such a rare creature.

"You would not dream of trading him back, would you?" There was the smallest hint of hope in James' question, though he hesitated to look Anteros in the eyes for long. Instead, he focused on the prince's blade, anticipating his first move.

This was his chance to make the fight interesting.

"I would not," Anteros replied. "I'd wager that you could try to win him back, but we all know you cannot beat me in a fight." Though he did not relish crushing his friend's hopes, he also knew none of his friends would allow him to live it down if he caved and gave away something of such value that he had won fairly.

Calix snickered from the sidelines. "You should have known that would never happen." His teasing made James tighten his grip on the hilt of his sword, his fingers turning red where he grasped it. Determination flashed in his green eyes.

Then he charged.

Anteros lifted his blade to repel the sudden onslaught of strokes, surprised by his friend's increased speed. "Have you been practicing without me?" the prince asked, his tone accusatory yet impressed.

Julian chuckled. "He catches on quickly!" He slapped hands with Calix in premeditated victory.

"Cheats, the lot of you," Anteros murmured as James reared back, giving them both a moment to catch their breath.

"Not cheating. Leveling the playing field," Julian replied. Anteros did not dare glance in his direction, but he could hear the smirk in his friend's voice. What he would give to wipe that cheshire grin off his so-called friend's face.

The prince didn't have time to linger on that thought because James was right back on top of him, rearing his blade down with impressive coordination and control. Not only had his friends been practicing without him—they'd truly improved.

If they could fight dirty, so could he.

"Why are you so angry, James? Did your father give you a lashing for stealing his firebird?"

His friend's cheeks bloomed deep red as he charged forth once more. Locking weapons with Anteros, both gritted their teeth in a struggle to overpower the other. Then, James leaned a hair closer and said, "No worse than any punishment your father could come up with."

Anteros flinched, giving James just enough leverage to send him stumbling back. Their friends clapped their hands, and Anteros dropped his gaze to the ground. His feet were barely within the sparring square. He clenched his jaw and stepped closer to James, distancing himself from the edge. "Now I'm dying to know what he chose. Scrubbing the floors? Polishing the silver? Or," Anteros paused, grinning in self-satisfaction, "no more money to pay for your whores."

James growled, the sound feral like that of a wild wolf protecting its lair. The rest of the hall grew quiet, awaiting his next move. "I won't need my father's money where he's sending me," he finally said.

"He's sending you away?" Anteros asked. He lowered his weapon, losing concentration on the fight. "Where?"

When James did not answer, the prince looked to the others. Julian's cold eyes stared back, not even offering a hint of pity. Calix's brows rose, his equal surprise not giving Anteros any more information.

"If it will help, I'll sell the ruddy bird back to him," Anteros said. As he turned back toward James, a blade swung diagonally in front of him. The prince leaned back, narrowly avoiding the swing, unable to wrap his mind around James' surprise attack. He had moved so quietly, nimble as a cat, that Anteros had not heard him coming.

James huffed. "He is not willing to pay twice for the same beast. No, I will be joining the king's regime come springtime."

"The army?" Anteros asked, incredulous. None of his friends had expressed any interest in joining Antoine's service. Bootcamp at Murmont was notoriously brutal— more so than practicing with any of the old militia members who hung around Graynor.

James brushed back the sweaty curls from his forehead and nodded. "No need to sound so shocked. After training, I'll be stationed in Lettras or Graynor. It could be worse." He smiled faintly, and the prince narrowed his eyes. Something was amiss.

His friend circled, watching the prince's weapon as he lifted it back to his shoulder. "It's a shame, though, that I will not be around for Sabine's wedding… or *yours*."

Everything flashed red as Anteros charged, putting all his power into each move. They parried once, twice, but on his third swing, Anteros twisted in an unexpected motion, avoiding James' blade completely. Instead, his weapon made contact with fabric and continued, slicing through the muscular flesh of James' chest. A tortured howl shook Anteros to his core, and he dropped his bloodied blade in horror. Blood continued to pour from his friend's chest as two men raced into the square with towels and water, trying to help stop the bleeding.

Anteros stepped back, his ears ringing as he watched blood drip onto the tile below James. He had not meant to injure him—not like that. His anger had gotten the better of him in the heat of the moment. As he tried to justify the accident to himself, Julian, Ryker, and Calix stared at him, murmuring in hushed tones. Anteros did not need to hear the words aloud as he watched Ryker's lips move.

Ruthless like his father.

Bile burned the back of his throat, and the prince rushed for the entrance. He had barely stumbled into the hallway when he keeled over to vomit. He had lashed out in a wave of rage—an act so grave he feared his very soul was in jeopardy. What if James succumbed to blood loss or infection? His arms shook as he pressed his hands into his knees, praying silently to whatever greater being was out there that his friend would live.

He had to live.

If he didn't, then Anteros would be no better a man than his twisted, murderous father.

25

NIGHTMARE

A black stallion galloped toward the horizon. A bitter wind bit at Elara's cheeks as she rode through the field behind Graynor Castle. Long had it been since she had stepped foot on the grounds of her childhood home, but she would always remember the deep, woodsy scent in the air and the way the sun glistened on the lake at sunset. It was breath-taking, yet for some reason, she felt an overwhelming fear creep into her chest.

This is not right. I left in the springtime. Why are the leaves red?

Elara shivered, pulling a heavy black cloak tighter at her chest. Then she realized she was not pregnant. She wasn't herself at all.

This was a vision.

As Idonea had taught her, she closed her eyes and took a deep breath, steadying her heart rate as the horse galloped on. Knowing this was a dream did nothing to ease her mind. Whoever was riding this horse was going much too fast. They were running away from something. And with Graynor just behind them, she could only assume that it was Antoine.

The autumn wind nipped at her cheeks, and she gripped the reins tighter as she glanced over her shoulder. Several guards with bows were in pursuit. She felt the urge to laugh at them, for they were quite a distance behind her. With luck on her side, she could reach the woods and lose them.

Then an arrow whizzed by her face, barely missing her horse. Whoever was being chased, Antoine wanted them dead. Elara felt pity for them. She had spent many years eluding his assassins. She hoped whoever it was would manage to reach the dwarfs before Antoine's men caught up to them.

A new fear rose in her chest, and Elara gasped. Judging by their size and attire, this had to be a young woman. What if it was Serena? What if she had failed to kill Antoine and fled?

The beat of two dozen horse hooves pounded in her ears. The men were gaining momentum, closing in on the lone rider. Another sharp sound echoed across the valley, and something sharp pierced her back.

199

She cried out, and seconds later, an arrow hit her horse in the rear, bringing them both tumbling to the ground...

Elara jolted awake, her heart pounding in her chest as she checked her body for injuries.

There were none, of course.

Gerard sat up beside her, rubbing the sleepiness from his eyes, and asked, "Another nightmare?"

"A vision, I think," she murmured, still feeling a sting where the arrow had embedded in her back. "Someone was fleeing Graynor on horseback. It was like I was them. Like I was not in my own body."

"What happened?" Her husband put an arm around her back, his other hand absent-mindedly caressing her belly. She shifted uncomfortably, feeling caged between his arms.

"Antoine's men shot me—or *her*—in the back with arrows. It felt so real," Elara said. A trembling hand reached across to gently brush her shoulder, relieved to feel nothing there. Her eyes welled with tears as she stared at the far wall. "What if it was Serena?"

Gerard made a gruff noise and pulled her into his chest. "You did not see their face, so you cannot fret over the possibility. Besides, she's safe in Ord Metsiilva, is she not?"

The queen nodded, temporarily reassured by his reminder. Serena was safe. She knew this to be true. Her niece had checked in when the group spent the night in Montaris. Elara had sent her away to train and recruit additional allies, knowing the elves were extremely protective of their territory. Crystal had assured them they would have a guardian with her at all times. Antoine could not reach her there.

But her niece was headstrong. She would leave eventually.

Sharp pain lanced Elara's chest. The burning sensation spread as it crept up her throat, the cold fingers of her fear wrapping tight around her airway, cutting her breath off. She couldn't go back to sleep now. Not after such a nightmare.

Pushing back the blankets, Elara slid her legs across the silk sheets and slipped off of the bed. "I need to see Idonea." She swooned on her feet, reaching out for the bedpost to stabilize herself. Her breathing was labored, though she tried to hide it from her husband, turning away from the bed to grab her silk robe off a hook on the wall.

Gerard blew out a puff of air and scurried off his side, hurrying around the foot of the bed to block her path to the door. "Get back in bed before you hurt yourself. You know that's what Ismenia would advise."

Eyebrows lifted, Elara finished shoving her arms through her robe. "You cannot speak to me like this," she said, harshness lacing her whispered words.

Her husband stepped closer, his height imposing as he looked down at her, the shadows over his features scaring her. She took a step back, but he reached out, grabbing her wrist gently and keeping her close. "I am your husband. You cannot continue to use your title against me. It is my duty to protect you." Pale eyes searched her face in the darkness, reminding her of the two moons over the mountain. Wide. Watchful. Pleading.

"I don't need your protection right now. I need you to listen to me. To respect what I want." Her heart pounded rapidly as she implored him.

He turned and slapped both palms down on the bed sheets in irritation. "How can I trust you when you constantly put your life at risk?"

She started to feel the muscles in her chest tighten again, and she crossed her arms over her bosom. "I am tired of having the same argument with you, Gerard. You knew who you were marrying. How could you expect me to suddenly be a complicit little wife?"

"Because you made a vow to me," he hissed, the increase in his volume making her gasp. He turned and seized her by the upper arms, this time less gently. "Why must you continue to push yourself knowing what's at stake?" His gaze dipped to her belly, and the tension in his body laxed. His hands slowly fell from her, and he backed up a few steps. "We cannot go on like this, Elara. We have to come to some sort of understanding."

A flurry of movement within her abdomen made her pause. She placed a hand against her swelling bump and whispered, "I know, my sweet. It has been a long day." Releasing a heavy sigh, she perched on the edge of her bed and buried her face in her hands.

Gerard sighed, obviously fighting the urge to get closer. To feel his child flipping and kicking within her. Scratching his salt-and-pepper beard, he finally said, his voice back to a gentle whisper, "These dreams are making you think irrationally. Will you at least sleep on it before disturbing the oracle?"

"This isn't easy on me either, you know," she whispered through her hands. Moving a hand from her face to her chest, Elara pressed and focused on breathing slowly, deeply. "Sometimes I can hardly breathe from the stress of it all."

Gerard knelt on the floor in front of her and took her hands in his. "Let me call for the physician then. Please?"

She shook her head. "Ismenia. She'll know what to do. This is not the first time."

Her husband rose wordlessly and went to address the guards posted outside of their bedchamber. The minutes ticked by slowly as they waited in silence, seated side by side with his hand on top of hers. It was heavy and hot, an added weight she would have rather brushed off, but Elara tolerated the gesture knowing it was all her husband could do to try to comfort her when comfort felt like a foreign concept.

When the herbalist arrived, her body wrapped tight in a burgundy robe that shuffled along the floor as she charged into the room, Elara sighed at the sight of her friend's small beaded bag. Coming over to them, Ismenia perched the bag on the bed to Elara's left and began sifting through its contents. "What ails you this night, milady?"

The queen narrowed her eyes, unsure why her friend had taken such a formal tone. Before she could answer, Gerard butt in. "She had a bad dream. When she got out of bed, she wobbled on her feet like she was weak. She said it was hard to breathe."

Ismenia turned, alarm and concern in her rich brown eyes as she pressed chilly hands to the queen's neck and checked her temperature. "No fever. Do you feel faint now?"

"Only tired." Elara shook her head. "And it wasn't a dream. It was a vision. Someone is going to die," she said quietly.

The herbalist lowered her chin, eyes flitting warily to the queen's husband before she hummed a half-hearted sound. "And you're certain you did not overdo it with Rilura today?" She leveled the queen with a knowing gaze, full of concern and disapproval. Elara winced.

"Rilura? What happened today?" Her husband rose from the bed, crossing his arms over his chest as he looked between the two women. "Have you been training again? After I asked you not to?"

"It was nothing, dear," the queen lied, pressing her lips together. Her brows lifted, and she hoped Ismenia would take the hint to let it go. She had sneakily met up with Rilura for another brief sparring session that morning while Gerard had been giving the new Denorfian ambassador a welcome tour.

But he did not need to know that. It was not training that ailed her, after all. It was her mind, not her body, which betrayed her.

"I leapt out of bed too quickly in my worry. I only wanted to see Idonea, but Gerard would not allow me to leave," she added, wringing clammy hands together in her lap.

Ismenia shook her head. "I'm not so certain of that, Your Majesty. You should listen to your husband and rest. There's nothing to be done about these visions, so at the very least, you should conserve your energy during the day." She pinched closed her beaded bag, her hands empty, and Elara sagged.

Gerard inhaled sharply, relief washing over his tired visage. "Thank you."

The queen stared in disbelief as Ismenia stepped back from the bed, shoving the strap of her bag over her shoulder. She seemed irritated. Perhaps waking her in the middle of the night had been a terrible idea. But the herbalist had never refused to treat her before.

"I will bring Idonea to see you in the morning. We can have tea *in your sitting room,*" she said firmly. Ismenia was not asking but insisting, and Elara knew she could not argue otherwise with her husband's focus on them. She felt like they were teaming up against her, and that made her grind her teeth, struggling to respond without snapping. No one had coddled her in such a way since she had a nursemaid and tutor who followed her everywhere in her youth.

"Very well." Elara sighed as her friend patted her shoulder and turned to leave them. Before Ismenia opened the door, the queen added, "Please inform Rilura as well."

The muscles in Gerard's back rippled as he rolled his shoulders and neck. "Good eve, Ismenia. Sorry for the trouble," he said as the door latch quietly clicked behind her.

A pregnant pause permeated the space until Elara shifted, resigning herself to attempt to go back to sleep. Gerard stalked toward her side of the bed. "Care to elaborate on your *strenuous* day?" Fingers drummed against his arms as he stared down at her.

Elara squirmed, her back aching as she rolled onto her side to face him. "It was not strenuous. You handled the envoy, allowing me to rest before hosting him for dinner." She stared back, the heaviness of her blatant lie sucking the air from the room.

Hurt flashed in his crystalline irises, and he shook his head knowingly. Turning away, he started around the side of the bed. "I thought you were smarter than this. More cautious. Certainly not this reckless. It appears I didn't know you at all."

She sat up as he slid into the sheets with his back facing her. "That's hardly fair." Grabbing him by the shoulder, she forcefully rolled him onto his back. She had the high ground now, yet the way he was looking at her—like she was a complete stranger and not the woman he was madly in love with—made her feel small. "Gerard, please. I am not being reckless. Most women do not confine themselves to their quarters for their entire pregnancy. I am healthy. The baby is moving regularly. I've not overdone anything."

"Why must you train with a sword?" His words were sharp, filled with hurt and displeasure. "Everything was perfect. We were both happy. Why must you drive this wedge between us?"

"Everything I've done has been to ensure I can protect our child. Every deal with every ambassador, every guard promoted, every sword lifted. All of it is for them. For *us*," she snapped, pressing her open palm to her stomach. "What kind of mother would I be if I cannot protect them after they're born?"

Gerard pushed himself up on one elbow. "If you did not think me capable of protecting you both, then why did you marry me?"

Elara huffed, indignant. "I married you because I love you."

He scoffed. "If you loved me, you would listen to me. You would respect me enough to stop this folly. That dwarf has filled your head with foolish notions. You're a pregnant woman, not a warrior."

"This has nothing to do with Rilura," she argued. "This is *my* body. These are *my* hands." She held them both out, palms up, in front of her husband. "What I do with them is my right. I'm not overdoing it. If anything, the child's powers are the issue here. I was fine until I had that vision."

Gerard clenched his jaw, eyes dropping to her abdomen. "I wish I could rid them of that curse."

Elara gasped at his blasphemous words. He might not have been an estrelle, but she had never heard him disrespect Divinity. To speak out against her very faith.

Sight was a rare and beautiful gift from Divinity. The chosen were revered among her people. Though the gift had been hard on her mind and body, it was not to be taken for granted.

"How can you say such a thing?" she whispered, leaning back. "Our child has been blessed with an extraordinary gift. To speak such disrespect against Divinity…"

A gentle breeze from the open window blew the canopy over their heads, casting harsh shadows over his features. His eyes were nearly lost in the darkness, his exhaustion evident. "Any god who would put such a strain on a pregnant woman does not care about you," Gerard said. Desperation seeped through the husk of his voice. He was tired.

So was she.

Elara dropped back onto her pillow and exhaled. A deathly silence stretched on between them until her husband began lightly snoring. What was once an endearing sound now irritated her. She stared at the back of his head for a while, feeling more unsettled than when she had first awakened. Her relationship with Gerard had taken an unfortunate turn over the past few weeks, and she saw no happy resolution to their bitter arguing.

Perhaps she should listen to him. Even Ismenia seemed to agree.

But if she bent to his controlling impulses now, would Gerard ever truly respect what she wanted?

That question unlocked a new fear within her heart—a fear that might have been worse than any vision could cause.

THE ACADEMY

Ord Metsiilva seemed to have a life of its own as Serena and their party traveled north from Montaris to Envyre. The wind whistled through the trees, sending a flurry of bright-colored leaves skittering to the forest floor. It reminded her of the woods behind her family's home in Durmak. While she loved the smell of fresh spring grass and new blooms, the changing of colors had also been a highlight on her morning walks when the air was crisp yet not bitter.

Serena paused in a patch of sunlight beaming down between branches. Tilting her head back, she closed her eyes and breathed deep, allowing the smell of lush grass and crisp cedar trees to renew her spirit. For a brief moment, it felt like she was back home.

"Come on. We're almost there," Crystal called back, waving a hand over her head. She was in a rush to get Serena back inside city walls where she thought she'd be safer, but Serena felt more at peace in the forest than she ever had in Symptee.

A hand grazed her lower back, and Serena's eyes snapped to meet Will's. "Oh. Hi."

"Hi," he replied, his dimples sending her heartbeat soaring. In the past week, they had spent most of their alone time wrapped in each other's arms, memorizing the feel of each other's lips and breathing in each other's scents as though they were making up for lost time. Perhaps they were. Long had she harbored feelings for the boy who grew up with her brother and apprenticed with her father. Now that she knew the taste of his lips and the warmth of his touch, nothing was more important to her.

Except ending the war.

After all, there was no hope for a peaceful future unless Rexton was dethroned.

Heat spread from his fingers through her back, and she shivered. "Are you cold?" Will's arm wrapped around her back, one hand hooking onto her waist as he led her forward.

Gideon and Madeline made retching sounds from behind them. Serena wondered if either of them had ever been in love. By the sounds of their joking, she assumed not.

"I cannot wait to see their faces when we've returned," Madeline said. There was a metallic sound like blades scraping against each other, and Serena turned to investigate, finding the other archer was twirling a pair of throwing knives around her fingers out of boredom.

"Are you quite good with those?" Serena asked.

Madeline grinned, catching a knife in each palm. "I'm the best."

"She thinks she's the best at everything," Kieran said, chuckling at her expense as he trudged past them. He swung wide, avoiding Will, who tightened his grip around Serena's waist as he watched the guardian pass.

"Could you teach me?" Serena asked. After hours of sword skill training, she was desperate to learn something new, and throwing knives seemed like an optimal choice. The thought of taking out an enemy before they could get close was exhilarating.

Will's arm slipped away, and Serena turned to find Crystal standing right in front of her, arms crossed. "Knives are only useful if you're trying to avoid a fight. You will have to go up against at least one man, so it's best you stick with your sword skills."

"Give her a break, Crys. We're going to war soon. She'll need all the skills possible," Xandra argued, patting her friend on the shoulder. "It might not be a bad idea for you to show her how the bow works, too."

"She's seen me shoot plenty," Crystal said. She had been especially irritable ever since visiting her father. Though Serena wanted to ask her a million questions, she could tell that the archer was not in the mood. Since they reached Montaris, Serena was certain that sharing personal matters was the last thing Crystal Windaef enjoyed.

"You know that's not what I meant," Xandra said. Her voice was stern, reminding Serena of her mother fussing the boys when they did not listen.

The archer pulled her bow and an arrow from the quiver behind her back. Stretching the string with one hand, she took aim at a tree ahead of the group. "You hold it like so," Crystal said, her voice dripping with sarcasm. Then she released the arrow, watching it soar a great distance before implanting in a tree trunk. "Aim and release. It's simple." She tucked her beloved weapon back into her quiver and returned to the front of the group without another word.

Madeline ruffled Serena's hair from behind. "That one isn't much of a teacher, but I'm sure the instructors at the Academy would gladly help broaden your skill set. And I would be honored to help you."

"Thank you," Serena said, offering the new guardian a smile.

When they caught up to Crystal and Rigel, she watched them carefully, noticing the small ways they reacted to each other. How Rigel would lean closer to hear her better and Crystal would lean away if he stepped too close, careful never to let their arms brush. So different from the time she used her bare hands to save him from bleeding out.

Before they knew it, a great wooden wall rose out of the forest floor before them, and four armed guards approached, all bearing the pointed ears and stern expressions customary of elves. They nodded at Crystal before surveying the faces in their group, each slowly seeming to register that the majority of the humans had a history in Envyre.

"Back so soon?" The closest of the guards lowered his weapon, speaking directly to Kieran and Madeline. His gaze flicked toward the unfamiliar faces. "And you've brought new friends?"

"I've brought them," Crystal said, bringing their attention back to her.

"You've been away a long time, Windaef," another guard noted, returning his bow to its quiver. The dark-haired elf crossed his broad arms over his chest and looked her over. "Haven't changed a bit, though. My cousin will be pleased."

Her cheeks pinked, and Serena narrowed her eyes at the man. "I've already seen him," Crystal said, shoving the guard playfully.

When he grinned, pulling the archer into a bear hug, Serena realized he must have been related to Deldrach. *Her betrothed.*

That still did not sound right.

Crystal smiled and hugged him back briefly before pulling away. It was a far warmer and more relaxed greeting than what she had shown Deldrach the day prior. Turning to face the group, she stood with an arm around the guard's back. "Serena, Will, this is my dear friend Ilrune Caimys. I'm convinced he is the happiest elf to ever live."

Ilrune laughed heartily, the sound warming Serena's spirit. "My friends call me Rune," he said, extending a hand to Will, then Serena. His disposition was certainly closer to that of his cousin than the Windaef siblings. It was a relief to know not all of the Silveryl Elves were as stern as her friends. "Come inside. The elders will want to meet you at once."

Led by Ilrune and Crystal, they walked toward the entrance where the other guards were already back at their posts. Men on the top of the wall watched as they walked over the drawbridge and entered the city. Envyre was much larger than Serena had imagined. While she only knew it as the home of their training academy, she was surprised to see it was as grand and bustling with life as their capital, Montaris. A thriving market to their left boasted brick-and-mortar stores, and pop-up vendors lined the roads.

"There will be time to explore later," Xandra said sympathetically, steering Serena to follow the others.

Ilrune led them down a road to the right between two rows of matching cabins. "These are where students, refugees, and guards stay," he informed them, gesturing toward the homes made of rich, dark timber. Their tall windows and the vibrant little gardens in front of their massive porches were inviting, and Serena wondered if there would be a house available to them during their unforeseen stay.

Madeline broke off from the group, heading toward one of the houses. Her initials were painted on the bright red door. She waved from the porch. "Seeing as some of us have not been gone long, our homes are still reserved. I'll see you all after a much-needed bath." Serena was almost envious as the lithe warrior slipped inside the house.

Kieran, Heath, and Wesley grinned as they parted ways for one of the larger homes with two stories. Remaining with the group, Gideon pointed in their direction and said, "That's the bunkhouse. Many of the men stay there. They don't care about privacy so much as the women do." Will nodded, seeming to understand that was where Gideon, Rigel, and he would also end up sleeping. If they were permitted to stay.

"Where will we sleep?" Serena asked Xandra, glancing at the doors of the past few houses. Each had two sets of initials painted on. "Do you have a house here?"

Xandra chuckled. "Not anymore. When we were selected as guardians, we wrote to the Captain to let him know we would not be returning. Mad-eye actually moved into our old house." She glanced back wistfully at the red door where Madeline had abandoned them.

"They'll find us a place. Don't you worry," Crystal said without turning to face them. She walked side by side with Ilrune, her posture more relaxed than when they were in the capital.

Toward the end of the road, the sound of arrows hitting targets amplified. Serena craned her neck in search of the training ground, but it was partially obscured by a massive structure. Several people—elves and humans—went in and out, most of whom were wearing the same brown pants and loose cream tunics. She wondered if that was a uniform or just the common way to dress in Envyre.

Rigel moved to hold the door open for everyone, and Ilrune led them into a maze of wide hallways housing a dozen offices. Humans and elves chatted excitedly as they passed. It was refreshing to see them convene together—so unlike the cold greeting they had received in Montaris. Many of them looked around their ages—late teens to mid-20s— with a few younger children mixed in. Orphans, most likely.

Orphans just like her.

Serena wouldn't dare venture to guess how old any of the elves were. Not after discovering Crystal was over 70, and sweet little Iriela was around 45. How they could look so similar to humans yet age so much slower, she'd never understand.

Finally, Ilrune paused in front of a door and knocked twice. A gruff voice called for them to enter. Their escort swung open the door and gestured for them to wait in the hall. Serena peered around Crystal, trying to get a peek at whoever Ilrune was telling about their arrival, but he managed to block the desk with his wide frame.

"This is Captain Aspen Smedley. He's responsible for overseeing all the human refugees and students in Envyre," Crystal whispered.

"All of them?" Serena asked, her brow furrowed. They had already seen no less than a dozen humans since their arrival, and she assumed there were many more in the Academy.

"Yes, all 74," a deep voice replied.

Serena straightened, realizing the captain was standing in the doorway looking right at her. His thick, short curls caught the light from a nearby window, revealing a hint of red that reminded her of Rigel. "I could not imagine watching over so many children. You must be very patient," she said hastily, holding out her hand. "Serena Finch."

"Thankfully, they are not all children." Smedley took her hand and shook it enthusiastically. "I knew your father well, long before the war. Good man." She itched to pick his brain more about John Finch's life in Graynor, but he turned to address the others before she could reply.

"Captain," Crystal said. Smiling, she shook his hand.

"Miss Windaef. 'Tis not often we see tournament winners return to the Academy. What brings you here?"

"We've come seeking asylum for Serena. It would be best if we could speak in private," the elf said, glancing down the hall. The captain nodded and turned, walking back to his desk and taking a seat. Crystal turned to Xandra and said, "The rest of you can go on to the dining hall. Eat and then show Serena the training grounds. She should get in some practice later."

"Need me to stay, help explain things to Cap?" Rigel asked, leaning an arm against the wall. Crystal hesitated, pursing her lips in consideration. "You know the man loves me. He was practically a second father to me." She exhaled and shrugged, gesturing for him to enter the office first.

As they closed the door, Xandra grasped Serena's hand and dragged her down the hall. "The cooks here are quite good." She smiled as she saluted Ilrune, who nodded before heading back in the direction they had come from.

A dagger whizzed through the air as though it were propelled by the wind. It moved so quickly that Serena lost sight of it until the blade implanted in the dead center of the painted target 30 feet away. "That was incredible!"

Madeline gave a dramatic bow before winking at Serena. "It's all in the wrist," she said, plucking another small knife from the stack between them. "Now you try."

Serena reached across and took the weapon from her new guardian. She hated the weight of the handle in her palm. The way it felt far more intimate than any sword in her hands. Perhaps it was because she had killed with a dagger previously. It was a weapon that required a firm grip and an iron conscience for you had to cut through the little air between yourself and your enemy to plunge it through their flesh.

A sharp, slicing sound of metal on metal rang out repeatedly behind her. She glanced over her left shoulder, eyeing the men practicing with their swords. Sweat glistened on Will's brow, drenching his off-white tunic in patches. He was actually starting to look like a skilled fighter… until he locked eyes with her, and Kieran whacked him in the nose with the hilt of his sword. Before the fight could escalate, Rigel and Gideon were between them, telling Will to walk it off. He tossed his weapon onto the ground, taking a towel from a young girl as he skulked toward the main building.

"Sorry," she mouthed as he walked by, but Will avoided meeting her eyes. His cheeks were flush—likely from embarrassment. Fighting the urge to go after him, Serena watched him disappear into the building before turning back toward Madeline, her stomach in knots knowing she had distracted him—not for the first time—and she was allowing him to distract her as well.

Knife throwing was to be her focus. That had been her request. She didn't know if she would ever have need for the skill, but in battle—and they were fated to one day face such a harrowing ordeal—a girl could use a number of skills in her arsenal beyond swordsmanship.

"What's the best way to hold this?" Serena asked, her fist tightening around the handle as she held up her hand to her instructor.

Madeline's pale fingers wrapped around hers, repositioning her hold, and Serena immediately noticed they bore many small scars. She remembered her own hands bleeding after the intense battle with Cameron and wondered if that was the price of wielding such a small weapon in close combat.

Perhaps that was what she deserved—to count her kills in marks on her skin.

"Have you ever taken a life with one of these?" Serena asked, her voice low and hesitant.

Her instructor lowered her hands to her hips and sighed. "While those idiots have tempted me over the years," she grinned as she pointed a thumb over her shoulder at the men practicing, "I have not. But when the time comes to face our enemies, I will not hesitate. No man who sides with that vile monster shall ever have my pity."

Serena nodded. If only guilt were such a simple thing one could elect to feel—or not. It would make her memories far less haunting. Her dreams, less nightmarish. Her heart, less broken.

"I am still jealous you faced a ship full of pirates while I was sleeping. Try not to go rogue without me next time," Madeline said, lifting Serena's arm to position the blade over her shoulder.

She turned and narrowed her eyes; the target seemed miles away. Almost as removed as her enemy felt. But even in Ord Metsiilva, Serena knew safety was an illusion. She practiced flicking her wrist twice before releasing the blade on her third snap. The dagger hit the edge of the wooden target and ricocheted into the grass.

A hand landed on her shoulder, and Madeline said, "Don't worry. Nobody hits a bullseye on their first try. This takes practice. I daresay even more than swordsmanship."

"Madeline Milliorva! You did not write to tell me you were coming back." The shrill female voice carried across the yard, making everyone turn their heads. A bouncy young woman with golden hair raced toward them, nearly tackling her friend to the ground. On her heels, five others followed. They stopped short of Madeline, some eyeing Serena curiously while two boys around her age took off toward the men who were sword training.

"My apologies. Our return was decided last minute. Mere days after Elara awarded us for our tournament performances," the black-haired guardian said. She held the bubbly blonde out at arm's length. "We actually were sent to Montaris, but you know how Daephyra feels about us."

The girl rolled her eyes before finally noticing Serena. "Hi! Are you new? Can't believe they've got this old grump teaching someone." She snorted, and Serena tried not to laugh at the sound.

"Serena Finch," she replied, holding out her hand in greeting. "I'm not exactly here as a student... Crystal thought this would be a safe place to stay temporarily."

The woman nodded. "Carissa Rycroft. Did you mean Crystal Windaef? I haven't seen her in years." When Serena nodded, the woman perked up; determined eyes skimmed the training grounds until they fell on the men training, and she inhaled sharply. "By the stars... Excuse me," Carissa muttered before taking off in a run.

Serena caught the end of a hug between Gideon and a boy around her age. Then his gaze flicked up as Carissa neared.

Rigel must have heard her coming. He turned just in time for her to dive, forcing him to catch her midair. Her legs wrapped around his waist as she clung to him and squealed.

Noticing the concerned look on Serena's face, Madeline nudged her and said, "They were a *thing* before Elara made him a guardian. Broke her damn heart when he told her not to wait around for him."

That was more information than Serena needed to know. From the looks of it, Carissa had definitely been waiting for him to come back. The poor girl. If only she knew that Rigel now looked at Crystal the same way she was looking at him.

Though she had never seen Crystal wrap her entire being around Rigel before. And he didn't seem to mind the attention.

The door to the administrative building flew open behind them, and more students poured out into the training area. A muscular blond growled in frustration, plodding toward Carissa and Rigel. "DeVarr! Get your hands off of her!"

Rigel nearly dropped the girl. "Cyrus, it's been a while." But the man offered him no greeting in return. He approached, his face reddening as he glared at them. If Carissa had not stepped between them, Serena was certain he would have thrown a punch.

"Oh, come on, Cyrus. Rige didn't do anything," a woman with auburn hair said. She caught up to him and took a place standing beside Carissa, linking their arms at the elbows. The blond—Cyrus, Serena presumed—exhaled, staring at the other woman. "She's just excited to see him. As is everyone else."

"He better keep his hands to himself, if he knows what's good for him," Cyrus declared before stalking over to an empty area. He lifted an axe and took a practice swing, embedding the blade deep in a hunk of wood. Serena swallowed, awe-struck by the power of his arms. They could use someone like him on their side.

As long as he didn't take a swing at Rigel.

Madeline wrapped an arm around Serena's shoulders and turned her back toward their target. Placing the hilt of another dagger into the girl's palm, her instructor nodded and said, "Again."

Serena tried her best to focus on the lesson, but over time, a small crowd of strangers gathered around them, eager to chat with Madeline about the Guard Tournament and their brief time in Symptee. She also suspected they were curious about her. It didn't seem like new faces came to Envyre often.

After many terrible throws and plenty of encouragement, Serena finally managed to sink a dagger into the outer ring of white paint on the wooden target. She leapt in the air, squealing excitedly at her progress. Clapping started behind her, and she turned to find Crystal and Will watching from a distance with proud smiles on their faces.

"Nice work, Finch," the archer said. The humans encircled behind them parted, leaving Crystal room to come closer. "Who knew Mads could be a decent teacher?"

Madeline rolled her eyes, the look on her face mirroring the archer's usual demeanor. Serena stifled a snort. How ironic that these two were rivals when they were so similar. "She is. But I wonder… which of you would be a better archery instructor?"

The women exchanged a contemplative glance before both replying, "Me." Their friends snickered, spurring them both on.

Xandra and Rigel walked over with Carissa wedging herself between them. Shooting a cold look over her shoulder at Xandra, she whispered something to Rigel and giggled. His face flushed, and he rubbed the back of his neck as he stole a glimpse at Crystal and Serena.

The archer wasn't paying them any attention. Something behind them had caught her eye. Ilrune waved emphatically as he approached. "Your housing has been prepared. You could have told me you were expecting one more!"

"What?" Her brows knitted together as she leaned to the side, realizing someone had followed him out of the main building. Her brother. Her jaw fell open as she watched him veer off, ignoring her and going straight for Xandra. The guardian's smile fell when she noticed him approaching, and she crossed her arms and pressed her lips together. Cole whispered something in Xandra's ear, and she stared at him for a moment, a look of uncertainty in her doe eyes, before following him toward another building on the far side of the training grounds.

Serena leaned over and muttered, "Typical cold greeting. Why am I not surprised?" Crystal shook her head, watching them as they trekked further from the group. When they reached the large structure, Cole held open the door and gestured for Xandra to enter first. "Where are they off to?"

"That's the indoor training facility where Cole taught advanced lessons," Madeline replied, her brows raised. "Are those two—"

Crystal grimaced. "These days I am not certain… But if he breaks her heart, we're using him for target practice tomorrow."

Serena and Madeline laughed. If that were the case, Serena would have to invite Will to join them.

27

HOME

Once they were safe inside the building, Cole took Xandra's hand, leading her down the hall to the room where he had first really noticed her. She was twenty then, full of grit and determination the likes of which he rarely found in human students. That was the only reason he had agreed to work with Xandra—and Rigel as well. They weren't just skilled. They were formidable. Though he would never dare admit it aloud back then, he was impressed and incredibly proud of their progress over that year of advanced lessons.

Now he knew he should have told them.

Several times, they both could have been killed on their mission. It was seeing Xandra bleeding and pinned down by an enemy that had finally made his composure snap. He worked his jaw at the haunting memory, tightening his grip on her hand. The same hand that wretched soldier had plunged her weapon through. The hand he now wanted to put a ring on. He knew with certainty that he would vow to protect her until her dying breath—or his, should he somehow perish in the battle by her side.

He could only hope that he wasn't too late in making such a promise.

"I'm surprised to see you back in Envyre," Xandra said quietly. "Did the queen not have work for you?"

Cole clasped his hands behind his back, kneading them anxiously. "I informed Her Majesty this morning that I would not be continuing in her service."

She gasped, one hand flying up to cover her mouth. "But why?"

The furrow of her brow made his chest tighten. Could she really have no idea he had done it for her? Cole ran his hands through his hair, tucking it behind his ears. "I realized home wasn't where I wanted to be anymore."

Xandra lowered her hand and fidgeted with the little silver band on her right middle finger. It had been her mother's—he'd heard her tell Serena about it on their long journey across the Athamar Mountains. He nearly zoned out watching her spin the band absent-mindedly, until she asked, "You wanted to be here instead? I didn't realize you missed teaching."

The ring box in the pouch tied to his belt was heavy against his thigh. He had spent over a hundred nights under the stars, sleeping mere inches away from this enchanting woman. His lips had laid claim to her after her persistent pursuit of the truth behind his feelings. He wanted her the way the autumn leaves longed for the wind. The way the flowers turned their faces toward the sun. He needed to see her smile as desperately as his body needed him to breathe. Yet now that he finally had her alone, he felt as though his chest might burst open.

"It wasn't teaching that I missed," he said, reaching for her hands. Her eyes softened as they searched his face, waiting for him to say more. Cole wasn't supposed to lose himself staring into those molten irises, yet he couldn't look away. If he ever wanted her to truly be his, he had to speak his truth. Every last word on his heart. After the way he'd left Symptee, he owed her that much. "I missed you."

Her chest rose; her eyes brimming with tears as he squeezed her hands in his own. "I missed you, too," she choked out. Sniffling, she dabbed the corners of her eyes with the back of one hand. "So, you don't intend to stay in Envyre then?"

Cole barked a laugh and pulled her a step closer. "I intend to stay as long as you stay and to go wherever you go—for as long as you'll have me, sunshine." He pecked her on the forehead, wrapping both arms around her back.

Her shoulders shook, and he held her tighter. "I thought if you went home, you would never come back to me. I thought you would always choose Daephyra."

He shook his head. Running his hands down the sides of her arms, Cole gently drew her back so he could look at her tear-streaked face. "I'm sorry I left, Xandra. I'm sorry I ever made you feel like I didn't want you for a second. Because you're all I've wanted since the last time I held you. I have ached for you far more than I ever ached for home. It took leaving for me to realize that you are my home now."

She stood on her toes and wrapped her arms around his neck then, one wet cheek pressing against his cheekbone. Burying his face in her neck, he breathed her in. How he had missed the subtle scent of her—fresh like the forest and sweet like honey. Like home. His fingers buried in her raven curls as he pressed a kiss to her neck.

She sucked in a breath; her fingers dug into his shoulders, the warmth of her touch making him hold her more tightly. "Where do we go from here? The elves will never approve," she whispered close to his ear.

"Envyre is different. I think we will be safe here. At least, for now," he said reassuringly. She relaxed into him and barely nodded her head.

A moment later, she tensed again. Lifting her head suddenly, concern etched her features. "What about your father? When Daephyra finds out, you'll be banished."

He caressed her cheeks between his hands and smiled bitterly. "I would choose that fate a million times over because you are far warmer than she'll ever be." Her lips parted to argue, but he pulled her in, sealing his mouth over her plump lips. A deep, moaning sound rumbled in the back of her throat, and she tilted her chin higher as he kissed her languidly, his tongue sweeping across her bottom lip. She pressed her body closer to his, igniting his senses. Cole cursed himself for holding her at arm's length for so long. Now his lips alone were unable to satisfy the way he craved every inch of her beautiful skin.

Pulling apart, their heavy breaths intermingled between them. "Perhaps we should have Ilrune show us to our beds," she murmured, lips brushing against his. Her cheeks, slightly flushed, rounded as she smiled, kissing the corner of his mouth.

Cole tensed at the mental image of her in his bed. "I do not want you for only one night," he whispered back. "I want all your nights. All of you. Your lips…" He stole a chaste kiss. "Your mind." He kissed her forehead, lingering with one hand on her cheek for a moment. "And most of all, your soul." One finger trailed down her neck, stopping at the center of her chest. Her pulse pounded heavily against his finger. He would savor the feel of her beating heart every day, protecting it at all costs. Her life was the most precious thing to him.

He reached for his belt and fumbled to untie the bag from it. Xandra tried to hold back her infectious laughter as she watched him. Stealing a glimpse at her smile, Cole's chest swelled with pride. He had once been the reason she was hurting, but he would never make that mistake again. Now, he would ensure that all her smiles began with him.

Finally freeing the pouch, he pulled out the red velvet ring box and exhaled in relief. He was all too aware that elves and humans had different traditions when it came to mating and marriage. Elves were more solitary, and most saved themselves until they were soul-bound to a spouse. That was how his parents had done things, and it was how he had always intended to do things as well. He thought there was something intrinsically romantic about finding the one person your soul was destined to bond with.

As agonizing as waiting for a century was at times, he knew that Xandra was worth it.

Xandra stared at the ring box, a look of sheer disbelief having replaced her shining smile. Cole grinned as he flipped open the lid, revealing the ring inside. "Xandra Stanton, would you do me the honor of binding your soul to mine?"

Shaking fingers cupped the bottom of his hand, lifting it higher so she could better admire the ring. "Was this your mother's?" Xandra finally whispered. He nodded, his heart bursting with pride at the notion of her wearing it. She stroked the gold band with one finger, admiring the jade stone at the center. "It's beautiful."

"It's yours, should you want it," Cole said. "Nothing should please me more than to call you my wife."

"When?"

The question surprised him, but he chuckled at her enthusiasm. "I want to do this right. A gown, flowers, your father. Perhaps during the winter solstice, or shortly after?"

Xandra's brow furrowed. "I do not need a big wedding. We aren't in Symptee. And if we are still here, my father will not be able to attend. Why should we delay?"

"I do not wish to simply bed you and call you my wife. I want you to experience everything you deserve. You'll only be married once," he said confidently.

Her lips curled. "How can you be so sure?"

Wrapping an arm around her waist, he yanked her closer. His nose brushed her cheek as he said, voice low and husky, "Because once I have had you, nothing—no king, queen, god, or mortal—will stand between us again. I will hold you each night, and tighter still when you take your dying breath. That is a promise."

"I want that more than you can fathom," Xandra said.

He reached into the box and removed the ring, holding it delicately between two fingers. "May I?" She nodded, her teeth sinking into her bottom lip as he slid the band onto her left ring finger, as was typical for human betrothals.

She caressed his cheek, tears filling her eyes once again. Her joy was infectious, as his own eyes were fighting back the same. "I will bind myself to you, Alarcole Windaef. Make plans for whatever traditions you'd like to include. You, as well, shall only have one wedding."

A quick wink sent his heart fluttering, and he lifted her feet off the ground, spinning her in a circle. "You're right about that," he said before kissing her again. "And I cannot wait for the world to know you're mine." He gently lowered her feet back to the floor, fighting the urge to kiss her again. If they stayed there too long, he just might lose his will to wait.

"Suppose they'll know as soon as we leave the building," she teased, lifting the hand bearing his family ring. It fit her hand perfectly, almost as though his mother had hand-selected Xandra for him from the great beyond. He would never tire of seeing her wear it.

"Some of us have known for a while," Crystal said, her voice projecting through the near-empty room. They turned to find her leaning against the doorway, a large grin spread across her face. "I'm glad to see my brother has finally come to his senses."

Xandra ripped out of his grasp and raced across the space to hug her friend. As they embraced, Rigel and Serena rounded the corner, both barely containing their sheepish grins. Cole crossed over to them and shook his friend's hand. While he wasn't fond of public displays, the elf couldn't have imagined a better pair to witness the fruition of their relationship. Crystal and Rigel were part of the reason his feelings for humans had shifted over the years. Now, he was pleased to call them family. And he would do everything in his power to keep his family intact when Serena Finch eventually leads them into battle.

28

SAVE THE DATE

When her father called for a special banquet with half of the court in the main hall, Sabine knew something was awry. He had been quiet since returning from the hunt. Too quiet. And if Antoine Rexton contemplated anything for too long, that was bad news for everyone.

A small part of her feared that he had learned of her visit to the dungeon. The supplies she had smuggled to Talitha. But it wasn't her life she feared for—it was her friend's. She would never forgive herself if she caused Talitha to be tortured again.

Sabine wiped her clammy palms against the silk of her deep coral evening gown as she and her mother walked toward the main hall side by side. Worrying was pointless. Whatever pain or punishment was to come was inevitable, and she would endure it. She always did. It only made her stronger.

Perhaps the greatest surprise that week was Ryker Umbryon's absence. Suddenly, he no longer stared at her at meals. There were no more coerced strolls, stolen kisses, or horseback rides. Ryker had distanced himself. Not just from her—but all her family.

She couldn't blame him after witnessing her brother slashing through one of his oldest friends in a rage. She had been shocked to hear about the accident in the training hall the week prior. The entire castle had. Her father had been thrilled, of course. The king did not have the least bit of sympathy for the boy who had landed in the infirmary, too weak from blood loss to get out of bed. In fact, she wouldn't be surprised if this very banquet were a celebration of his son's ruthlessness in battle.

The incident had sent Anteros into yet another downward spiral. Drinking from dusk until dawn. Slogging through half the day before passing out all afternoon. His bloodshot

219

eyes roamed the halls in search of someone to lift his spirits—but even the girls at court were reluctant to be alone with him now.

And no maiden could make him forget the guilt he allowed to suffocate him day and night.

As the Rexton women entered the hall, Sabine exhaled when her eyes fell on her brother, Calix, and Julian chatting, glasses of red wine in each of their hands. Her heart beat faster as she stared at the pale blond hair slicked back over Julian's head, a sharp contrast to the all-black suit he was wearing. She wanted to go over to them—to laugh and flirt and act the way they once had.

But she was no longer free to do that.

Her mother gestured to where her father was introducing Ryker to some of the nobility. He smiled and shook their hands with ease. When Ryker met her gaze but did not approach her, Sabine leaned closer to her mother and whispered, "I'm going to check on Anteros. Make sure he doesn't make a fool of himself." Her mother nodded in approval before walking away.

When the princess reached the young men, sharp crystal eyes gave her a once-over before Julian started chugging from his goblet. Up close, her brother looked worse off. The bags under his eyes were deep purple, and his breath reeked of alcohol as she leaned in to kiss his cheek. "Take it slow tonight, won't you? Who knows what father has in store."

Anteros scoffed loudly, and her eyebrows shot up in alarm. "I do not need a nanny, Sabine," he huffed, taking a long swill from his glass. Leaning closer, he added, "And if anyone should be concerned tonight, it's *you*."

She reeled back, looking to Julian for some kind of clarity. As soon as their eyes met, he turned his back, pretending to speak to Calix instead. Did they know something that she did not?

Before she could question them, Anteros walked away, his shoulder brushing hers as he headed toward their father. Sabine watched in disgust as their father greeted him with a broad smile, clapping his son on the back and delving into the tale of his son's proficiency with a sword. The nobles smiled and congratulated him on his skills.

The entire scene made her nauseous.

"How many times do you suppose your father will tell that story before Anteros has to be carted off to bed in a drunken stupor?"

She whipped her head to the left, stunned to find Julian standing beside her, watching her brother from afar. His words might have been said in jest, for he once would have relished Anteros' discomfort, but not this time. Now, Julian frowned, a harsh line cutting horizontally across his forehead as he watched his friend squirm. There was pity in his eyes. Sabine stroked the back of her hand against his, and he jumped at the sudden contact. "Julian, I—"

"Don't. We shouldn't even be standing here together. People will talk," Julian replied, a husk creeping into his deep voice. He closed his eyes and cleared his throat.

Sabine waited for him to say something, anything, to make her feel better. When he didn't, she leaned closer and hissed, "He would not want your pity, Julian, and neither do I." She tried to sound resolute when it felt like her heart had been shattered like glass. Turning on her heels, the princess blew out a breath, but a hand caught her arm before she could march away.

Julian pulled her back a step until his nose skimmed the top of her ear. "Don't think you are the only one hurting here, princess. This isn't what I wanted for us either."

His whispered confession sent goosebumps flaring up her spine and down her arms. Sabine blinked back tears, discreetly reaching a hand behind her back. She sucked in a breath when Julian took it, giving her fingers a gentle squeeze before letting them go. Her gaze roamed the hall, making sure nobody was watching them. The only eyes she met were Ryker's, but he quickly looked away.

"Come to my chambers after dinner. *Please*," she pleaded. This might be their last chance. At what, Sabine wasn't sure. There was so much left unsaid between them. But she could not leave Graynor without kissing Julian Malloy one last time.

Julian nodded, running a finger through her raven hair. His knuckle skimmed her bare back, and she fought the urge to turn and kiss him right there in front of everyone.

That would certainly piss off her father.

Realizing they had been standing too close for too long, Julian backed away, and Sabine took a deep breath, trying to steady her shaking hands as she crossed the hall to join her family.

While dinner was uneventful, Sabine was restless, drumming her fingers against the table as the minutes ticked by. Most people watched the dancers who had been hired as entertainment, but she was distracted by the family of blonds sitting on the far-left side of the U-shaped banquet table. One caught her eye, his casual smirk making her heart flip. She had missed that smile. Tonight, it would be hers again, even if only for a second.

When the servants began handing out dessert, a cherry tart that oozed blood-red juice when the crust was impaled, Antoine clinked his knife on his glass, and an overwhelming sense of dread filled Sabine. It was her birthday all over again; the reminder made her head spin. She dropped her fork, and it bounced off the edge of her plate before falling to the floor.

She shouldn't have been surprised when Antoine lifted his glass to toast the bride and groom, turning his torso to face her and Ryker. "What a blessing it shall be to both of our kingdoms when you are wed on the winter solstice. A worthy offering for the moon goddess and the wind god as we celebrate the survival of our people through this joyful union."

Sabine choked on nothing. It was as though all the air had been sucked from the room. She coughed, patting herself on the chest to try to diffuse the shock. The solstice? That was only two months away. It wasn't even spring, as Ryker had requested of her.

She clenched her jaw, turning to face her fiancé. Their audience was applauding, and she used the echoing noise to muffle her seething words. "Is this why you can barely look at me? Because you asked for an earlier wedding date? So much for receiving my consent." She smiled at her father, then the nobles, lifting her glass as though she were happy with this announcement when what she really wanted to do was bash Ryker's face in with her gold chalice.

The Denorfian envoy shook his head. His brown eyes were mortified, though she did not believe this was news to him. Her father liked to talk. Ryker would have known. He had probably asked for this. "No, Sabine. I promise you, I did not ask your father for this. It was his decision. He only informed me a few days ago. I had no idea you were unaware."

The princess lifted her cloth napkin and dabbed her mouth with it. Using it as a shield, she whispered, "Your promises mean nothing to me. Now I know who you really are."

This man was as cunning as her father was. Perhaps all men were. And she would never be fooled into trusting one of them again.

An hour after the banquet had concluded, Anteros rapped his knuckles three times on Sabine's bedchamber door before trying the latch. It was open, so he quietly slipped inside. "Bine? Are you still awake?"

"Anteros? Get out," his sister growled from her bed. She pulled the covers up to her chest and crossed her arms.

He sauntered past her vanity over to her red velvet sofa, leaning his rear on the hard cushioned arm of it, hands in his pockets. "I just wanted to make sure you're well."

Sabine took one of the pillows off her extravagant bed and tossed it at him, but Anteros caught it in both hands. "I am not *well*. I am *angry*. I want to break something, but that would not be lady-like!" Her mocking tone, mimicking something their mother no doubt said, made the prince chuckle. She sat up straighter and threw another pillow across the space, missing him entirely. "This is *not* amusing."

"I know, I know," he said, holding up both hands in surrender. A searing thought crossed his mind, and he gnawed at the inside of his lip. Sabine did not know about the incident with Ryker when they were hunting. How he had put his hands on the envoy, threatened him. His father had likely set this wedding date to appease the man. "I'm sorry it's coming to this. I should have made a better impression on Ryker. Then perhaps we could have prolonged your engagement."

"This has nothing to do with your impression," Sabine said, rolling her eyes. "This is my punishment for seeing Talitha again."

Anteros' head shot toward her, his dark hair falling messily over his forehead. "You saw her recently?" His sister nodded, flopping back onto her mountain of pillows. The prince's head reeled with questions, so many he wasn't sure where to start. "How is she?"

"She wishes she were dead, Anteros. What do you expect?" Sabine stared at the bright colored cloth that draped over the top of her canopy bed. It was vibrant, rich—every strand of pink and orange silk matched his sister's personality perfectly. "We should have snuck her out the day of the games. Or the night of the ball. So many wasted chances."

He locked in on a strand of orange fabric, and images of Talitha flashed through his mind. The pink ombré gown she had borrowed from Sabine for the games. The way the sunlight glinted off her hair. The emerald color of her ball gown that had made her hair stand out that much more. He remembered it all. He had relished every second of that evening because he'd gotten to spend it with her—even when she bit his lip and pushed him away.

Now, thoughts of her were still punishing him for every wrong decision they'd made.

He shook his head, ridding himself of painful memories and trying to refocus. He had come here for his sister. Sabine was the one who needed him right now. "What are you going to do, Sabine? Are you going to marry him? Or run away?"

Slowly, she sat up, resolve glittering in her eyes. "It would only bring Father joy to see me suffer. So I will marry the earl with a smile on my face. I'll be the most beautiful bride this infernal prison has ever seen. And then Father will no longer be my problem."

That was the Sabine he'd grown up with. Stubborn as they come.

But Anteros felt a wave of relief knowing she would stay. Running and hiding was incredibly risky, and he knew she would likely be miserable living in a brothel. "It's for the best. Ryker is a hound, but he's well off. You will be cared for. And if you give him an heir, I'm sure he will treat you like a queen for the rest of your life."

She wrinkled her nose, refusing to look at her brother. "You're not very comforting, brother."

A subdued chuckle escaped him, and Sabine stuck her tongue out. He would miss this. Being able to conspire together, to watch out for each other's backs. Comforting each other after their father's brutality left them feeling broken and downtrodden. The backs of his eyes stung as he thought about her leaving, and Anteros turned his attention to the bar cart in the corner of her room. The selection was pitiful in comparison to his own, only a bottle of Sabine's favorite red and some fruity-smelling white wine. Neither tickled his fancy.

"I shall have to write the Madam tomorrow," he muttered, more to himself than his sister. "I'll lose the sum I paid for a room and her silence, but that doesn't matter now. You're doing the right thing. The safe choice." The cadence of his voice lacked his usual confidence.

Blankets scrunched behind him, and Sabine's feet hit the floor hard. "What a stupid idea," she said. Rolling his eyes, he grabbed one of the glasses and began pouring the merlot into a glass. He picked it up and turned, nearly bumping into his sister, who had wrapped herself in a red silk robe as dark as the wine in his glass. She reached out and took the glass with a smug smile. "Thanks."

"That wasn't for you," Anteros grumbled, turning back toward the cart. He leaned both hands on the wall and hovered over the selection again. "Why don't you have anything good?"

Sabine snickered. "Because one glass at dinner usually suffices." She took a quiet sip before walking over to sit on the sofa.

"But not tonight?" He turned and frowned at her.

"Definitely not." Forsaking decorum, she chugged until her glass was empty. Then, to his surprise, she patted the seat to her left. Grabbing the merlot bottle by the neck, he reluctantly ambled over and sat beside her.

The silence stretched on, and Anteros waited for Sabine to break it. He could tell she had something more to say. Otherwise, she would have already banished him from her room. Her beauty sleep was important, after all.

Finally, she hummed pensively.

"Spit it out already, Sabine."

"If the Madam has already been paid, then your plan can still work," she said slowly, choosing her words with care. Tracing a finger around the rim of her glass, Sabine smiled in a way that spelled trouble. "We should use it for someone who is in far greater danger than I am."

Anteros blew out a breath, rested his elbows on his knees, and buried his face in his hands. He knew who she meant. *Talitha.* He couldn't speak her name aloud for fear his father might somehow discover his unchanged feelings. They had already learned the hard way that he had more eyes and ears within Graynor's walls than they ever imagined. "We can't."

She shoved his shoulder roughly, but he hardly budged. "Yes, we can! You said this would work."

"The plan was for you, not her," he argued, his voice rising an octave. "Do you really think she'd prefer to live in a brothel?"

"It cannot be worse than starving in the dark on the dungeon floor," Sabine snapped. She narrowed her eyes, scrutinizing him, trying to decipher his hesitation. Her glass clinked loudly against the nearest table as she slammed it down. "When it was my life on the line, did you not think this plan would work? That I could get there and remain hidden?"

Anteros couldn't look at her. He pressed his fist against his lips and considered the many variables in their way. Even when the plan was designated for Sabine, he had been uneasy, fearing what could happen if their father discovered their ploy, or if he found her hiding place. He couldn't bear the idea of his sister or other innocent people being brutalized because he had tried to make Sabine happy. It was a hefty risk, and one he did not take lightly. He was only willing to try because Sabine seemed desperate at the time.

Now, she was willing to placate their father and marry Ryker Umbryon.

Now, they did not need to risk anyone's life so she could have some semblance of freedom.

"I thought it would work, but no plan is without risks. You and I both know that to be true," the prince said firmly. Rising to his feet, Anteros gently put down her favorite bottle of wine on the table. His head was pounding after a long evening, and he was ready to nurse a glass of something strong before collapsing in his bed, alone with his fears and regrets.

Sabine leapt to her feet and grabbed his arm, her grip surprisingly firm. She rose up on her toes, but she was still comically short in comparison. Grabbing the front of his shirt, she yanked him down, forcing him to look her in the eyes. "Since when are you afraid to take a risk?"

Anteros brushed her hands off his shirt and stepped back. Turning toward the door, he paused, taking a deep breath. "What if something went wrong again?" His throat tightened with each whispered word. He couldn't bear to think about the consequences if Talitha were caught trying to escape.

He wouldn't be able to save her again.

A gentle hand squeezed his shoulder. "She is miserable here, Anteros. No one can thrive in the darkness." Sabine's hand slipped away, but her words repeated in his mind. *No one can thrive in the darkness.*

"It will kill me if something goes wrong," he whispered, turning to search her face. Anteros needed his sister to be the voice of reason. To think about the risks and whether they were worth it. To understand his hesitation.

A small but steady voice replied, "It will kill *her* if we don't try."

The weight of her statement settled in his heart, and he nodded. This place—the whole of Graynor Castle—was a prison. There was no hope for any of them to be happy under his father's rule. But being his prisoner was a death sentence. He had to somehow set her free.

Even if it meant he would never see the girl he loved again.

He owed her the chance to live in the light.

29

BED REST

When Commander Stanton called for an urgent meeting with the queen and council, Elara was hesitant to allow her husband to accompany her. Though she tried to dissuade him, Gerard insisted that he attend to offer his support.

Once seated around the great table in her conference room, Elara thanked everyone for gathering at such short notice and opened the floor to the commander to fill them in on the situation.

"Our spies say Rexton has begun mobilizing his troops, though their target is unconfirmed at this time," Alexander said. "We suspect they are preparing to march after the hoarfrost has passed."

Immediately, the council members erupted into whispers and outcries calling for reinforced measures to protect the citadel. Multiple scenarios flashed through Elara's mind. Her people cut down. Cities set on fire. Catapults launching. The wall that kept the refugees safe crumbling around them, leaving them defenseless. Her breath caught, hand coming to rest on her chest, as she leaned back in her seat.

"We knew this day would come," Alexander added. He looked upon his queen with sympathy.

She did not want his pity. She wanted options. A way to prevent the worst. "What can we do to stop them before they reach the citadel?" She looked between Alexander and the other council members, who all stared back, awaiting orders from her. These were the types of discussions Elara loathed. She had been raised to host balls and tea, not to run a kingdom and command its military.

"Should Rexton's men make the mistake of crossing the mountains, the dwarfs shall be the first in the fray," Rilura declared, one fist proudly pounding her chest. "I will write my father to warn them what may come. Know my people are always ready for a fight."

"Thank you. I know this is not the dwarfs' fight, but we are grateful for your aid in it," Elara replied, grateful to have the support of the dwarfs. But she knew that covered only one of the paths Antoine's men could take. He had control of the valley, the safest and easiest place for his men to cross the border.

Gerard reached over and squeezed her hand under the table. When she turned to him helplessly, her spiraling thoughts fell on difficult options. Did she call Serena and the guardians back to Symptee, despite the safety risk? Write to the King of the Eastern Isles and beg for them to send men to join their fight?

"What are your concerns?" Her husband gave an encouraging smile, nodding his head slightly, giving her permission to voice some options.

She took a deep breath, slow on the inhale and slower on the exhale, before speaking. "We will need greater numbers if they reach Symptee," the queen began. "Last I heard from Serena, Daephyra was not agreeable to lending her aid."

Alexander scoffed. "That was no surprise to any of us."

"Should I write to Boreas and Adrian? With the new treaty, perhaps they might lend military support?" As soon as she voiced it aloud, Elara knew it was a futile idea. Both Denorfia and the Eastern Isles wanted no part in this war. And asking Boreas for any sort of support would only result in hefty demands. She had already promised an engagement between her firstborn and one of his grandchildren. What more did she have to offer him?

Alexander stated what she already knew to be true. "Boreas is a fruitless avenue. He has never and will never elect to assist us. And as far as the Isles…" His gaze flicked toward Gerard, a silent question passing between them.

Gerard sighed, looking down at his lap. This time Elara leaned over and squeezed his hand. "We know the Islanders do not have a sizable military," she said. "They have helped so much through trade already."

"I will ask my uncle if there is anything more they can do," he replied, cutting her off.

While she appreciated the offer, she did not want him to feel pressured to ask. This was her people's fight, not his. Their strengths lay on the sea, while the Hyrosencians' fight was on land. No ship of soldiers could offer them protection.

"The number of guards in Symptee has risen in the past five years," Commander Jacob Maynard noted. Elara gave him a pitying look, for they both knew the recruits hired from the Guard Tournament were few and far between. They were young and well-trained, but most of them had never seen a real battle. She wished she could keep it that way. The guards who had come over initially were growing old, their reflexes not what they once were, and even if the whole of human refugees in Envyre were to take up swords and shields, their numbers would hardly eclipse that of Antoine's.

Turning back toward the commander, Elara asked, "What did John have to say about their numbers?"

"The rebellion is in the hundreds, though most remain underground or in their own dwellings. I think it is best they remain hidden until Serena is ready. She shall need all the help she can to siege Graynor," Alexander said.

Serena. When she would be ready, no one could guess. Elara had promised the girl she would not send her into battle until she was ready—and she had meant to keep that promise. But if Antoine was preparing to march on Symptee, how much longer could they hold off this war?

"You've spoken to the girl. How fares her training?" Commander Chester Moorfield asked. He scratched his auburn beard, a gleam of hope in his eyes as he stared at the queen.

Elara sighed. "She feels confident in her abilities with a sword, but I would be weary to send her into battle just yet. Her training has not made a year. She's young. She still has so much to learn. Strategy, giving commands…"

"But we are running out of time," Maynard declared, pounding a fist against the table. The wooden legs clattered against the floor, making everyone jump, leaning back in their chairs.

Gerard and Alexander reached out to stabilize the table, scowling at Maynard's outburst. "What would you suggest then?" Alexander snapped.

"Bring the heir back to the citadel, where she belongs," Maynard answered, gesturing about the room with a broad swoop of his arm. "Envyre may be able to teach her weapons, but it is us, the men at this table, the men who have seen bloodshed and know the depths of battle, who should be teaching the rest."

"No," Elara replied swiftly, rising to her feet. Her chair fell back, banging against the floor, as she leaned both hands on the table, teeth bared at the old men who dared question her. "Symptee is not safe. It is a prison within walls. If Antoine were to take the outer wall, there would be no way to protect her, or *any of us*. If Serena dies in the first battle, we are all dead, and Hyrosencia will be lost forever."

The council and her husband stared in shock. Some lowered their eyes to the table knowing she was right. Bringing Serena back was too much of a risk if Antoine might send men to their walls.

Without warning, a wave of pressure rolled through Elara's stomach, and she hunched over, clutching her swollen belly. A stunned gasp escaped her lips as her husband's arms grasped her hips from behind. "Elara? What's wrong?"

She nodded as spots clouded her vision, and then she was weightless. Her legs came out from under her, and she tumbled into the darkness, all thoughts and feelings fading into nothingness.

In her chambers, Elara blinked awake, finding herself enrobed in the warm blankets of her own bed. Several people huddled around the bed whispering until a familiar hush silenced them. As the queen tried to sit up, arms reached out to support her from both sides of the bed.

"Easy, Your Majesty," Ismenia said, shifting pillows behind the queen's back. "Best you stay right where you are."

Gerard perched on the edge of the bed beside her, one hand smoothing the damp hair from her forehead. "How are you feeling?"

Her chest felt constricted by some invisible weight, her breaths coming quickly. Too quickly. She tried to inhale deeply, more slowly, but her body fought against her. Even her abdomen felt strange, an uncomfortable tightness starting in the middle and spreading down. "My chest… and my stomach." She cupped a hand under her belly and inhaled sharply.

"Your body is in distress. You have not been resting enough," Ismenia scolded.

The physician, Eamon, stepped forward. Cold fingers pressed into her abdomen as he hummed thoughtfully. "And you are quite sure of when the babe was conceived?" He leveled her with a questioning look, leaning forward to look at her through bushy brows.

"Yes," Elara and Ismenia both growled.

"It's far too early for the baby to come," Gerard said, concern etched in his darkened features. "Is there any way to stop her from an early labor?"

The physician's frigid fingers made their way to the queen's neck. After a moment, Eamon shook his head in displeasure. "Her Majesty must stay off of her feet," he began. "That is a strict order, not a request." He shuffled back from the bed, and the herbalist slipped back to Elara's side.

Ismenia nodded in agreement. "There is only so much that can be done. No strenuous activities whatsoever." She looked up, fixing Gerard with a stern expression.

"Understood," her husband replied. His thumb rubbed soothing circles on the back of her hand.

Elara sighed, sinking further into her pillows. She was tired, more than usual, but she did not know how to rest. The last time she had taken to bed rest, she had lost something quite precious, and she couldn't bear to think of it happening again.

Turning from the bedside table, Ismenia lifted a glass of water to the queen's lips and said, "Drink."

Elara struggled to push herself upright, croaking hoarsely, "Might there be a remedy… some special tea that might alleviate… this?" She gestured from her chest to her abdomen.

Her friend shook her head. "We can certainly make tea to calm the nerves, but as far as your symptoms, the only way to manage it will be bed rest. No more council meetings, no meeting with refugees, and *absolutely no outdoor tea* for the foreseeable future." The herbalist looked down her sharp nose at the queen, her deep brown eyes full of warning. Then her friend ushered the rest of their party out of her bedchamber, insisting everyone leave her to rest. "I'll return shortly with tea."

Alone with her husband, the queen's chest constricted again. "How will I rule from this bed? There are discussions to be had, decisions to be made," Elara moaned, covering her face with her free hand.

Gerard shifted to stand up. "For the time being, the council can rule in your place."

If she made a poor judgment, Elara had learned to live with it as queen, but if others made mistakes while she was incapable of ruling, she feared that burden would weigh even more. "But they would bring Serena back," she argued, trying to sit up straighter. Tears pricked her eyes, hot and angry at the total loss of control—over her kingdom and her physical well-being.

Gerard reached out, gently pressing her shoulders back into the pillows. "With your permission, I will sit in your stead," her husband continued. "I will ensure your wishes are respected." He stroked her hair, and she closed her eyes, struggling to allow his words to bring her an inkling of comfort.

The silk caressing her body felt heavy, the sheets threatening to pull her back into a deep slumber. She shoved them back, itching to feel the cool tile against the bottom of her feet, the breeze against her face. Anything to relieve the buzzing energy stirring within her. Staying in this bed would drive her mad.

"Elara!" Her husband grabbed her arm, but she slipped out of his hold, her feet hitting the floor and bolting for the balcony. Gerard cleared the end of their bed, quickly closing the distance between them with broad steps. "Elara, the physician said bed rest!"

"I'm fine! I just need some fresh air," she shrieked, throwing the doors open haphazardly. As cool, fresh air hit her face, she inhaled deeply—but the moment was interrupted by her husband wrapping both arms around her waist and hoisting her off the floor. "Put me down!"

"No!" Gerard dragged her kicking and clawing across the room before carefully depositing her back into their bed. "They said bed rest—not quarantine. You must stay put!"

The queen pounded her fists against the silk covers and growled in frustration. "I hate this! I am the queen. I cannot give up now. My people need me!"

"I need you!" her husband roared, leaning a hand on each side of her body, hot breath hitting her face.

Elara froze, leaning back on her arms in shock. He had never raised his voice at her—not like this. This time, he was more than concerned. More than just angry. Gone was his usual calming presence, replaced by a desperate man who was done fighting for control in his marriage. His blue eyes threatened to drown her in their rough waves, and she knew she had crossed the line.

He took a deep breath, his eyes closing as he leaned forward, shadows overtaking his features as he lowered his chin. "I did not want to do this," he whispered, the cold desperation in his voice sending a chill down her spine. *Do what?*

Her husband rose, unable to look at her any longer. Making his way over to the nightstand on his side of the bed, Gerard pulled open the top drawer and reached inside. A haggard exhale escaped him as he removed an item, his body blocking her view of it.

Elara tensed, an overwhelming feeling of dread swelling in her chest. "Gerard? What do you have?"

When he finally turned to face her, she zeroed in on leather straps resting in his palms. Her breathing quickened, and she shrank away from him. "Are you going to beat me? Is this what we've come to?" Scanning the room, she wondered if she might be able to reach the servant's entrance before he could reach her.

"Don't," his deep voice demanded. As he took a tentative step toward her, his gaze softened, and he added, "You know I would never hurt you, Elara. I love you."

But his words felt cold, detached, rehearsed. They were missing the affection he once held for her. "Do you love me? Or do you only care about your child?" The harshness in her question made him flinch.

He came closer to the bed and started unraveling the leather strap in his hands. It was a few feet long with a loop attached to a metal contraption at the end. "I have always meant every word I said to you. My intentions were always pure," Gerard said, coming around to her side of the bed. He leveled her with an intense gaze, remorseful eyes peering down at her through thick, dark lashes. "I will love and protect you every moment until I take my dying breath, even if you hate me for it. I cannot sit by and watch as your crown puts you in an early grave." Then he turned away and tied one end of the strap to the nearest post on their bed.

"You cannot do this," Elara whispered. Her voice was half-shock, half-plea, willing her husband to take pity on her in this fragile state. "Ismenia, Alexander... They will never allow it."

There was a shuffling at the door, and she turned wide-eyed to see Ismenia and Idonea approaching her bed. "Actually, the strap was my idea," the herbalist said regretfully, setting a piping cup of tea down on her bedside table. "And everyone is aware of the situation. Your physician made it clear to the council how dangerous it would be for you to continue under such stress, so we all agreed."

"There will be no order in Hyrosencia, no hope for our people, if you are lost," Idonea added, her voice low and rich. She looked upon the queen with pity. "This is for the good of everyone."

The queen sobbed as Gerard took her shaking hand in his, her vision overtaken by a wave of tears she could not fight off. He gently folded a silk pocket square over her wrist before clasping the leather loop around it and checking that she could not wriggle her hand out. Her husband, her council, her closest allies—they had all turned on her. With one hand tied to her bed, she was nothing more than a prisoner in her own chambers. A purposeless body trapped in her own home. She was no longer queen. She was but a vessel in name, an image of hope they were desperate to keep alive, even if it meant taking her crown and the last shreds of her dignity with it.

"I will never forgive you for this," she murmured. The bitterness in her words was not lost on any of them as they avoided her tear-streaked face.

Ismenia exhaled and lifted the steaming cup of tea, no emotion to her usually uplifting demeanor as she asked, "Would you still like some tea, Your Majesty? It will help calm your nerves."

Elara scoffed, sniffling as she swiped the back of her unhindered hand over her wet cheeks. She hated all of them for what they were doing to her. For taking away her choice. But she nodded and inhaled slowly, trying to calm her pounding heart. She had lost control for now, so she would patiently comply until the birth of their child.

Once her child entered the world, she would take back control of the citadel.

And then, Elara Garrick would make them rue the day they shackled their queen.

30

OLD FLAMES

For nearly a month, they had lived within the walls of Envyre, safeguarded by the Elf Queen's guards, training, sleeping, and mingling with the Academy students and other Hyrosencian refugees. Not a toe stepped out of line, though they never allowed Serena to wander around alone. Everyone was friendly and eager to help the newest arrivals acclimate. It was comforting, being back in Envyre after years away, and the guardians basked in the warmth of their old friends, both elf and human, whom they had missed. This place was far more home to Crystal than the capital had ever been.

Keeping Serena's identity confidential—save for her personal guardian squad—was the best decision for the time being. The human princess was eager to show off her sword skills and learn as many other skills as possible during their time in Envyre. She was hopeful that training alongside the students would help win them over to her side when it was time to go to battle against Rexton. They would need all the help they could get without Queen Daephyra's army.

In the evenings when the younger students had completed their lessons for the day, Crystal, Madeline, and Serena headed out to the training facilities and staked their claim on the archery equipment. Serena, though quite eager to learn, still fumbled with the robust weapon, her hands not picking up the hold of a bow as naturally as a sword. Crystal assured her that this skill was unnecessary for her arsenal, but Madeline insisted anyone could be taught. They butted heads often, but the elf didn't mind. It reminded her of their rivalry back when they had both been students.

Besides, Crystal knew she would always be the best shot.

When the sun had descended beneath the bushy tree line, Crystal wiped the sweat from her brow on her shirt sleeve and smiled. Though an autumn breeze had overtaken

235

the air in Ord Metsiilva, it was still hot when the sun beat down on their backs. The evening shade was a welcome reprieve.

Serena loosed another arrow, and it actually flew forward for the first time that day, going higher and farther than her previous attempts. Though the arrow ricocheted off the top of the target, it was progress. She had to master holding the bow before she could master her aim. "Nice work," Crystal said, patting her ward on the back. "Perhaps by tomorrow, it'll stick on the target."

"Tomorrow? I'll bet she sticks it on the next shot," Madeline wagered. She grinned as she passed another arrow to Serena, who swallowed nervously.

Serena knocked the arrow and hesitated, glancing over her left shoulder at the elf. "Any advice?"

The guardian hummed, stepping forward to inspect the girl's posture. Wordlessly, she used her hands to help Serena straighten her spine and lift her chin, then moved her hand positioning closer to her face. "There. Take a deep breath, hold steady, and release on the exhale."

Serena did as she was told, and her arrow flew true, remaining perfectly parallel to the ground until it embedded in the upper right side of the wooden target. "I did it," the girl breathed, staring at the feathered end of her arrow in awe.

"Nicely done," Ilrune said, his deep voice carrying across the ground from the main building. A small group of their friends approached. Among them were Rigel, Gideon and his younger brother Malachi, Carissa, and siblings Declan and Gemma Fledger, the children of one of Elara's guards who had recently passed away. They were new to the Academy, having only arrived a few months prior to Serena, and they loved watching the older students practice. Trailing behind them were Cole with his arm draped lazily over Xandra's shoulders and Cyrus hand-in-hand with Emilia. The influx of people meant it must have been dinnertime already.

Crystal tried to hide her smile when Xandra skipped over to them, pointing at the target. "Is that yours, Serena?"

Madeline snorted. "Well, it certainly isn't ours." They laughed as she went over and yanked the arrow out of the wood, examining the tip. Still in good condition, she added it back to the pile near Serena. "Dinnertime already?"

"Almost," Rigel replied. "The captain has an announcement to make, so they've asked everyone to gather early."

That didn't sound good. Either new refugees had arrived unexpectedly, or the captain had received news from the citadel.

They quickly collected the practice weapons they had used and returned them to the weaponry for safekeeping before heading to the dining hall. Nearly 200 bodies of all shapes, sizes, and ages filled in the bench seats, most smiling and chattering away excitedly. For some reason, everyone there loved it when new people arrived.

Everyone except Crystal.

She was on high alert, watchful eyes scanning the crowd for unfamiliar faces. She had to know where they were, who they were talking to, and how close they were to Serena, who sat on her right. Though her identity was not public knowledge, she had announced it to the new guardians and a ship full of pirates mere weeks ago. They could never be too cautious when it came to her safety.

"Relax," Rigel said as he slid onto the seat beside her. His deep voice and proximity sent a shiver down her spine, and she wished she knew how to be at ease the way he usually was.

Peering to her left, Crystal noticed that Carissa had seated herself on the other side of Rigel. She had been obnoxiously clingy since their arrival, and it irked the guardian that she could not have a simple conversation with her comrade without an extra set of ears nearby.

Once all of the students, refugees, and off-duty guards had found a seat, Captain Smedley called for everyone to pipe down. It was then that Crystal realized a few familiar faces stood behind him. Ilrune gave her a thumbs up as she stared in horror at her betrothed. When Deldrach spotted her, a broad smile spread across his face, and he lifted his wrist, giving a casual wave.

That's when Captain Smedley broke the news. "We've had an influx of new and returning faces over the past few weeks, so we wanted to make sure everyone is aware and welcoming. This is Deldrach Erlamin, cousin to a guard you're all familiar with, Rune. Deldrach is a graduate of the Academy who has worked in Queen Daephyra's service as a guard for a few years now. He was granted a transfer to Envyre to be closer to his fiancée, Crystal Windaef, who recently accompanied new refugees from Symptee."

Her face burned as she sunk lower in her seat, feeling a dozen eyes snap to her as all of their friends started whispering to each other.

So much for keeping that a secret.

Once the captain was done addressing changes to the guard schedule, Ilrune and Deldrach approached their table. Emilia motioned for Cyrus to scooch over so the elves could sit across from Crystal. While Ilrune slipped gracefully into the seat across from her, Deldrach took the long way around the table, sauntering up behind her. Warmth spread through her back as his hand skimmed gently over her shoulder, and he asked Rigel, "Mind if I squeeze in by my lady?"

The guardian glowered as the people to his left moved over, wordlessly making space for the broad-shouldered elf. Rigel reluctantly slid away from his friend, opening a space for Deldrach to slip between them. His raven hair cascaded down his back, shiny in the sunset light coming in the windows. A tan arm leaned casually on the tabletop, his pointer finger gently brushing against her long sleeve. Crystal yanked her hands into her lap, avoiding his gaze.

Serena leaned around her and welcomed him. "I'm sorry to have kept her away for so long," she said sheepishly, giving Crystal a wink. The guardian's stomach flipped, realizing she had left Serena completely in the dark about the situation. She would have to confess the truth eventually.

Deldrach snaked an arm around Crystal and dragged her shoulder into his side. It was a gentle, light-hearted gesture that anyone else would not have minded from their betrothed. But for Crystal, the unwarranted touch set her body aflame—and not in the way it did for others. She wanted to push him away, to get up and leave the table, to pack her bag and leave town.

But she couldn't just leave Serena and the other guardians.

She had a job to do.

So she quietly tolerated every gentle caress throughout dinner, thankful for a reprieve from his gushing while they ate.

Serena excused herself from the table, taking both of their empty trays with her. Her friend struggled to return a cheery smile as she thanked her.

A giddy shriek from down the table drew her attention. Xandra and Emilia were admiring each other's rings, giggling, and cavorting about wedding plans. Apparently, Cyrus had also recently proposed to Emilia, though they had yet to set a date. "I'm thinking springtime. Pink and yellow flowers." Cyrus groaned, mumbling about hating pink.

Xandra chuckled. "I don't think I could manage to wait that long. I'd like to have it done as soon as possible," she said, turning and giving Cole a less-than-subtle wink.

He grinned and pecked her on the cheek. "Perhaps after the solstice?" It was a cherished time for the Silveryl Clan to gather with family and friends, resting and exchanging small tokens of affection during the hardest days of winter.

"I am eager to set a date as well," Deldrach chimed in, reaching under the table to grasp Crystal's hand. She coughed, reaching for her glass and chugging water desperately. "Now that you've returned, we can finally start planning."

Rigel blew out a breath, rising to his feet. Standing, Crystal realized he looked agitated, his brow knitted tightly. "Air's crisp tonight. How about a bonfire?" He nodded at Gideon and Kieran, who were sitting one table over with Gideon's brother Malachi and his friends. The boys' faces lit up, and they all rose from their benches.

"I'll make a run to the market!" Gideon called out, already on his merry way for the door. Half of their friends got up, chatting excitedly as they headed for the door. Rigel slung an arm around Carissa's shoulders on their way, briefly glancing over his shoulder at Crys.

If this bonfire was going to be anything like their gatherings back when they were students, Crystal planned to keep Serena far away from it. Luckily, it was her night for guard duty.

Serena.

Her head whipped around with the sudden realization that her ward had vanished. "Blazing embers!" The elf planted both palms on the table and shoved herself onto her feet. "Serena's wandered off."

Xandra and Cole hardly batted an eye at her outburst. "It's not her first day here. She knows the area. She'll be fine. It's still daylight, and there are people all over," Xandra said. She stood, picked up her tray, and headed for the dish rack with Cole following close behind.

Deldrach stroked her arm supportively. "Why are you so worried about her?"
She scoffed. "You don't understand."

"Then make me understand. Tell me why she's so important to you," her betrothed said, his voice rising an octave.

"I saved her life. More than once. I will not let her die on my watch," she snapped in reply.

Ilrune cleared his throat, snapping them out of the weird exchange. Crystal swung each leg over the bench seat and stormed for the exit, not bothering to bid them good-bye. She knew she would inevitably see them both again tomorrow.

Outside, the sun began to sink behind the tree line. Orange and pink streaked the skyline, fading into each other and becoming deeper and darker blue as she looked up at the barely speckled sky. The stars were always so bright from Ord Metsiilva, appearing before the sun completely disappeared below the earth. If she knew Serena, the girl would be somewhere with a good view, watching the day fade into another glorious night.

Gravel crunched beneath her boots as she headed toward the housing area. The autumn wind took hold of her loose hair, whipping it around her face and neck. It was refreshing, yet the guardian couldn't stop to enjoy her favorite season. Not with Serena missing.

Luckily, it did not take long to find her. She was tangled up in William Burroughs' arms on her little front porch, oblivious to the people grinning and pointing as they passed the house. Will leaned her back on the cushioned bench, his lips making quick work of hers as if they were on borrowed time.

Crystal grimaced. She almost hated interrupting them, but after a few more minutes, she could no longer bear to watch their tongues intermingle. "Hey," she called loudly, bounding up the four steps to Serena's porch.

The disheveled couple flung themselves into a seated position faster than Crystal had ever seen. Will rubbed the back of his neck as Serena cleared her throat, brushing messy curls behind her ears and avoiding the guardian's gaze.

"Hey," the girl stuttered. "You're on guard tonight?"

"Mhmm." Zeroing in on Serena, the elf added, "Next time, at least tell me where you're going."

Will stood abruptly. "Guess I should bid you good night then." He took Serena's hand and brushed his lips over her knuckles, causing her blush to deepen. "Sleep well, sweetheart. I love you."

"I love you, too." Serena stood and gave him a final, chaste kiss before he made his way toward the steps.

"Some of the guys will be in the east field being idiots, if you want to join them," Crystal said as the boy from Durmak plodded past her.

Serena crossed her arms over her chest and scowled. "And we aren't joining them?"

"No, we're not. You need your rest. Sword skills with Cole bright and early tomorrow," the guardian said. Serena groaned loudly, burying her face in her hands. Crystal turned the doorknob and entered the house first, making quick work of checking every nook and cranny in the small space. Finally satisfied, Crystal turned both locks on the front door, sealing them safely inside.

Two light raps, a pause, and then two more.

That was her sign that Xandra was there to relieve her from guard duty. Crystal stood and stretched her arms overhead on her way to unlock the door. It was shortly after dawn. Early morning light flooded into Serena's sitting room through one large window—the one Crystal had sat in front of all night.

"Good morn," Xandra greeted, pulling her friend in for a quick hug.

Normally, Crystal was not one for physical affection, but after a long night alone with her thoughts and little sleep, she sank into the comfort of her friend's arms. "Mornin'."

"Quiet night?" The human guardian walked over to the sofa and perched on one end. She was lucky to have the day shift this time. Being able to sleep in one's own bed was a luxury Crystal did not take for granted.

"Quiet as it could be with those drunken idiots crowing in the streets. I don't know how they didn't wake Serena," Crystal replied, rubbing circles on her temples. She looked forward to burying herself under a mound of blankets and getting some sleep.

Her friend tried to hide her smile. "Just like old times, isn't it? Being back here?"

The elf cracked her neck, pushing a thin curtain aside to peer out the window. A dozen students merged in the street, heading toward the dining hall before their early lessons. "Almost. Except I never intentionally stayed up all night." They exchanged a knowing grin, eyes flicking toward Serena's bedroom door. Then a loud noise burbled from Crystal's hollow stomach. She considered joining the early birds to breakfast after a long night with only tea and mixed nuts to munch on. After a few years at the Academy, she enjoyed having three warm meals a day with her peers. They were more than just students or friends.

They were like a family.

A *real* family.

"You should go eat," Xandra said, resting a hand on her friend's shoulder. "Once Serena's up, we'll be doing the same."

A shuffling noise came from the bedroom, and Crystal sighed, her hand flying to the dagger attached at her hip. "Serena, you awake?"

"Yes," came the girl's sleepy, irritated reply.

"Go. I've got things from here," her friend insisted. Grabbing her by the shoulders, Xandra steered the elf for the front door and practically pushed her out onto the porch.

Taking the steps sluggishly, Crystal headed toward the dining hall, hoping they would have some spiced porridge, jerky, and fresh juice to replenish her weary muscles. She passed by several houses, tracing the initials on each door in her mind.

First was CW and XS–her and Xandra's new home.

The next one said MM and JD for Madeline Milliorva and her little knife-throwing protégé, Juniper Drayton. They were certainly the odd pair.

The third house was marked with EA and CR for Emilia Ashbourne and Carissa Rycroft.

Before she passed the house, the front door creaked open, and she glanced up, wondering if the girls were off to an early breakfast. The porch was shrouded in shadows, the sun coming up behind the houses, and it took a moment for her eyes to adjust. Slowly, a man's bare chest came into focus. At first, she assumed it was Cyrus, Emilia's fiancé, and she turned back toward the road, uninterested in chatting with the underdressed human.

Then he stepped into the light. The sun coming through the trees reflected off his orange hair. He got about halfway down the stairs before he noticed her. There, he froze in place.

"Crys," Rigel breathed, his voice gruff. He cleared his throat, tossed the shirt in his hands over one shoulder, and stared.

She paused in the road, eyes widening as she realized which house he was leaving. Her brows lifted as she asked, "Had fun last night?"

He rubbed the back of his neck, unable to look her in the face. "Uh, sure."

The elf scoffed loudly. "I didn't expect you to go falling back into old habits the second we got to Envyre." She nodded at the house. "You haven't mentioned that girl in over a year."

"It's Carissa. You know her. And I don't have to answer to you. You're not my mother," Rigel argued, crossing his arms over his chest.

"I'm not trying to be," she snapped back, taking two steps closer to the porch.

He glanced over his shoulder at the house, and she wondered if he had snuck out before Carissa woke. "You may not like physical affection, Crys, but some of us crave it. I know you don't understand, but not everyone wants to spend their life alone."

She swallowed down the lump rising up her throat. She didn't want to be alone. She didn't want any of them to be. She just couldn't understand how humans craved the flesh with such blind desperation.

"So, what? Did you realize you missed her when we got back?" Crystal asked quietly. "Do you love her?" When Xandra had asked her the same, she knew immediately the answer had been no. She had never been in love—not with Deldrach or any other.

He ran both hands through his messy hair before taking a seat on the second to last step. Perching his chin on his clasped hands, he whispered, "I don't know, Crys. I didn't plan any of this. We were drinking, and it just happened."

She nodded, though she did not understand. "You'd better figure yourself out, or you're going to break her heart all over again. And I won't feel a shred of sympathy for you."

"Why do you even care? You never did before," he replied, wringing his tunic in his fists. Those bright eyes, full of hope and expectation, searched her face, unable to find what he was looking for. "Are you jealous?"

The elf barked a laugh, bending over and leaning her hands on her knees. "Of course not." Her body ached, her muscles screaming for food and rest. There was no point prolonging this fight. He was a grown man. He could do whatever he wanted. *Whoever* he wanted. "I'm just worried you're not thinking clearly. You're my comrade. Don't forget why we're here."

"I haven't forgotten anything." A small group of Elven guards passed them in the street. Rigel lifted a hand in greeting, watching until they were two houses away. "Since we're giving friendly advice, I should remind you that you have your own mess to handle with tall, dark, and cheery. Perhaps you should worry less about who I'm bedding and more about your impending wedding."

Her cheeks burned as she stared at him, feeling as though he had slapped her. The reality was that he spoke the truth. She did have her own mess to handle, and Rigel's discretions had no impact on her own situation. Nodding slightly, she turned on her heels and walked back in the direction of her own house, no longer feeling hungry.

31

WHERE THE RED LEAVES SCATTER

Anteros tucked a tightly folded cloak inside his suit jacket and peered at his reflection in the mirror. He had donned his best black suit with gold epaulets for the special occasion—his sister's formal engagement dinner. Raven hair slicked back and face razed smooth, he was the picture of a perfect prince on the outside, but his nerves were in shambles.

His palms were sweating, and he wiped them on a handkerchief, discarding the soggy pocket square on his bed for another one. The castle was humming with excitement for Sabine's wedding. Graynor Court had yet to see a royal wedding in the past 18 years, Antoine having wed Chelsea in private due to her delicate condition at the time.

Sabine had assured him this would be the perfect night. She had chosen a lavish gown made of mauve silk with several ruffled layers to the skirt—the more volume, the easier to keep Ryker Umbryon at arm's length. As usual, Sabine intended to have all eyes on her throughout the event, giving her brother the opportunity to do something absolutely mad.

Leaving his chambers, he took the stairs down to the main floor two at a time, a bottle of his favorite red wine gripped tight in one hand. His hands trembled slightly, but he tightened his fists, determined to follow the plan they had concocted over the past few days. This was their only chance to do the right thing, according to Sabine. There would not be a more opportune moment.

The plan had to work.

Anteros peered up and down the halls, ever cautious as he made his way through the labyrinth of Graynor Castle until he reached the correct wing. The halls were dark and quiet. No servants passed him as he stood in the doorway, staring down the spiral staircase as if he were facing the darkest depths of his father's soul. The darkness threatened to pull him under, and he took a small step back, willing the shadows to release their hold on his throat.

The bottle nearly slipped out of his hand, and he fumbled to catch it with both hands. That would have ruined everything. He took a deep breath, closed his eyes, and focused on steadying his heartbeat. There wasn't a dragon waiting at the bottom. Just four idiot guards and a girl that he would do anything to save.

Even risk his own life.

The prince pulled a crumpled handkerchief from his pants pocket and dabbed it against his temples. Talitha was down there. This wasn't the time to hesitate. It was time to stop living in his father's shadows. Time to finally keep his promise to Talitha.

So, into the darkness he descended.

When he reached the guards, Anteros held his head as high as he could muster, trying to draw upon the confidence his father had spent seventeen years instilling in him as heir to the throne. Tonight, these men were nothing but obstacles, and he would not feel guilt for removing them from his path.

The guards fell in line, greeting him with surprised faces. "Big night tonight, Your Highness. Shouldn't you be getting to the ballroom?" one guard asked.

Anteros' head snapped in the man's direction. "It is an important night, gentlemen. That's why my father has sent me on rounds to ensure the castle and grounds are secure." The guards nodded, none daring to question his reasoning. Relaxing his stance, Anteros held up the bottle in both hands and added, "We all know night duty in the dungeon is the worst assignment. Thought I'd bring a little something to help ease your boredom tonight."

The guards glanced between each other hesitantly. Anteros held the bottle out to the nearest one, who reluctantly took it from him. "We aren't allowed to drink on the job."

The prince scoffed. "I've seen plenty of bottles make their way down here. Don't act like you've never broken the rules." The men shrugged, none agreeing with or denying his bluff. As he expected. "One bottle between four of you should not a drunk man make. The cells are locked, the prisoners are sleeping. There's not much else for you to do down here."

The guard on the end eyed him suspiciously. He recognized the man—Emmaline's elder brother. He'd been on Sabine's payroll for months, helping her to secretly visit Talitha. Sabine had told him to take this shift and do whatever Anteros asked. He could only hope the man would comply. "You," he pointed at the guard. "Walk with me." The guard took the key ring from one of his comrades and led Anteros down the barely-lit hallway.

Anteros walked slowly, hands clasped behind his back. There was almost an hour until Sabine's engagement celebration would begin. An hour to get in and out unseen.

A cork popped behind him, making the hairs on the back of his neck stand up. The other three guards snickered as they started passing around the laced bottle of wine. In twenty minutes, they'd all be fast asleep.

He could only hope his father wouldn't execute them all when the truth finally came out.

They peered between the bars of each cell, making sure the prisoners who were supposed to be locked up were still alive and secured. When they finally reached Talitha's cell, Anteros motioned for the guard to unlock it. The rusty hinges creaked as he swung the door open, and his gaze fell upon Talitha, laying on the ground with her feet still shackled to the wall. His chest ached at the sight of her, a willowy heap of filthy limbs huddled on the ground.

Blue-gray eyes met his, unblinking in the dark as she waited. He wondered if she could see who stood there or if she was too withered away to care. Stepping toward her slowly, Anteros held up both palms and said, "Hey, Red. Miss me?"

She perked up a bit, pushing her head off the ground to look at him upright. "Anteros?" Matted hair clung to the side of her face where she'd laid on the ground. He fought the urge to reach out and brush it back with his palm.

"Yes, it's me." He crouched beside her, using the keys to unlock the heavy shackles from her ankles. Once freed, the metal plunked onto the floor. Her skin was red and blistered, rubbed raw in some places, and she winced in pain. "It's time to go. Can you stand?"

"Go?" The fear in her voice matched the horror in her eyes as she grabbed his arm. Her grip was terribly weak, and he feared she was too malnourished to walk out of there. "Am I to be executed?"

Anteros shook his head swiftly. He had made many mistakes with her, hurt her with his own two hands, but he could not deliver her to a swift execution. "No, love. We have something else in mind tonight."

Her hand slipped from his arm, and she leaned her head back against the wall. "I can't." Her voice broke, the hoarse sound barely understandable.

Taking her thin hands within his, Anteros nodded gently. "You deserve to watch the sun set from the surface." Tears sprang to her eyes, leaving streaks through the grime on her cheeks. She was right to be afraid. He, too, was terrified. Although the plan sounded foolproof, there were many variables to consider. If one person saw them and reported it, they were done for.

Anteros shifted his hands underneath her armpits to help her onto her feet. She wobbled at first, reaching for him and the wall to stabilize herself. The bones stuck out under her thin skin; her flesh had taken on a pale, gray tone from so long spent underground. Just the sight made Anteros' stomach turn. He had done this to her. He'd been so blinded by his guilt that he'd allowed her to starve.

But staying away only protected himself.

He shifted one arm behind Talitha's back and leaned closer, feeling her tense in his arms. "After I hurt you, I allowed my shame to drag me into the abyss. I thought you were better off if I stayed away… but I was wrong," he whispered near her ear, a slight tremor to his voice. His fingers skated over her cheek in a featherlight touch, brushing hair behind her ear. "Your suffering ends today. I promise."

Talitha trembled, clinging to him as though his promise might give her the strength to stand. She rested her head on his shoulder and shuddered. "Are you certain?" Her voice was faint as the early autumn breeze, sending a chill down his spine. All he could do was nod.

The guard behind them cleared his throat and tossed his head in the direction of the entrance. "Whatever you gave them worked." The prince sighed in relief.

When Talitha lifted her head, she pulled away, and he tried to give her space, his hands slipping back to his sides. "You did something to the guards?" She eyed the one at her cell door wearily.

"The right herbs crushed up in a glass of wine can put anyone down—even a bear," Anteros replied, a smirk tugging at his lips. Though she did not return his smile, he was pleased to see some relief in her stormy gaze. "Let's get out of here." He held one hand out to her and waited.

She nodded, hesitantly placing her hand in his, and allowed him to lead her into the hallway. Two prisoners—a shirtless older man and a bosomy woman—both reached out through the bars on their cells, begging for help. Anteros didn't turn his head, focusing on the dim torchlight where the hall met the staircase. Sprawled out on the ground were three sleeping guards, one of whom was snoring quite loudly.

The first part of the plan had worked.

Talitha ogled the staircase, shadows of dread overtaking her sallow features as she placed a feeble hand on the railing. Raised goosebumps peppered her bare arms. Anteros clenched his jaw and pulled the black cloak out of his jacket pocket, unrolling it and drawing it over her shoulders. "Here." She nodded as he lifted the hood to hide her vibrant hair. As she turned back toward the staircase, he stepped closer to her back, quickly scooping her up in his arms before she could hurt herself further.

She gasped, gripping his jacket sleeve in terror. "What are you doing?"

Just trust me. Please.

The prince adjusted his hold on her. "I'm carrying you." Her cracked lips parted, and he stared at them, tempted to lean in and kiss her before she could protest, but he knew that would only scare her, so he simply murmured, "Hold onto me. I've got you."

You're safe with me.

How he wished they could both believe that.

But he had proven time and again that he was not to be trusted. Not even the people he cared for the most were safe. He was Antoine Rexton's only son. Heir to a stolen throne bathed in blood. There was no escaping what coursed through his very blood. He was cursed to be a villain from the moment he was born.

She turned toward him slightly and wrapped her arms around his neck. When her frigid fingers brushed his bare skin, Anteros sucked in a sharp breath. Their faces were a breath apart, and they studied each other as though it were the first and last time they would ever be this close. When her blue-gray eyes brimmed with tears, he looked away.

A heavy clunk behind them made Talitha jump, and Anteros tightened his grip. Turning, they found the guard who had helped them had plopped on the ground among his comrades. In his hands was the near-empty bottle of wine Anteros had brought. Nodding his head, he brought the mouth of the bottle to his lips and finished it off.

"Thank you," Anteros said, nodding at the guard before he started his slow ascent upstairs. He would have thought carrying a young lady upstairs would be difficult, but Talitha was weightless compared to the last time he had lifted her, when they had danced at the Solstice ball. She was all edges now—a bony, broken fragment of the girl he met months ago.

And it was his fault.

When they reached the top, Anteros glanced each way down the hall. Finding it was still empty, he started for the nearest path to the far side of the castle.

"Anteros," she murmured, her lips tickling his neck.

Instinctively, he nuzzled closer. "I've got you." The words were more of a comfort to himself than he had intended. After so much time spent apart, he had her. Held her close as he could manage because their time was limited. Their opening to get her off the grounds unnoticed was shrinking with each step.

"I know," she whispered, smiling faintly. "But I think I can walk now."

His steps slowed until he stopped. "Are you certain?"

"Let me try," she pleaded, so he obliged, gently lowering her legs to the floor. Talitha gripped his neck tighter when her bare feet met the cold tile.

Anteros glanced down at her blackened toes and grimaced. They had packed two plain gowns and a pair of shoes in a canvas sack, which was left with the horse that would carry her away. He should have snuck the shoes down to the dungeon instead. He reached around her back to pick her up again, but her arms shot out from under the cloak, pressing firmly against his chest. "I'm fine, Anteros. Lead the way."

Her hands fell to her sides, and he took one in his own, interlacing their fingers as he led her quietly down the hall until they entered a corridor with large open windows to the outdoors. Talitha paused and inhaled deeply, dropping her head back to bask in the warmth of the setting sun. Her hood fell off, pooling on her shoulders, and Anteros smiled bitterly, reminded of the day his sister brought Talitha out to watch the games in the field. That was the day she became Lady Adelaide to everyone else at court.

But she'd always be 'Red' to him.

The sound of clanking armor grabbed his attention, and Anteros realized two guards were walking toward the castle. Toward them. "Red," he called, snapping her out of her trance. Anteros yanked the hood over her head before swinging her around and pressing her against the brick wall. Nestling his face as close to her cheek as possible, he whispered, "Pretend to kiss me. Otherwise, they'll stop. They'll realize what's happening."

Her breathing quickened, her heart pounding in rhythm with his own as her eyes danced between his eyes and his lips. When the guards reached the stone path, their conversation became clear. Anteros stroked her cheek with his thumb, using his head to hide her face from the approaching men. "Just breathe," he whispered, trying to calm her.

Then Talitha curled her fingers around the back of his neck and pressed her lips to his.

Anteros froze for a second, eyes wide as he realized what was happening. He had not expected her to kiss him, not now or ever again, merely to pretend. The voices approaching were nearly upon them, so he grabbed her by the waist and deepened the kiss, taking what little sweetness she had to offer, knowing this would be the last time.

And how sweet it was.

His lips worked against hers in a frenzy, all thoughts slipping away as she continued kissing him, her fingers burning as they skimmed up the side of his neck. Had she missed this, missed him as desperately as he had missed her night and day? Or was this moment born purely out of fear they would be caught?

His lips slowed, pressing gently to hers for one moment longer before they broke apart, heavy breaths merging under the cloak hood. Anteros realized it was deathly quiet. The guards were long gone. All that remained was the two of them, panting and staring at each other. The prince caressed her cheek once more and whispered, "You have ruined me, Talitha. I will never deserve these lips, yet I will always crave them."

Talitha pressed a hand to her chest, trying to calm herself. Something shined in her eyes, bringing out the blue in them. Understanding? She looked down suddenly, pulling the black cloak tight at her throat to hide her ragged dress. He needed to know what she was thinking. Had he said too much? Pushed her too far?

Finally, a feeble hand emerged from the cloak and took his. Anteros led them through an archway and down a stone path until it ended abruptly. Then he plodded on into the grass, dry and gold as straw. Talitha didn't seem to mind the feel of it against her bare feet. Her face remained stoic, her gaze shifting back and forth in search of other people.

Where they were going, there were none. All the servants had been summoned to work the special event that night. He did not expect to see any on the private footpath.

Cutting between a few trees lining the outskirts of the manor, the dead grass thinned out into a worn dirt path. There, tied to a tree, was a dark brown horse waiting to take her away. "This is Lucky. He's fast. He'll get you where you're going quicker than anyone else could." Anteros let go of her hand to pat the horse's muzzle.

Talitha stayed two steps back from the creature. When he finally turned to make sure she was still there, a quiet voice asked, "Lucky?" Recognition flashed across her face as new tears welled up.

"Yes. I named him—with your help, of course." Anteros began untying the horse's reins from the tree, making slow work of the knot. The seconds were ticking. He needed to get back to the castle and find his way to the banquet before his father noticed his absence.

A lump rose in his throat knowing their time together was up.

"This is the footpath that leads to Jessiraé. Follow it as closely as you can. In town, go to a place called the Untamed Mare and ask for the Madam. She'll be expecting you. Give her the name Ruby, and she will take care of everything. Got it?"

Talitha nodded, though her face was painted with concern. "The Untamed Mare," she repeated. Her face twisted then, her nose wrinkled in confusion. "Is that a... whore house?"

Anteros bristled, pressing his lips into a thin line. "It's an inn with a tavern... and some women offer *services*, yes." She took a step back, looking ready to run and take her chances on foot. His hands shot out to grasp her shoulders, gently holding her in place. "But you will not be employed there. I've paid the Madam to house and feed you. That is all. No one will touch you. I swear it."

Her cheeks reddened, and she couldn't look him in the eyes. Reluctantly, he let her go, hoping she would believe his intentions and trust she would be safe there. If she decided to ride for home or anywhere else, she'd be on her own.

"You'll be safe there, Red," he said, trying to keep his voice level. "Promise you'll go."

She nodded feebly before turning her attention to the horse. Her fingers skated over his muzzle before tracing the lining of the saddle on his back. Attached to it were two plain brown sacks, one with minimal clothes, the other bearing water and food for the journey. Anteros kept his distance, stuffing his hands into his pockets. "There are shoes in that bag. Dresses and food, as well." She reached into the bag and lifted out a plain pair of brown flats. Holding onto the horse, she slipped one onto each foot and shrugged. "There's also a bag of coins. The Madam can get you anything else you need."

The cage tied to the back of the saddle rattled, and Talitha jumped. The bird inside pecked at the black cloth tied loosely around its prison. "Don't worry. He's harmless," Anteros said, lifting one side of the cloth to reveal Phinnian the phoenix. The bird had nearly tripled in size since he won it. The scrawny thing had sprouted a beautiful array of red and gold feathers from his chest to his magnificent wings. Some evenings, he let it out of its cage to fly about the room. It always came back to him.

He wondered if one day Talitha might, too.

"Is that a phoenix?" She cocked her head to the side and stared at the creature, brows scrunched in confusion. "Why?"

Anteros lowered the cloth, and the bird squawked, rattling the cage again. "Phinnian is a loyal bird. If you ever need anything, write a note, attach it to his leg, and set him free. He'll find me."

"I don't think he likes being caged," she muttered. "How am I supposed to care for it?"

"There are instructions in the bag. Read them once you're settled in," the prince said. "For now, just worry about yourself."

Talitha rested both hands on the horse, one on each side of the saddle, with her back facing him. The wind lifted wisps of her hair, carrying them over her shoulder. The sunlight reflected off her vibrant locks; the pale orange blended beautifully with the changing leaves on the trees that lined the path. She glanced over her shoulder at him, her profile heartbreakingly beautiful. "How long do I have before someone notices I'm gone?"

He stared, trying to commit her face to memory, knowing it would haunt his dreams for years to come. "I cannot be certain... You should go while you have a head start."

She nodded, taking a shaky breath. Tears trickled down her cheek, and his fingers twitched from the urge to wipe them away. He knew she was scared. Setting her free came with its share of dangers. He was terrified, too. Terrified this would all be for nothing. Terrified she'd be captured and executed, and her blood would mar his hands yet again, leaving a permanent scar on his soul.

Talitha grabbed hold of the saddle and lifted one foot into the stirrup. She tested her hold, repositioning her hands. For a second, he wondered if she had ever ridden a horse—the afterthought making him feel like the biggest imbecile in the kingdom—but she managed to push off the ground and swing her leg over the stallion gracefully. He sighed as she settled onto the saddle. The stallion whinnied as she pulled the reins tight in her hands.

"I meant what I promised you," he murmured. The wind carried his whisper to her, making her pause. "I only wish I could have done this sooner. You deserve to live in the light."

Talitha met his watery gaze. His chest ached knowing this was likely the last time he would lay eyes on her. She pressed her lips together, trying to find the right words to say to him. "Thank—"

He lifted a hand, stepping closer to the horse. "Do not thank me. I caused you suffering, and I will not soon forgive myself." Anteros released a heavy breath, glancing down the dirt path behind them. Maroon and browning leaves skittered across the ground before the breeze swept them away. He wished the wind could carry them both far away—somewhere out of Antoine Rexton's reach.

Talitha frowned, leaning down toward him slightly. She pressed her frigid fingers against his cheek. The warmth of that gesture was something he would never forget. "You were never my enemy, Anteros. When I was down there… you were the only thing that kept me alive." He leaned into her hand slightly, closing his eyes. "You're not your father. There is still goodness in your heart. Don't allow him to snuff out that light."

He pressed his trembling palm atop her bony fingers, tears streaking his cheeks. He wanted to believe her. He wanted so desperately to be good. To break free of his father. To change the way this kingdom was ruled.

The first step was letting Talitha Vise go.

Anteros opened his eyes and withdrew his hand. The lump in his throat restricted him from saying anything further. Their time was up, and they both knew it. He stepped back from the stallion and lowered his chin, bidding her a silent farewell. Her eyes blazed the brightest blue he'd ever seen them, red-rimmed from her own tears. She nodded back, sniffled, and snapped the reins; the horse reared up on its hind legs before jolting forward.

The prince watched until her red hair blurred, blending and disappearing among the autumn foliage as the horse galloped onward, leaving only a handful of fallen leaves and his shattered heart at the end of the dirt path.

32

SACRIFICES

Everyone in Graynor had gathered in the main hall, dressed in their finest coats and most elegant gowns, to celebrate the official announcement of Sabine Rexton and Ryker Umbryon's engagement. Sabine glided about the hall, her mauve silk gown sweeping the floor behind her as she greeted each noble, her father and fiancé never far from her side. She was certain they found her sudden acceptance of the situation peculiar, catching the men exchanging a raised brow more than once, but Ryker did not question the change in her demeanor. Sabine was a princess raised to honor her father's will, and that was exactly what she was doing—wearing her carefully done-up mask and pretending all was well.

Until she caught sight of her brother's late entrance.

Excusing herself, she made her way over to Anteros, desperate to learn what had become of Talitha. The melancholy look on his face gave her no indication whether their plan had worked—or if he had even gone through with it. For all she knew, he could have forsaken the chance, giving in to his negative thoughts and accepting defeat at their father's hands.

She would not stand for that.

"Brother," Sabine declared, her voice high and chipper. Her voice clearly startled him from his thoughts as he turned toward her. She gently grasped his upper arms, leaned in to pretend to kiss his cheek, and whispered, "Have we good news to celebrate this eve?"

Anteros swallowed thickly, a harsh exhale escaping him as he drew back from her. "Of course, we do. You are to be married." There was no malice to his statement, nor joy, for that matter. Only careful words disguised in nonchalance.

Sabine feigned a smile, her gaze roaming the nearby party attendants. None were within close enough proximity to them, so she asked quietly, "And have *you* any reason for celebration?"

His hazel eyes shone with a mixture of acknowledgement and remorse. His response was a simple nod, and she breathed a sigh of relief. Tears pricked her eyes as she imagined that poor girl riding free on a horse, on her way to a life of freedom. She beamed as she pulled her brother into a tight embrace, not missing the way every muscle in his body tensed at the contact. "You did the right thing," she murmured, blinking away the tears that threatened to fall. She couldn't have people wondering why she was suddenly so emotional.

"We did." Anteros patted her back briefly before she stepped back. They stared at each other for a moment, bittersweet smiles on their faces knowing they had at least tried to right one of their father's many wrongs.

Then Ryker tapped her shoulder. "Apologies for interrupting. I wondered if I might have a dance with my betrothed? I'm afraid the last time we had the opportunity, we had yet to get acquainted with each other."

Sabine's bright eyes shifted to Ryker, and she nodded, placing her hand in his. With a final glance back at her brother, she turned and allowed him to lead her onto the dance floor with several other couples. While she feigned enjoyment during their turn around the room, she could not shake off the feeling that Anteros needed her. That he was struggling with letting Talitha go. Her gaze kept finding him, in the corner of the room chatting with his friends, a chalice of red wine in hand. She prayed he would not drink himself into a stupor.

"You seem distracted," Ryker noted before lifting her hand and turning her twice. Her heavy skirt flared out, grazing his legs as she whipped around in a circle.

A low, light laugh escaped her, and she shook her head. "Oh, it's nothing. I'm just a bit worried about Anteros." The way Ryker looked at her encouraged her to continue. She had to give him something, some valid reason for her concern. "I think he's taken the news of his own engagement hard. He had feelings for someone else, someone our father never would have approved of, but that's over now." She watched over Ryker's shoulder as her brother took a long swill, polishing off his drink.

"I do not feign to know the burdens of being a young royal—much less the heirs of the indefinable Antoine Rexton," Ryker began. Sabine stared at his deep navy jacket decorated with his family crest and other silver embellishments of unknown origin. They must have been Denorfian. She nearly asked him just to change the subject. She still did not trust him. Did not believe that he had nothing to do with the sudden, expedited scheduling of their marriage day. Ryker went on, "But I am quite aware of the sacrifices we make for our parents. I hope you are aware that it could have been far worse, for *both* of you."

She tensed, unable to look him in the eyes. His statement could hardly qualify as a comfort. In fact, it almost felt like he was once again trying to bolster himself in her eyes.

It didn't work.

As the song came to a crescendo, Ryker lifted her at the waist, and Sabine inhaled sharply, thankful the end was near—of this dance *and* their conversation. Her feet landed softly on the floor, and the sound of string instruments died off abruptly. Seeking a reprieve from his company, she curtsied, saying, "I think I shall go in search of my friend Emmaline, if you do not mind." Ryker nodded, and she allowed him to kiss the top of her hand before turning and retreating.

Before she could find her friend, Julian intercepted her. Sabine glanced back, pleased to find Ryker had been sucked into conversation with visiting nobles from his own kingdom. With a sigh, she turned back to the icy irises that had frequented her dreams for the past two weeks. "Julian," she said, greeting him with a curtsy and a genuine smile.

His lips curved upward, though his smile did not reach his eyes. She couldn't expect it to. Not when they were meeting at her betrothal to another man. Staring at his lips, memories of a dozen stolen kisses and secret rendezvous flashed through her mind. Moments in time she would cherish for the rest of her life.

He took her hand and kissed her knuckles, his lips sending a tingle dancing across her skin. She relished that feeling knowing the man she would marry had never elicited the same response from her. "Sabine," he murmured, the softness in his voice taking her back to one of their more intimate moments alone. No one else had ever said her name as reverently as Julian did. "Would it be inappropriate to ask for a dance this evening?" His pale eyes pleaded for her acceptance before seeking out Ryker across the room.

Her chest swelled with longing. This would be their last chance as she knew it would be unfitting at the celebration of her wedding, so she nodded. "Of course." She accepted his outstretched hand, but as they turned toward the dance floor, one of his father's officers came through the doors, stealing her moment of delight.

"Give me a moment. I need to speak to Anteros," she said, pulling her hand away from the blond.

The corners of Julian's mouth drooped in disappointment but did not argue as she turned; her heels clicked loudly as she walked quickly toward her brother. Anteros had already noticed the guards whispering at the entrance, the men appearing hesitant to approach the king. All color had drained from her brother's face. They both knew what this meant.

Talitha's head start to freedom was up.

"What do we do?" Sabine hissed, quiet as she could manage in her panic.

Anteros shook his head. "I'll speak to the captain. Try to send them the wrong way, buy her more time."

"Father is going to explode when they tell him," she murmured, spotting him with Ryker and the other Denorfians.

"I know," was all Anteros said as he plodded toward the officer, leaving her behind, her fear simmering at the surface. She watched as he greeted the captain, gesturing for them to step into the hall to discuss the problem, desperate to somehow help distract her father from learning the truth, even if only for a little longer.

Then she had an idea.

It was crazy, but if it worked, it would be worth the risk. Talitha would be free.

Sabine glanced over her shoulder at Julian, her chest tight knowing she would have to sacrifice one last dance with him. Then she put on her best smile, gently lifted the front of her skirt hem off the floor, and marched across the room until she was face to face with the two men she normally avoided. "Father, Ryker," she said, bowing her head to each of them. "This evening has been almost perfect."

"Almost?" Her father bristled, lowered his chalice, and cocked an eyebrow at her.

She chuckled uneasily, draping herself on Ryker's arm. "I wish this were more than an engagement banquet. I wish it were our wedding night, of course."

Antoine and Ryker gaped at her, both baffled by her declaration.

If anything could distract a ballroom full of people, it was an impromptu wedding.

"Why should we wait? Everyone is already here. The seamstress has been working on my gown, and it is truly stunning," Sabine babbled. Her fingers dragged down Ryker's chest seductively. Feigning such affection with him was far from easy, but she was out of ideas. If this was a way she could cause a distraction, she would do it for Talitha. "Please, Father. Let us be wed. Tonight."

Her mother's fingers curled over her shoulders and turned her away from her fiancé. "Darling, what are you saying?" Chelsea interjected, a look of absolute horror on her face.

"This is a surprise, after your mother has advocated to wait until your next birthday." Her father's eyes, dark as obsidian, narrowed. Being under his scrutinizing gaze made her want to hide behind someone, but she stood resolute, chin raised and proud. He needed to believe she was sincere. That she wanted to marry Ryker that very night.

"Now that I've gotten to spend some time with him, I realized we're only prolonging the inevitable. What's a few months compared to forever?" Sabine smiled, impressed with her quick thinking. She knew in her heart that this was what fate had in store, so the timing truly didn't matter. All that mattered was helping her friend the only way she could.

Being the most beautiful distraction this court had ever seen.

Her father pulled Ryker aside, and they whispered about her sudden urgency to be married. Sabine glanced toward the entrance, catching Anteros out of the corner of her eye. To her relief, the officer had not reentered the hall. He must have managed to convince the man of a course of action that did not include informing their father during such a grand occasion.

Anteros waltzed over to rejoin his family just as Antoine and Ryker approached. "Very well. If it should make you happy to rush into your marriage, then by all means… We shall have a wedding on this night," her father said. "Go, get ready. We will start in half an hour." Without further discussion, the king wrapped an arm around his wife and led her away to make last minute preparations.

Her brother's brow furrowed as he stared at her, having missed out on her unrehearsed plan. Ryker kissed her on the knuckles before exiting the hall himself. A safe distance behind him, Sabine lifted her skirts and muttered to her brother, "Walk with me."

Halfway up the steps, Anteros hissed, "What the blazes are you doing? A wedding? This was merely supposed to be a banquet."

"The guards noticed she's gone, haven't they?" she asked quietly, glancing up and down the empty hall of bed chambers. Most of their family and distinguished guests were still downstairs in the main hall. "What did you say to the commander?"

"That the guards should start with the east wing and spread out through the castle. That the girl would be weak and was likely still hiding on the grounds. He agreed," her brother declared. He ran a frustrated hand through his slicked back hair, causing locks of it to fall over his forehead. "Why did you change the plan? You had a few more weeks."

She whipped around on the balls of her heels and planted a finger in her brother's firm chest. "Because she didn't have *weeks*. She only had a few *hours* head start, if we're lucky. And in the long run, weeks do not matter, brother. I will end up in Ryker's bed, no matter the day. Might as well use the occasion as a distraction."

Anteros grabbed her pointy finger and lowered her hand, giving it a light squeeze. "You didn't have to do this," he whispered. "I could have found another way. I'm the one who should have had to sacrifice more."

Sabine shook her head. "You aren't the only person burdened with guilt over what happened. I, too, needed to atone. Let me play my part. I was born for dramatics, after all." She smiled bitterly, and her brother pulled her into a tight hug.

"Do you need anything?" Anteros asked, searching her face.

She shook her head. She felt confident in her choice, knowing this would help keep her parents occupied. Glancing out the nearest window, Sabine watched several guards fan out over the grounds, scoping out the gardens below. They looked like ants from this high up. If she had learned anything in her sixteen years, it was that they were all ants under Antoine's shoes. But today, one would escape his crushing step.

"You have done enough already. Go back downstairs. Help keep Ryker and the guests happy. Tell the servants to bring out champagne. I will change and see you shortly."

Anteros nodded and turned away from her swiftly, his steps more self-assured as he redirected to Sabine's new plan. She watched him for a moment before entering her bed chamber. With her time limited, the princess had work to do. She wanted to ensure there would not be a dry eye in the room when she came down the aisle.

Half an hour later, Antoine Rexton sat upon a large chair poised to the right of a wide aisle strewn with flower petals. His wife sat to his left, gnawing on her bottom lip, her eyes never leaving the entrance. Ryker returned from his chambers in an even nicer suit of deep navy, the color of his Denorfian ancestors.

Anteros was pleasantly surprised by the servants' quick thinking, pulling flowers from the gardens and lining chairs and tables on each side of an aisle large enough to accommodate Ryker and whatever monstrosity of a gown the seamstress had put together.

Then Captain Charles Thurwynn breezed past him in the main hall, making his way toward the king. Anteros twisted his torso, eyes blown wide as he watched the captain greet his father. He had been too distracted by the bustling servants and tipsy nobles to notice him. Now there was no way to stop his father from learning the truth.

Anteros watched helplessly as his father's grip tightened on the arms of his chair, his knuckles stark white as Captain Thurwynn informed him of the missing prisoner. A deep green vein protruded from his neck, pulsing with the rhythm of his elevated heartrate.

Then the prince realized how pale his mother had turned. She was terrified.

They all should be.

Taking a deep breath, Anteros straightened his jacket on his way toward his parents. He knew there was no hiding from his father's fury. He could only hope that Antoine's anger would not be directed at his sister, who had played little part in Talitha's escape. If anyone should be punished this time, it was him.

His father's cheeks were cherry red when he stopped beside the captain, whose legs were visibly quivering. Anteros clasped his sweaty palms behind his back and asked, "Is there a problem, Captain?"

Before the sniveling captain could explain the situation for a second time, his father lunged at him. Antoine grabbed his son by the throat and squeezed, his nose scraping his son's cheek as he yelled, "You know why he's here!"

Anteros tried to breathe. Tried to inhale sharply, but his burning throat would not allow it. His fingers came up to claw at his father's hand, and he bared his teeth. His eyes burned, his throat constricted, and his father seemed unphased by the fingernails digging into his flesh. *You're a monster,* the prince thought bitterly. *Do what you will to me. I welcome death knowing today you have lost.*

Chelsea's heels hit the floor, ringing sharply as she scurried toward them. She was not normally one to get between Antoine and a fight, but this was her son. She clawed at the king's arm and yelled, "Antoine! Antoine, you're killing him! Let the boy go. He's your only son!"

With a ferocious snarl, the king released Anteros and whipped around to slap his wife with the back of his hand. The sting was so sharp it sent Chelsea flying back onto the floor. "Wretched woman! You do not address me as anything but Your Majesty!" he snarled at her. She lowered her head in submission, shoulders trembling with her silent sobs.

Anteros coughed violently, his knees hitting the ground as he gasped for air. The king breathed heavily, his presence looming over his son's hunched form. A shiny black shoe nudged Anteros in his ribcage, and he leaned back on his haunches, glaring up at the monster with whom he shared a bloodline.

"I should have known you hadn't let your little whore go," the king hissed, lips curled in disgust. "But no matter… I will not show mercy this time. My men will hunt her down and kill her on sight like the filthy gutter rat she is."

His father turned to exit the hall, but Anteros reached out and grabbed his leg. "Wait! What about Sabine's wedding?" His throat burned, his voice coming out hoarse and low.

The king scoffed. "Do you think me a fool? This was nothing but a ruse meant to distract. I am done playing games in *my* court. After the fugitive is executed, both of you will be dealt with… swiftly."

"This wasn't a ruse," Anteros argued, scrambling onto his feet. Going to stand before his father, he held his chin high. "Sabine had nothing to do with the prisoner's escape. I swear it."

Antoine sneered and stepped closer to his son. His breath, reeking of old wine, fanned his son's face, and Anteros held his breath, holding his ground. "You have already proven yourself unworthy of my trust. I may allow this wedding to proceed this evening, but only so that I may be rid of that spoiled brat for good." He shoved past his son, shoulder nearly knocking the boy back onto the ground as he went.

At the doors, the king paused and turned toward the hall full of buzzing nobles who were already busy gossiping about the king's latest outburst. "No one leaves until I lay eyes on the fugitive," he declared, motioning for the guards to close the doors.

Then all Anteros could do was wait for his sister, or Talitha's cold, dead body, to arrive.

<h1 style="text-align:center">33</h1>

SHATTERED

Anteros paced up and down the aisle as the minutes ticked by. An hour passed quickly with servants flitting about like busy bees, setting up chairs and passing out wine to appease the nobles who were stuck waiting. When his father returned to the main hall, he stormed past his son to sit upon the largest chair in the hall, just to the right of the main aisle. Chelsea was already seated beside him, nervously gnawing the inside of her lip. She had wanted to help Sabine get ready, but Antoine had refused to let her leave the hall.

Ryker bounced nervously from one leg to another at the front of the room. His entourage from Denorfia whispered among themselves, casting suspicious glances at Anteros every so often. The prince knew what they were thinking. Was this wedding actually going to take place, or had this all been a ruse? With the king back in the hall, Ryker sent his fellow northerners to take their seats, expecting Sabine to make her grand entrance any moment.

An uncomfortable silence settled in the hall. Antoine's jaw was clenched so hard every muscle in his face and neck stood out. Ryker's pallor had paled even more, and the earl casually strolled down the aisle to meet Anteros, looking for some kind of reassurance.

"She'll be here. If I know my sister, she intends to make a huge entrance," the prince said, putting on a half-hearted smirk.

His sister lived for being the center of attention. Today would be no different. They could only hope that Talitha wouldn't be making an appearance on her big day. That would be catastrophic for all three of them, and losing their friend would certainly put a damper on Sabine's wedding night.

Ten more minutes passed before two guards heaved open the tall double doors to the main hall. Nobles gasped, scrambling to their feet. Some rushed to clear the center aisle. Everyone held their breath, awaiting the princess's entrance, but it was not Sabine who entered.

A small cluster of guards came up the center aisle slowly. Sweat tinged their brows as they looked forward, the captain at the head of their group looking rather green. As they passed Anteros, he realized the man in the center of the group, who had been shrouded by the others, was carrying something large wrapped tightly in a black cloth.

His stomach dropped.

No. It was a black cloak like the one he had given Talitha mere hours ago.

Anteros wanted to follow them—to follow what he feared was *her*—but his feet were frozen. He watched helplessly as the guards came to a stop beside the king's chair, none willing to look him in the eyes. The prince could not blame them. Even men who had done their duties correctly had found their heads on the floor from Antoine's temper. And he was in a horrendously foul mood about Talitha's escape.

The guard carrying the wrapped body laid it before the king and quickly stepped back in line with his comrades. They all bowed their heads in submission.

Bile rose up the back of Anteros' throat as he stumbled forward. He had only drank two glasses of wine, yet his limbs felt out of his control as they carried him closer. He didn't want to see it, to see what had become of the beautiful copper-haired girl his father had squashed like some insignificant bug, but he had to know. He had to see his failure for himself.

Anteros stepped into the space between the guards and his parents' seats and stared down at the floor, waiting for someone, anyone else, to unwrap it. He thought he might be sick from the overwhelming nausea roiling in his gut.

This was his fault. Once again, he had tried to help Talitha Vise, and once again, she had paid for his kindness.

He was a fool to think he could get away with freeing her.

No one ever escaped.

His father always won.

The prince took a shaky inhale as his father rose from his seat. "Well?" The king looked indignantly at his guards. Gesturing with a broad hand toward the body, Antoine shouted, "Show me the body!"

The men glanced between each other before shoving one of their own forward. He fell onto his knees with a heavy clank of armor. Swallowing thickly, the guard leaned over the shrouded figure; the sharp sound of his armor scraping against itself made Anteros wince. The guard peeled back one layer of fabric, laying it on the floor near Anteros' feet. A hush fell over the room as people leaned forward to watch the man unwrap the body. Their morbid curiosity made the prince's blood boil. This was not some hardened war criminal or traitor deserving of a swift end; it was a young woman, strong and beautiful and mutilated by a monster. By all of them. None of them would ever know the pleasure of her company. She did not deserve to be wrongfully imprisoned, to have her dignity and hope stripped away day after day in the darkness.

"We followed your orders, Your Majesty. Shoot on sight," the commander babbled, but Anteros paid him no attention.

As the prince held his breath, he closed his eyes and called forth his last memories of Talitha. The way she had kissed him out of fright would haunt him forever. He could only hope that her death was swift and painless, finally bringing an end to her prolonged suffering.

Then the guard finally peeled back another section of the cloak, revealing the poor girl's face. Now void of their bright blue hue, the lifeless eyes staring through him did not belong to Talitha; they belonged to his sister Sabine.

Gasps rang out through the main hall, and a heart-wrenching shriek left his mother, the sound sending a chill deep into his bones. Anteros collapsed to his knees, his hands pressing into the cool tile for support as he struggled to inhale. How had this happened? She was supposed to be changing dresses for her wedding. How could she be dead?

Chelsea flung herself down by Sabine's head. Choking sobs echoed through the chamber as chaos erupted around them. "Sabine? Oh, my darling! My baby! Why?" His mother wailed the last word over and over. Her face crumpled as she pulled her daughter's limp body into her lap. "Who did this?" She turned her tear-filled glare on the guards, anger seeping into the air around her. "Who is responsible? Who murdered my baby?"

The guards kept their heads bowed, splotches of red spreading from their cheeks down their necks. They were unconcerned with the queen's yelling. They knew their fates rested in the king's hands alone.

Ryker finally pushed past the crowd to get a look at her. "What in the heavens is happening?" He paled at the sight of his corpse bride, taking a step back and holding the back of his hand to his mouth. "How did this atrocity occur? She was promised to me!"

Hot tears streaked Anteros' face as he blinked at the floor in shock. His father had ordered the men to hunt down Talitha Vise. How had Sabine ended up in the crossfire?

"Well?" His father's deep voice was as cold and unfeeling as ever as he questioned his men. "You were sent after a missing prisoner, yet you bring me my only daughter's corpse."

Anteros chanced another look at the body, hoping beyond hope that it would change. That he would wake up from this horrid nightmare. But his dear sister, paler than he'd ever seen her, lay still beside him. He tried to hold back the urge to vomit as he turned toward the guards, as desperate as his mother for answers.

The commander's legs were visibly shaking as he stuttered, "A person in a black cloak was spotted riding in the field. Heading toward the mountains." He paused, but the king raised his brows, awaiting more details. "When pursued, she did not yield. She rode faster. Out of fear she might outrun us, the men loosed arrows to bring her horse down. She was hit in the back, but we think the fall is what killed her."

Antoine scratched his beard and inhaled deeply. The crowd waited with baited breath to see how the king would react to the loss of his daughter. He was known for his unruly temper.

"It sounds as though my daughter lied about wanting to be married," Antoine said coldly, his eyes flicking down to the corpse in his wife's arms for only a second. "What a waste."

A cold prickle spread through Anteros' blood as he watched his father. The prince already knew there would be no emotional reaction to the news—not from his father. The man was cold, calculating, and never the least bit caring to Sabine. Of his two surviving children, Antoine had always resented that the second was female. He pretended at court that he had the perfect family, but his son knew. The king loathed his wife and daughter, and he was probably glad to be rid of her, one way or another.

"We had a bargain." Ryker seethed, eyes burning in rage. "The girl was mine." He held no tears for the loss of his fiancé, only the loss of something he saw as his property.

"This is an unfortunate turn of events," Antoine replied. "Not to worry, Ryker. I will pay you in gold for the cattle, and you can assuredly find yourself another bride."

The prince pushed himself up onto his knees, then his feet. His hands balled into fists at his sides as he stormed toward the earl. Before anyone could register what was happening, Anteros threw a punch; the squelch of his fist sinking into Ryker's cheek carried through the chamber. Some envoys rushed to aid the Denorfian, who had stumbled back in surprise, bloodied spit trickling from his mouth onto his dress attire. Others tried to flee through the main doors.

"She was never *yours*, and she was not just some girl. She has a name: Sabine. Princess of Hyrosencia. Show some respect," he spat at the earl, certain the crazed look in his eyes was scaring everyone in the vicinity.

"That's enough, Anteros," his father's deep voice came down on his ears like a pile of rocks, too nonchalant, too impassive to belong to a man who had lost one of his children.

"No, it is *not*." Whirling around to face his father, the prince pointed at the king and shouted, "Your only daughter lies cold on the ground. What are you going to do about this, Father?" Chelsea sobbed louder, clutching her daughter to her chest. Anteros stared into his father's obsidian irises and panted heavy. One wrong word, and his bloodied knuckles were ready to throw another punch. He wanted blood to rain—and lots of it. His sister, his only true confidant, was dead. Someone had to pay for this egregious error. If his father would not do it, he would.

Antoine cocked his head to the side and considered his son for a moment. Finally, he turned toward the cowering guards, leveling the commander with his dark gaze. "Who shot the arrow?" He was no more angry than usual—not the way he should have been. Instead, he was eerily calm. All the times his family, his men, his court, had witnessed his brutality, and now, all he could muster was indifference.

Anteros flexed his injured fist and wished he had a sword at his side. He could think of nothing more cathartic than running a man through with it right now—be it Ryker, his father, or the guards responsible. He loathed them all with an unbridled hatred that spread through his body, burning in his veins like molten lava.

"We cannot be sure," the commander stuttered.

Antoine stepped closer, looming over the sniveling man. His broad shadow fell over the officer's face as he screamed, "Who is responsible for this?"

"You are!" Chelsea shrieked from behind them.

Everyone went silent. No one dared move a muscle.

Turning, Anteros found his mother's shaking hand pointing an accusatory finger at her husband. The prince stopped breathing. He knew that his father would not dismiss such blatant disrespect in front of an audience.

Antoine cracked his knuckles and asked through clenched teeth, "What did you say, wench?"

This time, Chelsea did not cower. She stared down her husband with her tear-streaked face lifted in defiance. There was something terrifyingly broken about the look in her eyes. They held no more fear for her husband's punishing ways. No. She looked deranged, daring him to lay a finger on her.

Perhaps the fragile threads of her sanity had finally snapped, and she wanted him to kill her.

Anteros moved in tandem with his father, reaching Chelsea just before the king could slap her. "Don't," the prince pleaded. "She's lost her only daughter. Can you not show compassion to your own wife?"

The king seethed, wild eyes widening under his heavy brows. He breathed heavily, gaze flicking from his son to the woman standing just behind his shoulder.

Just when the prince thought his father might listen and let it go, his mother spoke again. "I have given you everything I had all these years. Even as you cast me aside for lovers, I have stood by silently and done all you asked. Sabine was the only good thing you ever gave me. The only thing that was truly mine... and now, she's gone... by your orders. Your cruelty."

Anteros stepped back and clamped a hand over her mouth. "That's enough," he implored her. Staring at his mother's bright blue eyes, he was reminded of his sister. She had been so much like their mother—strong, stubborn, confident. But all the good things about them had been destroyed by his father, pummeled into dust and carried away on the autumn breeze.

Chelsea pushed her son's hand down and lifted her chin toward her husband. "You are a vile man. It should be you who died by that arrow's edge." Her scathing tone sliced through the quiet room like a knife, but his father barely reacted. The smallest tick in his jaw told Anteros he was holding back. Shocked gasps echoed around them, and Anteros tried to cover her mouth again, forcing her feet to step backwards, away from Antoine.

The king scoffed and snapped his fingers. "It appears my wife has reached a state of hysteria over the loss of our beloved Sabine. Guards, if you would be so kind as to escort Lady Chelsea to her chambers and ensure she remains there until she's come to her senses." The quaking guards moved swiftly, relief washing over their faces as they quickly ushered the woman out.

Anteros blew out a frustrated breath and shook his head. His father approached, pausing when they were shoulder to shoulder to whisper, "Do not think you have gotten away with your crimes so easily. Your sister may be dead, but that shall not stop me from hunting down that traitorous whore." The prince worked a swallow, staring at the people pouring out of the open doors in a frenzy. He could no longer look at his father—not after his heartless reaction to his own daughter's death. The king concluded, "And when I find her, you will have a front row seat to her execution."

His father's red velvet cape swished around him as he stormed for the doors, leaving his son and dead daughter behind. Anteros sucked in a haggard breath and turned back toward his sister's remains, the weight of her loss hitting him over again like a second wave capsizing a ship. Dropping to his knees, he used two fingers to gently close her unseeing eyes. His cheeks were wet, his chest constricted in anguish as he pulled the black cloak back over her, sealing her away gently like a mother tucking her child into bed for the night.

"I hope he never finds her," Anteros whispered to himself. He could not fathom why his sister had made so many rash decisions that night without first seeking his input. Perhaps if she had spoken to him, she would still be alive.

Now, he could only pray that Sabine's distraction—the sacrifice of her tragically short life—had given Talitha enough time to reach Jessiraé and hide where Antoine would never find her.

34

FAMILY

The simmering hate flowing through Elara's veins had tamped down with the passing of two weeks. A variety of people took turns coming to visit her. She suspected this was set up in an effort to keep her from hurting herself by trying to escape. In the morning when Gerard was ready to leave, the physician would pop in to check on her and the baby. Then Idonea would come by for morning tea, bringing with her whatever special brew Ismenia thought might help the queen feel better. But no tea could wash down the poison lingering in her heart from her court's betrayal.

Her husband came to see her frequently. After unshackling her from the bed, Gerard would help her over to the small table and chairs in front of the balcony window. As they ate lunch, she listened quietly while he gave her brief and uneventful updates from the council and court. She could tell that he was leaving things out—anything he thought could upset her—and she loathed feeling like she was missing vital information. When it was time for him to leave again, to meet with dignitaries or the council to continue preparing for what might come, he would try to kiss her goodbye, but the queen turned her head, only allowing his lips a gentle brush against her cheek.

One of her maids would come by to tidy the room while she read or took a nap. Some days, the poor maid would try to teach Elara how to knit to help her fill her time. She created the messiest baby blanket the world had ever seen, but she was proud of it. It was one of the few times she was excited to tell all her visitors about something. It was all she had to do, after all.

Idonea and Ismenia would take afternoon tea in her chambers most days, having the kitchen prepare an array of the queen's favorite treats. Though the infant in her womb leaped for joy at every delicious morsel, the gesture did nothing to thaw the icy voice in the back of her mind that constantly whispered, *These people betrayed you.*

If Elara was lucky, they would bring Rilura or one of the nobles' wives, and the conversation would be far more interesting. The dwarf sat on her plush chaise looking rather uncomfortable as Ismenia poured tea into their cups. Her eyes trained on Elara's bruised wrist, and she clenched her jaw in irritation.

"It is always men who think us to be weak," the dwarf remarked, turning to gaze out the window at the mountains.

The queen sighed. As her baby stretched its legs, crowding her organs and making it harder to breathe, she wondered if perhaps her husband had been right to worry. She was exhausted, and sitting idle in her bedchamber was not helping. Elara closed her eyes and leaned her head back against her chair, feeling the gentle sunlight on her cheeks. What she would have given for a walk in the garden. Even if the air was frigid, the change of scenery would have been worth it. Opening her eyes, she looked to the dwarf and asked, "And what of the man you had feelings for? How would he treat you if you carried his child?"

The coloring in Rilura's cheeks deepened. "I cannot guess such a thing. Children are so rare among my kind that mothers are revered."

"As all mothers should be," Ismenia said, lifting her teacup in a salute.

Elara pursed her lips and tamped down her aggravation at the herbalist. There was no use arguing with her anymore. She had tried to make an emotional appeal to Ismenia one morning when they were alone, but her friend insisted this was for the best.

"How have you been sleeping, Elara?" The oracle's question dragged the queen from her intrusive thoughts.

In truth, the line between her dreams and visions had begun to blur. Some nights, she awoke drenched in sweat and paralyzed by fear. Despite her protest, Gerard would wrap his arms tightly around her, his body heat and proximity forcing her to breathe and relax until she drifted back to sleep. "As well as you can imagine at this point," Elara said, her teasing tone eliciting chuckles as she rubbed her protruding belly. Rare were the moments of reprieve when she did not feel her child wiggling around. She was much rounder than she would have expected for six months pregnant, and she dreaded the idea of waiting three more months to give birth. Her belly might burst before then.

"Is the baby moving frequently?" Ismenia asked, eyes glued to the queen's abdomen.

Elara exhaled in frustration. "Constantly. Now, can we please discuss something other than this baby? I fear their head grows bigger with each question."

More laughter. Things almost felt natural between the four of them. Almost. Yet distrust clung to her like an itch beneath her skin, a constant reminder that even her closest friends had agreed to imprison her.

Rilura must have noticed the way Elara's smile had faded because she loudly dropped her teacup on the tabletop, missing the saucer entirely, and changed the subject. "Have you any updates on Serena? I miss watching her train in the yard. She's a sharp one."

"Sharp," the queen repeated with an absent-minded nod. Elara hated that her niece had to become such a thing. She had been attacked half a dozen times, circumstances forcing her to shift into constant fight mode. The once gentle features of a girl raised in a peaceful place were now jagged edges punctuated by quick reflexes and a sharp tongue.

She could relate in a way. She, too, had to adapt when Antoine seized Graynor. She was *still* adapting daily. To being a queen with no real weight to her title. To being married again. To her swelling bump. To the idea of becoming a mother after so many years believing it impossible.

"I have not been able to speak to Serena the past two weeks. By the time Gerard gave me the ring from my bedside table, she was not wearing its match," Elara said, hanging her head. She hoped Serena was alive and well where they had sent her.

"What day were you meant to speak again?" Idonea asked before taking a sip from her cup.

"Today, actually."

Ismenia stood and walked across the room to her bedside table. "I'm sure she's been worried about you." The herbalist opened the drawer and fished around in the back of it until she found the ring, her face lighting up in triumph. When she came back to the sitting area, she held it out to the queen on her open palm. "Go ahead. See if she's waiting."

Elara hesitated before taking it. It was late afternoon; Serena was likely training. Rolling the gold band between her thumb and index finger, she hummed to herself, looking out the balcony window. "What if I can no longer reach her? What if something terrible has happened?"

To her surprise, a large, warm hand came down on top of hers, squeezing gently. The queen turned to Rilura as the dwarf countered, "What if she be perfectly fine? You shall never know unless you try."

She was right. Of course, she was. Elara was starting to think the dwarfs were the wisest of the races. Rilura always knew the right questions to pose to make her think differently.

"You're right," she replied. Tightening her grip on the ring, she looked down and tried to ease it onto her middle finger, as she normally did, but she could not get it over her knuckle. Shaking her head, she tried the ring finger next before ending up with the ring loosely on her pinkie finger.

Immediately, her vision blurred, and she squeezed her eyes closed, waiting for the dizziness from the magic to dissipate. It was quiet for a moment as everyone held their breath.

"Aunt Elara?"

The familiar voice made her heart leap. "Serena! Oh, it is good to hear your voice." She brought a hand to her chest, relief washing away the tension from her body. Her eyes pricked with tears, and she tried to blink them back. "How are you, dear? Is this a good time?"

"Uhm, I suppose. I was just out for a stroll." Serena was outside at some sort of market. The tops of vibrant trees peeked over the high wall behind the shops. This was the first the queen had seen of Envyre, but the wall made her feel better about sending her niece there. The Burroughs boy looked at her strangely, asking what was wrong.

Elara rolled her eyes, and Serena exhaled, looking down. That's when her aunt noticed she and the boy were holding hands. She quirked a brow, wondering how long that had been going on since they left Symptee. "So sorry for interrupting," the queen said, unable to keep the snark out of her reply. "Would you like to resume this later… when you're *alone?*"

Serena looked back to those brown eyes full of concern and whispered to Will, "Sorry. It's Elara. I should go back to the cottage." Disappointment was evident on his face as he nodded.

She pulled her hand away and turned to face the other side of the road. "I'll be right back," she said to Elara. The girl yanked the enchanted ring off her finger, and the market around her dissolved away. The queen blinked until her vision refocused on her bed chamber.

"Well?" Ismenia leaned forward, waiting.

"She was with the boy from Durmak, Will," the queen replied with a wistful sigh. She had hoped he would heed her warning and keep his distance, knowing Serena bore royal blood. Clearly, she'd underestimated their feelings. "She's walking to her house and will be right back."

"You don't seem relieved to have made contact," Rilura said, taking a sip of tea. She wrinkled her nose at the pungent blend.

Elara shook her head. "I am happy to know she's alive and well. I just hope she isn't doing anything foolish. She is a princess by birthright. The boy has not a penny to his name. What good is there in getting their hopes up?"

"He's come a long way for her," Ismenia remarked, leaning back in her chair.

Rilura nodded. "Will is not just some boy to her. He's a hard working young man. I have seen the way he's trained since we arrived. He would do anything to protect her."

"Then he should be a knight!" Elara huffed, slumping back in her chair. She did not wish to always be the bad guy, but Serena had to know they were an unsuitable match. "She is the firstborn heir. The star-chosen savior of our people. When the war ends, should we be so lucky to finally have our crown and kingdom back, she should marry a prince. Someone who can share the burden of her royal duties. That's what she deserves."

Rilura scoffed loudly, and Ismenia tried to stifle her own grin. The herbalist sighed. "If I do recall, you were meant to marry the Prince of the Isles, yet you did not."

The queen froze, staring at her friend. She hated that they were right. She had chosen love over the original arrangement that had been proposed.

But Gerard was first cousins with the crown prince. He was still a member of a royal line.

She rose to her feet, and all three of her companions did the same. "Please, sit. I will just be a few minutes in front of the mirror. Nothing strenuous."

They were all hesitant to return to their seats as Elara slowly made her way across the room to a large mirror. Finally, Rilura lifted two chairs with ease and followed her across the room. She gently put down the chairs in front of the mirror, and Elara smiled as she sunk back down, thankful not to be on her feet for long. She was so much more tired than usual.

Rilura plopped down in the chair beside her as her vision blurred once more. As Elara's reflection disappeared, she squinted, straining to see through Serena's eyes. After a moment, the queen was able to make out two hands clasping a small hand-held mirror in her lap. The face that stared back reminded her of her brother and a bit of herself at that age. The bittersweet reminder that she had not laid eyes on her brother since their youth left a sour taste in her mouth.

"Hello again," Serena said, giving her a nervous smile. The girl was probably expecting a scolding for not having checked in for weeks, but Elara could not blame her for that, especially under her strictly-enforced bed rest. "Wow, you have gotten..." The girl hesitated, her eyes lowered to the queen's distended abdomen.

"Yes, I am very round. Thank you for the reminder," Elara said, waving off that thought with a hand. "Enough about me. I want to hear about your time in Ord Metsiilva. Envyre looks... *cozy*." The Cinderfell sisters snickered from the couch behind them.

Serena's cheeks flushed. "Err, I suppose it can be. Bonfires are nice. They remind me of home."

The queen tried to suppress the motherly urge to pry. *I'm certain that's not the only thing to remind you of home*, she thought to herself. Instead, she said, "That sounds lovely this time of year. And have you warm enough clothes? Blankets? If you need anything, do not hesitate to ask. I can send a guard with supplies or funds, whatever you need."

"I'm fine, Aunt Elara. Really. Envyre is beautiful. The people here are lovely. Even the elves, surprisingly. The students are like one big, happy family," Serena said. But her smile faded, her green eyes flashing with something Elara couldn't quite read. Was she homesick? Missing her own family? Elara wouldn't blame her. The girl stared at her aunt's reflection as though lost in thought, and Elara stared back, wishing she could console her from whatever thoughts were plaguing her mind. With that faraway look in her eyes, she looked so young—and it reminded Elara that she'd put the weight of a war on the girl's shoulders.

Serena cleared her throat and added, "I'm a bit jealous, in truth. I find myself missing my family more than usual. There are boys here, at the Academy, around the same age."

Elara closed her eyes and nodded. She understood the burden of losing a beloved brother. Poor Serena had lost three—four, if you included the missing Garrick prince.

Serena swallowed thickly, looking away from the mirror in her hands. There was something more on her mind—something burdensome. Elara smiled grimly and waited, hoping her niece would open up to her. Finally, the girl asked, "Have you any news from Papa—I mean, Sir John?" Tears shimmered, threatening to trickle over the red rims of her eyes. They held a million fearful questions, and Elara was relieved she could ease some of those fears now.

"Yes, we received word from him a few weeks ago," Elara said. Her lips curled in a genuine smile as relief washed over Serena's face. The girl wiped at her eyes before gripping the edges of the mirror again, bringing it closer to her face. "Your father is well. The loyalists have been steadily building their numbers and stockpiling weapons." She paused, uncertain whether she should concern Serena with his update on Antoine's forces.

"What is it?" the girl prompted, her brows knitted in concern.

Elara sighed. "It seems Antoine's armies are preparing for something in Murmont. Gathering supplies, buying up horses… They have not uncovered the reason yet."

"Do you think he's readying to attack Symptee?" Her eyes were dry now, her fear replaced with fiery determination. "I should come back."

"No!" Elara interrupted, her voice higher than she had intended. Sitting back, she folded her hands over her belly and exhaled. "No," she repeated more quietly. "You are safest where you are. Antoine's men will not go anywhere before winter's end. We're fairly certain."

Serena shook her head. "We cannot sit and wait for him to attack. Symptee is a beacon of hope. Should it fall… Should anything happen to you…"

"Do not worry about us. Our enemies would have to go through half the Guard to get to me."

"Such a fate will not befall Her Majesty," Rilura interjected. "The dwarfs would never allow it."

Serena's brows shot up. "Who is that?" Then Serena gasped. "Is that Rilura?" Her voice hit a higher octave, and the queen couldn't help but smile at her niece's returned enthusiasm.

"Yes, she is here. Have you anything you'd like me to tell her?" Elara asked. Rilura watched with fascination as the queen seemingly spoke to her own reflection, the dwarf unable to hear Serena's voice.

"Only that I miss her company," Serena said with a shrug. "As you can imagine, Queen Daephyra was not so warm and welcoming as the dwarfs."

Elara frowned. She knew the ancient elf had a deep-rooted hatred of humans, but she hoped Serena might find some sympathy in the woman's notoriously cold heart. The queen leaned over and informed the dwarf, "Their stop in Montaris was not successful. Daephyra still loathes our kind."

"Our feelings are mutual for Her Majesty, the Elf Queen," Rilura returned.

Elara covered her mouth, trying not to laugh out loud at the brusque reply.

Being alone in her home, Serena was not worried about offending anyone. She snorted, the sound causing Elara to lose her own composure. The queen could only imagine the smug look on Rilura's face as they both tried to compose themselves. "I wish you were here. It would be nice to have another friend to train with," the girl finally said, forgetting that the dwarf could not hear her. Elara leaned over and passed on the sentiment.

The dwarf smiled at their reflections. "It would be my honor. Perhaps one day fate shall see us fight side by side."

"Hopefully not anytime soon," Elara replied, straightening her spine. Her body ached, the baby within pressing hard on the left side of her abdomen, and she took a steadying breath.

"Does it hurt?" Serena asked, her voice breaking the queen out of her daze. "You look tired. Perhaps I should let you rest."

"No," Elara said hurriedly. "It's tolerable. Sometimes there are little pains. I can feel little feet kicking now. But it's because the babe is growing. It's all perfectly normal." She glanced over her shoulder at Idonea and Ismenia, who pretended they had not been staring.

"Take care of yourself, Aunt Elara," the girl said, her voice solemn. "I look forward to meeting my cousin soon. It will be nice to have another person to call family."

Tears pricked Elara's eyes, and she cursed inwardly at her overly emotional state. Family had always been important to her growing up. She hadn't realized just how blessed she was until her parents and brother were ripped away from her. Now, she questioned her every decision when it came to Serena, and she would do the same once her child entered this war-stricken world.

Guilt crept into her heart as she stared at her niece's face in the mirror and saw a younger, more stubborn version of herself. Her entire life, Elara had been taught to trust in Divinity, to be grateful for His gifts and prophecies. Yet the queen couldn't help but wonder if clinging to a years-old prophecy relying on her only kin to lead the rebellion was the right choice. The safe choice.

"If you cannot recruit anyone in Envyre to our cause, do not fret," Elara began, struggling to keep her voice from quivering. She cleared her throat and wished her tea was within reach. "No matter what Antoine does next… as long as you stay alive, he has not won. Do you understand?"

Serena nodded. Her head cocked slightly to the side as she studied her aunt's reflection. Understanding and determination reflected in her matching irises. Though Serena would not recall her brief time with him, Elara knew the girl was much like her birth father, Stellan. He would be proud of her for being so strong—both physically and mentally. She had faced terrible losses, yet somehow, she never gave up. "I will not let you or Hyrosencia down. I promise."

Elara knew she wouldn't. Garrick blood flowed through her veins, pumping her heart and flowing with her every movement. Serena was strong, and she continued to grow stronger every day. The queen had to believe that when the time came, her niece would have more than a fighting chance. She'd prevail.

Feeling a slight dizziness, Elara pressed her fingers to her right temple and winced. Using the enchanted rings for too long could make her feel queasy, especially during her pregnancy. It was best she ended their conversation before her friends intervened. She did not want Serena to know she had been made a prisoner in her own bed chamber. "It's been a long day, and I'm sure you're eager to get back to your friends." Elara pinned her with a knowing stare, one eyebrow slightly raised.

Serena's cheeks turned pink, and she tried to play it off. "I see them every day. It's no rush."

Her aunt grinned wider, a lightness settling over her usually tense shoulders and neck. She remembered what it felt like the first time she thought she was in love, before everything changed. She also remembered what it felt like when she started falling for Gerard. If Will made Serena feel that incandescently happy, then she could not fault the girl for liking him. She deserved every bit of the happiness Divinity provided. "Go. Enjoy your stroll. Tell Will and the guardians I wish them all well."

Serena blinked at her in surprise before a full smile stretched across her thin cheeks. "I will tell them."

Just before Elara could slip the ring off her finger, Serena stopped her with one final piece of news. "Oh! I meant to tell you: Cole and Xandra are getting married sometime after the Winter Solstice."

The queen's brows shot up. "Does her father know that?"

"I believe Cole wrote him a letter," Serena mumbled. Her confidence faded as she gnawed on her bottom lip, considering her next words carefully. "I had an idea for a wedding present, but it would require your help."

Elara leaned forward, eyes narrowed. Curiosity sparked her interest, and her headache seemed to have miraculously subsided. "I'm listening."

Serena grinned and leaned forward in her chair, all too eager to entangle her aunt in the most brilliant plan she'd heard in years. Elara was grateful to know they were finding their own happiness and making the most of the calm before the storm.

35

WASHED AWAY

It was the middle of the night when the trees thinned out, and the worn dirt path emptied right into the center of the bustling city of Jessiraé. Talitha was exhausted, her thighs and rear aching from riding on and off for over a full day. The serene silence of the forest gave way to drunken laughter as men and scantily dressed women traipsed the street from one establishment to the next. She flinched as men turned to gawk at her, quickly pulling her hood lower to hide part of her face. The last thing she needed was unwanted attention from a man.

After passing what she could only assume were a tavern and an inn, she finally noticed a rickety wooden sign with a black horse silhouette hanging above a doorway. The Untamed Mare. Talitha shivered to think of what types of unsavory men were inside such an establishment, trying not to think about the fact that Anteros and his friends had spent some of their leisurely time there a few months prior.

She dismounted from the black horse and hummed to herself, watching people pass by as she wondered what to do with the horse. Finally, a lady with piles of rich brown curls atop her head stepped through the doorway with a man draped around her shoulders. Her corseted dress hardly contained her large bosom, and Talitha tried not to stare.

"You be seeing the Joffrey boys down at the Dragon's Nest for a room," the woman said to the man, pointing the way down the road. The drunken imbecile stumbled out of her grasp, nearly running into Talitha on his way. They briefly made eye contact, and she quickly looked away. "There be no loitering here, miss." The woman's biting tone made Talitha jump and turn toward her.

"Apologies. I was told to find the Madam of this place for a room," she replied, wringing the horses' reins tightly in her hands.

The woman paused and squinted at her, seeming rather unimpressed with her appearance. "We don't be havin' any vacancies on this night, I'm afraid. And you're rather scrawny to be takin' any clients." She started to walk back into the building.

"Oh," Talitha murmured. "Prince Anteros said there would be a room waiting." She glanced down the road, uncertain where else she might find shelter.

That made the woman stop in the doorway. "Ahh, so you'll be Ruby then. You look far worse than he let on. Come with me." Without waiting, the woman disappeared into the boisterous building.

Talitha hesitated for a moment more, turning to pat the tired stallion on its snout. Then she quickly untied the two bags of supplies from Anteros and the covered cage concealing Phinn the phoenix. When she turned back toward the door, a filth-covered boy no older than eleven greeted her with a toothy grin. "I'll take 'im 'round to the stable, miss." She nodded, mumbled her thanks, and entered the place that would be her new home.

Inside, lanterns lined the walls and packed tables. Several men crowded around two tables placing their bets over cards, some with scantily clad women draped over their shoulders as they played. In the far back was a bar where a man and woman kept busy pouring ale and wine for their patrons. Some of the men were dressed more finely than others, and she wondered if they were nobles on holiday from Graynor Court. To be safe, she tugged her cloak down, careful to conceal the strawberry blonde locks that could give her identity away.

Coming out of a doorway behind the bar balancing a plate of food on each palm, the older woman she had encountered outside lifted her chin toward the stairs in the far corner and said, "Follow me." She dropped one plate of food at a table as she passed and carried the other up the stairs.

Talitha's feet dragged as she followed, wincing with each excruciating step. Upstairs was a U-shaped hall lined with identical wooden doors, the only difference being the simple black numbers on the center of each. She followed the woman around the curves of the hall to the very end, where she paused in front of room number eight. The woman turned the knob and pushed open the creaky door. "This'll be yours then. Best eat up quickly." She entered the pitch-black room and lit two sconces before returning to the hall and motioning for Talitha to enter the room.

It was modest but far cleaner than she was expecting for a brothel. Talitha eyed the plain bed that was centered against the back wall wearily before taking in the rest of the room. The wall sconces barely illuminated the space. The wood paneled walls did nothing to cut through the drab interior. On the far left was a tiny table with two wooden chairs.

On top of it was the plate of food the Madam had been carrying. Slowly, Talitha walked over to the table and placed the bags there, one atop the table and the other in a chair.

The woman shut the door behind them and leaned against it, keeping her distance while Talitha took a seat. The girl dropped her hood to help her eyes adjust to the dim light. She picked up the spoon and eyed the mystery stew for a moment. Deciding any food was better than nothing, she began shoveling it into her mouth. A thumping sound started in the room next door, and she wrinkled her nose, trying not to think about what was happening behind other closed doors. This place was a step up from the dungeon; this meal the best thing she'd eaten in ages. And in her exhausted state, she knew she could sleep through anything.

Talitha turned back to the woman and said quietly, "It's delicious. Thank you. Are you the Madam here?" Waiting for her answer, she shoveled another bite into her mouth. The meat and carrots practically dissolved in her mouth. She wondered if it would be rude to ask for more.

One corner of the lady's mouth turned up. "Madam Rosmerta at your service." Her gaze skimmed over the girl, still mostly concealed by the black cloak. "Finish up, and then we'll get you fixed up downstairs. You can leave your cloak and things here."

Talitha's lips parted, a knot catching in her throat. She pressed her lips together nervously. "I did not come here on pleasant terms, Madam. I would rather not draw attention to my presence. People will be… looking for me." She gestured toward her hair before moving the cloak hood to cover it again.

The woman's brows rose at the look of concern on her face. "In that case, keep the cloak. Do not fret. We'll do what we can to disguise you. You're not the first runaway to come here."

But I am likely the first fugitive.

Talitha nodded and rose from the table, taking her empty plate with her. As they stepped out into the hall, Madam Rosmerta pulled a heavy brass key out from between her cleavage and locked the door behind them. "Come," was all she said as she turned and headed back down the hall.

Downstairs, Madam Rosmerta led her past the bar through a small meeting room into a private bedchamber with an attached bathing chamber. The young woman from the bar had begun filling a large tub with lukewarm water. Talitha dipped her fingers in and cringed. She should have rejoiced at the sight of a bathtub, but after hours in the bitter night air, she already felt a biting cold deep in her bones. All she wanted was to bury herself under blankets and sleep.

"New girl?" the barkeep asked the Madam, not bothering to keep her voice down.

The older woman rolled her sleeves up to her elbows and nodded. "This is Ruby. She'll be boarding here. Room 8. Might help in the kitchen or cleaning if she wants to earn a wage."

Talitha tried to smile but feared it may have come across more like a grimace. In truth, she was still too tired and too afraid to summon a real smile. She also wasn't a fan of her new name and wondered why Anteros hadn't allowed her to choose her own.

"Nice to meet you," the girl replied. She was plucky, not much older than Talitha, with dirty blonde hair and a welcoming smile. Talitha wondered what had led the girl to work in such an establishment. "Name's Kaela. If you ever need anything, I'm in room 10."

Another girl popped in from the kitchen and dumped a massive pot of boiling water into the tub while Madam Rosmerta untied Talitha's cloak and laid it over a chair. Kaela stirred the water and fetched a towel and bar of soap from a shelf. Talitha held her breath as the woman pulled her dingy dress up over her head. A low gasp behind her made Talitha cross her arms tightly over her chest. She knew Kaela must have seen the scars from the lashings on her back. Part of her wished she could see just how bad they were. Another part was glad she couldn't. With the worst of her scars out of her sight, it was easier to force those memories to the back of her mind.

When Talitha shuffled toward the tub, Madam Rosmerta let out a heavy sigh, and a gentle finger traced a line on the girl's back. "You've been mistreated." Talitha closed her eyes and nodded. She didn't want to explain, and she was thankful when they did not ask questions. Instead, the Madam continued, "Many here are no strangers to unkindness. Rest assured you are safe here. We protect our own."

Talitha's eyes burned, not from pain, but from the simple, motherly touch. The promise of safety. She'd felt safe once before, back when she lived with her family in Durmak what felt like a lifetime ago. In the many months since then, she had been assaulted, tortured, and starved. Like the lack of sunlight, the lack of kindness and hope had diminished her spirit. If it weren't for the rare visits from Anteros and Sabine, she would have stopped believing compassion existed.

The two women each held out an arm to steady her as she stepped into the bath. The boiling water had done nothing to take away the chill of the well water. Talitha winced as she lowered herself on shaky legs to sit down, grinding her teeth together to keep them from chattering. After dunking her head underwater to get it over with, she took a deep breath, the fear that had coiled in her lungs chased away by the shock of the cold. She looked at the women and reached out for the soap, but Madam Rosmerta shook her head.

"Rest. We'll get you cleaned up," she said, lathering the bar on a small rag.

Talitha hated the idea of strangers' hands on her, but her limbs were heavy from riding and lack of nutrition. Through the bath water, her skin was nearly translucent. An array of scars lined her arms and legs, and her ribs stuck out at harsh angles from her deflated abdomen. Deep purple bruising encircled her ankles, the color harsh against her pale flesh. She felt shame for the poor state of her body, not knowing how she had managed to stay alive this long.

Looking between Madam Rosmerta and Kaela, she found only sympathy in their eyes, making her feel safe enough to allow their help. Talitha leaned her head back as Kaela started to work soap suds into her hair, gently massaging her scalp. It had been months since her last bath, and her scalp was extremely sensitive. She sniffled, trying to hold back tears as the girl gently worked the soap through her hair. The scent wasn't floral like Sabine's; it was plain, odorless. But it was getting the job done.

When her hair had been rinsed, Talitha opened her eyes and stared at the soap bubbles among the brown-tinged water while Madam Rosmerta gently bathed her with the rag. Kaela held her saturated hair up while the woman washed her back. The lash wounds no longer hurt, thankfully, but Talitha still thought she could feel them at times. The whip had seared her so deep she thought her insides might never fully recover.

Or perhaps that was just the emotional damage from it.

Hoisting her back onto her aching feet, the women helped her towel off before dressing her in a thick cream chemise that fell just shy of the floor. The fabric was coarse against her skin, but she was thankful to be in something clean, free of tears, dirt, and her own blood. She wrung her hair out again with the towel as the women tidied the space.

Then Madam Rosmerta turned to her and said, "We'll have to cut and dye your hair if you ever want to come out of your room."

Talitha ran her fingers through her long, damp tresses and swallowed thickly. She had not thought hiding would mean changing one of her favorite things about herself. Then she pictured Antoine Rexton. The horror of severed heads, knives searing flesh, and agonizing lashes ripping her back to shreds flashed through her memory. Having such a rare and vibrant hair color was a dead giveaway, and she knew it. This was a sacrifice she would have to make for her own safety. "Whatever you think is best," she replied, her voice low and full of trepidation.

"We'll let you get some sleep tonight. I can work on your hair after breakfast. This place is normally dead until mid-afternoon," Madam Rosmerta informed her.

Talitha nodded, her thoughts whirling with an overwhelming number of thoughts. She wondered how long it had taken Antoine Rexton to uncover her absence. His wrath was sure to be fearsome since she had managed to escape his men. She hoped Anteros would not suffer from his father's wrath as she had.

Remembering the bird she'd left covered upstairs, she paused and asked the Madam if they had anything she could feed it. The kitchen managed to scrounge up some grains, and she told the woman she could pay her upstairs. "Not necessary," Madam Rosmerta said, waving a hand. "The boy paid a hefty price for your stay."

She swallowed, reminded that she was only at the Untamed Mare, clean and fed and safe, because Anteros had paid handsomely to hide her there. Such was a debt she knew she'd never be able to repay.

Upstairs, the woman unlocked her door and then handed over the key. "Make sure you always lock the door, especially at night. Otherwise, I cannot promise you or your things will be safe." Talitha nodded, and then Madam Rosmerta left her.

Finally alone, Talitha turned the heavy lock with her frail hands. Then she pressed her back against the door and exhaled, wondering how safe she would be sleeping in a brothel. The bed beckoned her, but she first went over to uncover Phinn and offer him the bird feed. He fluffed his bright red feathers and pecked at it a bit before returning to sleep.

She dug through the bags on the table curiously, taking out two dresses and laying them over the back of a chair. They were ordinary—nothing out of Sabine's closet, she was certain. They would do fine for where she was. From the other bag, she pulled out a few apples, lining them up on the table far enough away from Phinn's cage. At the bottom of the bag, she found two sealed letters, and her heartbeat quickened.

Taking both, Talitha rushed over to the bed and pulled the blanket up to her chest. The first letter had a red seal with a rose on it, which she could only assume was from Sabine. She broke the seal and skimmed over the brief letter. It wasn't signed, but she knew who had written it from clues. It was addressed to Lady Adelaide and wished her well at her new home, noting that she would miss her company. She had signed it with an S with a little flower at the end of the letter.

The second letter had a black seal with the Rexton family emblem pressed into it. She shuddered as she stared at the bear, her heart rate accelerated in terror despite knowing it must be from Anteros. After a moment, she broke the seal, never wishing to lay eyes on that bear emblem again.

This letter was shorter than Sabine's, but each word pulled at her heart strings.

"I will always regret the way you were treated here and the ways in which I hurt you. If you're reading this, and I pray you are, then you're free at last. My hope is that you find the peace and happiness you deserve. I'll be thinking of you, as always. A"

Her cheeks were saturated by a stream of tears when she finished rereading it for the tenth time. It was everything he had said to her outside of the castle and more. She knew that he had taken a huge risk in letting her go—a risk that could end very badly for him. For that, Talitha would be eternally grateful to Anteros Rexton, the young man who had somehow turned out to be nothing like his cold, cruel father.

36

AN OFFERING

An uneventful autumn passed quickly in Envyre. The red and orange leaves fell from the trees as a bitter cold settled in over Ord Metsiilva in late November. Though the forest was nestled in the southern region of the continent, winter was as harsh and unforgiving as in the mountains. Serena was relieved to hear that it rarely snowed there. The climate reminded her of Durmak in that regard.

For over six months, Serena had spent endless hours training, and it showed in her enhanced sword and knife skills. Even Cole seemed impressed—though he never dared speak such high praise aloud. Alternating lessons and instructors kept things interesting. With Rigel's once-injured shoulder allowing him a greater range of motion, he was all too eager to challenge her to duel, and they kept score of who won, making it feel more like a game than a life-or-death practice session.

Nights when Rigel or Xandra were on guard duty were her favorite. Far more lax than their Elven counterparts, the other guardians often allowed her to attend bonfires, and she savored the chance to snuggle up or sneak away with Will whenever possible. Only when his strong arms wrapped around her did she feel truly at home.

The week of the Winter Solstice, many of the elves packed their bags to travel home and visit their families. Serena expected to remain in Envyre and continue her training. While she had made many new friends, both elves and humans alike, she found herself looking forward to the camp being nearly empty. The indoor training facility had become overcrowded since a cold snap blew in, and some days she'd had to cut back on her regimen to accommodate the students who were enrolled at the Academy.

She was shocked to find she had been sorely mistaken.

"But why would we go back to Montaris? We weren't exactly welcome there the first time," she argued, crossing her arms over her chest.

Crystal continued stuffing folded clothes into her knapsack. "This is one tradition I cannot ignore. My father expects Cole and I to come home. Deldrach and Ilrune's family always joins us for the feast. I was luckily able to convince him to extend an invitation to the rest of you."

"Will we stay at the inn again?" Serena asked, remembering how small the Elven cottages had seemed from the outside.

"Yes. I've sent word ahead to reserve two rooms. Cole and I will stay at our family home," the archer said. She flipped the top of the knapsack over, covering its contents, and fixed the buckle to hold it closed.

Serena begrudgingly returned to her own cottage and followed suit, packing a few spare articles of thicker clothing she had purchased from the market in Envyre. Unsure how formal the Winter Solstice feast would be, she picked up an emerald velvet gown that Xandra had recently talked her into getting, carefully rolled it up, and placed it in her bag. At least she would be prepared for anything.

Due to the weather, Crystal arranged horses for them to use on their journey to Montaris and back. Serena was relieved they would not have to walk, prolonging their miserably-cold journey. On horseback, they were able to reach the capital in one day's ride instead of two. After checking into the inn with no issues, Crystal and Cole left their human friends to bring their bags home and help their father prepare for the next day. That's when Xandra suggested that they should head to the market to pick up gifts for their host.

Will grabbed Serena's hand as they walked the quiet streets. Her gloves had nothing on the way his simple touch warmed her from her fingers to her toes. Flush from the breeze hitting her face as they walked, Serena's cheeks hurt from smiling so much. She couldn't remember the last time she'd been this happy. Before her brother and father left Durmak, perhaps. She had thought Will to be handsome a year ago, but she couldn't imagine him looking at her the way he was now. His eyes, as warm and welcoming as a crackling fire, looked upon her with such adoration. She still didn't feel that she deserved such affection, but day by day, Will's tenderness was healing the broken pieces of her heart, filling all the cracks with hopes and dreams for the life they could build together after the war.

From the middle of the road, Serena glanced up at the Elf Queen's castle and exhaled. She was still frustrated that Daephyra had refused an audience with her. Part of her wondered if the Silveryl elves' winter celebration might somehow manage to thaw the queen's icy heart, even for a day.

From what Crystal had told her, she doubted it.

The roads were nearly empty as they continued toward an area with several indoor shops. It seemed the cold was enough to keep most people indoors, cuddled up to their fireplaces by the looks of the smoke billowing out of chimneys all over the city. She stood up on her tiptoes and pecked Will on the cheek, hoping they would have the chance to do the same at some point on their little holiday. If they had to take a break from training, Serena wanted to make the most out of it.

In the first shop, they stopped for tea and fresh pastries. It was the best tea she'd ever had, rich and earthy but not too bitter, and she wondered if Elara might also enjoy it. Last they had been able to visit, she learned her aunt had been placed on bed rest for the remainder of her pregnancy. Serena could see the exhaustion in her face as Gerard held a mirror up for them to converse. She hoped there hadn't been any more assassination attempts since she left Graynor. Before they departed, she purchased two small sacks of dry tea leaves from a sweet elderly elf—one for her aunt and the other for Cassius Windaef. She didn't know the man, but she hoped he would appreciate something warm and Elven-made.

Xandra spotted a dress shop and grabbed Serena's hand, dragging her into a run as they crossed the empty road. "You boys can check out leathers next door," she called over her shoulder, leaving Will and Rigel in their dust.

Inside, Xandra giggled as she perused the luxurious fabrics on display. On one side of the shop were premade dresses with corsets varying from everyday to fancier attire. "May I help you?" the shopkeeper asked, approaching them. When she noticed they were human, she paused, keeping a few feet between them.

"I'm getting married in a few weeks," Xandra explained as her fingers skirted over gowns of deep gold silk, burnt orange velvet, and lush crimson cotton.

The elf's face lit up as she congratulated her, closing the gap between them. "We have many fine dresses. I'm sure we can find whatever suits your tastes."

Xandra's airy laugh had the elf eating out of her hands. Serena was starting to wonder if the sound contained a special type of magic that could quell even the most serious of elves.

Perhaps she needed to bring her along to meet Daephyra.

Serena's brows raised as she contemplated the crazy idea. They would only be back in Montaris for a few days. This was her chance to try bargaining with the Elf Queen.

When Xandra pulled Serena from her spiraling thoughts, she had four dresses draped over her arm. "How many weddings are you having?" Serena teased, shaking her head.

"One is for the wedding, one is for Crystal, and one is for you," the guardian said, lifting the top gown and passing it to her.

Serena had to admit her friend had exquisite taste. All the gowns were stunning. There were a few other items hidden under the pile on Xandra's arm, but Serena didn't bother asking about them. At present, she cared more about finding a way into the castle than discussing what her friend was skillfully hiding.

They paid the shopkeeper, who helped them to bag their purchases in a few burlap sacks for discretion. When they exited the shop, they nearly ran into Deldrach and Ilrune, who had stopped to speak to Ausha and Iriela. The elves tugged at their cloaks and thick scarves, fighting to keep the bite in the air off their skin.

It was the perfect timing. Deldrach had been in the Queen's guard for years. If anyone could possibly help her get in to see Daephyra, it was Crystal's fiancé.

"Well, if it isn't my favorite set of sisters," Xandra declared, accepting a hug from each of the female elves. "Everything ready for tomorrow?"

"Our mother has things handled. She sent us shopping to get us out of her way," Ausha replied with a grin.

The younger elf nudged her side and wagged her finger. "She sends *you* off because you burn something every year."

Serena chuckled. Seeing the two of them banter made her miss her brothers. They would have chased each other around the kitchen while she and their mother prepared a big meal. Roasted fowl and vegetables and a rich fruit pie would have graced their table— for the Winter Solstice, as well as for the double snow moons in January. Closing her eyes, she could almost smell her favorite scents of the winter season. Fresh baked breads that they'd meticulously braided into different patterns. Chopped fruit simmering over the fire with cinnamon and nutmeg. The memory alone made her mouth water.

"What brings you back to Montaris?" Ausha asked, directing her question at the humans.

Xandra lifted the bag in her arms and waggled her brows. "We were invited to join the Windaefs for the feast tomorrow. Today, I'm getting in some wedding shopping while I can."

Ausha's gaze dipped to Xandra's bare hands, immediately focusing on the gold band Cole had given her. With an excited yelp, she congratulated her friend, and they immediately delved into discussing every detail of the upcoming ceremony.

Seizing the opportunity, Serena turned to face Deldrach and Ilrune and feigned her best smile. "Gentlemen, it's good to see you." Her heart pumped faster, blood whirling in her ears as she studied their expressions. They seemed keen to discuss anything other than their friend Cole's marriage, especially knowing how their queen would feel about the situation. "Have you any plans to see Queen Daephyra while you're in the city?" She tried to sound nonchalant, but the question clearly surprised them both.

Deldrach crossed his arms over his chest and glanced at his cousin. "Of course. All Silveryl must pay their respects on the solstice. Her Majesty is carried through the city, and everyone bows, making an offering to her. Some she takes; others, she passes. If she takes a liking to your offering, she might bestow a special gift."

Serena bounced on the balls of her feet and clapped. If Daephyra would be walking the streets of Montaris tomorrow, that would be the perfect chance to gain an audience. "That sounds like great fun!" Her frozen cheeks hurt as her smile stretched wider. She had an opening and had every intention of using it to her advantage. She could not come back to Montaris for nothing.

"Solstice events are typically exclusive to Silveryl," Ilrune said quickly. There was no malice to his statement, but he avoided her eyes as though he felt guilty for saying anything.

Serena settled to a stop and twisted her lips in irritation. "But we were invited by the Windaefs." The light glistening off the queen's palace drew her attention, and she squinted at the golden-armored guards on the upper steps. *There has to be a way to get to her.*

An arm snaked around her shoulders, and she turned to find Ausha and Xandra had rejoined them. "Oh, it won't hurt anything if they attend," Ausha said. "Wear a cloak and stand in the back. You'll be fine. You're not the first humans from Envyre to come for the holiday."

Xandra smiled. "Rigel and I have been many times over the years. As long as you don't make a scene, nobody will bother you, not even the old human-hating shrew."

Deldrach coughed loudly, startled by her choice of words. The girls snickered, patting him on the back. Serena was surprised to hear Xandra speak so callously about the Elf Queen in the streets of the capital, yet none of their Elven counterparts moved to scold her. That did nothing to instill confidence in Serena as she went to work searching for the perfect offering for a queen who already had everything.

The following day, Serena and her friends departed from the inn early in the morning. The streets were already overflowing with elves eager to find a good place to watch the procession. Xandra led them down the street to the row of cheery cottages where the Windaefs live. In front of their home, they found Cole lounging in a chair on the front porch. His gaze softened and he leapt to his feet the moment he laid eyes on his fiancée. She bounded up the steps and pecked him on the cheek before asking, "Have they killed each other yet?"

Cole chuckled. "Oddly enough, no. I think he's happy she's back home. They've been quite civil while cooking."

"Do they need any help?" Rigel asked, his focus locked on the door.

"They already banished me from the kitchen, so I think they can manage," Cole said. He peered through the propped open window behind him and smiled crookedly, though he couldn't see anyone in the sitting area. Only the sound of gentle chopping drifted from the kitchen to the open window.

Rigel inhaled deeply and sighed. "Ahh, I smell your mum's legendary cookies!" He grinned as he yanked open the front door.

"It's tradition," Cole said with a shrug, following his friend inside the house.

Rigel's voice carried through the open window as he crossed the room. "We should see if she needs someone to taste test them."

Will laughed as he wrapped an arm around Serena's back. "You coming?"

She hummed, glancing back at the palace. There was no motion. The guards remained in their positions on the steps, the queen unseen.

Serena was more than happy to remain outside on the porch after what she'd learned about Crystal's father, but the bite in the air made her shiver. She allowed Will to guide her inside the cottage.

"Anyone want some tea?" Cole called from another room as Serena and Will joined their human friends in the sitting area. Several enthusiastic responses replied at once.

As Crystal made her way into the room in an emerald green sweater with a piping teapot in her hands, Serena hoped her plans for the morning wouldn't completely derail their family's celebration. Cole followed close behind with a stack of delicate cups and saucers stacked in his large hands. They worked together to pour and pass out the tea. Serena couldn't look Crystal in the eyes as she took her own, mumbling her thanks at the floor. They had no idea what Serena had spent half the night working on. She clutched her twine-wrapped package close to her chest with her free hand, using her cloak to protect it like a newborn. It wasn't her intention to cause any trouble, but she had to try appealing to Daephyra for her aunt's sake—and for the sake of all her people. There was no longer any time to be passive in this war. Not with Rexton preparing his army to attack.

"Where will we watch the procession from?" Serena asked loudly.

Crystal laid the teapot on the center table and wiped her hands on the apron hanging from her waist. Rigel stared at the small smudge of flour across her left cheek, but no one said anything about it. As she opened her mouth to answer, Cassius Windaef walked through one of the doorways with another tray in his hands.

The room immediately went silent.

Cassius' sharp gaze swept over their faces before answering, "We will greet Her Majesty from the yard in front of our home, as is customary." Now Serena knew where Cole had gotten his deep voice, and Crystal, her no-nonsense attitude.

Though Cassius did not smile, he stopped in front of Serena and held out the tray. To her surprise, it was covered in delicate cookies of a rich, dark brown cut into the shapes of leaves. "Thank you," she murmured as she picked one up. The warm scents of cinnamon and citrus hit her nose before she took a bite of the mouth-watering morsel that melted on her tongue.

Before long, the sound of trumpets boomed from outside, drawing everyone's attention to the open window. Cassius and Crystal stood abruptly. "That'll be her. Quickly, out on the lawn." The elves ushered the rest onto their feet and out of the door. They found Cole and Xandra sitting on the porch in separate chairs, smiles poised on their faces despite the obvious distance they were keeping for the sake of appearances.

Serena watched as Crystal cleared the steps with a covered plate in her hands. She joined her neighbors in leaving the offering atop a small wooden beam that sat two feet off the ground, safely keeping their gifts for the queen out of the grass and dirt. Serena clutched her own gift and breathed in, debating whether she should place hers beside Crystal's.

"Go on, Serena. Add yours to the row," Xandra encouraged from her seat, motioning for her to go down the steps with her hands.

"You have an offering for Her Majesty?" Cassius asked, blinking at her in surprise. His eyes flicked down to the parcel in her hands as she removed it from her cloak. The elf cleared his throat, trying to act indifferent. "What is it?"

"The inn allowed me to use the kitchen last night," Serena explained, swallowing loudly. Her throat was suddenly dry, and she wished she had brought her tea outside. "I baked my Mum's special bread. I made three actually. The first was a bit flat. The second burnt a bit around the edges—I've brought that one to share today. The third was as good as I could manage. I don't even know if she likes bread, but I wanted to give her something." Cassius eyed her curiously, and she stuttered to add, "For allowing us to stay in Envyre, I mean."

The elf nodded slowly, then raised a hand to point at his daughter. "Best join Crystalira then. Her Majesty particularly enjoys baked goods on this day." Serena beamed as she skipped down the steps to join her friend.

When Daephyra's entourage turned onto their street, Serena gaped. Four pallbearers held the queen up on a gold palanquin. She lifted one hand lazily, waving her long, rouge-painted claws at her subjects as they bowed. Her hair was silver. Not the tired, sagging gray of an elderly human, but vibrant and shimmering like stars in the morning sun. As Serena had expected, her sharp features made her both beautiful and lethal-looking. The girl watched as the house across from them presented their gift. The queen nodded, her lips barely curled into a pleased smirk, and a guard walked around to collect the gift and deposit it into a matching gold wheelbarrow.

Everyone stood and bowed when Daephyra's palanquin stopped before the Windaef home. Serena glanced to the side nervously, waiting for Crystal to lift her head first. The elf held her bow for another minute before rising. Immediately, she picked up the covered tray and lifted the lid, revealing more of the delicious leaf-shaped cookies they had eaten earlier.

But when Serena looked up, there was no smile on Daephyra's lips. Instead, the silvery pools of her hardened gaze were fastened on Serena, her nails tapping her golden ride in discontent. "You are not one of my own," the Elf Queen said, peering down her nose.

"I am not," Serena said. Her heart raced as she stared at this elf who looked as though she might rip out the girl's throat with her fingernails. She touched her throat and swallowed. "I am Serena Finch—I mean, Garrick. I believe Your Majesty is familiar with my aunt, Queen Elara of Hyrosencia."

A hissing sound came from the back of Daephyra's throat, and she pointed an accusatory finger at Crystal. "How dare you orchestrate this after my explicit refusal?"

Crystal and Serena exchanged a nervous glance. "We meant no slight, Your Majesty. We simply invited our human friends from Envyre to join us at our table tonight."

"I meant no disrespect, Your Majesty," Serena added quickly. "I baked you a loaf of bread as thanks for allowing me to stay in Envyre—and not just us. All of the refugees. We are so very grateful for your hospitality." She lifted the bread she had carefully wrapped in a shawl and tied with twine, bowing as low as possible while she held it up.

The street was silent save for the rustle of what few leaves held on in the trees. Everyone held their breath, awaiting Daephyra's reply.

Finally, Serena felt someone lift the offering off her hands. Popping up like the first daisy of spring, she expected to come face to face with one of Daephyra's armored guards. Instead, she found that the men had lowered the palanquin, bringing Daephyra nearly to eye-level with her. Serena sucked in a breath as she met the queen's cold, scrutinizing gaze. Without looking away from her, Daephyra unwrapped the parcel and lifted the loaf, inhaling deeply. Serena could smell the herbs from where she stood on her shaking legs.

Crystal remained prostrate on the ground beside Serena, as did Cassius a few feet behind them. Serena wondered if she should do the same. Fall to her knees and be silent.

No.

Serena had finally come to accept that she was also royalty, and she would not cower under the calculating gaze of the Silveryl Queen—or any other monarch. Garrick blood ran through her veins, hot and determined and blessed by Divinity. She was the true heir to the throne of Hyrosencia, the star-chosen savior of her people. Tipping her chin higher, Serena held the queen's gaze.

Daephyra slapped the half-wrapped loaf of bread against the nearest guard's chest and leaned closer to her. Wrapping one hand under Serena's chin, Daephyra cocked her head to one side and hummed to herself. "You are a brazen little thing, aren't you?" Her sharp nails stroked up the side of Serena's neck, and the girl held her breath.

Then she just as quickly dropped Serena's chin and turned away. "I know why you came. You want me to send my people off to war for you. To fight a human war."

Daephyra shook her head and made a tutting sound. "Why do you think I should send Silveryls to spill their blood for humans who will soon enough be dead?"

Serena clenched her jaw, leveling the queen with her own somber look. "Though we may not live as long, that does not make our lives any less valuable. All life is precious, and all people deserve to live in peace, not in fear—be they human, elf, or dwarf."

The Elf Queen sneered at her final word, eyes narrowing in dissatisfaction at the mention of the other races. Turning her gaze toward the neighbors waiting next door, Daephyra seemed to be done with her. As her servants lifted the palanquin back to shoulder-height, Serena stared up at the queen, willing her to turn back and see her. To see that the humans gathered in friendship with the Silveryl elves were accepted. Loved. Worthy of respect.

"Antoine Rexton is known far and wide for his hatred," Daephyra said, still not looking at the girl. Serena held her breath. "If he wins your war, he will want more. Men always do. And I will not have him trample the peace we've fought hard to maintain in Ord Metsiilva."

Serena stepped around Crystal, trying to get in front of the queen's face. She could not tell from the shrewd woman's voice where her statement was going.

Finally, those silver pools turned toward her, catching the sunlight like a freshly polished blade. "I will not force my men to fight your battles. Not when you've yet to prove yourself."

Serena felt her cheeks flush in disappointment, her eyes dipping to the ground in shame. The queen was right. She had never fought in a battle, merely small skirmishes. She was far from ready to lead a troop into the throws of battle. "I understand, Your Majesty." She bowed her head, the heaviness of defeat settling on her shoulders.

"Rexton's reach extends beyond Hyrosencia's borders. Perhaps you can prove yourself to be a capable leader by liberating the land which once had no ruler," the queen suggested.

Crystal's head shot up then, and Serena glanced between the two elves. "You mean the valley?"

Daephyra shrugged and turned away from them both. The slightest smile was visible on her red-painted lips as she waved a slender hand, and the bearers started walking toward the next home. Serena and Crystal watched her go, both too stunned to speak. The Elf Queen had accepted both of their offerings, but beyond that, she had given them a gift greater than either could have anticipated.

Hope.

If there was any chance Daephyra could be persuaded to send guards and healers to aid them when they siege Graynor, Serena was willing to take the gamble.

37

COLD

Anteros was floating.

No.

Drowning.

The last thing he remembered was flopping onto his bed. The silk cushioned him in its cold embrace, making him sink deeper into the fabric until the bed swallowed him whole.

Weeks under confinement had passed in a blur. On this night, the whispers in his mind were particularly loud, so he chugged his last bottle of heavy liquor, desperate to drown it out. In his drunken stupor, he shattered glass decanters against the wall in fits of rage and cried out to the gods for answers.

The gods were silent.

He was left alone with his spiraling thoughts, his life a waking nightmare plagued by memories of vibrant hair blowing in the gentle autumn breeze and dead eyes staring through his soul.

She's gone. Sabine is gone.

The thought echoed through his mind like a ghostly whisper, threatening to drag him down into an early grave with his sister. He stared at the balcony and contemplated his options. After his outburst that dreadful night, the prince was restricted to his bed chambers with two guards posted outside the door. He wished his father had punched him. Whipped him. Anything to make him feel something. But his father chose to torture him with the brutality of silence instead.

Anteros wondered how his mother was doing. She, too, had been locked up. Last he'd heard from the servants, she was in a state of delirium, talking to herself as though someone were in the room. As if *Sabine* were there.

Not being able to see his mother, to grieve with her, was agonizing. No one else knew the pain they were feeling.

But not even his mother could have felt the unbearable guilt that pressed down on his chest daily, making it hard to breathe.

He didn't deserve air. Only desolation.

The loneliness sank deep into his bones as he lay in bed waiting for his sister to barge in with some silly problem, knowing deep down she never would again. Tears streaked down the sides of his cheeks, soaking into the gold-threaded blanket underneath him. He squeezed his eyes shut. All he needed was to go back to sleep. Hunger eluded him; his stomach twisted in agony from his worries and his grief. He wished he could somehow speak to Talitha. To make sure she had made it somewhere safe. But he knew better than trying to reach out. His father and half of Graynor were watching closely. Guards were still on the lookout, and as far as he knew, she had yet to be found.

He fell prey to the insufferable silence and allowed his mind to wander into alcohol-induced dream-states where he, Sabine, and Talitha were all together having a picnic in the field overlooking the lake. Talitha had meat on her bones; she looked far more like the girl who had first been brought to Graynor. Sabine complained about the dirt on her frilly pink gown, and he laughed at her. The sound of his laugh felt foreign. Forced. As though he could not remember a time when he had been happy enough to produce such a sound.

Then he'd remember that they were both gone, and the darkness would creep in through the edges of his mind, consuming his dreams and crushing him down until he felt helpless like an infant. He couldn't move, couldn't stop the pain, could only cry until he drifted back into a restless slumber…

Cold water slapped his face, shocking him from his sleep.

Anteros sputtered as the assault came to a stop, and he sat up, gasping for air. The bed was soaked, and he was certain it wasn't from his tears alone. Looking up, he found a small audience huddled around his bed. Julian Malloy held his wash bin in his hands, looking rather disgusted by the state of the prince.

"What in the nine realms are you doing?" Anteros snapped, yanking the bin away from his friend. He tossed it haphazardly toward his bedside table and missed. The vessel crashed to the floor and shattered loudly, making everyone wince.

Julian shoved his hands into his pockets and shrugged. He wore mourning black, his shirt the only thing about him that looked clean and put-together. His blond hair was disheveled, his facial hair grown out in a way Anteros had never seen before. The bags under his eyes were dark purple as though he had hardly slept. Had he been crying, too?

"Your father sent us. He expects you at the feast tonight," James said sheepishly, poking his head out from behind Julian.

Anteros rubbed his hands over his face. "I'm not going."

Julian huffed an unamused laugh at the arrogant remark. "Yes, you are. Everyone at court is expected. *Including you.*"

Anteros threw his legs over the side of the bed, recoiling at the feel of the cold, wet blankets underneath him. Shoving himself onto his feet, he swayed a bit, several hands shooting out to steady him. "My mother is beside herself. My father has not mourned the loss of his own flesh and blood in any way, and he's to blame for her death! You can tell him that I will not be a pawn in his absurd show any longer." Not bothered by the audience, he shoved past his friends and started stripping out of his soaked clothing.

"Do you wish to see us beheaded?" Calix asked.

The bluntness of his statement made Anteros pause midway through pulling on clean trousers. He stared at the floor for a moment before returning to the task at hand, muttering, "He wouldn't behead you."

Julian scoffed. "You really don't care for anyone but yourself, do you?"

Anteros turned on his bare heel, teeth clenched like a mad dog as he barreled his way toward him. "My sister is *dead*, and my mother blames *me*." His finger jammed hard into his own chest as he got in Julian's face, but it was nothing compared to the ache he felt inside his chest. Like his ribcage had been cracked open and his beating heart had been ripped out, stomped into a bloody pulp on the cold cobblestone. His face burned as he leaned closer to the wide-eyed blond, his voice raising an octave. "And the bastard I call my father is *hunting* the girl I love. So, tell me: why should I give a damn about anyone else in this infernal place?"

Julian's hands gripped the prince's biceps, barely holding his trembling frame at bay. His pale brows furrowed as he took in Anteros' fragile state. Anger and heartbreak soaked his friend's reddened cheeks as he breathed heavily, wishing he were back in his bed succumbing to the numbness he could only find in slumber. Then Julian released his hold, and Anteros went to step back from those pity-filled blues.

But before he could, Anteros was encased in a tight embrace.

"I'm sorry you've suffered so many losses," Julian whispered, patting the prince stiffly on the back. "Know that you do not grieve Sabine alone."

Sabine.

Anteros choked at the sound of his sister's name, fists curling into the back of Julian's tunic as his knees threatened to give out. It was all too much, too heavy. His entire world had been ripped in half, his life separated into two distinct parts: before Sabine's death and after.

After, there was nothing but hollowness. Endless darkness and pain he knew he'd spend the rest of his life never being able to outrun. It wasn't fair. She was only sixteen. She should have been having tea and flirting with her brother's friend.

Instead, she grew cold in the ground.

He had felt that piercing cold deep in his bones as he wallowed in his bed chamber alone for the past few days. Until now. When Julian, Calix, and James huddled around him, tears staining all their faces as they held him up. For the first time in days—in his entire life even—Anteros felt seen, and it was a comfort he hadn't realized he'd desperately needed.

When he stopped quaking, Anteros wiped his face with both hands, and the boys backed away from him, all turning and doing the same. A heavy, uncomfortable feeling permeated the air. No one spoke as they cleared their throats and tried to collect themselves. They were boys on the cusp of manhood. They had been taught to hold their heads high and never show this type of emotion to anyone. Sadness and tears were a weakness. Yet how could one not weep at the loss of such a vibrant young soul?

Anteros pulled a dry black tunic over his head and leaned against the back of his sofa. "I do not want to see him." He ruffled his mussed hair and stared at his bare feet.

"I cannot blame you," Julian replied, cautiously walking over to him and leaning against the sofa beside him. "But we all know it will be more trouble than it's worth if you refuse."

The prince nodded, pinching the bridge of his nose with his fingers. "I'm going to need a drink."

Calix eyed the empty bottles piled up on his bar cart and muttered, "Perhaps you should take it slow tonight."

Anteros grumbled under his breath, already feeling a dull pulsing in his temples as the earlier buzz began to fade. Without something to take off the edge, it was going to be a very long evening with his father.

At the feast, Anteros did his best to ignore his father entirely, despite being seated inches to the man's right. His mother was notably absent; a younger woman with dirty blonde hair and a voluminous bosom occupied her seat. She was so young, in fact, she would have made a more suitable conquest for the prince than the king. Anteros clenched his fork in a death grip, trying to tamp down the rage he felt from seeing another woman sprawl herself in his father's lap.

"Where is Mother this evening?" he asked, grating his fork against the porcelain plate.

Antoine nudged the woman off his lap into the chair beside him. She landed with a thud, her lower lip jutting out in discontent as the king raised his chalice to his lips. He didn't look at Anteros when he replied, "In her chambers."

The prince laid his fork down and exhaled through his nostrils. "Do you ever intend to let her out?"

His father turned toward him and said rather bluntly, "Not after her hysterics at the memorial. She can spend the rest of her days in that room if she cannot control herself."

Anteros reached for his goblet and frowned at the water within. He still didn't know why he'd allowed his friends to convince him not to drink that evening. The three of them were seated beside him—though he was not sure whether that was a blessing or a curse at present. They were watching him closely, trying to steer his gaze away from his father and his latest mistress with chatter about James preparing to leave them. His friend had thankfully made a full recovery from the sparring injury he received back in autumn, but his father was still adamant about forcing him to join the king's service to learn discipline and respect.

"It's going to be dreadful without you lot there," James moaned. He lifted his glass to chug its contents—earning a pointed glare from the sober prince.

Calix slapped his friend on the back. "Perhaps I will join you. I'm a second born, so it's not like I'm going to inherit anything." He turned toward Julian and lifted a brow expectantly.

There was no humor on Julian's face as he chuckled. "Oh, no. You may need a calling, but I will inherit my father's title. I'll be staying put until then."

Something stirred in Anteros' heart; the urge to chuckle at the way his friends never changed. But the feeling died out as quickly as it appeared, no sound leaving his lips. He sat in silence, sipping his water and pushing food around on his plate for what felt like the longest stretch of time. Occasionally, he dared lift a roasted potato or carrot to his lips, but every bite was bland. All he could think was that Sabine and Talitha would have been pleased with the meal. Thoughts of them left a sour taste in his mouth that no mere water could wash away.

After a while, it became hard to drown out the drunken laughter from his father's mistress. Anteros gripped his chalice tight in one fist, feeling the gold ridges dig deep into his palm. Seeing the woman's subtle movements out of the corner of his eye nearly drove him mad.

Standing, the prince nodded at his friends. "I think I'll retire early." He didn't turn to acknowledge his father, marching swiftly in the opposite direction.

As he rounded one corner of the table, a deep voice called out his name, the sound so loud it seemed to reverberate at him from every direction. Anteros froze but didn't turn. He knew his father would be on his feet from the shrill scraping sound of his chair against the floor. Eyes closed, the prince could picture the way the veins bulged in his father's cheeks and neck when he got angry. The way his pupils blew out until there were only black holes glaring at you. He had seen it all before, and this time, he welcomed it.

Glancing over his shoulder, Anteros ran his fingers through his messy hair as he skimmed over the wide eyes of the other guests. "Yes?" he replied, intentionally forgoing a formal address.

Boots plodded against the floor, the sound growing closer with each heavy step. Anteros counted them, goosebumps trailing up his spine as his father's menacing presence approached.

Sixteen. It only took sixteen steps before Antoine came to a halt just behind his back, the heat of his heaving breaths burning the back of Anteros' neck.

"You have not been excused," his father said. His son recognized the distinctive edge to his voice that came from clenching his jaw when he felt disrespected.

Anteros smirked slightly and turned to face the bear on his heels. Though he was a few inches shorter than his father, he held his chin high, determined not to cower to the man's brutality. He had seen too much suffering from the man's ruthless hands and callous orders. Now, he would not give him the satisfaction of bowing or addressing him like a king.

All he would ever see when he looked at his father was a monster.

"I'm afraid I am not feeling up to socializing this evening," Anteros said, cocking one eyebrow in defiance. "I finished my meal, so I should like to return to my confinement."

The king took a deep breath, causing his heavy fur-trimmed cape to brush against his son's chest. His father's breath was hot on his face; the foul smell of rancid wine and meat made him want to step back. "You leave when I say you may leave."

Anteros wished his buzz had not worn off. He could have used the confidence boost as he stared into the cold, unfeeling darkness looming over him. "Then by all means, grant me your blessing, Father, because I am already on my way out." He threw his arms out at his sides in exasperation.

He turned away from the king, pride swelling in his chest at the way he'd handled the situation, but his father did not let him get far. Antoine's heavy hands landed hard upon his shoulders, yanking him back roughly. The prince stumbled but managed to keep his footing. Suppose he had sobriety to thank for that.

"You insolent brat!" His father gripped the back of his jacket and turned the boy back toward him. Spittle flew from his lips as he got in Anteros' face, his own having turned a vivid shade of red that almost matched his cape. "You will show your king respect, or I will send you to the abyss."

"The way you sent Sabine?" Anteros snapped back. He searched his father's face for any sign of remorse, knowing in his heart there was none.

The man didn't flinch at his accusation. He held his son's gaze, his nostrils flaring with white-hot anger. "I did not lay a hand on your sister that night. Her death was the result of her own stupidity."

Anteros lurched forward, grabbing his father's tunic in both fists. "She died by your orders! You may have executed the guards, but everyone here knows you're the real monster!"

"That girl was as useless to me dead as you are presently," the king said through clenched teeth. Shoving Anteros' hands off his shirt, Antoine grasped the boy by the throat and backed him into the nearest wall. When Anteros' head and shoulders slammed into the stone, he winced, prying desperately at his father's fingers. "All this time I have raised you, and you turned out to be weak and pathetic like your mother."

The prince growled, feeling the vibration of his throat against his father's hand. To his surprise, Antoine's grip slackened, though he continued to press his son against the wall. "I would choose mother's love over your cruelty any day," Anteros declared.

An unsettling smile curved his father's lips then. Anteros' heart rate quickened as he considered that perhaps his statement might have just endangered his mother's life. He hoped his worries were for nothing, for the woman did not deserve to meet a cruel end after such a miserable life.

The king leaned his head close to his son's right ear and chuckled. "You believe me to be a monster, but you have yet to make any sacrifices for your crown. It's time we change that."

I've already sacrificed everything, Anteros thought miserably. He stared back at his father in silence, awaiting further monologue from the ruthless tyrant.

Antoine released his throat and turned back toward the banquet table, where all his esteemed guests were staring at them. The man zeroed in on the place where Anteros had left his three friends and smiled cruelly. "Pack your things. When your friends leave for Murmont, you will join them."

When the king turned back toward his son, Anteros shook his head in quiet protest. He had no interest in joining the king's service, no need to ever feel his blade slice through the flesh of another again. Chills racked his body as he remembered the incident with James—how one of his oldest friends had nearly died by his hands. He had felt like a monster that day, the obvious heir to a ruthless tyrant who had slaughtered innocents to take the throne for himself.

The same throne Anteros would inherit should his father manage to maintain his power.

As if he could read his son's swirling thoughts, Antoine stepped closer and patted his son roughly on the cheek. "Cheer up, son. There are worse places than Murmont to learn to be ruthless. Like your father, you shall learn on the battlefield."

Anteros clenched his fists at his sides in a futile effort to stop them from trembling. "We aren't even at war right now," he said, his voice coming out like a childlike whisper that made him curse inwardly.

The king chuckled loudly, the eerie sound echoing through the hall. "We are not at war *yet*, but I will not sit around and wait for Elara's loyalists to make their move. No, I have plans to show those fools just who they are dealing with." Something truly sinister reflected in his eyes as Anteros stared up at him, unable to breathe a word of protest. He was cornered like a mouse, frozen in fear, stuck staring into the eyes of the beast that intended to devour him whole. "When we are done, you will have earned your title. I will make a monster of you yet."

Without another word, Antoine Rexton waltzed back to the table, offering his hand to the blonde tramp who awaited him. She tried to feign a smile as she took the king's hand, but she looked more like a doe than a vixen then. Watching them leave the hall together, Anteros knew his father was serious—and he was terrified that he might succeed.

38

FAMILIAR

Talitha stared into the dusty mirror on the wall in her room, running her fingers through her tresses. Even a few weeks later, it was still like looking at a stranger. Her hair, dip-died in black tea, had taken on a deep burgundy color. The Madam had cut it so her waves barely touched the top of her shoulders.

The plain brown dress she wore covered her marred skin effortlessly, the back rising to her neck and the sleeves coming down to a point at her middle fingers. Still, she tugged at the sleeves before exiting her room to join the others downstairs. She was lucky it was currently winter. It would be much more difficult to hide her scars come next summer.

In her short stay at the Untamed Mare, she had come to know a few of the other tenants. Kaela the barkeep was kind, taking the time to teach her a few things behind the bar during the daytime. After their overnight guests filed out of the place, back to their homes, jobs, or wives, all the women gathered for a late breakfast, rehashing the most hilarious and horrendous stories from the night before. Talitha didn't know how these women did it—entertained these awful men night after night yet maintained such high spirits and boisterous personalities.

At the bottom of the steps, several young ladies cheered at her arrival, beckoning her to join them at the table. The perky blonde named Alya slid over on the bench seat to make space for her. "Ruby! Join us! You *must* hear the latest news out of the capital."

Talitha nodded her thanks as she took a seat. Her heart rate quickened at the mention of the capital. "What news?" Her first thought was of Anteros. She hoped his father had not harmed him when he learned about her escape. His cruelty was unmatched, and she would never wish it on another.

A broad grin spread over Helene's face as she leaned forward on her elbows. A curtain of black hair cascaded over her shoulder, sweeping the edge of the beer-stained table. She might have been the oldest of the ladies of the night, but her beauty was unmatched. "Last night, the son of Duke Malloy had much to say after a few drinks."

Malloy. Talitha racked her brain and tried to remember him. Had Sabine mentioned him during one of their encounters? She couldn't remember.

"As did his friend Calix. Apparently, they're off to Murmont next week for military training," Rhea said.

Helene rose from the bench, gaining their attention. "That's not all I heard. After his recent outburst against the king, the crown prince will be joining them."

Talitha perked up. "Prince Anteros? What sort of outburst?" She hadn't intended to allow her interest to be so obvious, but she couldn't help herself.

The other blonde, Callisto, eyed her suspiciously. "Who else?"

Her cheeks burned. She was thankful when the other women did not seem to notice. They continued gossiping without paying her any mind. "I cannot say I blame him after what I heard from Cal," Rhea said, taking a more somber tone. "The poor boy is absolutely heartbroken. Blames his father for the tragedy that happened."

Talitha furrowed her brow. "What tragedy?"

"Ah, I forget you're new. You've missed so much over the past few weeks," Rhea said, tucking a strand of red hair behind her ear. The color reminded Talitha of her natural locks. She looked away, trying not to allow that to dampen her morning.

"The princess tried to flee her wedding on horseback," Helene declared. She certainly liked to be the center of attention when there was a scandalous story to tell. "There was some confusion that night. A prisoner had escaped or something." She waved a nonchalant hand in the air. "The guards shot at her by mistake, and she died."

Talitha's heart leapt into her throat, and she forgot how to breathe. *Sabine is dead?* She shook her head in disbelief. "When... when was this?" she barely stuttered, staring into the space between Helene and Callisto's heads.

"A few weeks back?" Alya said, sounding uncertain.

"Yeah, around the time you showed up, actually," Callisto pointed out, one brow raised as she stared at Talitha.

Then the girl realized how horrified she must have looked. Rising from the table, Talitha tried to breathe normally, but the air filling her lungs made her chest ache. Her friend was dead, likely had died on the night of her escape from the dungeon. But why?

"Apparently, the king's wife and son have been confined to their chambers since the incident," Callisto said before sinking her teeth into a plum. Juice dribbled down her chin, and Talitha squeezed her eyes closed, suddenly nauseated by the sight.

"They both openly blamed the king for the poor girl's death," Helene added.

Talitha blinked at her in shock. "And he did not execute them for such disrespect?"

The girls chuckled. "Heavens, no. He only has one heir. He wouldn't dare kill Anteros." The way Rhea said the prince's name made her grimace. It was familiar. *Too familiar.* And being reminded that Anteros had spent time at the Untamed Mare for his last birthday made bile rise in the back of her throat.

Talitha pushed herself onto her feet and released a shaky breath. "I'm going to take a walk," she mumbled, her feet leading her toward the exit on their own. She didn't know where she was going, but she needed to get out of there—away from the girls and their gossip and her spiraling thoughts.

She had yet to wander the city since her arrival. Too afraid Rexton's men might find her in the streets. But after several weeks, the guards who made their way through were no longer looking for a missing prisoner—only a good time.

For hours she roamed the bustling streets, taking in the market shops with no intention of purchasing anything. She already had more than a fugitive could ever need thanks to Anteros.

Midday when her stomach rumbled angrily, Talitha decided to go into a different establishment for lunch. She patted the outside of her pocket, relieved to feel the coins she had hidden there through the thick fabric. As sick as the news had made her feel, she knew Anteros would be worried sick if she starved herself because of it.

Talitha eyed the sign over the tavern, a simple silhouette of a fox reminding her of home and of the masquerade ball. Inside, she took a seat at the bar, avoiding the eyes of any strange men who looked her way. The barkeep delivered a steaming bowl of venison stew that smelled heavenly. She inhaled the steam, allowing the heat to thaw her wind-whipped cheeks.

Two men entered the tavern in heated conversation and seated themselves beside her at the bar. Talitha didn't look over at them. She pulled her arms in tighter, careful not to touch the back of the man beside her. She didn't want to give him the wrong idea.

"Haven't seen you around before. Passing through?" Talitha glanced up and realized the barkeep was leaning on the bar across from her. He cocked his head to one side, awaiting her answer.

Talitha stuttered, not wanting to admit she was living in the whore house. "Uh, not exactly. I'm... staying with a friend."

"Well, I wouldn't advise walking around alone at night," the man said, straightening. Pushing up his sleeves, he turned to the men beside her and asked, "The usual?"

"Yeah, and add a pint," a deep, familiar voice said.

Her head whipped around, causing her hair to slap her cheeks as she stared wide-eyed at the familiar profile. It was like seeing a ghost. Though his dark hair was longer than she remembered, she would know his face and voice anywhere. She had been to his home hundreds of times. He might as well have been a second father to her.

"Mister Finch?" she asked incredulously. Her chest rose and fell quickly, completely caught off-guard by seeing him outside of Durmak.

John Finch turned, thick brows furrowed as he took her in. The change to her hair was drastic, but it only confused him for a moment before he asked, "Talitha?"

She shushed him, terrified someone might have heard her real name. "It's Ruby now, sir," she insisted. "What are you doing here?"

Her friend's father huffed a little laugh and scratched at his neatly-trimmed beard. "I should ask the same of you. How did you end up all the way in Jessiraé? Your parents must be worried sick."

She glanced down at her bowl and dragged the spoon through it, embarrassment flush on her cheeks. Of course, she missed her parents desperately, but it was in their best interest that she did not return to Durmak. She wouldn't be able to live with herself if they were ever killed for harboring a fugitive of the crown. "It's a long story," she murmured.

Then it dawned on her that John Finch might not know what had happened to his family.

She swallowed thickly and pictured Serena's tear-streaked face. The last time she had seen her friend, she disappeared into her family's cottage. By the time help arrived, Serena was long gone. She hadn't even said goodbye. Talitha could only hope she was still alive.

"Do you know what happened back home… back in the spring?"

John lowered his chin and nodded. "Yes, I received word," he said solemnly. A darkness crept into his face as he zoned out, staring right past her. Talitha wanted to know who had sent word when no one had known where he went besides his wife.

"Have you seen Serena? Is she safe? There were men looking for her. When they couldn't find her, they took me," she said, her voice trailing off with the terrible memory of her kidnapping. The cruel soldiers' faces were burned into her memory, and she shivered at the thought of those restless nights in the dark.

John groaned apologetically. "I'm so sorry, Tal—Ruby. We thought everyone was safe. If I had known—" His voice was hoarse, full of regret. She almost pitied him.

But he hadn't seen the carnage. Two boys not yet old enough to be considered men and a hard-working woman who put love into everything she baked, all mercilessly slaughtered. He wasn't there to protect them. He wasn't there to bury them in their backyard. And where the last of his children were, she could only guess. She prayed they were safe, wherever they ended up.

"How could you have known? We all thought we were safe, too," she replied, using her palm to wipe away the moisture gathered in the corners of her eyes.

The man worked his jaw, clearly holding back something he wanted to say to her. After a long pause, he asked, "Are you staying somewhere safe?" Before she could answer, he glanced over his shoulder at his friend, a much younger man she had not paid any attention to until now. "Is there any space in the bunker?" She heard John whisper, nearly inaudibly.

The man peered over John's shoulder at her and shrugged. "I'm sure they could find a place somewhere for her." He ran a hand through his shaggy dirty-blond hair and smiled timidly at her. His face flecked with day-old stubble, he couldn't have been much older than Cameron.

"Leo, this is Ruby," her best friend's father said, careful to use her new name. "Ruby, this is my right hand, Leo Albright. He knows everyone and everything there is to know in these parts."

"It's nice to meet you, Leo," she said, tucking hair behind her ear.

The barkeep returned and placed two bowls of stew in front of John and Leo. John paid him, and the man added a pint of ale beside each bowl. "Eat up," John said to her, picking up his own spoon. "Then you can come with us."

"Where?" Talitha asked before scooping a spoonful into her mouth. It had already cooled but was still far better than the stale bread she had grown used to over the past few months.

John grinned between bites, eyes flitting about the small pub. Seeming to think the other patrons were no threat, he answered, "The underground camp."

39

RISK

Back in Envyre, Serena threw her everything into training with Cole. Her aunt had informed her that Rexton's men were preparing for something big, and Daephyra's suggestion that they fight for possession of the valley weighed heavily on her mind. She had thought they had more time. Time to train. Time to rest. Time to strategize. Time to be spent in their loved ones' arms.

But time was a fleeting thing. It would never stand still. If they remained idle for much longer, Rexton would come for them—for Symptee, for Elara, for the refugees, and for everyone she held dear. And Serena could not risk that.

She chugged from her canteen, eyes trained on Will sparring with Gideon. The confidence in his smirk stirred something within her chest. The sun glinted off the sweat on his brow, and he quickly swiped his shirt sleeve over his forehead. Her gaze snagged on his biceps, the way they strained against his tunic. Serena swallowed thickly, imagining being wrapped up in those strong arms.

Rigel gently elbowed her ribcage, stealing her attention away from Will. "You're drooling." He chuckled.

She scowled, shoving the redhead away with both hands. "I am *not*." He stumbled back a couple of steps, laughing on his way to face off with Kieran. Her heart swelled as she watched her friend twirl the hilt of a blade around his knuckles; the confidence he had been missing for months had finally returned along with the renewed strength in his arm. Now he was eager to practice against even more skilled opponents in preparation for the battles to come.

"You're up," Cole said as he waltzed past Serena, two standard issue swords in hand.

Serena exhaled and plopped her canteen in the dead grass, ready to face another brutal round against her trainer. She wiped her sweaty palms against the tops of her thighs. When she finally made eye contact with Cole, he tossed one of the swords up diagonally, and she caught the hilt in her right hand. "Thanks," she muttered, adjusting her grip. This blade had obviously been used by many students over the years, the worn-down hilt making her long for her own blade. She paused, considering how strange it was to think of Sannarvin as her own when just a year ago she had never held a blade at all.

Now, she was a fighter. Garrick blood flowed through her veins, thick and hot and heavy as the weight of the prophecy that weighed her down with every step.

Spurred on by her hatred of Antoine Rexton, Serena lifted her weapon and charged toward Cole. She was done waiting for him to make the first move. Done waiting for Rexton to do the same. She would run headfirst toward her destiny and give each swing her all—even if it wasn't enough. Her friends deserved that much. They deserved to bask in the sun in the land of their fathers once more. And she was willing to die trying to give them that.

After months of training, Cole's decisions in a fight were still unpredictable, forcing her to always be on her toes. She tried to focus on each of his carefully selected counter moves, but the clatter of swords from the other pairs around them were distracting. Each clang had her fighting to keep her eyes on her own opponent, especially as the others shouted profanities and egged each other on.

"Is that the best you can do?" Gideon chided from behind her opponent.

"I've hardly begun," Will replied.

Without thinking, Serena's gaze shifted over Cole's shoulder, scanning the terrain for the face of her favorite person. Her concentration broken, Cole quickly knocked her weapon aside with a skillful stroke, a thin slice to her forearm forcing her to drop her weapon. Serena seethed as the pain from his slash seared up her arm. She didn't see it coming when Cole stepped closer and knocked her in the face with the hilt of his blade. The cold ground was no cushion for her weak knees as she came down hard.

"On the battlefield, it is kill or be killed. If you cannot focus, you're dead!" Cole snapped, completely unconcerned with the bloody mess spewing from her nose.

Her eyes welled with tears—not from the pain, but from the deep-rooted fear that she was not ready. That she never would be. "I know." Pushing herself upright, Serena rested her elbows on her knees and dropped her face into her hands in defeat.

"Serena!" Will's voice called out for her from across the training ground, but she ignored it. There was nothing he could do to quell the fear clawing at her heart—unless he decided to return to Symptee, where he would be safer.

As he crouched beside her, a sturdy hand lightly gripping her shoulder, she dropped her hands and mumbled, "I'm fine, Will. Just got distracted."

His kind face turned cross as he whipped around to face Cole. "What is your problem?"

"She must focus. If this were a real battle, she'd have been gutted already," Cole argued, crossing his arms over his chest. The other guardians and students around them seemed to agree, turning back to their own training without an inkling of support for her.

Will offered her a hand, but she brushed it off, using both hands to push off the ground instead. "I'm fine, Will. Really. He's right. I shouldn't have looked at you in the middle of sparring. That was foolish," she grumbled, her own words like a dagger in her chest.

How would she fare in a real battle knowing Will was fighting nearby?

It would be impossible not to worry about him.

Serena wiped the blood from her face onto her shirt sleeve. A deep crimson streak soaked into her thick beige sweater. Bloodied like she'd seen the heat of battle, she wondered if the wound on her nose made her look weak or formidable. Probably the former.

She shooed Will off, urging him to go back to his own practicing.

When Xandra finished scolding her fiancé, he walked over to Serena and offered a damp handkerchief to her. "Here. I'm sorry for hitting you in the face," Cole said, his reluctant smile more like a grimace.

Serena took it and gingerly touched the fabric to her nose. "An enemy would have done far worse." She winced as she dragged the rag over her top lip and chin, blindly trying to remove what was left of the blood on her face. "You're doing what you're supposed to do: preparing me for battle."

Cole nodded, icy gaze cutting toward Xandra and Rigel having a heated argument with Will across the yard. "Let's take a walk. Get your nose fixed up before farm boy tries to break mine." He nodded toward the main building.

Following him away from the training grounds felt like failure. Serena's chin pointed at the ground as she walked beside Cole. At the building, he wrenched the door open and gestured for her to enter first—much to her bewilderment.

Inside, they walked the shadowed halls until they reached the small infirmary manned by two Elven healers. It was no wonder they only kept two beds in that small room. The male healer had her nose fixed and a glass of water in her hands within minutes.

Serena paused to glance at her reflection in the mirror on their way out of the infirmary. A few flecks of dry blood peppered her lips and chin, although there was no trace of the cut Cole had inflicted on the bridge of her nose. She was hesitant to touch the freshly healed skin on her face, fearing she would find it still hurt, but the searing pain was completely gone as though she had never been injured at all. Will would be relieved to see that.

"What's changed since the Winter Solstice?" Cole asked. His blunt demeanor left no room for her to bluff. He did not often interfere in personal matters. The fact that he was asking at all was a shock to them both. "Are you really so worried about what Daephyra said to you?"

A silver-haired, sharp-nailed woman flashed through her memories, and Serena turned away from the mirror to face him. "Of course, I am. I knew one day we'd face Rexton, but the idea of waging battle against his men on the valley's border is..."

"Terrifying," Cole finished for her. She studied the far away look in his eyes before he started down the hall.

Hurrying to keep up with his long strides, Serena took a huge breath and asked, "Why are you terrified? You're the best fighter in Envyre. Perhaps even all of Ord Metsiilva."

Cole paused and shook his head. "I am not worried about myself." His hushed confession sent a chill through her. He was thinking of Xandra, perhaps even his sister. In that case, they weren't so different as she once thought.

Serena swallowed, flashes of their friends and loved ones flooding her mind. The last image was that of Cameron Finch clutching a bloody wound in his abdomen. A wound she had inflicted when he tried to kill her. Will had told her he wished he would have been the one to save her, to take that burden off her shoulders. Yet she feared Cameron's skills would have overpowered him back then. Just as Rexton's highly trained soldiers might still be stronger and more skilled than they were.

"How do you maintain your focus knowing she fights as well?" Her whisper hung in the air between them for a few minutes, the reality behind her question plain.

Finally, the elf exhaled slowly. "I was taught that to succeed in battle, one must be selfish. You cannot think about the other warriors fighting beside you. You must trust that each has the skills needed to survive on their own. Otherwise, you put yourself and others at risk."

He continued down the hall in the direction of the training grounds, and she followed a beat behind his right side, contemplating his answer. Growing up, she had been taught the exact opposite. She knew how to be selfless and sacrifice her needs when her family needed more from her. Family was everything, and she had always been willing to be flexible if it meant helping her parents or her brothers out.

So, when it came to Will, she didn't know how to stop worrying about his safety. He was the star her world had come to revolve around, and she couldn't imagine losing that light. She needed it to tether her to the girl she once was, to help her remember that fighting and killing their enemies did not take away the good in her heart.

"I've seen you lose your temper over Xandra getting injured," Serena reminded him. Cole jolted to a stop just before the exit. "She will soon be your wife. How will you fight without worrying the same thing will happen to her again?"

He stared through the glass pane on the door. Serena could see Xandra crossing the yard, a big smile on her face as she spoke to the younger students. She had a light that summoned people to her; it was no surprise Cole fell in love, despite his icy demeanor and their differences. "I do not want her to fight," he whispered, a hint of shame in his deep declaration. "But I know what this rebellion means to her. I know how desperately she wants to settle down in her homeland. It's where she was born, where her mother died. I could never ask her to stay behind. Just as you cannot ask such of Will, much as you want to."

"What if we lose them?" Serena choked, fear seeping into her bones at the question.

Cole turned toward her and planted a hand on her shoulder. It was the most comforting thing her instructor had done in the past year. The gesture felt forced coming from him. "Make no mistake, we are going to lose people when we go into battle. It's inevitable. The ones who are meant to survive are already pre-destined to. Worrying over that will only weaken your resolve."

"I don't know how to not worry about him. I love him!" Serena crossed her arms over her chest.

"I know. And I love Xandra. So much that it is hard not to succumb to the fear that she will one day be taken from me. But we must believe in them the way they believe in us. It's the only way we can go into battle with clear minds and strong hearts," the elf concluded.

His hand slipped from her shoulder, but he waited, not pushing the door open yet. As though he knew she needed a moment more for his words to soak in. Will had full faith that she was capable of anything she put her mind to. Perhaps it was unfair for her to worry that he wasn't strong enough when he had been training for just as long.

Maddie and her protégé Juniper came walking down the hall, their hands full of freshly polished knives. Cole and Serena shifted to one side, allowing them through. When the hall was quiet again, Serena asked, "Do you think I am ready? To lead the rebellion and… to fight Rexton? Be honest."

"I'm always honest," Cole quipped, a smirk softening his sharp features. "I think you're capable of everything your people expect of you and more." There was not a hint of sarcasm in his voice as he met her eyes. An ocean of pity and pride swirled in his irises. He meant every word.

"Thank you," she murmured, fighting the urge to throw her arms around him and squeeze.

"We have them today, Serena. That's what matters," he said firmly. "We have a few weeks before we'll go on the offensive. Let's make the most of it." Then he turned and pushed the door open, not stopping to hold it open for her.

Serena huffed a small laugh and allowed herself out of the building. She watched as he stalked over to Xandra and wrapped his arms around her from behind, pulling her back flush against his body. The guardian's smile deepened as she laid her head back on his shoulder, and he leaned forward to kiss her openly, a declaration to the world that she belonged to him.

That's when Serena realized he had not been referring to training at all.

40

A FAMILY AFFAIR

Crystal adjusted the collar of her brother's fancy tunic—black, as were most of his clothes. Even for his own wedding, she could not convince him to lighten up. Luckily, Xandra had found a gorgeous black tunic with gold leaf embroidery up the sleeves while shopping in Montaris, and Cole had liked it so much he insisted he wear it that day.

"You should be with her right now," Cole said. "She doesn't have any family here besides us."

"Actually, she does," the archer said with a slight grin. Crystal had only left to check on her brother because Serena and Will were with Xandra. Using Serena and Elara's enchanted rings, they were going to allow Xandra's father to watch the wedding through Will's eyes that evening. It was a truly touching gesture—one that left Xandra in an absolute puddle of tears—which was the elf's cue to step out for a moment.

Cole looked at the mirror on the wall and ran his fingers over his grown-out waves. His sister smiled at the way he tugged at his shirt sleeves. She had never seen him so anxious about anything—much less a woman. "You really do love her," Crystal said, shoving his arm. "I never thought I'd see the day you married."

"Neither did I," he replied, turning away from his reflection. He sighed, crossed his arms over his chest, and watched her study her own reflection, fingers fluffing and tucking the hair around her ears. "And what about you and Deldrach? Are you ever going to discuss the future with him?"

Her cheeks burned, and she couldn't bear to look at herself in the mirror anymore. Looking down at the bronze velvet gown that Xandra had chosen for her, Crystal suddenly felt exposed. She didn't want to have this conversation—not with her betrothed, and certainly not with her brother who was set to be married in mere minutes. "We're planning to attack Rexton's men in the valley soon. There's too much to do before then."

"Crystalira." His use of her full name made her flinch. It reminded her of their father. Of being scolded for breaking the rules.

"Alarcole," she replied, sharp eyes cutting toward him. "Do not ruin a good day."

Her brother shook his head and waved a hand. In a few steps, he closed the distance between them and gently grasped her shoulders. "Nothing is going to ruin this day," he said. His voice was calm, assured. Something she never felt when considering the subject of marriage. "You're the bravest person I know, Crys. If you don't want this, then tell him as much. It's for the best for *both* of you."

Her bottom lip jutted out in a pout. "Easy for you to say. You're Father's golden child."

Cole belly laughed, nearly keeling over from loss of control. She had not seen him laugh like that since they were children. "Not anymore. I'm binding myself to a human, remember?"

Crystal paused, eyes widening. He was right. He had gone against Daephyra's edict—something their father took very seriously. Once they were bound, Cole would never be permitted in Montaris again.

And the craziest part was that he did not seem to mind.

For the first time in years, they had enjoyed a wonderful holiday with their father and friends. It was the perfect day. Despite Serena's shocking conversation with Queen Daephyra, their father held his tongue, opened his doors, and hosted the humans with grace. He didn't say a sour word to either of his children all day, choosing not to mention either of their engagements for the sake of their guests.

It made her miss him and their home terribly. If every visit could be like that, she'd be happy to return to Montaris more often.

But Cole's wedding was the firm closing of a door. In order for their family to be whole going forward, their father would have to leave the capital and come to them.

She wouldn't hold her breath.

Rigel knocked twice on the door before it swung open. When his face appeared, his gaze immediately snagged on the archer, his carefree smile slipping as he took in the blonde hair cascading over her shoulders. Her pale arms peeked out from underneath the fox fur shawl resting in the crooks of her elbows. The fur matched his slicked back hair.

"Wow, you look—" He paused, swallowing as his bright blues dared drift lower. Crystal shook her head and turned away from him.

"Like a lady, for once," her brother quipped, shooting her a teasing smirk. She scowled at him. His demeanor was much changed. Now, his quips were light-hearted, not full of snark and venom. Xandra had worked her way into his heart and given him something he had lacked for so long: a reason to be happy. Crystal would do anything to protect that.

The archer watched as their friend sauntered over and held out a hand to Cole. The elf scoffed, the grin on his face growing as he shook Rigel's hand. "I'm so happy for you guys." Then, their human companion yanked him forward into a tight hug. She was surprised her brother didn't immediately shove Rigel away. Everyone in their family avoided physical affection—at least, they had since their mother died.

Once Rigel had released his hold on Cole, the elf stepped back and readjusted his tunic sleeves for the tenth time. *He's nervous*, she thought. In all their years as siblings, she'd never had to comfort him. She crossed over to her brother, a nod of her head signaling for Rigel to slip back out of the room. Hesitantly, she rubbed her hands up and down her brother's arms as affectionately as she could muster—the way their mother had when they were little.

Cole caught her eyes and breathed in sharply. His sister wondered if he was thinking about their mother as much as she was. Her death had been a sucker punch to them both, and it felt cruel for her to be absent on the most important day of her son's life. "I wish they could be here," he finally admitted, looking down at his boots.

Cupping his cheek in her palm, Crystal nodded. "As do I." As her hand slipped back to her side, she cleared her throat, fighting back her warring emotions. "At least Father gave you her ring. We both know Xan deserves it. She's—"

"Every bit as kind-hearted as Mum was," Cole finished for her. There was a bitter gleam in his eyes as they spoke to each other about Lyrissana for the first time in over a decade.

"It's really no wonder you fell in love with her," Crystal said, giving his shoulder a small shove. She dabbed at the tears in the corners of her eyes with her fingertips. Xandra had spent all morning applying kohl and rouge to her face. She'd hate to mess it up before the wedding even began.

"She was your friend first," her brother noted. She could feel his eyes bore into her back as she walked toward the door, ready to head back to her friend's room. "Did you ever stop to think that's why you gravitated toward her?"

Crystal paused. She had never considered that. In all the years they had been friends, she never once thought to compare her temperament to their late mother. Now that Cole had pointed it out, she couldn't unsee the similarity between them. "I did not befriend her because she reminded me of Mum," the guardian whispered. Her words couldn't quell the insinuation that hung between them. "She isn't a replacement for who we lost."

"That's not what I meant," he said sternly. Dropping his head back to look up at the ceiling, Cole ran his hands over his face and sighed. "I just mean she's been good—for *both* of us—after what we lost." Crystal nodded. That they could agree upon.

A knock on the door drew their attention. "It's time," Serena declared, her high-pitched voice and excited clapping carrying through the closed door.

Crystal glanced back at her brother. His arms were relaxed at his sides; his face, serene. Gone was his nervous energy. All that remained was hope in his eyes. Excitement. Joy.

The archer smiled, her heart pounding faster in her chest as she pulled open the door. While she had never been in love, Crystal envied that blissful look on her brother's face. Everyone deserved to feel that kind of joy. "Come on, Cole. Can't keep your bride waiting."

Outside, the students and instructors of the Academy had transformed the outdoor training facilities into the perfect setting for a wedding. Gone were the targets and piles of weapons. Instead, chairs lined each side of a flower-strewn aisle, and the still-lush forest at the end made the perfect backdrop.

She walked up the aisle arm-in-arm with her brother, nodding at guests as they passed. The number of elves in attendance surprised Crystal, given their queen's feelings toward humans. It warmed her heart to see so many gathered in support, especially Ilrune and Deldrach. The latter beamed as he watched her walk past, and her chest constricted knowing he must be thinking of his own wedding. What he expected to be *their* binding day.

At the front of the makeshift aisle was a wooden arch that Serena and the other ladies had decorated with long, thin vines covered in tiny white flowers. When they reached the end, Crystal hugged her brother, feeling him stiffen momentarily in her grip before he squeezed her back. "I love you," she whispered before drawing away, the words feeling foreign on her tongue.

Cole stared at her as she stepped to the side and took a seat in the first row beside her betrothed. Across the aisle was an empty seat beside Will and Serena. Most of the other humans from the Academy filled the rows behind them—among them, Maddie, Gideon, Carissa, Emilia, and Cyrus. Everyone was cleaned up and looking their best, eyes turned toward the main building in anticipation of the bride.

When the harpist began playing a different tune, the buzzing among the guests quieted. The captain opened the door, and all eyes fell upon the bride. Xandra wore a beautiful Elven-made gown in a deep scarlet with intricate embroidery along the bust and down the bell sleeves. Her raven curls cascaded freely down her back and over her shoulders, framing her face as the golden rays from the setting sun made her glow.

As she exited the building and made her way toward the aisle, Rigel met her and offered his arm. Xandra beamed as she took it, tears gleaming in her eyes. Crystal knew she was having a hard time missing her father during that moment, but she was grateful Serena and Elara had been able to arrange for him to witness the ceremony. It was a delightful surprise when the commander requested that Rigel step up so she would not have to walk by herself.

Crystal turned to watch her brother as their friends walked down the aisle to meet him. He looked as if the mere sight of her had stolen all the breath from his lungs. His ocean eyes shimmered, studying her with reverence as though she were the most beautiful creature on earth. His gaze swept appreciatively from her head to her feet before quickly returning to her face, trying to commit every thread on her gown and hair on her head to memory.

When Xandra reached the first row, she reached out and squeezed Crystal's hand before joining Cole before their audience. Captain Smedley and Ilrune stepped forth to lead the ceremony, which was to be equal parts a human wedding with vows before Divinity and an Elven binding ritual.

They began by exchanging vows, opting for a more traditional set commonly used by the Hyrosencians rather than writing their own. When Cole had finished repeating the sappy exchange, he glanced his sister's way, but something behind her caught his attention. His smile faded into a shocked expression, unable to tear his gaze away.

Suddenly, the worst flashed through her mind. What if Daephyra had sent soldiers to stop them? To arrest Cole? To send away the humans in her outrage?

She whipped her head around to find none other than Cassius Windaef standing in the grass between the building and the back row of chairs. She sucked in a breath, unable to peel her eyes away as the captain began feeding Xandra her vows. Her father's arms were crossed, wrinkling his cream tunic, but he did not look displeased. Watery eyes and flushed cheeks watched his son closely. Crystal wondered if they were tears of sadness or joy. When he moved to take an empty seat in the back row, she felt like she knew the answer.

Then Cassius' gaze shifted to her. Her mouth went dry as their father nodded in acknowledgement, a small, sad smile making an appearance.

"You're about to miss the best part," Deldrach whispered close to her ear.

Crystal turned abruptly, his proximity having sent a chill down her spine. "Sorry," she muttered, trying to refocus on Cole and Xandra. Ilrune wrapped a beautifully braided rope of red, white, and green strands around their joined hands, chanting the prayer of Eternal Devotion in Elvish.

A warm hand curled over her own, gently encasing the fist resting on her right thigh. Crystal glanced at her betrothed, who leaned back in his seat as he watched Cole and Xandra with a broad grin. She stared at their hands before turning back toward the bride and groom. Their skin was a stark contrast of dark and light intertwined under the multi-colored ropes, yet the caramel and cream tones melded so naturally. She glanced down at Deldrach's hand; his deeply tanned skin was streaked with tiny white scars from years of training and working as a guard. He was an honest, hard-working elf. A kind person. She tried to envision a rope wrapped around their hands, the words of the binding ritual being chanted for the two of them, sealing their souls as one forever, and her stomach lurched. She quickly withdrew her hand and pretended to adjust the fur shawl higher on her arms.

Crystal could sense Deldrach's disappointment, though she did not dare look over at him. Instead, she focused on the conclusion of the ceremony. Cole and Xandra had begun chanting the sacred prayer in the ancient language while staring deep into each other's eyes. This part of the binding ritual was so intense emotionally, physically, and spiritually, that neither noticed when their hands began to glow faintly where they held fast to each other. The couple gazed at each other as though the rest of the world had melted away, and no one was there to witness their bonding.

Ilrune began chanting the closing to the prayer, and everyone in attendance held their breath as the glow between them shone bright white before dissipating. Silence stretched over the crowd as they waited, counting the seconds until Ilrune began unraveling the rope.

When the ceremony concluded, Captain Smedley stepped forth to congratulate them before declaring that Cole could kiss his bride. Without a moment's hesitation, her brother stepped closer, pulling his bride flush with his chest. One hand curled into the hair at the base of her neck and pulled her face closer, drawing her in for a deep, impassioned kiss.

Their guests rose to their feet, clapping and hooting their approval. When Cole finally drew back, he studied her face up close for a moment before leaning in to whisper something that made Xandra giggle.

Yuck.

Their human friends tossed flower petals in the air as Cole and Xandra came down the aisle holding hands. When they reached the main building, Gideon's brother Malachi was waiting to open the door for them. Then their guests moved into the aisle to follow them inside for the wedding feast.

Crystal lingered behind the rest, watching the crowd head inside. Her father had stepped to the side, waiting for her. As the last of the guests made their way inside, Crystal had to encourage Serena and Deldrach to go ahead without her. Deldrach was smart enough to realize why. He lifted a hand to wave at her father before disappearing through the doorway.

Finally alone, Crystal fidgeted with her shawl as her father approached. "Crystalira," he said, leaning forward to kiss her cheek. "You look marvelous."

"As do you," she replied, hardly able to look him in the eyes. She wanted to ask why he had come. Why he had lingered in the back instead of joining them before the ceremony. Instead, she said, "We weren't expecting you."

Cassius pressed his lips into a thin line. Staring at the arch where Cole and Xandra had just taken their vows, he seemed at a loss for words.

"Will you be joining us for the feast?" She hoped he would say yes, head inside, and have a pleasant evening without need for any uncomfortable discussion.

But Cassius had other ideas.

Taking his daughter's hand, he squeezed it. "I would like that very much," he said, giving her a grim smile. For a man attending his only son's wedding, he could not manage a proper smile.

"Is something wrong?" Crystal dared to ask. If he was too uncomfortable attending their wedding, she did not understand why he had made the trip to Envyre.

"You don't look at him the same way," her father finally said.

It felt like her heart stopped beating. His sudden statement had shocked her. She knew he meant Deldrach, and she did not want to argue with him about her dragged-out engagement when her brother had just married the love of his life.

"Now really isn't the time to talk about that, Father." Crystal turned toward the door, but her father reached out and grabbed her arm, stopping her from running.

When she looked at Cassius, he pleaded wordlessly for her to stay—to finish the conversation she was always running from. Crystal took a deep breath and nodded. "Fine," she gritted out between her teeth. For so long, she had held the truth in her heart, allowing the weight of it to drag her down. If he wanted the truth, she'd give it to him. "I do not love Deldrach Erlamin. Is that what you want to hear? That I am a terrible, dishonorable woman for saying yes in a moment of shock when I never intended to marry him or any other man ever?" Her chest heaved with her pounding heart as she stared, waiting for her father to say something, anything.

"I do not think you a terrible, dishonorable woman." He reached out to cup her cheek, and a fire quickly spread through her face. This kind of affection was strange for them. Warm but foreign, she leaned into his hand and closed her eyes, fighting back a wave of unwanted emotions. "You are one of the bravest fighters to come out of this Academy. I know I have not always made your life easy, but you are now and will forever be my only daughter. I would be a poor father to force you to marry someone who doesn't bring you comfort and joy."

Crystal shook her head slightly and removed his hand from her face. "How did you figure it out?"

Cassius grinned slightly, his resemblance to Cole shining through. "At the solstice feast, the boy kept trying to touch you, talk to you, and you avoided him as best you could by cooking, serving, and chatting with anyone but him." She winced, realizing how terrible she had been toward him since her return. Deldrach had to know she was avoiding him for a reason. That she was not in love with him. "He's always been infatuated with you. But if you do not feel the same, you should not hold fast to your betrothal after all these years. He deserves to find someone who will appreciate all the affection he has to give."

"I know," she whispered, so low it was barely audible. "He is going to hate me for wasting so much of his time."

"Two years is nothing between elves. He will bounce back," Cassius reassured her.

She nodded. He offered his elbow to her, and she wrapped a delicate hand around its crook. They entered the feast together, finding some people had already taken to the makeshift dance floor in the center of the room. Among them were Cole and Xandra, arms wrapped tight around each other as they swayed and spun in the glittering sunlight coming through the windows. Serena and Will were also dancing near them, gentle touches and whispered words causing the girl to blush as he tucked her in close to his chest. They all looked happy.

No, happy was not a strong enough word for it.

They were elated, spinning around in their blissful, contented states as if war did not loom in their near future.

"I wish it could stay like this," she confessed to her father. Her gaze trailed after the couples on the dance floor before it snagged on Deldrach, making a beeline straight for them. For *her*. She blew out an exasperated breath and removed her arm from her father's.

When Deldrach reached them, he greeted her father with a firm handshake. "It's good to see you again, sir." Turning toward her, she offered a feeble smile in anticipation of the question in his eyes.

Surprisingly, she realized she wanted to dance. To join all the cheerful wedding guests in celebration. Only she did not want it to be with Deldrach.

"Crystalira," her father interrupted, much to her relief. "My apologies, Deldrach. It's not every day I get to see my daughter. I wondered if she might grant me a dance?"

"Oh, of course, Mister Windaef. After you." Deldrach bowed his head slightly before backing away, stealing a wistful glance at Crystal before finding some other elves to occupy his time.

Crystal beamed and nodded. There were few times she remembered doing anything fun with her father—dancing included. Perhaps on a rare holiday when she was a child. But when she thought back, she could only remember watching him lead their mother in circles around the kitchen in their old house. Her melodic laugh would fill their cottage, her joy summoning her children out of their rooms to join them.

On the dance floor, Cassius kept his eyes on his son over her shoulder. She wondered if he was feeling nostalgic, seeing Lyrissana's ring on Xandra's hand. "We talked about Mum earlier, how we wish she was here," Crystal admitted. She tensed, afraid of how her father might handle the mention of his late wife. She prayed that she would not sour his mood and send him running when they were finally seeing eye to eye for the first time in decades.

Cassius focused on her face. His lips drew back into a sad smile. "I think about her every day," he replied. In the silence that followed, he lifted his daughter's hand and spun her around. "You look so much like her now."

Crystal looked down, suddenly self-conscious of the comparison. Her mother was beautiful—far more than she thought of herself. In truth, the only similarity she clung to was her healing magic, though she never wanted to pursue the same path as her mother. Healers were patient, kind, hard-working. Many became mothers. That wasn't how she saw herself. She was a fighter. Hard edges and sharp sticks and sharper words that were necessary to keep people safe.

All she wanted was to keep her family safe.

Not just her brother. But her chosen family. The humans who had managed to weasel their way into she and Cole's hearts. These were the people she fought for—would die for, if it came down to it. She had lived with the unbearable pain of losing the person she loved most and the guilt that came with being unable to save her. She couldn't imagine feeling such pain again.

"We intend to attack the border, try to take down Rexton's walls into the valley, as the Queen suggested," Crystal informed her father.

His ears and brows perked up. "Waging war so close to home? When?"

"It will be best for everyone in the long run if Rexton no longer controls who can cross through the valley. Even Daephyra knows that," she replied. Her father's cheek twitched slightly, and she realized she had forgotten a formal address when speaking about the queen. She winced, fearing he might scold or slap her.

Instead, the hand at her waist squeezed lightly. "You're a great shot, but have you the numbers for such a siege?"

Her gaze shifted to scan the crowded dining hall. There were easily sixty or more people gathered to eat—not including the Elven guards and some students who had not attended the wedding. She knew it would be difficult to recruit most of these people to run into battle, but Serena was determined to try. Soon, she'd have to take her shot.

"We are hopeful most at the Academy will join us. Perhaps even some of the guards," Crystal said, trying to maintain a confident stance as Cassius studied her face.

He finally said, "I only hope you will be careful. Consider your own safety when you run into battle. If not for your sake, then for mine." Her father brought one of her hands to his chest and squeezed it.

She stared at their hands for a moment, a tight feeling in her chest as she considered how her father must have felt when she left home two years prior. All she had wanted was to fight, to lead her team, to save lives. She had never stopped to consider what it would do to her family if she never came back.

Now, she understood why her brother came after her. Why he joined her unit, despite his reluctance to help the humans. It wasn't just about being overprotective or controlling. It was about preserving what was left of their fractured family at all costs.

When Cassius released her hand, she stepped closer, wrapping both of her arms under his and pressing her face to her father's chest. He breathed in sharply, waiting a moment before wrapping his own arms around her back and stroking a hand over her hair. Though music continued playing, they just stood there, quiet and still and finally at peace with who they were to each other. "I am proud that you choose to fight for those who cannot," Cassius whispered. "And I will always love you, regardless of who you fight for or whether you marry."

Crystal's chest tightened, a lump rising in the back of her throat. Her father was proud of her. He finally understood and accepted her. And that was the most unexpected outcome of her return home. "Thank you, Papa."

"Are you two feeling well?" Cole asked from beside them.

They immediately shifted apart, sniffling and wiping at their watery eyes. "Never better," Crystal replied, somehow managing a smile.

Before she had fully composed herself, Xandra threw her arms around her friend and squeezed tight. "Need anything, my beloved sister?" They grinned at each other, thrilled to now be family.

"Actually, I need to have a chat with Deldrach," she said, her voice trailing off with the end of her sentence as she perused the hall. When she spotted him, something in his usually chipper demeanor was off. That was her fault, of course, for leading him on. But after tonight, they would both be free—him to find someone who could love him back, and her to focus on the battle ahead.

41

ETERNALLY YOURS

After hours of feasting, dancing, and celebrating with their loved ones, Cole took Xandra by the hand and led her to a cabin on the outskirts of Envyre that would be their private retreat from the bustling Academy area. Approaching the porch, he surprised her by scooping her off her feet. A vibrant laugh bubbled out of her mouth as he bounded up the steps to the front door.

"Someone's eager," she teased, running her fingers through the blond hair at the base of his neck. Tingles shot down his spine at the feel of her nails against his scalp, and he pulled her even closer as he opened the door with one hand.

Inside, he gently lowered her feet to the ground, but Xandra's arms remained around his neck, keeping him close. "I have waited a century to find my *saluna*," he whispered. His face lowered, his nose skimming along her cheekbone, lips peppering her with reverent kisses. "Welcome home, sunshine."

"You are my home, *saluna*," she replied, her smile broadening.

Hearing his language roll off her lips stoked the fire he usually kept under control. Cole used one foot to shove the door closed behind them, their hooded gazes locked on each other. As soon as the door slammed, his lips were on hers, hot and urgent. As close as they were, it wasn't close enough for either of them. Xandra's fist gripped the front of his tunic, bringing his lips back to hers between hurried breaths. One of his hands laced into the bouncy curls at the back of her head, the other pressing into the small of her back.

He started walking them backwards through their new home in the dark, unwilling to part from her lips as he guided her. A few steps into the seating area, Xandra tripped on the edge of a rug and yelped as she stumbled backward. Cole quickly reached out to grab the back end of a sofa and steady them. She breathed a sigh of relief as she regained her balance, one of his strong hands still splayed protectively across her back.

"That was close." She chuckled nervously, releasing the firm grip on his upper arms. "Might want to watch where we're going."

"I'd rather watch you," Cole replied, catching her hand in his as she threw a wink over her shoulder.

Xandra finally glanced around the house for the first time. Even in the dark, the house only illuminated by the moonlight shining through the uncovered windows, she could tell each furnishing had been specially chosen. Every piece had been created by an elf of great skill. She even recognized the rug she had tripped on from one of their walks through the market. The red, orange, and cream strands swirled around the border in an intricate leaf pattern.

"Do you like it?" he asked. A gentle tug turned her toward him. His eyes searched hers expectantly. Uncertainly. She'd never seen him so vulnerable before; the unexpected change was endearing.

The cottage was homey and modest. Everything she could have hoped for. And best of all, it was *theirs*. She beamed, reaching up to trace a thumb along his jawline. "I love it. Did you pick everything out yourself?"

He nodded, leaning forward to press his forehead to hers. "Except the sofa. That was Crystal and Rigel. They seem to think they'll be visiting us a lot."

"You don't seem thrilled by that." She shook her head as she laughed at him.

Strong arms wrapped around her waist and hoisted her feet off of the floor, spinning her around. When he stopped, a mischievous grin had found its way onto his face. "I don't intend to share you anytime soon," Cole declared, his mouth devouring hers once more.

Xandra hummed in approval, her fingers finding the back of his head. A gentle stroke of her fingers along the point of an ear sent a shiver through him, and he gently bit her bottom lip.

"You haven't seen the rest of our house yet, Mistress Windaef." Her husband tugged at her waist, carefully trying to guide her toward the back of the house.

Her cheeks burned as she let him lead her by the hand into a hall with three doors. "Spare room." He gestured to the first door. "Bathing room." He nodded his head to the second. Then he paused in front of the final door at the end of the hall.

"Ours?" she whispered, biting her lower lip in anticipation.

He caressed her cheek. "Ours." Cole turned the doorknob and gently pressed the wooden door open. They both stood in the doorway for a moment, taking in the sight of a dozen glowing lanterns placed about the tables in the room. Someone had obviously come by the house before they left the celebration.

Finally, a warm hand pressed against the small of her back, encouraging her to step inside. The paneling on the walls was painted a deep gray, a stark contrast to the nearly-white bedding. A pile of plush pillows were propped up against the wall, and a thick crimson blanket lay draped over the end of the bed—the same color as her bridal gown.

Cole shuffled behind her, and a black blob landed at the foot of the bed. Xandra's cheeks warmed as a hard plane of muscle came up behind her, bare arms capturing her waist. Using one hand, he drew her raven curls to one side of her head. "I have something to show you," he whispered, lips brushing against the side of her neck.

Xandra's brows raised. "Oh, do you?" She turned, a sly smile on her lips that faded when she laid eyes on him.

She had seen him shirtless before—a beautiful specimen of porcelain skin stretched taut over the contours of his arms and abs.

What she had never seen before was the small black half-sun tattoo on his ribcage.

She stared long and hard at the dark lines, a permanent etching on his perfect skin, and her brow furrowed. "When did you get this?" The question came out in a whispered breath as her fingertips reached for him, tracing the fine lines in disbelief.

Cole lowered his chin as though he might be embarrassed by her reaction. "I got it on my third day back in Montaris. I had gone to visit an old friend, and he strong-armed me into getting something."

"What made you choose the sun of all things?" She glanced up at his face already suspecting the answer, but needing to hear it from his mouth.

Cole took her hand and removed it from his abdomen. "You know why." A warm hand caressed her cheek as he gazed at her with unbridled affection. Xandra had always wanted him to look at her like that. Like she was the sun his universe revolved around.

"Tell me anyway," she whispered, taking a small step closer. Her gaze dipped back to the tattoo, the permanent ink on his skin that would tell the world he belonged to her. His sunshine. His wife.

Cole's fingers sunk into her curls, his other hand grabbing her waist and yanking her forward. Their noses brushed, breath hot on each other's faces. "Long ago, I allowed an unimaginable loss to harden my heart. I lived under a storm cloud until the day I opened my eyes and finally *saw* you. You didn't fight for revenge. You fought for hope. For the future. Your light brought me back to life. And though I tried to fight it at first, I realized the morning I left Symptee that I couldn't go back to living without the sun. Without *you.*"

A tear trickled down her cheek as she pressed up on her toes, wrapped her arms around his neck, and captured his lips. His arms and chest were warm against the bodice of her gown as he tightened his hold on her.

When they parted on a deep inhale, Xandra stroked her fingers over his sharp cheekbone down to his bottom lip. Her amber eyes glowed in the lantern light—warm and light like honey when the sun hit a glass jar at the right angle. "I wish you had turned back and told me that months ago." She fussed, resting her forehead against his.

"So do I." He chuckled, pressing a kiss to her cheek.

For months, they had planned their wedding day together, yet there were still so many things for her to learn about him. She couldn't wait to uncover everything he'd kept hidden for so long.

"My heart has been yours for a long time." She paused, smiling up at him, at the warmth swirling in those deep blue irises as he hung on her every word. "For so long as I live, I promise to be your light, just as you are mine." Her lips brushed against his, punctuating each word.

The air grew warm and heavy between them as his lids lowered, his gaze sparking with hunger. Slowly, he snaked a hand to her front and teasingly pulled at her corset strings. A smoldering stare pleaded silently for permission, and Xandra nodded faintly. He made quick work of the strings, allowing the outer part of her gown to fall to the floor around her feet. Still in her chemise, he lifted her feet off the ground and placed her gently on their bed.

Safely cushioned on top of the blankets, Xandra sighed, pulling him down for another languid kiss, convinced she would never tire of the taste of his lips. Cole climbed up and leaned over her, his body weight propped up on both forearms. "For so long as you live, and all the days thereafter, I am eternally yours," he said before pressing his mouth fully to hers again.

Heat pooled in her belly from his proximity. So close and yet still too far. She needed more. More of the warmth of his skin. The wet heat of his lips worshipping his way across her skin. The callouses on his palms. The deep blue of his eyes as he searched hers, tentative and reverent and full of adoration. She would have happily drowned in that blue for eternity.

Now, there was nothing more they needed to say with words, and in the gentle glow of the lantern light, they sealed their sacred promises to each other.

42

NIGHTFALL

Anteros pawed at his sore muscles as he and his friends headed to the stables. Their superiors had ordered all the new recruits to assist with loading wagons and preparing horses, though no one would say why. It had been three weeks since the young men had arrived at the base in Murmont. Three weeks of workouts, intense drills, yelling captains, and sleeping in a bunkhouse full of rowdy young men—not all of whom had chosen to be there.

And worst of all, a month without a drink to numb his pain.

Some of the men looked at him through narrowed eyes, as though they were aware who his father was. Anteros hoped not. He did not need to find himself at the end of a livid blade in the middle of the night. Not when he was just beginning to breathe the fresh air away from his father's cruel presence.

Being in the Enforcing Army was hard work—and certainly not something he ever imagined for himself—but hard work kept him busy. Staying busy kept the worst memories at bay. At least, until nightfall.

Night was the worst. Lying in his bunk in the pitch black, listening to the varying snores of other exhausted young men, his darkest memories came in flashes. Autumn leaves skittering across a dirt path. Red hair peeking out from under a black cloak. Cold fingers caressing his cheek—gentle yet abrasive at the same time. Guards in a panic. His father in an uproar. The thick glaze over his sister's eyes. Her cold hands. The echo of her last words to him. His mother's screams.

A familiar voice whispered from the bunk below him. "Ant? You awake?"

He waited a moment, debating whether to reply to Julian. The duke's son had been forced to join the rest of his friends in training, urged by the king to keep an eye on his son. Julian had been furious at first. He didn't speak a word to Anteros on their four-day journey to Murmont. But since their arrival, he'd cooled down. It was hard to stay angry when your body ached, hands made to train and work until they were cracked and bleeding. When you realized the person who had put you there was miles away, eating, drinking, and pretending none of them existed.

The prince scrubbed his hands over his face. "Yeah. I'm awake."

He could hear the shuffling of a body moving against the itchy sheets, adjusting on the hard mattress. Then a tuft of short blond hair appeared beside his bed. Julian hoisted his feet onto his mattress and folded his arms over the edge of Anteros' bed. "Want to take a walk?"

Anteros frowned. Barely on the cusp of spring, he had no interest in freezing his toes off walking the grounds after curfew. "It's too cold," he mumbled. His head lopped to the side, hair flopping over his forehead as he returned to staring at the ceiling.

Julian huffed a breath. "Fine then. I guess I will listen in on the commanders meeting by myself."

Anteros sat up abruptly. "Commanders meeting? How would you know anything about that?"

"Overheard the captain while we were hauling barrels this afternoon. They're to discuss your father's latest orders," Julian said, raising his brows.

The prince wrinkled his nose. His father had done enough damage. He did not want to have a hand in any further schemes. Yet he could not help the curiosity that had edged its way into his mind over the past three days. Why were they packing a dozen wagons with weapons, armor, a strange black powder, and food preserved in salt barrels? As if they were going off to war. What could his father have been planning?

He shoved the sheet off his legs and sat up. "Fine. Let's take a walk." Forgoing the steps, Anteros leapt off the top bunk, his bare feet slamming hard into the cold tile between bunks. The floor shook slightly, and his friend covered his eyes with a hand. The cabin remained quiet.

"Try not to wake everyone," Julian hissed, stepping down beside him. The two sat on either end of Julian's bunk and quietly laced their boots.

Anteros glanced at the lower bunk beside them where James was fast asleep. With his hair cut shorter and his face clean shaven, he looked younger than 18. He looked like a boy among grown men. Perhaps they all did. "What about them?" He turned his questioning gaze on Julian, who wrinkled his nose and swiped a dismissive hand through the air. Leaving them behind was probably for the best. James and Calix were not known for being quiet.

They stood and quietly worked their way toward the cabin's exit. Outside, a waning moon offered little light. The second moon hid behind heavy gray clouds as though it were afraid to witness what they were about to do. Anteros squinted, his eyes straining to adjust to the near darkness. Only two of the buildings and the fort wall held torches, the light from which did nothing to illuminate their path.

Julian started in the direction of the main building where the officers could usually be found. When he spotted two older men, their deep crimson uniforms cutting through the darkness like a lit beacon, his arm shot out, shoving Anteros behind the nearest cabin. They waited patiently, watching their breaths come in shallow white puffs, until the men disappeared inside the main building.

"How do you suggest we eavesdrop on this meeting without being spotted?" Anteros asked, crossing his arms over his chest. The wind nipped his cheeks, but he refused to show any sign of discomfort, clenching all his muscles against the urge to shiver.

The blond peered around the cabin and surveyed the main building silently. Anteros could tell his friend had an idea—Julian had never been one to run with a half-baked plan. He was cautious, calculated. A planner. He'd inherited that trait from his father. "I propped open a couple windows while everyone was in the dining hall."

Anteros blinked at his friend in surprise. "So, we just have to find the right room then," the prince said slowly. Julian nodded his head and slunk around the corner of the cabin like a slippery snake. Anteros followed close behind, his feet trudging sluggishly through the grass as a weight settled in his belly.

What if he did not want to know what his father was planning next? It wasn't like he was in the position to change things. He was an outcast prince, sent to join their military to toughen him up. To make him as lethal and ruthless and cunning as his father.

They crouched low to the ground when they reached the main building, careful to keep their heads below the windowsills illuminated by lanterns. The first office was quiet. A lone man hunched in the light from a single lantern to write a letter at his desk. They crawled to the next one, pausing briefly at the faint sound of moans coming from the cracked window. Julian and Anteros made eye contact for a split second before clamping hands over their mouths, stifling the urge to laugh. At least someone was having a good night.

Finally, the sounds of several deep voices carried across the wind to their ears. The voice of their own captain, Marcus Pelham, rose above the rest, volunteering his horde for the king's task. "They're young, but they're strong. They'll be able to manage the long journey, the heavy lifting."

Anteros dared lift his face, his eyes barely peeking over the windowsill into the room. There sat two dozen officers of various ranks, all arguing over who should be sent on the King's Mission, as they were calling it. Older commanders argued that Pelham's horde was mostly new recruits, including the king's own son.

"That's precisely why His Majesty suggested it," another man said from the head of the table. He rose to his feet, drawing the attention of his comrades. "The king is still quite displeased that none have uncovered the whereabouts of the escaped prisoner, Talitha Vise. We have reason to believe she'll have headed south, back toward her home."

Anteros dropped to his knees in the grass and gripped his chest. "No," he breathed, clutching the dark fabric in his fist. "She wouldn't be that foolish." But the words tumbled out more like a question, his uncertainty making his stomach flip.

His friend tensed beside him, icy blues narrowed as he observed Anteros' reaction. Finally, he asked calmly, "She's the one who escaped the night Sabine was killed?"

Anteros scrubbed his face with both hands, the motion warming his cheeks. "Yes," he hissed through his teeth, not wanting to answer the next question that twinkled in Julian's eyes.

"You care about her? Is that why you put your own sister at risk?" Julian sneered at the intrusive thought.

"Yes, and no," Anteros answered quickly. Then he realized that the room behind them had gone quiet. Grabbing Julian's arm, he nodded his head toward the cabins, dragging his friend away from the window before they could be spotted.

Halfway back to their quarters, Julian whipped around and shoved his chest. "You fell for a traitor and got your sister killed. Tell me that's not what happened."

"You know I would never have risked Sabine's life like that," Anteros yelled back, the blood in his veins feeling like molten lava at his friend's accusation.

Of course, Julian was still hurting over the loss. They both were. But he was wrong to try to blame Anteros for a decision he played no part in. Sabine had foolishly gotten on that horse all on her own, dooming herself with one final impulsive action after a summer of boredom built up her feelings of guilt about Talitha.

"Sabine was the one who wanted me to help Talitha escape the dungeon. I waited. Hesitated. Ignored her suffering for as long as I could manage. But Sabine was right. She was withering away, and we were the only ones who could save her," Anteros said, his voice breaking as he recalled how thin and pale Talitha had become. "Sabine was never supposed to leave the castle. The grounds were locked down. She never said anything about running or riding her horse. I would have stopped her."

Julian breathed heavily, white puffs of shallow breath dissipating around his head as he stared the prince down. His fists clenched at his sides. "Where's the girl? The one your father is so desperate to hunt down?"

"I cannot say," Anteros replied, glancing behind them at the main building. No one had left to check outside. They were lucky about that. He was lucky.

While he was distracted, Julian charged at him, fists clenching Anteros' thick brown tunic. "You cannot expect me to believe that. I saw the way you reacted to her name. *Talitha.* You love her, don't you?" The accusation settled heavily in the silence between them.

"I cared for her as much as you cared for Sabine," Anteros finally whispered.

Julian released his hold on the prince's shirt and stepped back. His tired eyes fell on the starless sky, and he blew out a long, slow breath. "If that's true, then I hope you've hidden her so far away that the king will never find her." With that, his friend turned and marched back toward their cabin, leaving Anteros alone in the dark again.

43

SEEING STARS

It was late in the evening, the air crisp, the floor tiles cold against Elara's bare feet as she paced the space beside her bed while the squeezing sensation in her lower belly came and went, growing more frequent with time. Her husband had left to fetch the physician half an hour prior, and she had sent one of her personal guards for Ismenia as well, who would be assisting with the birth. It felt too early for such a thing. The entire pregnancy had seemingly passed in a blur.

The herbalist arrived with a slew of baggage—towels and tonics and everything in between. Ordering the queen to lay on her bed for a check, Ismenia rolled up her sleeves and scrubbed her hands in the extra basin she'd set up on the breakfast table. Once Elara was in position, she rolled up the queen's night dress and declared, "You're right. It's time."

Elara tensed with another wave of contractions. "And you're sure it's not too early?" She pressed a hand to her abdomen, breathing slowly and deep like they had practiced.

"You've been measuring above average for weeks. We knew it was only a matter of days," Ismenia replied. Her friend rolled down her nightdress and clasped her hand, giving an encouraging squeeze. "Don't fret. You're in capable hands, milady."

The queen nodded and squeezed her friend's fingers tight. She knew Ismenia was right. Women gave birth all the time. Between Eamon the physician and Ismenia with her unique set of skills as an herbalist and midwife, the queen knew she was under the best care imaginable.

But that did nothing to quell the rising fear in her heart.

By the end of the next day, she would be a mother.

She would hold the greatest thing she ever wanted within her arms.

Yet her child would not call Graynor home. Their birthplace would be this citadel, the refugee city. Their legacy still indefinite.

As she came down from the contractions, a worse thought crossed her mind. Her ex-father-in-law, the self-serving King of Denorfia. During his visit, Boreas had been determined to arrange a marriage between her firstborn and one of his grandchildren. Her child had yet to see the light of day, and she had already been forced to make promises in an effort to keep her people safe and fed. Promises this child may one day resent her for.

Elara's eyes stung. As if sensing her friend's welling emotions, Ismenia grabbed her handkerchief off the bedside table and handed it over. "I cannot believe it's nearly time," the queen said, a nervous laugh bubbling forth. "All our talking and planning and worrying, and I might finally hold this child in my arms come morning." She gently splayed her hand over the center of her belly, feeling the baby's gentle movements against her palm.

"There is nothing wrong with being afraid of the unknown." The herbalist offered a timid smile, her eyes twinkling in the dim light coming from the balcony window. "But don't forget that there is peace to be found in Divinity's promise. You have held fast to the faith of our forefathers, and soon, you will be rewarded with a healthy babe."

No sooner had the queen nodded when the door opened, and Gerard ushered Eamon into their room. "Good evening, Your Majesty. I hear we may be ready to welcome a new Garrick into the citadel?"

Gerard paused at the man's wording. "Garrick-Stirling," he finally corrected, crossing his arms over his chest. The physician made his way over to bed and dropped his heavy bag at the end of it, clear of the queen's feet.

"I've just checked her, and she is showing progress. It will likely be several hours before the transition," Ismenia informed the gray-haired man as he pulled out a pair of spectacles and adjusted them on his nose.

Ignoring her update, the physician addressed the queen directly. "I should like to check for myself as the head physician." Elara caught notice of her friend's eyeroll but nodded for the man to proceed. Ismenia squeezed her friend's hand supportively as cold hands pushed her dress back up.

Her husband made his way over to the other side of the bed, carefully crawled up beside her, and cradled her belly as the doctor performed a quick examination. Elara winced, leaning her face into her husband's shoulder. Gerard leaned over and kissed the top of her head. "How are you feeling? Is there anything I can do for you?" he whispered into her hair. She sucked in a shaky breath, unable to respond as another contraction hit her.

The doctor rolled her nightdress back down and declared, "Right. You are most certainly in labor. Send a maid for some fruit and water; a full belly helps keep your strength up. Walk around the bed—*with help*." He leveled her husband with a look above his spectacles. "Sleep if you can manage. It will be a long night. I'll return in a few hours to check your progress."

"You're not staying?" Gerard asked, bewilderment apparent in his furrowed brow. The queen smiled sleepily, patting the hand that rested on her belly. She knew he was concerned but was thankful Ismenia would be the one to stay the night with them, not Eamon.

Eamon grunted, wiping his hands on a damp towel. "No need, my lord. Labor for a firstborn takes hours. It's best we all try to rest while it's early in the process. Should there be cause for concern, Miss Cinderfell can send for me."

Ismenia nodded. "Don't worry. I will be here for whatever you need until the babe comes," she assured him, settling into the large chaise closest to their bed.

"How many times have you done this?" Gerard asked her. His tone wasn't harsh or doubtful, merely curious.

The herbalist fiddled through her bag of supplies, seeming like she was counting to herself. "Oh, twelve, maybe fourteen times. I've assisted with all the births in the citadel in the past decade."

"She is very knowledgeable," Eamon said as he turned to leave.

Gerard didn't seem encouraged by those words. Hours passed, and he proceeded to fawn over his wife during every wave of contractions. She knew he was trying his best to be supportive while she suffered, but every tightening in her abdomen only reminded her that *he* had done this to her. This and so much worse.

It was early morning when her contractions were finally close together. Ismenia held a cup of water to Elara's lips, encouraging her to take a sip while they awaited the physician's return. The queen's heart raced as she gripped the bed sheets tightly in her fists. Her hair, damp with sweat, was plastered to her forehead, and her friend gently smoothed it out of her face. "It's almost time. You're doing great," Ismenia said with a reassuring smile.

A guttural growl of pain left Elara as another wave swelled. When it subsided, she collapsed back onto her pillows, breathing heavily. She had heard stories of other ladies' labors, but nothing could have prepared her for the toll it took on her body. Her arms felt weak and shaky. Breath came in haggard inhales.

Her husband pressed a damp cloth to her face and neck, the cool sensation a welcome reprieve from how warm she felt. "You are incredible," Gerard whispered, his focus so fixed on her it was as if he'd forgotten Ismenia was there. "I am so lucky to have you."

Elara allowed him to continue doting, despite her exhaustion. She was tired. Tired of the pain. Tired of being touched by so many hands. She wanted this baby out, and she wanted it out *now*.

When Eamon returned, he wasted no time checking her progress, but then he paused, not giving the queen an update. After a moment, he leaned forward and pressed his hands to her abdomen, feeling for the baby's positioning. "Is something wrong?" Elara asked.

The physician looked at her before shaking his head. "May I see you in the hall, my lord?" Her husband froze, looking between the concerned physician and his wife as though moving from the bed might be a grave error. "Just a moment. No need for Her Majesty to worry," the physician added in a monotone voice.

As Gerard got up, Elara felt panic rise in her chest. Despite the shackles having been removed a few weeks ago, she still felt trapped, unable to move or take control of her body in the moment. If something was wrong, she deserved to know. She was the one giving birth. She wore the crown. They could not keep the truth from her.

Attempting to push herself upright, Elara asked, "Why do you need to speak privately? If it concerns me or the baby, you can speak it here. In front of your queen." Just as quickly, Elara wailed in pain, dropping limply onto her bed. Something felt wrong, but she didn't know what. She could feel the baby move slightly, yet she felt like pushing would be futile.

Ismenia leapt to action, fluffing the pillows and offering the queen another drink.

The physician sighed. When Gerard came to stand beside him, he said, "There may be a *complication*. She is in transition, but I fear the babe's shifted. If it is breech, it could get stuck, and she would have difficulty pushing."

"What can we do?" Gerard asked. "You cannot just leave her to suffer like this."

Eamon lowered his face, and dark hair fell over his forehead. "Ismenia or myself can try to rotate the babe's positioning, but there's no way to see it. And it would be terribly unpleasant for Her Majesty."

"Ismenia," the queen breathed, and her friend clutched her hand.

"I've done it once before, but it's been years," the herbalist said nervously. She looked over the queen's sweat-drenched nightdress and shook her head. "I don't wish to hurt you."

Elara grabbed her by the wrist and looked her dead in the eyes. "Do what you must. I trust you."

Ismenia nodded and went to scrub her hands in the wash basin, careful to get between her fingers and all the way up to her elbows. Her friend approached slowly—too slowly— as the physician whispered with her husband across the room. Elara could make out words here and there—"complication," "death," "only save one." Each word sent her head spinning.

"What are you saying?" she asked loudly, her question punctuated by another pained wince.

Ismenia's hands skimmed over her abdomen, and a deep worry line appeared on her forehead. "Your body is nearly ready to push, but the baby isn't quite in position. With your permission, I can try to turn them. It won't feel pleasant." The queen nodded, though the words went right over her head. She was staring at her husband. All the color had drained from his tan face.

"Ismenia," Elara said quietly as the healer pressed gently on her abdomen, feeling for the baby's positioning. The woman hummed without looking up, focused on applying gentle pressure. Gerard and Eamon reappeared, both concerned that Ismenia might hurt the queen. Elara ignored them, asking her friend, "What will happen if you cannot turn the baby?" Her friend paused, fingers splayed on stretched skin but unmoving.

It was Eamon who finally answered. "In a breech birth, the baby could get stuck, leading to complications for both mother and baby. We could lose one or both of you."

The herbalist gnawed her bottom lip, not meeting the queen's eyes, and pressed again. Elara winced as the baby kicked roughly, wiggling and thrashing against the pressure. "I'm fine," the queen wheezed, breath coming in heavy puffs. "Keep trying."

"We need not worry. Idonea has seen you holding an infant. She has never been wrong," the woman assured her. But Elara and Gerard exchanged a weary glance, unconvinced by her comment.

Finally, Ismenia stopped applying pressure and wiped her forehead on her sleeve. She turned toward the physician and whispered something, pointing and gently touching the queen's abdomen. Eamon stepped closer and felt her exposed skin, gently skimming his hands over her bump. His eyes widened as he said, "We will find out soon enough."

They checked Elara again and agreed that it was time. Gerard offered her a sip of water before taking her hands in his. The queen was thankful to have something to squeeze tightly as she gave her first big push. It took a few tries, though time seemed to elapse in slow motion, and then the heavy pressure in her pelvis was gone. Elara collapsed back onto her pillows, panting heavily. Ismenia and Eamon turned their backs, going over to the wash basin behind them and working quietly. There was a moment of utter silence in the room as Gerard brushed sweaty hair back from his wife's face, the only sound his whispered words of praise in her ear.

A moment later, the most beautiful cry Elara had ever heard graced her ears. Tears pricked her eyes at the sound, and Gerard planted a kiss on her cheek. Ismenia walked over to them, a tiny baby wrapped in muslin cloth nestled in the crook of her elbow. "It's a girl," she told them, a relieved smile on her face as she handed the infant over to lay on her mother's chest.

Elara blinked down at her tiny miracle. The baby looked at her with pale, curious eyes. "Hello, my sweet girl." She touched the baby's little fingers, and a tiny hand wrapped instinctively around her fingertip.

"She is perfect, just like her mother," Gerard whispered, leaning closer to observe her. "Do you still like the name we had discussed?"

Elara nodded, feeling nothing could fit their child better. "Maristela Eden—firstborn daughter of the sea and stars."

Their moment of bliss was cut short when Elara winced, feeling another wave of tightening pain in her pelvis. "Something's wrong," she whispered, grateful for her husband gently scooping Maristela into his arms.

From the foot of the bed, Ismenia patted the queen on her knee. "Nothing is wrong, milady. As we suspected, you were doubly blessed by Divinity. We did not wish to alarm you because we could not be certain."

"Double?" the queen asked, her voice rising an octave.

Eamon nodded, getting back into position between her knees. "Yes, there is another."

"Another baby?" Gerard breathed, glancing from their daughter back to the doctor.

The queen cried out as another wave of contractions racked her body. She was tired, so very tired, and now she knew she had to muster the strength to do it all over again.

"I can see the head of the second," Eamon said. "Take a few deep breaths and then push!"

Elara did as she was told, though no amount of deep breathing brought her energy back. Gerard cradled their daughter in one arm and gripped her limp hand in his other. "You can do this. You're so strong." His words bolstered something within her. She *was* strong. She had fled her kingdom, suffered the near-unbearable losses of her father and brother, taken up the heavy burden of a crown preparing a rebellion, lost her first pregnancy and her first husband, and somehow, she was still there, pushing and praying and rising above all the pain.

A thunderous growl ripped free of the queen's throat as she pushed with all her might. The physician encouraged her to go again, and she clamped her eyes shut as she screamed through another push. This time, she felt the pressure ease. She blinked twice, seeing a quick flash of another baby in Eamon's arms before she laid back. Relief washed over her as she murmured to herself, "It's over. I did it. Twice." She still couldn't believe there was a second baby all that time.

Then she realized she had yet to hear the same beautiful cry that Maristela had made.

"Ismenia… is something wrong?" she asked wearily, unable to sit up.

Gerard held his breath beside her, cradling their firstborn in the crook of his elbow closest to her mother. The baby made a cooing noise, her little lips quivering in search of sustenance. "I think she wants you," her husband whispered, carefully passing Maristela back onto her chest.

Elara stared at Eamon and Ismenia, who were working in tandem with the second baby.

It was silent.

Too silent for too long.

She couldn't focus on the child in her arms for fear of the fate of the other. She had only just learned the second existed, yet she loved them equally. She couldn't bear to lose them. Not another beloved child. It would tear her apart.

Eamon landed gentle slaps on the infant's backside. Each made the queen jump. Her lip began trembling, a sob lodging in the back of her throat. Then Gerard caressed her cheeks, drawing her face away from them. Pressing his forehead to hers, he whispered, "Maristela needs you right now, my love. Please."

Elara clamped her eyes closed and nodded, holding back a flood of emotions. As she untied the front of her nightdress with one hand and pulled the fabric down to feed her daughter, she thought she heard a small cry coming from the other side of the room. Eamon delivered one more slap to the infant's back, and a tiny cough echoed through the room.

Then, another cry filled the chamber. This one was higher, sharper—a cry of discomfort. Elara's heart ached to hold them, to lay eyes on her other tiny miracle. A ragged sob escaped Ismenia as she and a maid finished cleaning up the second child. When they were done, her friend brought the baby over wrapped in a yellow cloth and said, "You have another daughter."

Gerard shook his head, his smile broadening as he accepted their second child from Ismenia. "Thank you," he whispered. Tears streaked his cheeks as he nestled his daughter, studying the faint brown hair on top of her head. Light blue eyes blinked up at him— eyes very much like his.

"What will you call the second?" Eamon asked. He wiped his hands on a clean towel as he approached the bed, observing the queen and her husband with their two daughters. "She's a lucky one. Quite small and weak compared to the first. Feed her as often as you can."

Elara nodded, eyes darting between the two girls. "We only had one name for a girl," she said, her voice weary.

"You've time to think about it. For now, get some rest. You've earned it," Ismenia said.

The queen offered a weak smile before turning back to her babies. It had been the most exhausting night of her life, but this moment—this beautiful, peaceful, perfect moment—made every second of strife and worry worth it. She was a mother, and she had never felt more proud to hold such a worthwhile title.

44

RARE

The Untamed Mare was packed for breakfast that morning. Two dozen members of the rebellion's leadership had decided to meet there with the blessing of Madam Rosmerta. Talitha wasn't sure how to feel when she came downstairs to a room full of strange men and women, the only familiar faces being John Finch and Leo Albright.

The ladies of the house had crowded around a small table in the corner. They ran fingers through their hair and adjusted the bodices on their day gowns, hungry eyes more focused on the men at the main table than their breakfast. Talitha shook her head at them before John Finch's voice drew her attention back to the main table.

Leo's endearing crooked smile greeted her as he beckoned with one hand for her to sit beside him. She slid onto the empty seat, her arms pressed tight to her sides, careful not to touch the man on either side of her. Leo leaned over to whisper, "Sleep well?" She leaned slightly to the other side, avoiding his gaze as she nodded. "I don't know how you manage it. We can hear this place into the wee hours of the morning."

Talitha huffed a laugh. "I help cook and serve. By the time I'm off to bed, I'm far too tired for the noise to disturb me."

She scanned the tabletop, quickly realizing that most of the men had piled their empty dishes on one end, unfurling several maps and coded letters in their stead.

"The latest correspondence stated that the heir will be leading the charge against Rexton come spring," John said, his voice faltering as he gripped the edges of a letter tight in his fingers. Thunderous cheers rang forth, and many lifted their glasses in celebration. John waved his arms, urging them to settle down. "They will not start in Graynor. They hope to take the valley back from his forces, freeing travel between the

341

two sides of the mountain once more. This would allow more reinforcements to join us and keep the citadel safe."

"How are we to aid them?" She didn't recognize the middle-aged man who spoke up, but his comrades nodded, their own concerns echoing after his. He scratched his graying beard, the wrinkles in his forehead deepening as he eyed the blank side of the letter from across the table.

"We aren't," John replied, folding the letter and tucking it back into his jacket pocket. "The heir has gone to recruit aid in Ord Metsiilva. It was the Elf Queen's suggestion that they take control of the valley if we want the elves' aid."

A broad-shouldered man two down from John stood abruptly. "How can the Garrick heir be ready for such an undertaking when they are still so young? Not even twenty years of age, and he's to lead a siege? This seems like a fool-hearted plan."

"I agree," the gray-haired man chimed in. "It's an unnecessary risk. With the support of the dwarfs, they can cross the mountains and avoid the king's men altogether when the time comes."

"I've been assured they are ready for such a task. They'll have spent a year training with the best sword master the elves could provide," John assured them. Talitha noticed the way he wrung his hands together, the confidence in his demeanor wavering. "Elara would never approve such a thing if the heir's instructors did not have full confidence—"

"So, all we can do is wait and pray the heir survives their first battle?" a woman at the other end of the table asked. Her roots had begun to grow silver, the bottom half of her tight braid still a vibrant orange.

John flexed his fingers and planted both palms on the tabletop, leaning over the pile of maps. "By all means, pray. But in the meantime, we have our own work ahead. I have full faith they will be joining us in Jessiraé soon. We must have things in order. Weapons, a discreet route, a strategy for getting past the guards and into the castle."

"Graynor Castle?" Talitha asked, louder than she had intended. Her cheeks burned as she looked down at the map closest to her. The hand-drawn map of the castle was rudimentary at best. There were many blind spots: mislabeled rooms and missing pathways, including the commoners path she had taken from the servants exit all the way to Jessiraé. Pointing a finger at the east side of the grounds, she said, "This layout is not quite right. The gardens are more on the south-east side."

Everyone was silent, staring at her in disbelief until John asked, "When were you at the castle?"

Talitha swallowed audibly. "I—well, I lived there for a few months," she stuttered, brushing hair behind her ear.

John's eyes widened as he leaned over the table. "How?"

She glanced around at the unfamiliar faces, all eyes locked on her. She didn't know any of these people. Even John Finch had become a stranger over the past year. Her palms clammed up as she considered how to answer him, the seconds stretching into minutes, and with it, scrutinous gazes. "I'd rather not say," Talitha finally mumbled.

John nodded, his brown eyes softening in sympathy. He still saw her as a young girl. The same age as his daughter, Talitha wondered if he would always look at her like she was one of his own children. Like a little girl who had skinned up her knees running through the woods.

But she wasn't a little girl anymore. Her eighteenth birthday had passed sometime during her imprisonment. No cake, no candles, no presents. Just a girl forced to grow up far too quickly. She couldn't bear to tell John or anyone else what had happened—not what the guards had done to her, or Anteros, or the king. She didn't want people to look at her with pity. She was strong enough to survive it. She was free now. She did not need their pity.

What she needed was the downfall of Antoine Rexton.

And if she could help take out the tyrant, she would.

Talitha cleared her throat and refocused on the map. "As I was saying, your map has inconsistencies. I can try to correct them if you'd like. I know about a few of the servants' paths, the lesser-known shortcut from the castle to Jessiraé."

"We all know of that path," a stocky man with blond hair interrupted from Leo's other side. "Who's to say we can trust anything this girl says? She's just a child. She only showed up a few days ago."

"I beg your pardon, sir, but I am *not* a child, and I daresay I have seen worse than all of you combined," she snapped.

Leo reached out and placed a warm hand on top of hers. She flinched at the sudden touch, instinctively wanting to yank her hand out of his. But then she remembered Anteros, the way he touched her so gently the day he freed her from the dungeon, as though he were scared he might break her. He hadn't. In fact, he had done the opposite.

Like Anteros, she knew Leo did not mean any harm, so she took a deep breath. The tension eased from her shoulders as she focused on the comforting weight of the hand on top of hers.

"She is no more a child than I am," Leo declared, giving her hand a light squeeze before releasing it.

The blond man on the other side of Leo rolled his eyes. "But you are my son. You have been with us since you were a boy."

"That's enough, Leonardo," John said, the tone of his voice silencing the man's argument. "Tal—Ruby grew up in Durmak with my children. She's helpful and honest. If she has information we're lacking, I trust her." He turned his attention back to Talitha.

"Take the map. Make any adjustments you can. We appreciate any information you can contribute."

She nodded. The parchment was rough against her fingers as she slid it closer, eyes darting back and forth over the scribbled words. With each label came a memory—some better than others. Her gaze snagged on the second floor and lingered on the room labeled *Prince's Quarters*. She had only been there once, but she could not help reminiscing about the only good night she had in Graynor. She had slept like a baby in Anteros' bed. How could she not when wrapped in the warm, comforting scent of whiskey that clung to his bed sheets?

The Madam placed a plate of hot eggs and buttered toast in front of her. The plate covered most of the map, breaking her train of thought. She stared down at the hot meal, still in disbelief that this woman continued to feed her without being asked after months of begging the guards and kitchen wenches for extra scraps.

"That bird of yours is making quite the commotion," Madam Rosmerta said, pulling a small bag of feed out of her pocket and dropping it on the table. "Best feed it soon."

"Ah, sorry about that. I'll do that right now," Talitha said, rising from her seat.

Rosmerta's hand landed on her shoulder, and she gave her a stern look. "Not before you've filled your own belly." She nodded at the plate.

Talitha pressed her lips together as she sank back onto her seat. Quickly, she shoved the food into her mouth, hardly listening as John and the other elders of the group finished their meeting. Her mind kept drifting back to the map. To the feisty phoenix. To Anteros.

When she had finished eating, she scooped up the bag of feed and waved a silent farewell to those at the table. Leo looked disappointed as she turned and walked away. He had shown an interest in her the last two times she saw John and the loyalists. She wasn't looking for anything romantic, but she appreciated his kindness. After all, she was a wanted traitor.

In her room, she poured the bird seed in one of the two bowls attached to the side of the cage. Phinnian allowed her to scratch at the feathers on the top of his head before he attacked his breakfast. She was about to take a seat at the little table in her room when someone knocked twice on her door.

"Ruby, could I have a word?" John's voice carried through the door, much to her relief.

Talitha swung the door open and found that John had not come upstairs alone. She gestured for him and Leo to enter and closed the door behind them. Phinnian squawked at the strangers, and she went over to cover his cage. "How can I help you?"

"Is that a phoenix?" Leo asked incredulously, coming up to stand beside her. "May I?" He reached for the cloth, awaiting her permission to remove it.

She held her breath for a moment. The word "no" died on the tip of her tongue. She did not want to draw attention with the firebird, but they had already seen it. There was no hiding it now. "Sure," she said hesitantly, pulling the cloth back off. Her stomach twisted in knots knowing they'd have questions about the rare creature. Questions that would give away more information than she wanted.

"Magnificent," Leo whispered, holding a hand up to the cage as though he intended to stroke the bird's tail feathers. Phinnian chirped, then quickly pecked the young man's fingers. With a hiss of pain, Leo withdrew his hand. "Feisty little thing. How did you come by him?"

Talitha wrung her sweaty palms on her skirt. "A boy I met in Graynor. He gave it to me. Said if I was ever in trouble, I could write to him."

Her best friend's father eyed her suspiciously. She could see the deeper questions swirling in his brown eyes. What boy? Someone in Graynor? What happened when you were there?

But John waited and held his tongue.

"Such a rare bird. Hard to imagine anyone giving such a thing up," Leo said, glancing over his shoulder at her.

Talitha's cheeks burned as she considered how this looked. Like she had stolen it.

"He cared for me when nobody else did. He's the reason I was able to escape the castle and come here," she said, her voice low. The last thing she wanted was for the ladies of the house to overhear the truth.

John stepped closer, catching her eye. "You're the escaped prisoner Rexton is searching for?" Though it came out like a question, the sadness in his eyes told her he had already figured it out. She nodded. John ran a hand over his face and groaned. "Divinity on high. Why would the king want you?"

"He didn't! He wants you!" Her eyes burned as she stared at the man who she had been interrogated about repeatedly. She kept her mouth closed. Not that she had known where John Finch had gone last fall. But for Serena's sake, she did not want to help Rexton find either of them.

Leo cleared his throat and excused himself from the room. With the click of the door closing behind him, silence settled between them. Talitha couldn't bring herself to look at John anymore. She sank into one of the two chairs at the table and exhaled, hoping he would follow Leo's lead.

The legs of a chair scraped against the floor as John pulled it out and took a seat across from her. He clasped his hands on the tabletop and waited a beat before whispering, "I knew there was a risk to my family when I agreed to recruit for Elara... but I don't understand why they would take you."

"When the king's men came for your family, Serena ran off. I was in the forest looking for her when they found me. They thought I might have been Serena. I told them I wasn't, but they were suspicious. I was right outside of town. They kept asking about your family and where you were, but I didn't tell them anything. How could I? I didn't know where you'd gone… so they dragged me to Graynor."

Her cheeks were wet when she finished explaining, her throat tight and raw. The faces of the men who had captured her flashed before her eyes. The wet squelch of one of their heads landing on the ground beside her making her stomach turn. She may have imagined their deaths more than once, but witnessing such violence… It still haunted her.

When she finally met John's gaze, tears streaked his face too. "I'm so sorry, Talitha. I never meant for any of you to get hurt." He wiped his face with the back of his hand and sniffled.

Talitha blinked rapidly, dabbing at the damp streaks under her eyes. "I know you didn't," she mumbled, her voice hoarse. She cleared her throat, her gaze fixating on the bright red feathers to her left. She reached out toward the bird, and it nudged the side of its beak against her knuckles.

When they had both composed themselves, John asked, "Who really helped you escape? He must have been a noble if he owned a phoenix."

Talitha froze, fingers perched atop Phinnian's head. She pictured Anteros and wondered how he was handling things. Especially the loss of his sister. Slowly, she lowered her hand. The ladies of the Untamed Mare had said his father was sending him to Murmont to join the army. If that were the case, giving her the phoenix had likely been futile. She doubted the bird would be able to find him if he wasn't at the castle. "He was no one. Just a boy who brought me food from the kitchens and felt sorry for me."

John quirked a brow. "You expect me to believe a kitchen servant gave you a phoenix?"

She laughed at how silly that sounded. "I suppose not." The smile on her face quickly fell away. It still felt foreign to laugh and smile after so long. She couldn't tell John the truth about Anteros. He wouldn't want to believe that Rexton's only son had a heart. The loyalists would want more information from her—information that could put Anteros' life in danger, and she didn't want that. "When the rebellion attacks the castle, what will happen to all of the nobles? To the servants? And the king's family?"

"The servants will be spared, of course," John replied quickly. He leaned back in his chair and crossed his arms over his chest. "But anyone who holds a weapon in Rexton's favor will be considered an enemy."

"And if a noble did not join the fight? Would they be spared?"

John studied the look of concern on her face. "I suppose they might be spared when it's all over. It's not our intention to slaughter the entire court."

She was quiet then, too scared to ask what would happen to Rexton's wife and son if the king were dethroned. As if John could read the worries on her face, he asked, "The person who helped you escape. Do you think they would consider turning sides? Being an inside person, providing information to us?"

Knowing what she did of Anteros' conscience, she could see him being willing after the horrendous crimes his father had committed against his own family. But would any loyalist ever trust someone who shared Rexton's blood and name? While she trusted Anteros with her life, she doubted others would entrust him with theirs.

"I'm not certain. He may not even be in Graynor anymore," she said, gnawing on her bottom lip.

"He gave you the phoenix to contact him, right?" John picked up a piece of parchment that she had addressed a few nights prior to "A" and passed it to her. "Perhaps you could write to him and see where his loyalties lie."

Each night as she readied for bed, Talitha thought of Anteros. Several times she had put a quill to parchment but could not find satisfactory words to say. She wanted to tell him how sorry she was to hear about Sabine, but no apology could lessen the pain of such a devastating loss, just as no letter could ever adequately thank him for setting her free. Words held power, but sometimes, no words felt strong enough.

John stared at her expectantly, as though this boy who had freed her from the castle dungeon might be the key to the rebellion's victory. What a foolish notion. If John knew who Anteros really was, he would never have asked her to write to him.

But as he did not know the truth, Talitha picked up the quill, uncapped the tiny jar of black ink, and allowed John to help her form a coded message for the king's heir, knowing deep down that it was unlikely this letter would ever reach Anteros' hands.

45

HOPE

The week of Serena's birthday, the bitter cold had improved enough for everyone to ditch their heavy layers and resume outdoor training. Serena threw herself into training, cycling through practice with different guardians. Adjusting her grip on Sannarvin, Serena grinned, the heaviness of the weapon in her hands feeling natural. Powerful. Sweat pooled along her hairline; her breath came in steady inhales after the conclusion of each fight. The cold bite of the wind kissed their cheeks. She welcomed the harsh sting—a welcome reprieve from the intensity of battle.

Despite their years of training, the guardians were no longer impossible to defeat. Serena had learned a few of her master's tricks and made sure to utilize them when her opponents least expected it. While Cole and Xandra were tucked away in their home enjoying time together, she had managed to defeat Gideon, Wesley, and Rigel—though the latter swore it was only due to her awareness of his prior injury.

During a particularly intense clash with Kieran, Serena glanced wearily at Will, whose stern expression was fixed on her opponent. Kieran, who had avoided her since their arrival, relished the opportunity to fight her. "What's the matter, Princess? Worried I'll knock you on your back?"

Will clenched his fists, starting forward as though he were about to start a brawl. Rigel was quick to block his path, and Serena shook her head, warding him off.

Turning back to Kieran, she countered, "I'd like to see you try." She twirled Sannarvin's hilt twice around her knuckles, feeling a tingle pulse up her arms as she captured it in both hands.

Bystanders whooped and cheered as they took their positions to start the duel. A small crowd had forgone their own training, opting to form a wide circle around them and

349

watch. Though most of the Academy was still unaware of Serena's true heritage, the other humans never failed to notice when she was training nearby. Their eyes gravitated toward her the way Serena's once followed a shooting star flying across the night sky. Like she was some rare sight that burned white-hot like a fire, demanding everyone's attention.

Serena would have preferred not to have such a large audience. It only made her feel that much pressure during training. In the heat of battle, she would not be concerned about who was watching, only who her opponent was and where her friends were. Whether they were safe.

No. I can't worry about them, she reminded herself. Eyes narrowed in on her target, she abandoned her worries and plunged into the fray.

While Serena often wondered if Rigel or Will went easy on her, she had no doubt that Kieran Brooks threw his all into each fight. Having been scorned, this man didn't care about her royal blood, only his ego. He was much too proud to allow himself to be shown up by a woman. He came at her with his sword poised to kill. Tightening her grip on the Sannarvin, Serena met his feverish succession of blows. Her teeth ground together as she pushed back, his strength and speed undeniable. This match would be her greatest challenge of the day.

Against the others, she felt confident. Cocky, even. But against Kieran, an edge of uncertainty sat heavily upon her chest. There was venom in his bright blues, and she wondered if he actually intended to harm her. "Scared, Princess?" the new guardian sneered, one corner of his mouth raised in a smirk.

She couldn't risk training getting out of hand—not with so much at stake in the near future–yet she could not help taunting him. It would have brought her immense joy to knock him on his back. "I see nothing to fear here." Serena lunged forward, sword swiping down toward Kieran's opposite shoulder. Her blade came down at such a sharp angle, he shouldn't have been able to block her.

Yet he rolled his shoulder, turned in three quick steps, and slammed his sword down on top of hers with a harsh clang. His speed baffled her. She moved to draw her sword back, but he twisted his blade around hers like a snake entangling with prey. Serena's jaw ached from clenching it. She loathed the thought of losing to anyone so quickly.

Thinking on her feet, Serena released the hilt of her blade, and it fell over, coming to rest on the trampled yellow grass. "You surrender then?" Kieran asked smugly, lifting his sword nonchalantly. It gave Serena the opening she needed. She dove onto the ground, rolled over her back, and snatched her blade out from under him.

Brows raised, Kieran barely leapt over her blade as she swiped at his ankles. As she pushed herself back onto her feet, his blade swiped through the air in a move far less tactful than usual. His confidence was wavering. Serena flashed a pleased smile that only seemed to irk him more.

The sound of a horn rang out overhead. All eyes lifted as the shrill note echoed through the training grounds. "What is that?" Serena asked, lowering her weapon.

Kieran grumbled at the sudden stop in their duel, hesitant to lower his weapon and end the fight prematurely. "It's the queen's guards. They sound off when potential danger is near. Unknown faces bearing weapons. Magical creatures that have wandered north."

"I don't recall hearing that when we arrived," she commented. Following the curve of the brick wall that surrounded Envyre, Serena wondered which was the case.

Then Ilrune came running around the main building, calling her name. "Serena! You're needed at the main entrance."

Her lips parted in surprise. Before she could reply, Rigel was beside her, asking, "What's going on?"

"There's a rather sizable group here looking for you. They say they've been sent by your queen," Ilrune said. He waved a hand as he turned, ushering her to follow him. "And that's not all. There are... dwarfs among them."

"Dwarfs?" Serena asked loudly, her voice hitting a higher octave. "How many?"

"Two or three. It's bizarre, really. We've never seen dwarfs from the north enter Ord Metsiilva," Ilrune said. "And why would Elara send them here?"

Rigel exhaled and glanced sideways at her, waiting for her to take the lead. Their mission to attack Rexton's men in Norlee was known, as Ilrune had been there when Daephyra suggested it. But the elves still did not know the depth of their plans. The celestial secret that had been under their noses all this time.

"They're reinforcement," Serena answered nervously as they walked hurriedly down the road past the cabins that housed them. She hadn't expected them to arrive so soon. She had intended to brief Daephyra's guards and the Academy staff before their arrival. "In a few weeks, we intend to attack the valley walls. To try to take that land back from Rexton. Elara has sent whoever she could spare from Symptee to aid in the fight. I wasn't expecting them so soon."

When they reached the entrance, which was firmly shut, Ilrune directed Serena, Rigel, and Will to ascend a set of stairs on the outside of the perimeter wall. At the top, some of the elves watched them curiously while others held fast to their bows, which were pointed down at the unexpected visitors.

Serena leaned over the edge and gasped. She had expected twenty, perhaps thirty men at most, knowing Elara would need to retain many guards to keep the City of Mercy safe. What she hadn't expected was more than double that, all decked out in armor and carrying with them an abundance of weapons and supplies. The troop below spanned so far back it disappeared into the trees out of sight.

"Blazing embers," Rigel whispered, running a hand down his face in disbelief.

"Do you recognize any of them? We want to confirm they are who they say before the gate is opened," another elf said.

Serena and Rigel leaned further, squinting at the faces shielded by shiny helmets until they spotted a few familiar faces. Rigel pointed first and said, "There. That's Atlas and Nyra. They trained here. They've been in Elara's Guard for a few years."

A short, thickset woman with a long black braid and shiny steel armor raised a hand and waved at them. "Rilura!" Serena shrieked, waving back. Will wrapped an arm around her, anchoring her to the wall as she leaned half her body over the edge. "I can't believe she came." Ilrune and the other Elven guards exchanged a glance. When Serena realized they had not ordered the gate to be opened, she turned and frowned at them. "She is the Steelcast *princess*. Open the gate *now*."

Reluctantly, Ilrune's friend nodded and called something out in their language. With the crank of a massive wheel and a bit of magic, the gate lowered. Serena turned and bolted for the stairs, ignoring Rigel and Will calling out her name. As her feet hit the dirt, she came face to face with several guards, who parted, opening a path for her to run straight to the dwarfs. When they came face to face, they greeted each other warmly.

"I cannot believe you're here!" Serena threw her arms around the dwarf, pulling Rilura's face into her neck. "Just when I was starting to worry we didn't have the numbers for this fight."

"Oh, we wouldn't miss it for the world. 'Tis not every day we get to put our axes to proper use," Rilura replied. Over her shoulder, she shot a grin at Bandan and Thomli. Serena was pleased to see the two of them looking in good health. A heavy hand landed on Serena's shoulder. "And there's more to come when the time is nigh."

The members of Daephyra's guard whispered behind them. Serena turned to see what was happening and spotted a concerned-looking elf with a half-shaven head scolding Rigel. "That cannot be good," she muttered, making her way over to them.

Rigel exhaled in exasperation when she approached. "It seems the elves are concerned about allowing the dwarfs to enter their city. They're also concerned there is not enough room for the entire brigade to stay within the walls."

"That is no issue," a deep voice said from behind her. Serena turned to see Commander Jacob Maynard, who had sat upon Queen Elara's War Council. He had been a key advisor, as well as a trainer for all new recruits to the Garrick Guard. He reached a deeply tanned arm toward the elf, who hesitated before shaking his hand. "We've brought our own provisions. We'll set up camp outside of the city—if that's acceptable. We only wanted to alert the guardians and Daephyra's guard to our presence."

The elves nodded, relief spreading over their faces as they headed back toward their posts. "You should head back. Only so much light left today," Ilrune said as he walked by.

Rigel and Will seemed to agree, moving to follow the elf back into Envyre while Serena remained. "I'd like to speak with the Guard and Rilura more. See you for dinner?" Serena called out to them.

Both young men paused, turning back to look at her. Rigel grimaced. "I can't just leave you outside of the wall. Crystal would kill me."

"We're going to move west and set up camp. Why don't you join us for dinner later this evening? Bring whoever you like," Commander Maynard said. He nodded at Rigel in acknowledgement.

"Really?" Serena asked, her voice spiking an octave higher as she whipped her head around to smile at the dwarfs. They grinned at the way she leapt up and down before taking off toward the gate. "We'll be back in a few hours!"

She ran right past the guys without slowing. Will called after her, "Wait up! Where are you going?"

With a broad grin, Serena turned, continuing to walk backwards toward the gate as she said, "To the kitchen! I feel like baking."

His dimples appeared as he jogged to catch up to her. "I told you," he muttered, wrapping his arms around her and planting a kiss on the top of her head.

She pressed against his chest, her brows pinching together. "Told me what?"

"That you're still the same girl I grew up with," he replied, tucking a piece of hair behind her ear. "Only now you have a sword and can beat me in a fight." His arms slipped back to his side as she playfully pushed him away.

Her cheeks hurt from smiling. She had been doing that a lot lately, despite her trepidation about the battle ahead. "I think you like it when I beat you," Serena argued.

Will snaked an arm around her shoulders and turned them toward Envyre. "Sometimes," he said, giving her a wink.

They walked through the gate side by side. Behind them, Rigel made hooting noises. "Get a room!" His taunting made them both laugh, though Serena could feel the sting of embarrassment burning her cheeks. Her brothers would have acted like that if they ever saw her kiss a boy. *Especially* William Burroughs.

Her chest tightened at the harsh reminder that none of her brothers ever had seen her like this. Madly in love with a boy who looked at her like she was made of stardust. Neither had her mother. And now, they never would.

Serena pushed that thought to the back of her mind. There was work to be done. Easy work she could use to knead some of the stress from her mind. Bread and cookies. Those were things that she enjoyed making. Things that could bring others comfort. For once, she wanted to focus on creating something that made others happy instead of fighting against someone who stole happiness. She needed that more than she had realized.

As they neared the main building, Serena asked, "Meet me in two hours?"

"Yeah, of course," Will replied, stooping for a quick kiss goodbye.

She marched toward the building, determined to find space in the cafeteria kitchen to get to work. To her surprise, Rigel followed, and shortly after, Crystal and some of the others joined them. The kitchen came to life with the pouring of ingredients and the overflow of laughter that filled the space, their hard work concluding with the heavenly scent of a job well done.

Nearly all the human students at Envyre Academy joined Elara's troop outside of the wall for dinner that night. With them, they carried freshly baked rolls, a vat of venison stew large enough to feed an army, and an array of cookies made from both human and Elven recipes. Everyone gathered around three large fires. The students mingled between the Guard members. Some knew each other from their time at the Academy. A few were even related.

When Serena had finished eating, she set her bowl aside and admired the faces lit by the fires. All these people had traveled from Symptee to fight for Hyrosencia, or to train to fight in the future. To fight beside *her*. For her family's throne. And many of them still did not know it.

She leaned closer to Rilura and whispered, "I did not think Elara would send so many, and so soon. Do they even know why they're here?"

The dwarf smiled faintly. "They know they need to liberate the valley. And as loyal soldiers, they did not question her orders."

Serena's stomach twisted. These men and women would soon march into their first real battle—and some of them would die there. They deserved to know the full truth. That she was the star-chosen savior they had been waiting for. That this battle had been her decision, not Elara's. That if they won, they might have the aid of the Silveryl elves when they siege Graynor.

"I need to tell them. I just don't know how." Serena wished she sounded confident in that claim, but her voice wavered. To announce her true lineage now would be a huge risk—one she knew Crystal would not condone. There could be more spies among Elara's men, or even the young people at the Academy. There was no way to know.

Rilura leaned back on her hands and stared up at the sky. After a moment of gut-wrenching silence, Serena followed suit. The stars were especially bright in Ord Metsiilva. Her thoughts drifted back to her family. They'd been heavy on her mind all day. Likely because her birthday was in a few days. The first she'd celebrate without them. Tears welled in her eyes as she stared at a cluster of twinkling stars just south of them. "Maybe

I'm scared to admit the truth because then my life as Serena Finch really will be over. At least now, I still feel tied to them. Even if my name is a lie."

Will reached over and squeezed her hand. He was obviously eavesdropping but pretending not to be. It was sweet that he wanted to allow her to talk to Rilura without disrupting them. Glancing his way, she tried to smile and squeezed his hand back.

"You have been through more pain than most here," Rilura noted. As if she knew which stars Serena gravitated toward, the dwarf lifted a thick hand and pointed. "Speaking the truth cannot erase the life you lived, nor the people you loved. The Finches were your family, and no one can take those memories from you."

Serena sniffled loudly, wiping a stream of tears away with the back of her hand. "Thank you." A deep breath helped to steady her emotions. She closed her eyes, blacking out her view of the stars above. But even in the dark, she could feel their presence, and it gave her strength.

"Do you remember what I said to you as we came down the mountain all those months ago?" Rilura asked, one thick brow quirking higher than the other.

Of course, Serena remembered. Her words had offered comfort and strength when she was guilt-ridden after killing Cameron, watching Rigel nearly die saving her life, and finding out the truth about her identity. Her eyes snapped open, seeking out the watchful eyes in the night sky. One was half-full while the other was a mere sliver in the sky, nearly invisible beyond the trees. It almost looked like the moons were winking at them, as though they were privy to her secret. "The moon is not always full, but it always has light to offer. So do I." Yet at that moment, Serena did not feel this light Rilura was referencing. She felt the heavy burden of destiny pressing down on her shoulders.

"Correct." The Dwarven princess's smile broadened. She pointed to the sky again. "And there are two moons. Just as there are two sides to who you are. Sometimes one offers greater light than the other, but both are important. They exist in harmony."

Serena was awestruck by the dwarf's wisdom once again. "Two sides," she murmured. Sitting up straight, she glanced around the camp once again. Everyone there had hope in their eyes. Hope that the upcoming battle was the first step toward taking their kingdom back. Toward returning to their homeland.

That hope stemmed from a prophecy.

A prophecy about her. The last Garrick heir.

Pushing to her feet, Serena went to stand on a fallen log and cleared her throat. As everyone's attention slowly found her, she studied the curious looks on their faces before settling on Will and Rilura. In that moment, their gentle smiles encouraged her to speak.

"Good evening, everyone," she began, nervously tucking stray hair behind her ears.

Everyone was staring at her now. The guardians and students waved and smiled, most having no idea what she was about to say. Crystal's jaw clenched, her mouth pulled into a flat line as she watched. She did not move to stop Serena, but it was plain by the fear in her eyes that she wanted to.

But Serena had to do this. She had to embrace who she was and tell her people that she was ready to take this fight all the way to Rexton's doorstep.

"Some of you know me as Serena Finch, the daughter of Mary and Sir John Finch. Or Fritz." She paused. A few of the older guards lit up in recognition of the names, but many of the younger people did not know about her parents' significance. "I was raised in Durmak until Rexton sent men to slaughter my family. He's done that to so many here. Slaughtered innocents. Chased us out of our kingdom. Burned our homes. Hunted us like animals."

Many people nodded their heads in solemn agreement. She took a deep breath and continued, "Last summer, I thought he was after us because of my parents' loyalty to Elara. It wasn't until we had safely crossed the mountains that I learned the truth." She swallowed thickly. Everyone seemed to be holding their breath, brows pinched in anticipation of her next words. "Almost eighteen years ago, the Finches took me with them when they fled Graynor. But Mary Finch had not given birth to me. She had been my caretaker. My birth parents were Stellan Garrick and his wife Gwen. And Queen Elara is my aunt."

Gasps echoed through the darkness. All eyes remained fixed on her. Some of the students looked confused, turning to whisper questions to the older students and guards. At first, no one moved or responded.

Just as Serena was going to speak again, Commander Maynard rose from his seat and approached her. He paused before the log where she stood and studied her face for a moment as if looking for pieces of her father in it. As understanding dawned in his dark brown eyes, Maynard dropped onto one knee. "Your Highness, it is an honor to meet you at long last."

Her heart felt like it was lodged in her throat. To her horror, the other members of the Guard slowly joined him in taking a knee, heads bowed in reverence. "Oh, no. Please don't. You can sit. Really. I am just like any of you—a Hyrosencian who wants her home back." She didn't want anyone to kneel to her. She only wanted them to know she was there to fulfill Divinity's promise to her people.

At one of the other bonfires, she heard whispers. Questions regarding the truth of what she was saying. Asking for proof. Rigel stood then, his red hair reflecting in the fire light as he turned toward her. He beamed with pride as he proclaimed, "She speaks the truth. We were sent to retrieve her. Nearly died saving her. And I would do it again. Serena is the heir we have all been waiting for. Look her in the eyes and you will know it to be true. She has the Garrick eyes, and she has trained long and hard to live up to that prophecy. To lead us to liberation."

Some of the younger people, students and recent graduates, cheered at his words. They, too, fell onto a knee as shouts of "Long live the Princess!" rang out in the night.

Serena stepped down from the log and sighed. "Can everyone please take a seat?" Slowly, people started to return to their seats. All eyes remained on her. Hungry. Hopeful. Anticipating more. When the camp fell quiet, she said, "I have told you our kingdom's greatest secret—not so you would bow to me—but so you would know why I am making the decisions going forward. I do not seek to take Elara's place. She is the crown, and I am the sword. We both know our roles. I am a fighter like the rest of you. If there is one thing I have learned this year, it's that blood means nothing. Blood may link me to a prophecy, but it has never limited my family. The Finches were my family for eighteen years. And now…"

She scanned the crowd, finding the faces of her closest allies. "Now I have a new family. This is what I'm fighting for. Each of you. For our homes. Our safety. Our futures."

Someone sniffled in the back. Xandra had tears running down her cheeks as she watched in awe, her husband's arm resting gently on her lower back. Even Cole met her gaze with pride. The guardians had such faith in Serena, even when she did not have faith in herself.

Looking back to the guards who had traveled all this way for a battle at the border, Serena addressed them. "You should know: I have been trying to recruit the elves to aid in our plight. The challenge to take the valley back from Rexton came from Queen Daephyra. It is my hope that should we win, the elves will join us for the siege of Graynor."

Some of the guards glanced at Crystal and Cole. Crystal then stood and proclaimed, "I will stand with Serena, regardless of my queen's choice. Now each of you must decide whether you will fight with us."

Maynard was the first to stand. Crossing one arm and placing his fist over his heart, he said, "It has been my honor to serve the Garrick family for thirty years, and I will not stop today. Say the word, and I will follow you into battle."

The members of the Guard all repeated the motion, chanting, "It is my honor to serve you."

As the students passed out cookies and extra blankets, many of the older students and Academy graduates approached, eager to shake Serena's hand and pledge their service as well. On the walk back into the city, their friends were rather upbeat considering they had committed to going off to war in a few weeks.

The weight of a secret had been lifted from her heart, and the truth had brought hope to so many who had been waiting in anticipation for their star-chosen savior. Hope was a funny thing. It filled the night air with pleasant warmth and eased the fears that normally chilled Serena to the bone. Everything felt lighter. She turned her face up to the sky and smiled at the moons knowing they had a fighting chance.

46

HEARTS TAKE FLIGHT

Talitha stared at her last piece of parchment; her bottom lip protruded as she racked her brain for what to say. Phinnian reached his beak through the cage bars and pecked at a crumpled, discarded page—one of several failed attempts to write Anteros. She knew she needed to be careful not to give away either of their identities in case the letter fell into the wrong hands, but nothing she wrote seemed adequate. The letter she'd started with John's help had been too cold, devoid of anything she wanted to say to Anteros. She wanted to offer her condolences. More than that, she longed to apologize. Since learning about Sabine's death, the girl's face had been haunting her dreams. She knew she was to blame for the incident that had taken his sister's life, and the guilt was eating away at her.

That morning, she had gone underground to deliver food to the rebellion. John had asked again about the boy who had helped her escape the castle. She lied and said she had not heard anything. The truth was, she had never sent a letter in the first place.

She tapped the quill on the corner of the parchment, leaving behind splotches of black ink. Staring at the ink as it soaked in, the face of an animal stared back at her. A cat or a fox. The pointy-eared creature judged her failure to put words down and send this letter.

Phinn squawked loudly, breaking her concentration. Dropping the quill, Talitha sighed in frustration. She reached out her fingers to scratch under the phoenix's chin. Her mind drifted as she pet the firebird. Anteros' face was clear in her mind. Waves as black as night that she wished she'd reached out and touched. Hazel eyes flecked with green and gold that held a world of sorrow. Hands that were always gentle with her. Lips that—

Sharp pain made her snatch her hand back from Phinn. The rotten firebird had bitten her!

359

Talitha growled under her breath and snatched the quill back into her hand. A single drop of blood dripped from her finger onto the page as she scribbled:

A,

I've heard that time heals all wounds but personally know that to be false. My heart aches over this loss, so I can only imagine your pain.

I wanted you to know I am doing well. Please do not worry for me any longer. I have caused you enough trouble. I want for nothing but your peace and happiness.

There are people here I would like you to meet one day. They do not know who you really are, only that you saved my life. For that, I will always be grateful.

I hope we will meet again under better circumstances.

T

She paused, rereading her words before realizing that using her real initial was dangerous. With a frown, she scribbled over the T and reluctantly drew a terrible sketch of a gemstone over the place where her blood had soaked into the parchment.

Leaning back to admire her handiwork, Talitha groaned. "Why did I do that? I am no artist," she muttered crossly. She folded the sheet until it was smaller than Phinn's leg, then tied it to the bird with a piece of twine. The creature made an indignant sound and pecked the piece of parchment once, quickly deciding it wasn't food. Talitha said a silent prayer to Divinity that the stupid phoenix would not lose the letter before finding Anteros.

A tightness in her chest made her hesitate for a moment more. What if he doesn't get it? Or what if he does, but he never intends to come to Jessiraé? She really had no way of knowing unless he wrote her and sent the phoenix back. Even then, there was no guarantee Phinn would find his way back to the Untamed Mare.

With a heavy exhale, Talitha reached into the cage and allowed Phinn to step onto her arm. She lifted him out carefully. Once free of his confinement, he spread his wings and shook his feathers out. Red feathers transitioned to yellow at the base of his wings and on his belly. He was the most majestic creature she had ever seen. She still couldn't comprehend how she'd come to possess such a magnificent creature.

Knowing she might never see him again, she took an extra moment to admire his beautiful feathers and proud face. "You really are marvelous," she said, hesitantly patting his head. Phinn squawked in approval and dipped his head, allowing her to continue showing him affection.

Finally, she lifted the letter that Anteros had written her weeks before to the creature's beak, and he sniffed the parchment. Immediately, his feathers lifted, and his eyes sparked in recognition. Or at least, Talitha hoped she wasn't imagining that reaction.

Going to the window she hardly ever opened due to the bitter cold, Talitha looked at Phinn and said, "I need you to find our friend Anteros. Do you think you can do that?"

The phoenix just stared at her, head cocked to one side. She felt silly for talking to the creature, but some nights, he had been all she had to combat her loneliness. Now she'd be alone with her thoughts.

With her free hand, Talitha reached out and unclasped the wooden shutter that kept the elements at bay. The breeze gently pushed the shutter open. Cool air hit her cheeks as she shuffled closer. Phinnian the phoenix shivered in anticipation, giving her one last look before he pushed off her arm. As soon as he cleared the window, the phoenix spread his wings and soared. Talitha watched until he disappeared, wishing more than anything that she had wings of her own.

Sometimes, weapons were far easier to handle than people. Crystal counted in her head as she collected the sheathed blades that Will and the younger boys had spent the day sharpening and placed them in long, thick canvas sacks. *Fifty.* Enough for the students and graduates who had committed to joining Serena and the Guard at the border.

The archer propped the last bag up against the wall in the armory. She wiped the sweat from her brow on her sleeve. Thankfully, Heath, Gideon, and Malachi were set to load the supplies onto the horses the morning they would leave. With each passing day, the time grew nearer. That day had been another whirlwind of intense training and preparing for battle. At the end of it all, Crystal was happy to sit alone in the armory and finish making new arrows for the battle.

They were all nervous—Serena more than anyone. The last thing they needed was for the Garrick heir to be sleep deprived and sick with worry, so Xandra gave her a bottle of wine and banished her to her house early in the evening, insisting she get some rest. Comforting others had never been Crystal's strong suit. The elf was thankful the others could take the lead on easing Serena's growing fears. She preferred to busy her mind to keep her own worries at bay.

In a few days, they would move out, opting to sleep under the stars in lieu of the comfort of their beds in Envyre. They couldn't take these final nights sleeping in peace and safety for granted. In mere days, they would incite a battle, and no one was guaranteed to survive, not even their princess. They would all have to fight for their lives.

A loud creak drew her attention to the door. Leaning on the doorframe, Rigel stood watching her, arms folded over his chest. The way he looked at her made her stomach flip. Something in his bright blues was wild. More bold and mischievous than usual. Like he had drunk some Elven wine and found the courage to say things he normally wouldn't.

Crystal cleared her throat and returned to checking the arrow shafts she had created a few days before. Pretending to check that each was perfectly straight, she thought about ignoring her comrade in hopes that he might lose that terrifying spark in his eyes and leave.

He didn't.

Stepping into the room, Rigel allowed the door to swing shut behind him. "Need some help?" She blew out a breath as he made his way over to sit beside her on the bench.

As she eyed the final shaft, Rigel leaned over. His face hovered over her shoulder as he pretended to inspect the piece of wood. Thankfully, he didn't know the first thing about making arrows by hand, or he would have realized that Crystal had already prepared the shafts and added a groove on each. She was only inspecting them now to avoid eye contact.

A strong, fruity scent overwhelmed Crystal's senses, and she wrinkled her nose. "You've been drinking," she noted, not looking him in the eyes.

Her friend chuckled and leaned back on his palms. "Can you blame me?" His blithe reply made her frown, but there was no point chastising him. He was a grown man who could do whatever he wanted, even if he made stupid decisions at times.

"Surprised you're not with the guys… or Carissa," the elf said nonchalantly. She would have preferred that over the feeling of his gaze following her every move. It made her skin itch.

"I'm not with Carissa. That was—" He cleared his throat abruptly. "That should have stayed in the past. We didn't work then, and we still don't."

"And she understands this?" Crystal laughed, recalling the way the bubbly woman followed Rigel around at the wedding reception, desperate for a dance.

"Explicitly." He ran his hands over his face. When they dropped to rest atop his thighs, Crystal glanced sideways and felt a pang of guilt for questioning him. His relationships. He stared at his lap looking cross.

"So, there's nowhere else you'd rather be tonight?" One brow raised in disbelief, she waited for him to look up and answer her.

The moment he looked at her, she regretted asking. His entire body turned toward her, their knees brushing against each other. Rigel searched her face, longing plain on his handsome features. *He's definitely drunk*, Crystal reasoned as she stood and went over to the steel arrowheads that she had asked Will to forge for her. They were perfectly pointed. A lethal tip for a skilled archer.

"Crys." His voice was a desperate plea from just behind her. His proximity sent a chill down her spine. "I heard Deldrach returned to Montaris. Why didn't you tell me you ended your engagement?" Her heart sank. She didn't want to have the conversation he seemed set on. Not tonight. Not ever, knowing her words could be as sharp as an arrow to her dear friend's fragile heart.

She hesitated, lips parted but her back still facing him. "I figured Xandra or Cole would tell you," she lied. Snatching one of the arrowheads from the basket, Crystal focused on fitting it into the slot she had cut onto the shaft. Once placed, she began wrapping sinew around the arrowhead to secure it in place.

Rigel stepped into her peripheral and huffed in exasperation. "That's bullshit, and you know it. You've been avoiding me, haven't you?" When she didn't reply, he reached out and yanked the arrow out of her grasp.

She gasped. "Rigel, I'm working," she snapped, turning to face him. "I can't do this right now. There's too much to be done."

He set the arrow down on the table and stepped closer. Gentle hands came up to either side of her face, and she pressed her lips together, bracing for an argument neither of them would win. "Stop worrying about weapons. We have time," Rigel said gently. His thumb brushed back and forth against her cheek in calming circles. His hands were warmer than she'd expected. Oddly comforting, considering she usually disliked being touched.

Crystal closed her eyes in exhaustion. "I am sorry I did not tell you," she finally whispered. "Once it was over, I just… needed time to breathe."

"Why did you do it?" Rigel asked. The warmth of his hands disappeared, and she opened her eyes to meet his. All humor was gone from his bright blues, replaced with the most somber look she'd seen in a while. Even more serious than Deldrach's face when she gave him back his ring.

Turning her face up toward the ceiling, Crystal counted the wooden beams in her head. "I never loved him. My father said he could tell. He told me it was acceptable to end it. So, I did."

Rigel loosed a brief chuckle. "I'm still shocked he came for the wedding."

"As am I," she replied, feeling some of the tension in her face and body relax. She couldn't help the smile that found its way to her lips as she recalled that day. Her father had surprised them in the best way.

"He actually gave his blessing to Cole?" Rigel's question was weighted. He was looking for permission. For hope that nothing stood between them.

Crystal nodded, unwilling to say it aloud. She couldn't encourage him. This was the way things had been for months. He leaned closer; she leaned away. He was a good friend, a skilled comrade and honest confidant. That's all this would ever be. "Rige, I—"

Before she knew what was happening, warm lips crushed hers, cutting off what she was about to say. Rigel's hand sank into her hair, gripping the back of her neck. Crystal tensed, though her eyes closed on instinct. Her hands found his chest, pressing gently into his leather vest, but he didn't take the hint to pull away.

When he finally withdrew, his hands lingered on her neck and hip. Tears pricked her eyes as she stared at him, both catching their breath. His eyes were so full of adoration. As they dipped back to her lips, she shook her head and said, "Stop."

Rigel's arms dropped to his sides as he stared at her, bewildered. She clenched her eyes closed, fighting back the tears she refused to let him see. How dare he do this to her? She cared about him. He was one of her closest friends. How could he kiss her without asking? Her skin felt like it was boiling from the buildup of sadness and rage in her. Her lower lip trembled as she clenched her fists, knowing he had crossed a line that would alter their friendship forever.

A loud crack echoed through the armory as her hand made contact with his cheek. This slap wasn't playful, nor a warning. It was pure anger. A reiteration that he had crossed a firm line. That she was quaking with quiet fury at his foolishness.

A hand pressed against his red cheek as he stared in shock. Crystal growled in frustration. Flinging the back of her hand out, she knocked over the bucket of steel arrowheads. The clatter of metal pieces hitting the ground made him wince and squeeze his eyes shut. Her cheeks flooded with her grief as she breathed in shakily. "I am not my brother," she whispered, surprised by the crack in her voice. She didn't know what had become of her usual calm demeanor.

Rigel opened his eyes—now filled with his own tears—and reached a hand toward her, but she flinched back from him. "I'm sorry, Crys. I didn't think—"

"You can blame the wine for that," she snapped. A thin finger jabbed into his chest as she stepped toward him. "I did not end my engagement for you, Rigel. It was never about you. It was about not wanting to get married. Not just to Deldrach, but to anyone. Do you understand? I will never love you the way you want."

Hurt flashed in his water-logged eyes, and Rigel hung his head in defeat. She had always appreciated the spark in his heart, the hope he had in the world, the prophecy, and the future. She had never wanted to be the person to crush that light.

"I tried so hard not to encourage you. I didn't want it to come to this." Crystal gestured between them with her hand. "I've spent so long tied to what other men want for me. For my future. For the first time in my life, I'm free. My father has accepted my choices. And I don't ever intend to give up that freedom. Not for you or anyone else."

Rigel didn't meet her gaze as she rushed past him out of the armory. Outside, Crystal gasped, the burst of cool air making her chest hurt even more as she broke into a run. Cutting through the night air like an arrow set on a target, Crystal ran down the street toward the cottage where she now lived alone and wept silently. When she saved Rigel's life in the mountains, she never imagined she'd rip his heart out days before going off to war.

47

FEET IN THE FIRE

A few days into their trek south, the pit in Anteros' stomach intensified knowing there were only so many places they could be going. When they reached the border to Norlee, half of the horde was ordered to set up camp and wait there. The remaining thirty men, including Anteros, were sent south. That was when the prince knew for certain where his father had sent them.

Silently, he sent desperate prayers out into the universe. To the gods. To Divinity. To the stars. Whatever unseen force dictated their fates. He pleaded for Talitha to be kept safe. Were he not surrounded by others, he would have fallen to his knees and begged. As they approached Durmak, he could only hope that she had stayed in Jessiraé and not returned home.

"Hey, Captain," Calix said loudly. Pelham turned to glance back as his horse led the group down a worn dirt path. "Why would His Majesty send us out before winter's end? The nights are still chilly, and the ground is cold."

The captain chuckled, dark eyes flitting to Anteros knowingly. "Because everything is dry. Much easier to manage than the rainy season."

Anteros swallowed. The few leaves that clung to the trees for dear life rustled in the wind. The fallen crunched under their horses' hooves. Everything was brown and dried out—devoid of the moisture needed to grow and thrive.

That only mattered when building a fire.

Drawing the hood of his cloak over his head to protect his ears, Anteros tamped down the panic rising in his chest. His armor threatened to strangle him; the steel and chainmail sat heavy on his shoulders. The leather sheath strapped to his hip clanked against the metal as his horse trotted onward. His friends seemed unphased by the secretive nature of their mission, but Anteros knew now that his father had sent them to Durmak purely out of spite. He must have assumed Talitha would make her way home, and he wanted Anteros to be there when his men captured her.

They entered the town in the late afternoon when the sun had begun to descend beyond the tree line. The sky had shifted from blue to lavender; a pop of pink surrounded the quickly setting sun behind the trees. Small children chased each other across the dirt road, shrieking and grinning until they noticed the soldiers coming their way. Then their smiles fell, dissolving away into looks of fear as they bolted for their homes. That was the safest place they could go.

When they reached the center of town, an older man and woman approached while others lingered in open doorways, concern etched on their faces. The elders held their chins high as they greeted the captain and asked how they could help the king. Captain Pelham produced a scroll from within his uniform and unrolled it, making a show of their business. Anteros already knew what it would say. *Anyone found harboring known fugitives, Talitha Vise, Serena Finch, or John Finch, will be found guilty of treason and promptly executed.*

He nodded as Pelham read the paper nearly word for word. But the king's decree went one step further than that. "Where is the home of Caelum and Alba Vise? We have orders to search their properties."

The elderly woman shifted back and forth on her feet. Her eyes shifted to a house beyond the king's men before answering. "Why would the king want those girls? Neither had ever left home until they disappeared last spring."

"They've been linked to a known loyalist who has gone by the alias of John Finch. Perhaps you've heard of him?" Pelham asked, leaning down on his horse to look her in the eyes.

The woman stepped back and averted her gaze. "No one by that name has been here in well over a year." Her hands trembled as her eyes flitted over the soldiers, likely counting them in her head. They were thirty strong, dressed in shining armor and all carrying a blade at their hips.

The other elder cleared his throat. "I can assure you none here had any knowledge of his loyalties. I'm quite certain not even those girls knew."

The captain swung one leg over his horse and dismounted beside the elders. Marching up to the gray-haired man, Pelham kicked one of his legs, bringing the man to his knees. "And who are you to make such a statement?"

Quiet gasps sounded behind them, and Anteros glanced over his shoulder. Several men shoved their wives and children into their homes and closed the doors. Their eyes trained on the captain; their hands perched on the hilts of their daggers in anticipation.

Fools, Anteros thought. Even if every man in this town bore arms, they would not stand a chance against the king's men. The soldiers had swords and training, where these simple farmers had dull daggers and no experience.

Someone cleared their throat beside him, and the prince whipped his head around to his left. Julian and Calix were staring at him, eyes wide and full of trepidation. "All this for one girl?" mouthed Julian incredulously.

A metallic sigh rang out as Captain Pelham unsheathed his blade and pointed it at the elder's neck. The man froze, tears springing to his eyes as he stared back in horror. The captain leaned closer and asked, "Who are you? And where is the Vise residence?"

"I am Varren Borgh, an elder of the Durmak Council." The man's deep voice faltered.

With a roll of his eyes, Captain Pelham straightened his stance and hummed thoughtfully. His gaze swept from the elderly woman to the nearby houses. Terrified faces peered hesitantly out of windows, ducking out of sight when he looked their way. Pelham seemed to relish their fear—especially the apprehension on his new recruits' faces. He held eye contact with Anteros, a dark smile creeping onto his face.

Then he turned and swung his blade, swiftly beheading Varren the elder.

Screaming ensued. The elderly woman, now covered in blood splatter, dropped to her knees and burst into tears. Anteros' stomach lurched at the unexpected violence. His friend Calix leaned over the side of his horse and retched.

Before anyone could move, Pelham turned and issued orders to his men. "Search every house in this wretched town. When you find the Vise household, bring them to me. Set fire to their property and any other that dares defy the king."

"You cannot do this," the elderly woman said from behind him. She was back on her feet now. Clenched jaw and fists kept her shaking to a minimum, but the terror in her eyes was still there. She knew there was no use arguing with the king's men. "These are good people. We have done no wrong."

Pelham chuckled darkly. "The king does not care about you or anyone else in this pathetic town except traitors to the crown. If you have nothing to hide, stand aside." Hanging her head, the woman stepped aside and gestured for him to enter the house behind her.

The captain waved toward the men who remained on their horses, including Anteros and his friends. "Get to work!" With that, the men dismounted from their steeds and fanned out toward the homes lining both sides of the road. The soldiers approached each in pairs, pounded their fists on the front doors, and then forced their way inside.

Julian charged toward a home with James rushing after him. Anteros lingered behind as Calix recovered from puking. Neither of them were quick to follow these orders, which Pelham noticed. They made their way toward a house further down the road and knocked, not using the sheer force that others were. No one answered at first. The young men exchanged a look before Calix announced, "Open the door or we will break it down!" The prince cringed at the idea of invading these innocent people's space.

The door slowly creaked open to reveal a little girl—she couldn't have been older than ten—with unruly brown hair and a knife that was much too large for the size of her hand.

Anteros balked at the brazen girl, then crouched to address her at face level. "Hi there. What's your name?"

She narrowed her eyes. "Lena Burroughs. Who are you?"

"I'm Anteros. Are your parents home?"

She peered over her shoulder at the empty sitting area before nodding. "Papa's in bed sick. Mama went out to the barn."

Calix nudged the prince, but he ignored it. "The king wants every house searched. He's looking for two girls from here—Serena Finch and uh…"

His friend sighed and said, "Talitha Vise. Recognize those names?"

"Of course. They're friends with my brother," Lena murmured. She shuffled a step back from them, fiddling with the knife behind her back. Another glance over her shoulder told Anteros she was scared. He was familiar with the clammy hands and shifty eyes, having grown up under his father's iron fist, and it killed him to have someone look at him the same way people looked at his father.

Calix wasn't fazed by her fear. He took a step closer to the girl and held out his hand, wiggling his fingers to silently demand she hand the weapon over. Without looking up at him, Lena pulled it from behind her back and placed the hilt on his palm. "Are either of them in the home? Best you tell us now. Save your family the trouble." She shook her head vigorously.

Still squatting beside her, Anteros offered a half-smile before standing. "We'll make the search quick. Why don't you take a seat over there so you aren't in the way?" He pointed at a time-worn sofa in their sitting area that had seen better days. On it lounged a shabby gray cat. Lena nodded and scurried over to where he pointed, pulling her cat into her lap and scratching behind its ears.

Calix nodded his head toward the back of the house. "Let's get this over with." Anteros followed him, one hand on the hilt of his sword in case they found any trouble with her father. Luckily, the man slept through their search. His obnoxious snoring somehow managed to muffle the sounds of their digging around. Once they were certain the king's targets were not present, Calix marched through the sitting room and back out into the road. Anteros paused and nodded his head at the girl, placing her knife on the corner of a small table before exiting.

Outside, chaos ensued as soldiers dragged people out of their homes into the road. Children were crying, parents were screaming, and soldiers were barking orders without bias. Anteros watched in horror as a couple was shoved down the road, stumbling over their feet as they approached Pelham. The stout man's sideburns had begun to gray, but it was the woman's hair that snagged Anteros' attention. It was a vibrant shade of orange. Like falling leaves. Like Talitha's.

Before he could think, the prince was running. His chest was on fire. The air in his lungs was suddenly hot, a heavy weight pressing down and choking him, making it impossible to catch his breath. All he could see was red. *His* Red. Even as the woman's tired, wrinkled face turned, Anteros didn't slow. She wasn't Talitha, but very likely her mother. Soldiers forced her onto the ground. The look on the captain's face reminded him of his father the day he dragged them all out to the gardens. An ominous feeling crept into his heart at the reminder of that terrible day.

Anteros slowed to a stop as he reached them. Bile rose up the back of his throat as he stared at the couple on their knees in the dirt. The woman looked so much like Talitha it took his breath away. She had the same weary look on her pale face that Talitha had after months in the dungeon, yet that didn't take away from her beauty. But when he turned to her father, it was like looking directly into Talitha's eyes. Pale blue gray like the sky just after it rained. Melancholy, yet achingly beautiful.

"Anteros! Just the man I was looking for," Pelham boomed.

A heavy hand clapped down on the prince's shoulder. The weight reminded him of his father, sending a chill down his spine. Anteros clenched his fists and shrugged out of Pelham's grasp. The captain narrowed his eyes before sauntering over to the man on the ground. He pulled his sword from its sheath again. As he paced around the Vises, Pelham tapped the sword gently on top of each of their shoulders.

Tap, tap, tap.

Quiet settled over the town, the only sound the crunching of boots as the rest of the horde made their way back toward the center of town. Anteros held his breath as Pelham began questioning the couple. "Where is your daughter?"

The woman, Alba, began crying. Her shoulders trembled as Pelham's blade tapped her on the shoulder again. Her husband reached for her, but a blade swooshed through the air between them, slicing his wrist and cutting him off from her. Caelum Vise hissed as he held a hand over his wound, blood pouring out between his fingers. "Leave her alone," the man growled. "We haven't heard from our daughter in a year. Not even a letter. She could be dead for all we know." Alba wailed louder, leaning over and burying her face in her hands.

"An unlikely story," Pelham said.

Then he looked up at Anteros and summoned the boy over with the waggle of two fingers. The prince's boots dragged through the dirt as he forced himself to approach. Sweat pebbled along his hairline and dripped down his temples. He pulled at the neck of his shirt. His armor was suddenly too tight. His chest, too restricted. The air, thick and heavy. Downright suffocating. Pelham grinned as he unsheathed a glistening dagger and held the hilt out toward Anteros.

A sharp inhale felt like knives piercing his chest. The prince held his breath, staring at the steel without moving. "What's this for?" His brow furrowed, he studied the captain's face.

Pelham thrust the blade closer, jabbing Anteros in the chest with the hilt. "It's your father's orders. To teach you a lesson in maintaining power."

Anteros reluctantly clenched a fist around the hilt, and Pelham released it. He wasn't sure why the captain had given him a dagger when he had a sword attached at his own hip. Staring at the cold steel, he asked, "What are his orders?" In his heart, he already knew the answer.

Kill anyone linked to known traitors.

Stepping behind the prince, Pelham grabbed him firmly by the shoulders and shifted him to stand in front of Talitha's father. Then the captain came to stand beside him, addressing the man before them. "Your daughter, Talitha Vise, escaped from the king's custody three months ago. Now, I want you to tell our young prince here where she's hiding. Otherwise, he'll start cutting off appendages."

"What?" Anteros whipped his head around, eyes wide and horrified.

Pelham chuckled. "Someone here knows where that stupid whore's hiding."

"My daughter is no whore!" Caelum Vise lurched forward, but Pelham's right-hand man grabbed a fistful of his dark hair and forced him back onto the ground.

A dark chuckle sent chills through the prince. "The king says otherwise. She got very cozy with his son before her mysterious escape. Right, Anteros?" The captain leveled him with a knowing look, and the prince turned away.

The seething man in front of them was innocent. A man who had not seen or heard from his only daughter in a year. He was likely overjoyed to hear that she was somewhere out there, alive. Anteros wished he could tell her parents the truth. That he had spent time with her. Fed her. Kissed her. After months of confinement, he finally set her free—and he would die before handing her back to his father.

But he couldn't give away Talitha's location, not even to her loved ones. Not after all the trouble he went through to save her.

"One way or another, we're going to find out the truth," Pelham said, shoving Anteros forward. "If they won't talk, cut off a finger."

"No," Anteros replied, his tone firm and stern. He had taken the whip when his father threatened Talitha last summer. Watching his father hurt her had been torture. He had thought doing it himself was the lesser of two evils at the time. Now, he knew better. Pain was pain, regardless of who inflicted it, and hurting innocent people would always mar the abuser's soul as much as it scarred their victim.

He could not do it again.

Anteros tossed the dagger into the road. A small puff of dust exploded up into the air as the weapon bounced before settling on the ground. "These people are innocent—just as their daughter was. I will not torture them for nothing."

A crazed look entered Pelham's eyes as he got in Anteros' face. "And how would you know they're innocent?" Spittle peppered the prince's face, and he closed his eyes momentarily, wiping it away with the palm of his hand.

"Because I freed her." When he opened his eyes, Anteros half-expected to see his father.

Instead, he found his captain, long dark hair nearly covering his threatening eyes. There was no surprise behind the crazed look—only fury that one of Rexton's own would betray him so blatantly. The captain reared back his arm and smacked Anteros so hard across the cheek that he flew back, landing hard in the dirt. "Your father was right. You are a fool. How did she do it? How did she seduce you into setting her free?"

Anteros sat upright beside Talitha's father and exhaled. "She didn't need to seduce me. I knew she was innocent from the first time I spoke to her. She never knew where the Finches were hiding, and no amount of torture was ever going to yield information she didn't have." He peered sideways at Caelum, who was staring at him, understanding blooming on his face.

Behind him, Alba crawled forward, her voice cracking as she begged. "Please. Tell us you know where she is. Tell us she's safe. I'm begging you."

"Silence!" Pelham shrieked, kicking her onto her side.

Anteros ground his teeth and pushed himself off the ground. "Don't touch her! Don't touch any of them. None of these people know anything. Only I do!" Pieces of his dark hair fell over his eyes as he charged at the captain, but there were too many soldiers there. Arms grabbed him quickly, restraining him. Seething, Anteros fought against them, unwilling to make it easy for them. "Coming here was futile! No one here knows anything."

The soldiers forced Anteros onto his knees and bound his hands before stepping away. Then he realized one of them had been his friend James. His green eyes surveyed the prince with a mixture of sadness and disappointment. Was this quiet compliance revenge for taking his father's phoenix months ago?

Pelham crouched down in front of Anteros and huffed a laugh. "You think this was futile? I think otherwise." He grabbed the prince's chin roughly and forced him to look up into his eyes. "You have one chance to tell us where she is before we start killing these innocent people you care so much about."

His heart started beating faster, his chest rising rapidly as he scanned the town. Some men stood guard outside of their homes, awaiting the inevitable confrontation to come. Children's faces peeked out of windows, fearful yet too curious to hide. Little Lena poked her head out of a crack in her front door, and Anteros squeezed his eyes shut knowing someone would get hurt no matter what he said or did.

"Don't do it, son," Caelum said from beside him. He held his head up stubbornly. "Divinity holds our hearts. Rexton can never take that from us."

Pelham growled as he unsheathed his sword and pointed it at Anteros. "Their false god cannot save them! Now tell me." He pressed the tip of the blade into Anteros' sternum, drawing blood. "Where is the girl?"

Anteros didn't flinch. Nearly eighteen years under his father's thumb had exacted a world of hurt—both physical and emotional. He shook his head slightly, a smug grin spreading across his face. Nothing Pelham could do would possibly compare to the pain of his own father tormenting and tearing their family apart. "Was that supposed to hurt?"

The captain worked his jaw, a green vein bulging in the side of his neck. "Insolent prick. I'll show you pain," Pelham sneered. Then he turned and jabbed Talitha's father through the center of his chest.

Blood splattered across Anteros from his face to the chest of his armor. Suddenly, the atmosphere shifted in Durmak, and bodies clashed in the pandemonium that followed. A high-pitched scream pierced through the air as Alba Vise dove forward, hands clawing at the dirt as she crawled to her husband. His twitching body slumped to the ground, and she cradled his head in her lap until he fell still. The soldiers around them didn't move to stop her. The men of the town raced toward them with a fearsome battle cry, and carnage ensued.

Sudden pain shot through Anteros' scalp as Pelham lifted him by a fistful of his hair. Nearly eye level, the captain gestured with his free hand. "See this? This is all your own doing. Had you been a dutiful prince, the king never would have sent us here."

"I don't understand," Anteros barked. "Why do all this for one girl?"

Pelham released his hair, and the prince stumbled, struggling to remain on his feet. "This has nothing to do with that girl and everything to do with your treason. Had your father another heir, you'd have been beheaded for your disloyalty."

"If I am the problem, then kill me! Torture me. End this misery and spare these people." He yanked his wrists, trying desperately to free them of their binding, but the rope did not budge.

"And leave our kingdom without an heir?" the captain said with a faint laugh.

The sound of steel clanging and clashing rang through town. Over the captain's shoulder, Anteros watched as women raced for the forest, their children on their hips or dragged along by their hands. The men kept the soldiers occupied, and Anteros held his breath, praying none would get the chance to follow them.

"No, Anteros, your father believes any man can be turned for the right price," Pelham continued, pacing around the prince like a cat stalking prey. "And if he cannot be bought, then he can always be broken. Every man has a weakness—and I suspect yours is your bleeding heart."

That's when it dawned on Anteros that his father *couldn't* kill him, but the king was willing to torture and slaughter any number of innocent people that it would take to force

Anteros into total submission. To make sure he would never stray from his duty as the Rexton heir to the throne.

This wouldn't stop at a brawl in the road.

"Start a fire, men." Pelham turned to one of the other officers and pointed at the hall at the center of the town. "Start there."

"No!" Anteros yelled. Panic crept into every crevice in his mind and heart at the thought of this quaint town on fire. Talitha's hometown. All because he had chosen to let her go. "Don't do this! I'll do anything. I will apologize. Atone. I'll do whatever my father wants. Please."

A short distance away, a small fire burst to life in the grassy area between two soldiers. The men made quick work of rudimentary torches, lighting them and passing them out to whoever was left after the altercation with the townsfolk. Anteros watched helplessly as his own friends stepped up to take torches from the officers—Julian refusing to look his way as he shuffled up last to join them. No one else argued with the captain. No one dared say a word, despite a few of the men clenching their jaws and looking visibly unsettled by the situation.

"It's much too late for that, Anteros. You chose the girl from Durmak over your own father, so Durmak must burn." Pelham waved a hand signaling for the men to begin. The first officer tossed a torch through the main hall's window. It only took a minute for the flames to spread and consume the wooden structure. The fire climbed high, eating into the roof and spreading up toward the pastel sky. "Leave no home standing." The captain's final order bellowed over the crackle of the burning building before them.

Pelham turned and seized Anteros by his arm, walking him in a circle so he was forced to watch as their comrades tossed torches through open doors and onto every roof. Being a town built on the edge of a forest, everything was made of timber. Dry. Flammable. Kindling for a careless king. The prince's eyes fell on the house he had searched earlier. "Wait! There could be people inside," Anteros pleaded. His insides twisted as James tossed a burning torch onto the roof. Had Lena and her father made it out?

The captain leaned close to his ear and said, "You'll do well to remember your place in the future."

Soon everything was on fire, the bright orange flames and black smoke stretching their arms toward the tangerine sunset. All Anteros could do was watch the grieving woman who sat in the center of town, her weeping face illuminated by the flames.

As darkness overtook the sky, the captain called for their men to move out. Anteros stared into the flames that licked over the homes. The stench of burning wood filled his nose, making him want to hold his breath. Houses shuddered and caved in under the weight of his father's cruelty. For a moment, he thought he saw red feathers flapping through the smoke. Blinking his eyes, he focused enough to see the phoenix soar over a burning building before disappearing into the trees. He wondered if his mind was playing a trick, or if Talitha had sent Phinnian in search of him. If she needed his help. Bile rose in his throat knowing she'd be heartbroken over what had just taken place.

He had no idea how many people had escaped into the woods, but he was thankful Pelham did not send men in search of them. They had accomplished what they came for. Anteros had been taught a brutal lesson he would not soon forget.

Julian patted him on the back of his shoulder and nodded toward the men who were moving out. As the horde departed Durmak, they were all quiet. The sound of wailing people and crackling wood trailed them with each step until the noise finally faded into the distance. Even then, Anteros knew those heart-wrenching screams would haunt his dreams as often as Sabine did.

48

SLEEPLESS NIGHTS

The night was quiet as Elara cradled the sleeping babe who had just finished feeding in her arms. Already a month old, Maristela favored her father. Not only did she have a head full of black hair, but this child seemed to have inherited his calm and quiet temperament as well.

Cordelia was another story. An unexpected miracle, she had been born smaller and weaker than her sister—a physical manifestation of the weakness her mother had felt throughout her pregnancy and her entire life. It was no surprise this child favored her— a featherlight layer of light brown hair over the cradle of her head. Despite this, Elara felt disconnected from her second born daughter. Every time the queen held Cordelia, she cried louder. She was tiny but loud, fighting for her life and commanding her parents' attention from the moment she was born. She never seemed satisfied when the queen fed her. Cordelia was only satiated when they finally brought in a wet nurse—much to Elara's disappointment.

The queen glanced sideways as the wet nurse from the city, Tayla, handed Cordelia back to her husband. Gerard stared at the little girl in his arms, his eyes full of unabashed love and admiration. Part of her missed when he had looked at her like that. Like she was the center of his world. But she was still furious over his choice to take her autonomy away when she was at her most vulnerable. Seeing him with their daughters had not helped thaw her heart. If anything, having daughters had made her that much more upset about the situation. Sleeping beside him made her blood boil. She often lay awake at night, the phantom feeling of a leather strap tight around her wrist making her teeth clench. Some nights she thought about tying his arms to the bed and leaving him alone with his guilt.

375

But that was no way to live.

Gerard walked over and perched on the edge of their bed beside her. Bright blues met her eyes as his hand skated over the blanket covering her legs. Chills ran down her spine, and she quickly averted her gaze, fixating on the sleeping infant in her arms. She could feel his eyes on her. So many unspoken words hovered in the air between them.

"How are you feeling?" His quiet question cut through the silence abruptly, and Maristela stirred in her arms.

Elara shushed the baby while rubbing gentle circles on her back. "I'm fine." The lie tingled on her tongue, sour like sucking on a lemon slice. In truth, she wasn't sure things would ever be fine between them again.

Gerard smiled gently. "Why don't we send the girls down to the nursery?" He rose from the bed, adjusting his hold on Cordelia as he walked toward the door to their bedchamber.

Before he could summon the nursemaids, Elara called out, "Wait!"

His shoulders sank. He paused, staring at the closed door in defeat for a moment before turning to face her. "You selected the nursemaids yourself and have yet to accept their help in the evenings. Why? Are you that afraid to be alone with me?"

Her breath hitched. Her pulse quickened. She adjusted the infant in her arms, suddenly wishing their two small children weren't standing between them and the truth she needed to say. Hanging her head, Elara tried desperately to hold back the tears burning her eyes. "Fine. Summon them. Then we can talk."

A vein bulged in the side of Gerard's neck as he clenched his jaw, still facing the door. He stayed like that for a minute, not reaching for the door right in front of him, his fear suddenly turned palpable. She knew he wasn't looking to have that talk. Not about what he had done to her. Not about the unspoken tension between them.

Breaking free of his trance, Gerard finally sent for the nursemaids. Then he sat in a chair in the sitting area, quietly cuddling Cordelia while they waited in silence. When the two young women arrived to take the babies from them, Elara's heart ached to let Maristela go. She needed the break desperately, but it was never easy to let the girls out of sight. And the prospect of being left alone with her husband twisted her insides into knots.

The click of the door closing behind the nursemaids was louder than usual, slicing through the fog in the air that choked back their words. Gerard sat on his side of the bed and exhaled, the sound carrying all the anxiety and exhaustion he was feeling. Elara stole a glance at the man who had once cradled her heart with such delicate tenderness, coaxing the fire in her back to life after so many years in seclusion. This man had earned his place by her side through patience and reverence. Through their love for each other, they'd welcomed the greatest miracle—two beautiful, perfect daughters.

She never would have imagined that he would betray her.

That he would take her power and her choices away.

It was the total breaking of their trust that had caused this rift between them, a dark cavern of hurt and anger that made her want to scream and kick and run away at the sight of him. The idea of him touching her made her skin crawl.

Gerard shifted beside her, drawing his legs under the blanket. She stiffened and inhaled sharply. Unable to look at him, she busied her hands picking at the frayed edges of the blanket in her lap. "Elara."

"Yes?" Her brows rose slightly at the question, but she still did not look his way. She wanted him to feel the weight of her discomfort. To sit with the knowledge that he had caused it.

"Darling, would you please look at me?" His fingers skirted over the blanket to rest on her knee, but she jumped, shifting away from his touch. "Elara, look at me." The sudden increase in his volume forced her to turn and face him. "I have done nothing but love and protect you since you first let me in."

Her cheeks flushed as angry tears burned a trail down her face. "Was tying me down and taking control of my court protecting me? Because being tied to the bed with a leather strap did not feel like an act of love."

Suddenly, her husband could not look at her—and she desperately needed him to. Elara wanted him to see all the pain and anger she had been holding in. To realize what she wanted without having to say it.

She wanted him to leave.

"I know how much that upset you, and for that I am sincerely sorry," Gerard began.

"You have no idea just how angry I am," she snapped, cutting his apology off.

Her husband made a ticking noise in the back of his throat. Straightening in his seat, Gerard shook his head. "We have just welcomed two children together," Gerard argued. "Every night I have been up with you, caring for our babies as a team."

"I never asked that of you," Elara argued, raising her arms in the air as she turned her entire body to face him. "Honestly, I would sleep better if you weren't present."

Gerard's face dropped. The shock on his face looked as though she had slapped him. His voice shifted between a disbelieving whisper and an angry argument when he finally replied. "That's preposterous. Do you hear yourself? We have two babies. We need each other now more than ever."

"I do *not* need you," Elara sneered. With a toss of the blanket, she leapt off the bed and plodded across the room. Her face was so hot, she thought steam might pour out of her ears. She made a beeline for the balcony, hoping the cool night air might relieve the heat seeping from her pores. She tossed open the door and stomped outside, praying her husband would leave their chambers while she cooled off.

But Gerard was persistent as ever, a quality she had once found attractive. As he waltzed through the doorway, she backed away until her calves hit the parapet. He leaned forward, pressed his palms into the parapet, and boxed her in. Their breaths mingled, heating the air despite the gap between them. "Don't do this, Elara. Don't push me away now that we have everything we've ever wanted."

Staring into the deep blues looming dangerously close, a sob erupted from her mouth. She had broken out in a cold sweat, every inch of her frozen in place. She couldn't move. Couldn't speak. Could only stare as her fear trickled from her body in terrified rivulets.

Her husband's face softened then, and he straightened, taking a step back from her. Elara didn't move. "Elara," he whispered. One hand lifted toward her but stopped midway. Thinking better of it, he dropped his arm. "Are you afraid of me?"

The queen didn't answer at first. She averted her gaze, looking over the city wall at the Athamar Mountains looming in the distance. She had been scared when she had to flee her home and make the crossing. Terrified when she came face to face with the Steelcast King. Horrified to learn her family had been slaughtered.

Yet she had never felt more alone than in the weeks following her husband's betrayal.

"I want you to stay in your old chambers," she whispered, her voice cracking.

"No," Gerard answered firmly. He stepped closer, the sudden movement making her flinch. "Elara… you are my wife. We made vows to each other. Til death do us part. Married couples do not live apart."

"They do when trust has been broken," Elara replied, strength returning to her voice. She was the queen. She couldn't be weak. She had two girls to raise.

And she would raise them to never allow a man to steal their voice.

"I have been faithful to you from the moment we met," Gerard argued, anger seeping into his tone. "You cannot shut me out of your life. Our souls are bound to each other."

"You broke my heart, Gerard. You took something from me, and I can no longer rest with you sleeping beside me. I need—I just want to feel safe again," she insisted, pushing past him to return inside.

He followed on her heels. "You once said you felt safe because I was here with you. Has so much changed in so little time?"

"Yes!" She threw her hands in the air in frustration. "Everything changed the moment you confined me to my bed and took control of my council."

"This isn't even about me. This is about Serena and the council. You don't feel safe because Rexton nearly killed both of you. That is not my fault." He ran his hands over his face, exhaustion setting in. "We've been up for hours. You'll feel better after you get some sleep."

Elara crossed her arms over her chest and shook her head. "I'll feel better if you listen to me for once. I want you to sleep elsewhere."

"If you insist… but what about the girls?" His brows lifted in anticipation of her answer.

The wind from the balcony blew the canopy hanging over their bed. A tendril of the light fabric drifted to hang between them. Elara lifted her chin, mustering her confidence. "They are equal parts yours and mine. I would never keep them from you."

He stepped closer and brushed the falling canopy to the side. "And what about us? Will you ever have me by your side again?"

She bit her lip and looked at their bedchamber door. "I cannot answer that. Not now. I need time." She sniffled, cursing her fragile heart for breaking over again.

Her husband shook his head in dejected understanding. As he walked toward the door, he paused beside her, his thumb gently brushing away the wet tracks down her cheek. "All my time is yours, my love. And I'll do whatever it takes to earn your trust back." Gerard placed a gentle kiss on the side of her head, and she squeezed her eyes shut. The echo of his footsteps was agonizing as the distance between them increased. She stared at her bare feet on the stone floor. They were cold. Her entire body was.

The door opened and shut behind her, and then she was left alone.

A queen with no kingdom and no real power.

A new mother of twin daughters.

A broken-hearted wife.

Elara shuddered as she crawled into her bed, increasingly aware of the empty space to her left. Sleep eluded her, and the silence filled her with dread. All she could do was sit with the knowledge that she had dismissed her husband, birthed the next great oracle, and awaited her niece inciting a war any day.

49

SHIELDS

The eve before they intended to attack the border, the Hyrosencian forces made camp near the edge of Ord Metsiilva, just out of sight of the border patrol. They numbered well over one hundred fighters between Elara's Guard and the older students and graduates from the Envyre Academy who had volunteered. Seeing the dwarfs come to their aid, even a small number of Silveryl elves joined them, including Ilrune and Ausha. Crystal thought perhaps even more would arrive the next day when the battle began.

The week leading up to that night had been tense. Rigel had been avoiding Crystal, and everyone noticed their unease. As the troop gathered to leave Envyre, he made sure he was on the opposite side of their party, never glancing in her direction. The elf found herself searching for him more than once. Her heart was heavy with guilt after the way they'd left things, and she did not wish to go into battle without amending their friendship—if that was possible.

Huddled around the fire, everyone ate quietly that evening. One by one, the men and women retired to their bedrolls until few remained. When Crystal noticed Serena and Xandra stargazing, she went over and sat beside them. They spoke about growing up in Hyrosencia and the family members they'd lost there. That was the driving force behind many of the volunteers who joined them, even the elves. Rexton had been responsible for so many deaths, both directly and indirectly. His hatred—an extension of his own father's prejudices—had spread like a plague across the lands, inciting unnecessary disputes and encouraging discourse between the races for decades.

"With any luck, tomorrow will be the first step toward our liberation," Xandra said wistfully. Her eyes locked on something behind Crystal and lit up.

Cole, Rigel, and Will rejoined them, having finished setting up a few small tents near the marquee at the center of their makeshift camp. Their intention was to give Serena some privacy after a long day of conversing with Elara's guards and their friends from Envyre. Everyone wanted to know her—the star-chosen savior of Hyrosencia. Looking from Serena's weary face to the others, all illuminated by the moonlight, Crystal frowned at the thought that this might be the last time the six of them sat under the stars together. She wished she could somehow preserve that moment and these people indefinitely, but none were fated to live forever.

The creatures of the night chirped and shifted, rustling the leaves and grass. After a while, Crystal reluctantly said, "You all should get some rest. Big day tomorrow."

"I'm not sure I'll sleep at all. I could take the first watch?" Serena suggested. There were already a few members of the Guard positioned around the exterior of their camp, a rotation established so that everyone would be safe and well rested come morning.

"Not you," Crystal replied. "You need to rest up. I know you're anxious about tomorrow, but losing sleep tonight won't help." Turning to address Will, she added, "Please make sure she sleeps."

Serena exhaled in frustration as Will helped her onto her feet. "You got it," he said, nodding at Crystal before guiding Serena toward the second biggest tent in the camp, the one set up specifically for her.

"We can take watch if needed," Cole said.

Xandra yawned as he draped a blanket around her shoulders. "Speak for yourself. I'm exhausted." Her husband gave her a mischievous grin, pulling her closer and pecking her on the side of the head.

"I wonder why," Rigel muttered from beside them.

Crystal snorted. Covering her mouth, she looked up to find all three of her friends staring. "He's got a point, lovebirds. Make sure you get some sleep tonight," she said, shooing her brother and best friend off to bed with one hand.

"You can't stay up alone," Xandra argued, shrugging off Cole's arm.

"I'll stay with her," Rigel said, much to everyone's surprise.

Crystal met his piercing gaze and swallowed thickly. So many thoughts swirled in her mind that she couldn't string together a coherent sentence. Instead, she nodded, offering a flimsy smile to convince the others to leave them.

Finally alone, they moved to sit by the nearest fire, an arm's length between them as they sat in silence for a few minutes. As her friend's lips parted to speak, Crystal blurted out, "I'm sorry for the other night."

Rigel's shoulders drooped, and he shook his head. "I crossed the line. You have every right to be upset."

She turned to face him, her own uncertainty reflecting in his eyes. "I shouldn't have slapped you," she countered.

"You know that's never bothered me before." A familiar smirk appeared, and she shook her head. He was still the same Rigel, even when he was trying to hide his disappointment.

The elf pressed her lips together and turned back toward the fire. Remembering why they were there, she forced herself to continue. "I shouldn't have said what I did either. The last thing I wanted was to hurt you, Rigel. You're one of my closest friends. I don't… I don't want to lose you."

He shifted beside her, resting his elbows on his knees and leaning his chin on his hands. Staring thoughtfully at the fire, her friend smiled bitterly. "You haven't lost me. You mean too much for me to let go completely."

She swallowed hard, surprised to feel a prickling behind her eyes, a tightening in the back of her throat. She hadn't realized just how scared she had been to face him, to find out if he would still want to be friends when the idea of being something more was so harshly snatched away from him. Brushing the back of her wrist against the corner of her eye, Crystal sniffled.

Rigel scooched over and hesitantly rubbed up and down her back. "I'm sorry I upset you," he whispered. "Do you want me to leave you alone?"

She shoved him playfully and blotted at her face in aggravation. "No." This wasn't like her. Crying. Moping. Being terrified. She felt like a child again, forced to hide in the cupboard and watch her mother's murder through the cracks. She hadn't realized just how much fear she had been tamping down during their training and preparations. Now there was nothing to hide behind. No cupboard to conceal her distress. Her friends would go to war tomorrow, and some of them might not return. The mere thought of losing anyone clawed at her heart.

When she was more composed, Crystal leaned over and rested her head on Rigel's shoulder. "We've faced danger a dozen times over, yet this time feels heavier. Scarier. Perhaps because we're inciting this battle ourselves? If we lose anyone, it will be our own fault."

"Don't speak like that," Rigel said, putting his arm around her and squeezing her shoulder gently. "We're going to win. We have the numbers, the element of surprise."

"And we will still lose people. People we call our friends," she murmured, her usual hollowness creeping back into her heart. As an elf, she had been taught to release those fears and charge into a fight with a clear mind. Worry about herself and trust the rest to their own fates.

Now she realized that was all a moon-damned lie. When you love someone, it's impossible not to care about their well-being.

"We might," Rigel agreed, his grip on her arm slackening. "But we shouldn't mourn them before they're dead." He leaned back on both of his hands, looking up to the stars.

She blinked, his words somehow relieving some of her anxiety. "You're right." Crystal pushed her hair off her face with both hands and exhaled as though she had been holding her breath all day. "When did you get so wise?" They grinned at each other.

"Around the time you saved my life, if I had to guess." The playfulness to his tone was gone then, snuffed out by the reminder of his own mortality.

The elf's smile faltered. Her vision clouded over, smears of crimson speckling the fresh white powder that coated the mountain. His pallor turning gray. Her hands stained red. She reached for the hand on the ground beside her. "Let's not relive that awful day."

A spark of mischief lit up his eyes. "Are you sure you aren't madly in love with me?"

Instinctively, she punched his arm, and they both chuckled. "I do love you, you big idiot. Just not in a romantic way. Do you know what I mean?"

Rigel nodded. "Of course. You feel for me the same way I feel about Xandra or Mads." He blew out a breath, eyes skimming over her hair and face wistfully. His gaze reflected heartache—an ache she had caused and feared she could never quell. "You're too good for me anyway."

"No, I'm not. You're a great guy," she argued. His brows furrowed, confusion flashing over his features as he leaned further back. There was one way she might be able to make him understand why. Something she'd never said aloud—not even when telling her father she never wished to marry. "It's not about you, Rigel. It's not that I'm not attracted to you. The truth is… I'm not attracted to *anyone*. I have no interest in a physical relationship of any kind. That's why I don't wish to get married or have children. I'm… I'm content with being single. I have my brother, my friends, my work, and that's enough for me."

His brows raised slowly as realization dawned on him. Her rejection wasn't about him at all. It wasn't that he wasn't good enough or handsome enough or strong enough. She was just different. A kind of different many people couldn't understand. But it was important that he knew her truth. Perhaps that might lighten the sting of rejection and help him to move on.

Rigel scrubbed his hands over his face and cleared his throat. "I didn't realize."

She smiled timidly. "No one does. And no one asks. But I'm telling you now, as my dear friend. If you're content to be just that."

He smiled back. This time, it was one of his big, full-hearted smiles that told her they would be just fine. They always were. "If this is all there is for us, then I'm honored to be among your friends. I'd rather have a small part of your heart than none at all."

Crystal smiled knowing she could not have said it better herself. And tomorrow, she would do all she could to protect the people she loved the most.

Will stroked his fingers through Serena's hair as they lay on their bedrolls facing each other, the tent shrouding them from the rest of the camp. Bugs and nocturnal creatures chirped and rustled in the darkened forest surrounding them, the sounds bringing an inkling of comfort to them both. It was familiar, a reminder of many late nights spent in their hometown. It gave Will hope that they'd return to Durmak after the war was over.

Lying on his stomach, he rested his chin on his folded forearms and studied her. "How are you feeling?" He wanted to kiss her then. To take possession of her lips until that wrinkle of worry on her forehead vanished. As much as he hoped for their success, he knew this might be his last chance if anything went wrong, and he did not want to waste a minute of their time together. He reached out and tucked a lock of hair behind her ear.

"I'm fine." She shifted onto her back, focusing on the top of the tent. Not a single star shone through the fabric.

He leaned forward on his forearms, his face hovering slightly over hers. "I've known you for a long time, Serena. You don't have to lie to me." He traced the line on her forehead with his thumb before skating down her temple to caress her cheek. The guardians were depending on him to make sure she went to sleep, so if she needed reassurance or distraction, he would offer it in any capacity.

Serena allowed her head to lull to the side, so she was nose to nose with him. "I'm scared, Will. You know that already." Her eyes pleaded with him not to push her. She'd already agonized over the potential of losing friends in battle for weeks. The possibility of dying herself. Had probably already spoken to every one of the guardians about her fears. But she never allowed Will to steer their conversation toward that for long.

While he loved being the person who brought her comfort, he was terrified at the prospect of her getting hurt during the battle, or worse. "I'm scared, too, but more for your safety than anyone else's. It's not fair that Elara put all this pressure on you."

"I've made my peace with Aunt Elara and my destiny. For years, she has worried about the fate of Hyrosencia. I cannot blame her—or anyone else—for clinging to that prophecy," Serena said. "Besides, this battle was my choice, not hers." She glanced away from him, her eyes fixing on Sannarvin, resting in its scabbard against the side of the tent. "In another life, I would have been raised a princess, but Rexton stole that from me, just as he's taken two families from me."

Will gently grabbed her chin and turned it back toward him. "I'm sorry he's taken so much from you… but I cannot be sorry you ended up in Durmak. We would not have met otherwise." He leaned forward and pressed a lingering kiss to her forehead.

Eyes wide and red-rimmed, she stared at him, a bitter smile making its way onto her face. "I am glad to have met you. I couldn't imagine coming this far without you here. You've kept me sane through all the training and planning and grief."

"And I will continue to do so until my dying breath," Will insisted.

Serena flinched and looked away. "Don't say that," she whispered, her voice suddenly hoarse. She sat up abruptly. Fear took possession of her features as she shifted her legs, preparing to get up and leave the tent, but Will wouldn't let her.

He sat up, shifting closer to her. "It's true. I love you, and I would do anything to keep you safe." A tear slipped silently down her cheek, and he reached out to brush it away with his thumb.

"I love you, too, Will. You're the one person I cannot live without." She shuddered, leaning forward to rest her head against his bicep. Fingers latched onto his shirt—one near his heart, the other on his sleeve. Holding on tight as if she were afraid he'd disappear. As though her grip might somehow shield them both from the dangers ahead.

Will ran a hand over her dark tresses and inhaled her scent. His heart swelled knowing she felt exactly how he did. "Then marry me." He hadn't planned to ask her that night, but the words felt right as soon as he said them.

Serena jolted upright. Her bright eyes met his, and they sat in stunned silence for a moment. Then Will realized she still wasn't smiling. She looked as though she had seen a ghost. His hands fell into his lap, and he cursed inwardly for blurting it out without thinking—and without a ring—like a lovesick fool. "I'm sorry. I shouldn't have—"

Her hands grasped his and squeezed. "Oh, Will, I—I would like to… one day… but I have sworn to be the sword of justice for Hyrosencia. I cannot marry you until I have fulfilled that vow."

Will cleared his throat, fighting the uncontrollable heat that spread through his cheeks and the burning behind his eyes. After all they had been through and all they had said to each other, he wouldn't have expected her to say no. Yet he understood why.

"I'm so sorry." She hung her head, her cheeks tinged pink. "Do you hate me?"

He shook his head. "I could never hate you." His pride stung, but his love for her remained. Nothing could diminish that. "I will wait for you to fulfill your destiny, if that is what you want. I'd wait an eternity for you, and it would be worth it."

Serena nodded, one corner of her mouth pulling into a reluctant smirk. "Ask me again when the war is over?"

He returned her bittersweet smile. His thumb stroked her bottom lip, his focus shifting between her eyes and mouth. "It would be my honor." Then his lips captured hers, gentle, hesitant, waiting for her to react. To encourage him. To let him know they would be fine. That nothing had to change between them.

Her fingers scraped his scalp as she wrapped her arms around the back of his neck and pulled him closer, deepening the kiss. One hand splayed against her lower back as they clung to each other. With frenzied lips and gentle touches, she kissed his doubts away. When they finally paused to catch their breath, that worry line on her forehead had disappeared. She rested her forehead against his, and they breathed each other in.

Finally, she whispered, "Do you think I can do this? Do you think we can win the war?"

Will drew himself back to look at her. "Of course you can." She chewed her bottom lip, her reservations returning. "If you are the sword of justice, then allow me to be your shield. At least, until you grant me another title." He grinned, knowing that was what their families would want. They'd be proud of him for putting her first—her safety and her heart.

A chuckle escaped on her exhale. "I don't need you to protect me, Will. I just need to know you can protect yourself out there."

"I can handle it. I promise." He had spent nearly as long training as intensely as she had. Now he felt confident that he was fit to fight alongside Serena and the others, and he wouldn't need any of them to save him.

Will turned and started digging through his knapsack, suddenly eager to give her something he had been holding onto for a while. It was not a ring, but he hoped it might help her in her role as Hyrosencia's savior. "This is for you." Facing Serena, he held out his hand. A small, thin dagger set with an amethyst stone to match Sannarvin balanced on his palm.

Serena gasped. "Where did you get this?" His heart swelled as she reached out and accepted the weapon. One hand on the hilt, she yanked the simple silver sheath off, revealing the shining blade beneath. "It's beautiful. Sharp. Must have cost you a fortune."

"Actually, I made it for you during my apprenticeship in Symptee." He ran his empty hands through his thick hair, cheeks burning.

The blade glinted in the dim lantern light. She leaned back, that stubborn wrinkle back on her forehead. He wanted to pull her close and kiss it away again. "You made this? That's incredible, Will." Serena sheathed the blade and placed it on the ground beside her bedroll before pecking him on the cheek. "Why did you hold onto it for so long?"

"At first it was because Elara asked me to stay away." He clenched his fists in his lap, knowing the queen felt he was unworthy of the amazing young lady he sat beside. "Then I wondered if you would want a dagger as a gift. It almost felt silly when you carry that sword everywhere." He nodded toward the place where Sannarvin lay. They both smiled a little. "Tomorrow is our first step toward freedom. I'll do my best to stay by your side, but it cannot hurt for you to have extra protection."

She nodded. "Thank you. This… It means a lot to me, Will."

Will wrapped his arms around her in a tight embrace. "I'm honored to fight by your side as whatever you want me to be, Princess."

Serena cringed and shoved him away. "Do not call me that." She flopped back on her bedroll and shook her head.

Will settled in beside her, lying on his side and facing her. He pressed a gentle kiss to her cheek, slipped an arm around her, and whispered, "Whatever you say, love."

Her fingers laced with his at her waist, and he waited until the sound of her breathing evened out. Her shoulders relaxed as she succumbed to sleep wrapped in the warmth of his arms. Will held her even more tightly knowing it might be the last time he could. He kissed the back of her head and said a silent prayer to Divinity to protect the love of his life. He would give anything to make sure she came home from this battle unscathed.

50

DOWN SHE GOES

Standing in the open field before the border wall, Serena gave orders for the archers to ready. The dagger Will had gifted her was tucked through the top of her braid, easily accessible were she to find herself disarmed. Having something from Will on her made her feel slightly safer—but not by much. In a moment, this field would become a warzone.

Crystal, Madeline, Juniper, and a dozen others lined up with their bows. "Take aim and await Serena's signal!" Crystal called out to the archers. Each pulled an arrow from the quiver on their back, knocked it, and drew back the bowstring, aiming just over the wall. Everyone held firm, awaiting the call from Serena. The wind whipped the stray hairs around their heads, and they waited with bated breath.

When the breeze had blown past and the air was still, Serena moved beside Crystal and waited for reassurance. Without looking away from her target, the elf gave one small nod of her head, signaling to Serena that it was time. Unsheathing Sannarvin, Serena lifted it in the air. Slicing the weapon down swiftly, she shouted, "Fire!"

The simultaneous snaps of bowstrings rang out as arrows flew upward. They sliced through the air like birds soaring parallel to a tree trunk to find their nest. As the barrage of arrows cleared the top of the wall and veered down, panicked screams carried across the field, and several bodies dropped off the edge of the wall, falling like flightless birds. First blood.

"Ready again!" Serena called out. Most of the archers had already pulled another arrow, holding for her orders. "Take aim! Hold for Crystal's signal."

A small smirk on Crystal's face told her things were off to a good start. The guardian exchanged a glance with Madeline as they knocked their arrows. The elf took a deep inhale and waited. Seconds passed achingly slowly before Crystal finally yelled, "Fire!"

They had barely loosed their second round of arrows when a counterattack came their way. Members of the Garrick Guard stepped forward, lifting their shields to form a barrier over the archers' heads. Will and Rigel caged Serena in, holding their own shields over them. Metal battered against metal as enemy arrows rained down on them. A lone cry in the middle of their party made Serena's heart pound faster. One of the men had taken an arrow to the top of his foot. The rest had missed their targets.

With a sigh of relief, Serena turned to Commander Maynard. "Have him carried back to camp. The rest of you prepare the catapults. We must take down this wall for Hyrosencia!"

"For Hyrosencia!" An array of voices echoed in succession, swords and shields lifted in the air amidst their battle cry. Their impassioned reply bolstered spirits, and everyone leapt into action. The archers reloaded while half of Elara's men moved two massive wooden catapults into position. With Divinity's blessing, their projectiles would batter the wall that separated Rexton's territories from the free lands.

Serena breathed deep, the scent of anticipation ripe in the air as the guards made haste, hopeful the act of surprise would give them the advantage against the border patrol. Rexton's men bore plentiful bows and swords, but there was little they could do to combat the catapults from so high and so far away. This was their moment. Their chance to destroy part of Rexton's stronghold. The first crack in the monster's empire.

Six men drew back a thick braided rope attached to each catapult as guards loaded large spheres made of lead into the buckets. Maynard raised his sword in the air and yelled, "Ready!" Several guards moved clear of the devices. Grips tightened, the ropes pulled taut. Beads of sweat pebbled foreheads as the guards breathed heavily. The rest of the camp collectively held their breath.

Then Maynard yelled, "Launch!"

The guards released the ropes, and the catapults' arms flung forward, slinging the projectiles in quick succession. The archers lowered their bows. All paused to watch the lead balls soar through the air. Serena swallowed, her throat parched. Her eyes trained on the first ball until it made contact toward the center of the wall, a great crash sounding as the metal broke bits of stone free.

A resounding applause broke out among the loyalists and their allies. But it was much too early to celebrate. While minimal pieces had been broken off the wall, the whole of it remained intact. Serena lifted the Heir's Blade and shouted, "Reload!"

Each side exchanged another set of arrows, and the loyalists suffered their first loss: one of Elara's guards. Staring into the pale gray eyes of the dead man, time seemed to move slower as Serena contemplated what they were risking. She knew they would lose people, but now she knew there was no way to prepare for it. Not for the blood nor the desperate pleas of his comrades as they tried and failed to save him. She did not even know this man's name, yet her heart ached over the loss of life.

But there was no time for mourning on the battlefield.

On Crystal's order, the archers readied again, releasing a barrage of arrows moments before the catapults launched once more. One struck slightly lower than its predecessor while the second fell short.

"We should move closer, I'd wager," Rilura said.

Serena and Maynard glanced at each other and nodded silently. Getting closer was a risk. It would give their enemies' arrows an easier target. But the wall had to come down, and there were only so many projectiles.

"Very well," Serena began. "Allow a half hour reprieve. Then have the guards move forward with the catapults."

"Fifty paces should do it," one of the guards said.

The commander nodded. "Aye. Give word for the men to rest and hydrate. The real fight is impending."

"Do you want the archers to move forward with them?" Crystal asked. One hand poised on her hip, the other holding her bow down by her side.

"No. The archers seem well placed. Better to keep them at a safe distance for now," Serena answered. Crystal lowered her chin in acknowledgement before going to relay the update to the other archers.

"What should ye wish us to do?" Rilura asked. Behind her right stood Thomli, his axe balanced on one shoulder.

"Anyone waiting for a foot fight should remain behind the archers until the wall comes down. Hold fast to the shields." Serena turned to relay the orders to her friends and nearly ran smack into Will's chest. "Oh. Hi."

"Hi," he replied. His dimples greeted her as he reached out to tuck stray hairs out of her face. "What are the orders? Are we moving closer?"

Both of Serena's hands shot out to his chest, holding him back. "Not you. Only those on the catapults. You're staying back with the archers and swordsmen. It's safest that way."

Will's brow furrowed. "And where will you be?"

Her lips parted, but she hesitated to reply. Truthfully, she had intended to go forward with the catapults for a better vantage point, but she did not want him to follow her there. They had already lost one man to Rexton's archers, and two others had been injured. "I will go between the catapults and the rest relaying orders." She turned away from him then, eager to find Rigel so she could avoid a confrontation with Will.

Naturally, he followed her. "Then I will go with you." When she did not stop, Will quickly caught up and grabbed her arm, forcing her to turn and face him. His dimples were nowhere to be seen. His thick russet hair, matted to his forehead with sweat, cast a shadow over his honey brown eyes as they searched her face. "What did I say? I am your shield. Where you go, I go. That's not a request."

Hearing those words, seeing him in his leathers and chainmail made her want to vomit. He wasn't meant to be a soldier. War was no place for a gentle soul. "If I had my way, you'd be waiting back in Envyre," Serena snapped, yanking her arm away from him. "I've already looked into the eyes of one dead man today. So, like it or not, you're staying back until the wall comes down."

"I don't need you to protect me, Serena. I'm supposed to protect you," he argued. She rolled her eyes, knowing she was far better off with Sannarvin than most of the other fighters in this troop.

Rigel and Xandra approached them cautiously. Xandra grabbed Serena by the shoulder and whispered, "This isn't the place for a domestic spat."

Serena and Will both crossed their arms, seething from their disagreement. "When everyone charges in, I know I won't be able to stop any of you. But I can do my best to keep you safe until that time comes," she said, her tone returned to normal. Not allowing further argument, she shrugged off her friend and marched across the field, dried leaves and grass crunching beneath her boots with each step.

"Wait up," Rigel called, jogging until he fell in step with her.

She paused and blew out a frustrated breath. Even from afar, the wall towered over them, seemingly impenetrable, and she watched the tiny figures of Rexton's men marching back and forth, readying for the next wave of attack. "Better rest while you can. With Divinity's blessing, we're hoping the wall will be down before nightfall."

A round of arrows came up from the top of the wall, and several people cried out in warning. Without thinking, Rigel grabbed Serena's hand and yanked her against his chest, using his shield to cover them both as arrows rained down. Once satisfied there was no longer danger, he released his hold. Serena stepped back, swallowing thickly as she peered back at the wall. "Thanks," she mumbled.

"I promised Elara I would keep you safe," he started, and she looked down at her feet at the mention of her aunt. The fact that so many had vowed to follow her into battle made her stomach tense. "But even if I hadn't made that vow, I'd do the same. I like to think we've come to be friends. Have we not?"

Serena nodded. "Of course we are."

"Right. So, as your friend, I must remind you that your safety is more important than anyone else's. You're the true heir to the crown."

She knew he was right but hated to admit it. Hated every time someone referenced that title. Rigel reached forward and gently grasped her chin, lifting her face. "If you won't let Will go with you, allow me. It will put everyone at ease."

Looking at his kind eyes, full of unadulterated hope, Serena couldn't argue. "Very well. Be sure to tell him?" Rigel smirked and gave her a salute with two fingers before jogging back to where they'd left their friends.

A short time later, he found his way back to her side. With a fleeting glance back at Will and the others, Serena gave orders for the catapults to be rolled forward. It took ten men to push each vessel, the wheels creaking as they approached their target. Fifty paces made a world of difference. Now they stood on the edge of the shadow cast by the wall, a dark reminder of the wretched evil they were up against.

The passing hours felt like days. With each pluck of the bowstring and fling of projectiles, their apprehension increased. Chunks of stone crumbled away from the wall, tumbling to rest in the parched grass below. Two areas having been battered repeatedly, they waited in anticipation of their triumph. When the skyline began to look like it was on fire, Serena took a deep breath, fear inking into her heart with the rapid setting of the sun. Only a couple hours of daylight remained, and they were down to their last two projectiles. A final chance at taking out part of the wall that closed off the Valley of Norlee from the east.

Another wave of arrows rained down upon them. Serena huddled close under Rigel's shield, not meeting his gaze. She squeezed her eyes shut, wishing for the briefest moment that he was Will. Then the battering of metal against metal shocked the thought out of her mind. It was her destiny to fight at the front lines, not his.

As Rigel lowered his shield, her gaze swept over the sweaty, dirt-streaked faces of the other guards. What a long, difficult day it had been for everyone. And it would only be more intense when the wall came down. "Wait," Serena ordered. The men paused, yet to load the projectiles onto the catapults. "Perhaps we should fall back. Rest for the night."

Maynard shook his head. "I would advise against such. We risk Rexton's men coming down in search of us in the middle of the night."

The wall loomed over them as Serena contemplated his advice. There were one hundred strong awaiting her decision. A decision she would have preferred to fall on someone older and more knowledgeable. She glanced from the commander to Crystal and Rilura, who had approached for an update.

"Would it not be a risk should we lose the light?" She was reaching now. Desperate for a reason to postpone the inevitable. A way to keep her loved ones safe but one night longer.

The dwarf princess looked to the sky and squinted into the bright sunlight. "I dinna' believe so," Rilura countered. She rested her axe on the ground at her side. "'Tis best we go forth with our advantage whilst they scramble."

The archer rested a hand on Serena's shoulder. "I must agree. By now, they've sent for reinforcements. We should handle the border guards before additional soldiers arrive."

"This battle will not end at the border," Maynard said, fixing Serena with his dark brown eyes. "It will be fought in waves. And whoever wins the first fight will have the advantage come tomorrow."

The apprehension must have been plain on her face as Crystal squeezed her shoulder and Rigel nodded in silent support. Even the commander—far more versed in these matters—awaited her agreement. The burden of being looked to as a leader had never felt so heavy. Serena could easily carry the weight of a sword, but she would give anything to not have so many eager eyes looking at her with anticipation.

"We can do this," Rigel insisted. She turned to face him, his blue eyes hopeful as ever. "You can do this, Serena. Just give the word."

Serena swallowed hard. She glanced behind them at the many people waiting to fight on behalf of Hyrosencia. Because they believed in a prophecy. In her. Then she turned toward the guards handling the catapults and declared, "Ready yourselves!"

The guards hurried to load the final projectiles into the catapults. Crystal and Rilura turned and rushed back to inform the others to be ready. If they aimed true, the wall might yet come down. Then the real fight would begin.

Once the steel was loaded, the guards pulled back the ropes, readying to send them flying once again. Serena looked to Maynard, who nodded when his men were ready. She breathed deep, relishing in the crisp air that filled her lungs. This was it. One last moment of quiet. Either they would fail and return to Envyre defeated, or the wall would break open and battle would ensue. She counted slowly in her head.

One. Two. Three.

"Launch!" she screamed, slashing Sannarvin through the air once more.

The guards released the ropes, and the projectiles flung high in the sky. Everyone watched as the lead moved achingly slowly before ramming the border wall. The first hit low on the left, not causing any substantial damage. The second aimed true. It slammed into the same fragile, crumbling area two other projectiles had hammered previously.

The wall seemed to explode on impact. A massive chunk of stone came crashing down, each falling stone chipping away at what was left below. When the dust from the avalanche started to settle, Serena stepped closer, squinting at their handiwork. There was now a sizable hole in the wall, large and low enough for their troop to enter the valley. Triumphant cries rang out across the field, swords lifted in preemptive victory. "For Hyrosencia!" The loyalists cheered as they rushed forward.

Serena lingered for a moment, the pounding of feet on the ground matching the rhythm of her wildly beating heart. The catapults were already abandoned, the guards pulling swords from their sheaths and joining their comrades in the charge. As the troop reached them, Serena unleashed a war cry bearing all the pent-up rage she held for Antoine Rexton and his men. Then she took off running for the border, followed closely by Rigel and the rest of their comrades.

When the rebels reached the wall, they avoided the shattered chunks of stone that scattered the field and made their way to the opening, prepared for a fight. Rubble crunched under boots as they started to climb. Frantic yells echoed from beyond the wall, and they knew Rexton's men awaited.

Weapons sheathed, Rigel started to climb the pile of shifting stone to reach the opening a few feet above them. The first men to climb had dropped ropes to aid the others. Once Rigel found a stable foothold a few feet up, he turned to offer Serena a hand. As he pulled her up, strong hands found her waist and lifted. Once she'd made it up, she realized Will and Cole were climbing up behind her.

Rigel nodded at his comrades before trudging on, pulling his sword in preparation for what lay ahead of them. Within the crater in the wall, shadows shrouded them, but even in the dark, Serena could see the worry in Will's gaze. It mirrored her own fear. Taking his hand, she drew closer and pleaded, "Please be careful in there."

He pressed his forehead to hers. "I love you, and I will see you on the other side when this is over. I promise."

Tears threatened to fall, but there was simply no time. More loyalists were climbing up the ropes, ready to face the fight they'd willingly begun. No one could rest until the battle was over. Teeth gritted to steel her resolve, Serena sniffled once and blinked away her anxiety. "I will love you so long as the stars burn and longer still." His arm wrapped around her waist, drawing her flush against him. He pressed his lips to hers, hard and brisk and bearing all the words they did not have time to say. She told herself it wasn't goodbye. That this was not the last time he would hold her close. Then they strode through the jagged stone tunnel into the light of war.

When they emerged, there was hardly time to survey the area. Will grabbed her arm, helping her keep balance as they hastily climbed down the rocky ledge to the ground. Three dozen soldiers in crimson uniforms were already on the ground, quick to defend themselves against the intruders. The first to come through the rubble had already taken on those men. Several writhing bodies already covered the ground—men from both sides. Metal on metal rang out. The metallic scent of blood permeated the air as fighters cried out in pain.

A flash of red hair caught Serena's attention, and she spotted Rigel taking on a middle-aged man in a crimson uniform. His brown hair and beard were peppered with gray, but he moved as quick as lightning. They parried twice before Gideon boxed the enemy soldier in. The distraction proved enough for Rigel to slash through the crimson-coated man's right arm. As the man bellowed in pain, Gideon brought down a fatal slash on his throat.

Serena winced and looked away. A slew of soldiers were scrambling down the crumbling stairs on the backside of the wall. Rilura and Thomli headed them off, swinging their axes out at the nearest soldiers. For such cumbersome weapons, the dwarfs wielded them with lethal grace—a testament to their strength and discipline. The dwarf princess nearly took off a man's head while Thomli slashed through another's arms. That man's blade fell to the ground still clutched by his severed hand.

While the dwarfs held their own against multiple enemies, several managed to run past them, weapons reared for battle. Serena and Will leapt into action. She felt a surge of energy rush from her fingertips up her arms the first time an enemy's blade met the Heir's Blade. Lips curling with renewed confidence, Serena pushed back against the black-haired soldier. He paced toward the right, and she turned her body as he circled before thrusting his blade forth again. She leaned to the right, avoiding his blade and clamping down on his arm underneath her left armpit. The soldier's eyes widened, and he stumbled, trying to recover use of his weapon while she swung Sannarvin with one hand, carving flesh from the man's calves. A blood-curdling shriek pierced her ears as he dropped to his knees, her weapon still lodged in bone. With a yank, the Heir's Blade came free, and blood spurted from the man's wounds. He slumped over sobbing, as pathetically wilted as the brown grass underneath him.

Serena didn't bother to finish him off. There seemed no point when he was obviously no longer a threat. Other enemies posed a far greater threat at that moment. Beside her, Will fought a young soldier with black hair and eyes the color of a dying pine tree. He reminded her of Cameron—young, impulsive, erratic. Fear crept into her heart as she watched Will hold his own, employing quick thinking to conserve his energy. Before Serena could join their duel, Will managed to elbow the soldier in the nose, the top of his metal arm bracer cracking hard against it. Blood gushed down the soldier's face to blend with his jacket. Will lifted his blade but hesitated. She wondered if he, too, saw Cameron as he stared down this soldier.

Just then, an arrow pierced the young man's chest. Will's shoulders dropped as he lowered his sword. Serena turned in the direction it had flown from and met Crystal's icy gaze. With a lifted chin, the elf lowered her bow and nodded once at Serena before turning her attention elsewhere.

As more loyalists clambered through the hole in the wall, additional soldiers seemed to appear out of nowhere. Some of Rexton's men lifted bows, sending arrows flying at the unprepared loyalists. Will quickly covered Serena as metal rained down, some striking shields while others struck softer targets. Screams of agony ripped through the battlefield. Rilura had taken an arrow to her leg, which Thomli was already inspecting. Maynard clutched at one protruding from his shoulder—somehow it had managed to find the small opening between his breastplate and pauldrons which allowed him to move his arms. A female guard collapsed nearby, the feathered end of an arrow sticking out of her neck. Serena's heart skipped as she watched blood gurgle and trickle out of the corners of the woman's mouth. There was nothing any healer could have done to save her.

As soon as Will lowered his shield, more of Rexton's soldiers spotted them. Serena could no longer worry about Will or anyone else. Sword raised to her shoulder, she defended herself with swift, steady movements. With each powerful stroke of her blade, she aimed to push back her opponent, distancing them from the rest of the skirmish. More arrows whizzed by their heads, and people yelled from all directions. As the fight continued, dust kicked up from the rubble on the ground. The middle-aged soldier she was fighting coughed and tripped over a fallen stone, landing on his rear.

In another life, she would have pitied the wide-eyed man who trembled in her shadow. The kind girl who had grown up in Durmak would have shown him mercy. But staring at his coat—a shade of red that could only remind her of the absolute carnage caused in Rexton's name—she thought of her mother and brothers and the fallen Garricks before her. Of the good people who had been and would be lost in that very battle. Reminded of all she'd already lost, she fixed her jaw and slashed through the soldier's chest with no remorse. Any man who fought for the tyrant who slaughtered women and children with the utmost prejudice would find no mercy at the end of the Heir's Blade.

51

ENEMIES

In the shade of pine trees, Anteros sat and stared at his rope-bound hands, unable to move from his location. Captain Pelham had led his father's men across the border into the valley two days prior, joining the other half of his forces where they had been camping outside of the city of Noomi. Pelham boasted loudly about their successful raid of Durmak and its subsequent burning while Anteros fumed in silence.

It was there, tethered to a tree, that Anteros learned his father's greater plan. The king intended for them to attack the city that safeguarded Elara and her Hyrosencian refugees. Anteros couldn't say he was surprised by this plan. But after his disobedience in Durmak, he was shocked that his superior still intended to drag him along for the raid.

For the second night in a row, most of the men went into town in search of libations and entertainment, including their captain. Anteros tried to get his friends' attention, but they all ignored his whistles and whispers. The one time he caught Calix glancing his way, the young man shook his head and turned his back. As his empty stomach growled in displeasure, Anteros looked up at the stars and wondered how Talitha had survived feeling so hollow for so long.

Remembering he had abandoned her to the darkness for weeks, he thought perhaps starving was the least of what he deserved.

The following day when the camp was quiet, Julian meandered over. A bowl plopped in the grass at Anteros' feet, some of the deep brown contents sloshing onto his boots. The prince wrinkled his nose and sighed in defeat. "Thanks, I guess." He grasped the edge of the wooden bowl and dragged it into his lap. The sad stew was the first food he'd been offered all day. Using two fingers like a spoon, he scooped a chunk out and forced himself to eat it. Cold. Lumpy. Containing questionable meat, it could hardly qualify as a proper meal. He'd be lucky if he did not expel the contents later.

His friend shrugged, not having anything to say to the disgraced prince as he turned back toward the camp. Most of the men had gone into town seeking reprieve from the midday heat. The few who were posted on guard had dozed off in the shade. No one was around to hear them.

"Julian," the prince pleaded. His friend stopped and waited, back still turned. Anteros wiggled and sat up straighter. "Be a friend and loosen these bindings for me." He held up his hands.

His friend scoffed and ran a hand over his head. In anticipation of the heat, he had shaved his hair close to the head. Missing his signature slicked back locks, Julian looked quite different from the young noble who had been raised at court. One of the few permitted to be the prince's friend. "Do you have any idea how much more difficult you've made this assignment for the rest of us?" He finally turned to glare at Anteros.

The prince dropped his hands into his lap. "How have I done that? You complied with your orders. You aren't the one tied up."

"Believe me, Pelham considered it. I'm only enlisted because your father *encouraged* me to keep an eye on you. And by encouraged, I mean forced me to join you on this ridiculous escapade," Julian snapped, storming closer. The trees cast ominous shadows over his tired features as he approached. "Now my future is tied to that of a traitor!"

Anteros flinched. "Have you forgotten who was responsible for Sabine's death? If anyone has betrayed us, it's him!" His chest rose and fell quickly as he returned his friend's hostility.

At the mention of Sabine, Julian's spine went stiff and his gaze softened. Anteros had hit a nerve, a soft spot he knew would likely never go away. After all, one could never forget the first girl they loved.

"Don't drag her name into this," his friend whispered, his chin dropping. He couldn't look Anteros in the eyes then. Julian's hands remained clenched at his sides as he swallowed down their bitter reality once more. Everything had changed between them, having lost the only person they both cared about in equal measure.

Anteros cursed his father for having driven a wedge between him and his fickle friends. Without their support, he had no good reason to return to Graynor at the conclusion of their mission. Perhaps dying in battle would be a welcome reprieve.

As Julian's lips parted to say more, a commotion drew their attention toward the city. To their disbelief, Rexton's men were running toward camp in droves, yelling at the guards. "Ready the horses! The loyalists have attacked the border!"

Anteros and Julian shared a brief glance before his friend took off for the horses, leaving him still tethered to the tree. The prince looked down at the bowl of cold stew and frowned. His last chance of an easy escape had been thwarted by this uprising against his father. He couldn't say he blamed the rebels for finally making their move.

Carnage awaited when they reached the eastern border wall. They had heard the projectiles battering the wall from afar, but none expected part of the wall to be blown wide open when they arrived. His father's border guards, clad in the usual crimson, engaged with the rebels who had entered the valley through the pit in the wall. The rebellion's numbers were surprising, considering they had attacked from the isolated part of the continent. They must have numbered a hundred or more. Anteros' mouth gaped as he watched them engage in battle, all lithe, fitted with armor, and poised to kill. Bodies already littered the ground—some writhing from injuries, the bloodiest ones obviously deceased.

Rexton's troop quickly dismounted from their horses before entering the fray. Anteros tossed one leg over his steed, jumped down, and called out for assistance to no avail. His wrists were still bound in front of him, and his weapons had been confiscated following his insubordination. He ducked behind the horse, careful to stay out of sight as he tugged at his bindings. In his futile struggle, the knots only grew tighter, the ropes rubbing his wrists raw.

His father's men did not get far before they were greeted by rebel weapons. A dozen fighters threw everything into close combat, their swords like a living extension of their bodies. Each slash was an exhale, hot and fast and gone in an instant. An elf with blond hair showed impressive skill, staving off two soldiers at once. Despite being outnumbered, he managed to run through one of Rexton's less competent men rather quickly. Against a captain, the elf would have his work cut out for him.

The troops were evenly matched in both number and skill. Anteros scanned the terrain in search of his friends. Dust clouded the air, making it nearly impossible to tell the soldiers apart. During his perusal of the battlefield, several of his father's men were slain. An arrow pierced through a bearded soldier's chest, another through someone's eye. Wherever they were, the rebel archers were lethal. The prince lowered his head, anxious to remain out of their view.

As the battle raged on, the rebels pushed further into the valley. Most of the horses charged off into the trees, leaving Anteros with little shelter from the enemy. He stumbled through the war-torn landscape over fallen rubble and bloody corpses with no idea where he was heading. At the sound of a woman's scream behind him, Anteros looked over his shoulder, tripped, and landed on top of someone. Recognizing the crimson coat underneath his hands, he hastily pushed himself off his fallen comrade's body.

Then an idea struck. Anteros couldn't help the laugh that escaped him at finding a dagger still strapped to the man's hip. Unsheathing it with some difficulty, the prince managed to tuck the dagger underneath his bindings and saw through them. A heavy sigh escaped his lips as the ropes snapped and fell away, his marred hands falling limp at his sides.

Then he caught sight of the man's face, brown eyes wide and motionless.

It was Calix.

"Sun and moons," Anteros murmured, sinking back onto his haunches. He dropped the dagger on the ground and scrubbed his dirt-caked hands over his face, fighting back a wave of sorrow. The sounds of war roared from all sides, robbing him of proper time to mourn his friend. Using two fingers, he gently closed Calix's eyes, regret squeezing his heart.

Swords clashed nearby, and Anteros rose to his feet. Peering in the direction of the closest combatants, he spotted Pelham right as he ran his blade through a young man. The captain breathed heavily as he straightened his stance and met the prince's gaze. Blood dripped from the edge of his chin as his lips curled. "Best take a weapon before you join the fallen." He nodded his chin toward his most recent opponent before walking away.

Anteros swallowed thickly, his feet dragging as he approached the man Pelham had just slain. He reached the abandoned sword first and stooped to pick it up by the hilt. His stomach lurched when he faced the fallen loyalist—a youthful face topped with brown curls, hardly the age of a grown man. The prince wondered what drove someone so young to go to war. The bloodshed caused by his father never seemed to end—only to increase tenfold with each passing day. The unnecessary loss of life felt so wasteful.

"No!" cried a female voice from behind him.

The prince turned to face her. His jaw slackened when he laid eyes on a young woman about his age. A thick rope of dark brown hair fell over one shoulder of her leather armor, the hilt of a dagger poking out of the top. Her pale visage was splattered with blood; bright green eyes rimmed with tears bore into him with a hatred the likes of which he had only seen aimed at his father. She pointed a large sword at his chest, an amethyst gem glinting from the hilt near her grip. "You will pay for that." She seethed.

"What?" Anteros followed her gaze down to the young man behind him and winced. She thought he had done this. He had done some awful things in his short life, but he had yet to end a life. "No, I didn't—You're mistaken."

She scoffed. "Lies. You bear the king's emblem!"

He winced, glancing down at the threadbare crimson uniform. A black bear proudly emblazoned on the right side of his chest. A mark of wickedness for all to see.

The girl shrieked as she ran at him, her sword raised overhead. Anteros moved quickly to block her first swing. His instincts were sharp. Years of private training with the best instructors had prepared him for this moment. For a blow aimed to kill. The only time he had ever feared an opponent's blade was when he faced his father. Yet the skill and strength behind this girl's assault shocked him. They matched each other swing for swing, engaging in a perilous dance, a push and pull led by vengeance and desperation to survive. A glowing green glare affixed on his sword, never wavering, never venturing to look him in the eyes.

Their swords locked in a standoff. Anteros pressed harder, eyeing the sweat drops along her brow. "Don't make me hurt you. This is not my fight," he insisted, a quiet reassurance in his voice.

Those green eyes met his at last. A flash of uncertainty. She wet her lips but said nothing, continuing to press her blade into his with all her might. "No. It is mine." She reared back her head and kicked underneath their blades, her foot knocking the air from his lungs as he stumbled back.

Anteros found himself grinning as he regained his footing. He had never met a young lady like her at court. Her tenacity reminded him of Talitha.

"You dare to smile after slaying my friends?" She came at him again, her movements quick and sporadic. Mindless swings led by a woman's fury.

He had fought like this once. Blinded by anger, he had nearly killed his friend James. Rage could wash over a person like the sea during an unforgiving storm. Uncontrolled waves that aimed to drown an opponent. Unfortunately, unrestrained anger often dragged the wielder down to the depths first. His father was an example of such hatred.

And that hatred was spreading to the innocent people he hurt.

"I am no enemy of yours. I've slain no one," Anteros said, defending himself against a barrage of wild swings. With each clang of the metal, he could feel the animosity permeating from her pores.

She attempted to kick him again, but he was ready for it this time. Unluckily for her, the crown prince had learned how to read his opponents—and had plenty of tricks of his own. Anteros continued to parry with the young woman until the right opportunity arose. She swung her arms at just the right angle, and he was able to dodge the blade. Quickly, he wrapped his own arms around her wrists, using his sword to pin hers down. Their arms now entangled, her sword was locked in place, unable to strike him. She struggled in vain. He tightened his hold, and she cried out in pain. A final twist, and her sword plopped onto the dirt, kicking up a cloud of dust. Watery eyes stared into his, anticipating the end. She tried to escape his grasp, but he held her arms firmly in place. "This is over," he said through his teeth before releasing his hold.

Glancing about, Anteros realized the battle was dying down. The number of fighters was dwindling. The ground was covered in red coats who had been cut down. They nearly doubled the number of fallen loyalists. His father's men were losing the fight.

Quickly, the prince shed his coat and tossed it aside. He could no longer bear to have the shadow of the bear mark him as a villain. A flash of red drew his eyes to the sky, and Phinnian the phoenix swooped over their heads, squawking at him before disappearing into the woods to the north. Hope swelled in his heart. With luck on his side, he might manage to catch up to the beast and find a message from Talitha waiting.

The sharp sound of metal scraping metal caught his attention, and he turned just in time to catch the girl's hand over his face. She held a simple dagger in one fist, a determined glint returned to her gaze. "This will not be over until Antoine Rexton and all of his men have grown cold," she spat, trying to wrestle her hand free. The fingernails from her other hand dug into his raw skin, making him wince.

Anteros growled under his breath at her stubbornness. She stumbled back, losing her balance as he released her arm. The prince dropped down, swinging one leg underneath her. Her hip hit the ground hard, and she exhaled roughly, the wind knocked from her lungs. Knife beside her on the ground, the prince quickly kicked it away. The metal flung across the dirt, landing far out of her reach. He pointed his sword at her chest and said, "Again, I am not your enemy. Count yourself lucky of that."

She stared up at him from the flat of her back, a quizzical brow revealing her confusion. He assessed their surroundings before sheathing his weapon. Finding no other fighters in their proximity, he deemed them both safe for the moment. With hope that freedom was in sight, Anteros turned and raced for the edge of the woods, ready to leave the carnage of his father's war behind in the dust.

He had nearly reached the trees when he spotted Pelham and another officer—Captain Corrigan—engaged in a fierce clash against two loyalists. Upon closer inspection, he realized the man with raven hair tied up and a deep tan was an elf. As the warrior spun and swung his weapon with lethal grace, Anteros watched in awe. He had never seen an elf in person, but this one seemed as formidable as those his nanny had told tales about in his youth. His sister would have appreciated the man's face—sharp, yet undeniably handsome. A cut above most humans.

His father had a particular hatred for the elves that stemmed from their longevity. The man would have done anything to be able to extend his life a few more centuries. Anteros always suspected his father might invade Ord Metsiilva if he ever eradicated the loyalists on the east side of the mountains. There seemed to be no end to the lengths Antoine Rexton would go to keep hold of his power—even if it meant inciting a war between the races.

Anteros shook his head at the idea of his father attacking yet another innocent realm. The elves kept mostly to themselves. The fact that some elves had joined the Hyrosencian loyalists in a siege on the border showed that even they knew of his father's hatred. Knew he had to be stopped at all costs before the entire continent went up in flames.

The elf flourished a wide blade made of deep gray metal around his hand as though it weighed nothing. In a swift move, he countered against Corrigan, knocking the bald captain's blade aside with ease. Corrigan growled as he wound his arms around, rearing for the next swing. When the elf came out with a quick succession of ferocious swings, the captain's heels slid in the dirt, kicking up a puff of dust around his feet.

Pelham ground his teeth and charged at the human—a young man with unruly chestnut waves. He couldn't have been that much older than Anteros, or that girl who had attacked him earlier. With a thin but sturdy shield in one hand and a blade in his other, the loyalist fended off every one of Pelham's strikes. With every swing, Pelham's frustration became more evident. Perspiration dripped down his face and soaked through his garments. His hands flexed and tightened around the hilt of his weapon, eyes narrowed in on his opponent.

Anteros could have slipped into the forest, never to be seen again by his captain or any of his comrades. But watching these two engage in close combat, his stomach twisted, and he found himself drawn toward the fight. A few steps closer, and Pelham noticed him in his peripheral. "Ahh, our fool-hearted prince lives. Come to your senses, boy?"

The prince glanced from the captain to his opponent. He was panting, his chest rising and falling with rapid breaths. Thick brows furrowed as the young man scrutinized him in silence, sword still raised above one shoulder in anticipation. As though he were considering turning his fury onto Anteros instead.

"I bested a girl back there," Anteros said, nodding his head. He'd left the girl alive. He hoped she was smart enough to find some of her comrades before someone less merciful found her.

Pelham grinned the most malicious smile Anteros had seen—besides his own father's. "Good man. Now, let us best this loyalist scum." The captain nodded toward the young man circling and watching them.

Fear flashed in this man's eyes as they bobbed between the three enemies in close proximity. While the elf was holding his own, this man was smart to keep them within his sight. In battle, the tides could shift in an instant. One misstep could cause a sudden, gruesome death.

Anteros did not have the heart for killing loyalists like his father and his officers did. The prince pretended to paw at his shoulder and rub his aching wrists. "I'm feeling quite sore from my confinement. I think I'll watch this match up." He grinned at the captain, whose face was already turning purple with his rising anger.

Before the captain could unleash his belligerence upon the prince, the loyalist leapt into action. Taking advantage of Pelham's distraction, the young man slashed out strategically. Against an amateur opponent, he could have caused a fatal wound.

But Pelham being a seasoned soldier, he couldn't be surprised. He thrust his blade forth, their weapons crashing loudly and ricocheting apart. "A foolish boy is no match for a man of war," Pelham declared. The loyalist clenched his jaw and parried with him over and over, their skills and strength a fair match. However, Pelham's experience and intelligence ultimately surpassed that of the rebel. Once the captain managed to find an opening, he bashed his head forward into the young man's nose. With a loud crack, the rebel fell back and collapsed onto the ground unconscious.

Instead of turning toward the prince, Pelham then turned his attention toward the dark-haired elf, who was quickly wearing down the other captain. The sky behind them looked like it was on fire. But not like Durmak. This fire was peaceful, patient, a quiet beauty. The gradient of orange and pink that stretched across the sky signaled the end of a long day. The merry shades reminded him of the marigolds and roses in the royal gardens that his sister so loved. His stomach churned at the reminder that she would never witness another sunset. Never again smell the roses when they bloom in the spring.

As Pelham lifted his sword, stalking toward the back of the unsuspecting elf, the knots in Anteros' stomach suddenly unfurled. Thoughts of his sister put the entire battle into perspective, and he ran toward the captain, wishing he could somehow knock sense into the man. To somehow make him see that his father wasn't worthy of their blades or their loyalty. Corrigan's eyes shifted ever-so-briefly to meet Pelham's, and Anteros panted in his rush to reach them. As Pelham slashed his blade across, intending to slay the elf from behind, the prince swung his weapon out between them and deflected the blow at the last minute.

"You…" Pelham seethed, turning his wrath upon Anteros. The tip of his blade left a line in the dirt as it dragged against the ground.

The prince straightened his back and held his chin up. "Yes, me. Did you not know that it's cowardly to stab a man in the back?"

Beside them, Corrigan and the elf continued to parry. The sharp sound of their swords clashing was the backdrop to Anteros' thoughts of life and death. Life seemed so short then, surrounded by bloodied corpses and reminded of his own beloved sister's cold remains buried in the cemetery of a castle they never should have lived in.

None of this would have happened if his father had stayed in Nyzenard. If he had not been selfish and desperate for power, a title, a crown, none of these people would have had to die. Even after he had acquired all he ever wanted, Antoine Rexton was still not satisfied. His son knew he never would be.

Looking at Pelham was like looking at his father. They bore the same black hair and darkness to their eyes. A look Anteros loathed that he shared with them. A darkness that beckoned him with gentle whispers to kill.

Anteros lifted his blade and blocked Pelham's initial attack. Engaging in close combat was like dancing at a masquerade. One had to use an array of skills to quickly get to know who they were partnered with—or against. Luckily for him, Pelham was a hands-on captain, so he already had an idea of how to bring the man down. A faulty left ankle.

"You are a disgrace to the Rexton legacy!" Pelham shouted as he swung for the prince's neck. "Your father shall thank me for ridding him of you! The stench of your betrayal will be left among the fallen on this field."

They fended off each others' advances several times before fatigue got the better of his captain. In a moment of the captain's sluggish recovery, Anteros dared to make his move. His elbow jammed into the captain's throat, knocking the air out of his lungs, and then he aimed a kick at the old injury the captain tried so hard to hide. The prince's heel made contact with Pelham's ankle, and the man cried out in pain as he dropped onto his knees.

Anteros pressed the tip of his blade into the side of Pelham's neck and shook his head at the pathetic man before him. The captain sneered and said, "Do it already! Should you find the balls to look a man in the eyes when you kill him, I'll have trained you well."

The prince twisted his mouth in contemplation. Much as he loathed this man, he had no intention of killing him. No, what he wanted more than anything was to get far away from this battlefield. To find his way back to the one person who made him forget he was the son of a monster. The girl who reminded him to cling to the light.

A solemn smile curved his lips, and Anteros replied, "A foolish man is no match for the King of War's son." Pelham's eyes widened with understandable fear. Even the greatest of warriors could not help but fear the end of a blade. Before his opponent could move, Anteros slammed the hilt of his sword down on Pelham's face with an agonizing crack. The captain's body flopped forward onto the ground, blood oozing from the fresh wound on his nose. This was all the victory Anteros needed. Freedom from one of his greatest oppressors.

Corrigan cried out then, and the prince looked up to find the elf had stabbed his broad blade right through the man's midsection. Anteros gulped and stepped back from the terrifying warrior. Nearby, soldiers and rebels approached to aid their respective allies. When Pelham awoke, his wrath would blaze like a wildfire.

Out of self-preservation, Anteros took off running for the mountains, easily disappearing among the thick trees and brush. The prince had come too far to perish on this battlefield. Finally free from the burden of his father's vile expectations, Anteros breathed a sigh of relief as he started making his way back toward Hyrosencia. With a little distance between himself and the battle ground, Phinnian the phoenix finally swooped down to greet his owner and deliver a message that would set Anteros on a new path. A path toward the familiar face he longed to see. Toward the heart that had changed his own for the better.

I'm coming, Red.

52

RETREAT

Serena lay on her back, staring up at the sky as it darkened, fighting to catch her breath. The ground beneath her was hard and uneven, yet she was grateful she could still feel it. Exhaustion dragged at every part of her. She was so drained she had made reckless mistakes and nearly lost her life in her first battle. She blinked, feeling tears trickle from the corners of her eyes down her temples into her hair. No matter how many times she faced certain death, she somehow was still breathing.

Hearing metal clash in the distance, Serena finally hoisted her aching body back to its feet. The remaining fighters were near the border wall and the southern woods. She turned north toward the towering mountains she had not long ago had to cross. The mountains where she had first taken a life to save the boy she loved. Where her brother became her enemy and her destiny came to light. The woods were dark and still. Eerily familiar. Haunting. Somewhere in that darkness hid the young soldier who could have brought her life to an end but didn't. She would always wonder why.

Especially since she had tried so very hard to kill him.

Turning away from the dark, Serena sought out Will's dagger and the Heir's Blade. Her braid falling apart from the previous fight, she sheathed the dagger and tucked it into her boot. Her palms ached, skin screaming with cracks and blisters under her gloves as she adjusted her grip on the hilt of her sword. But she persisted, moving quickly toward the nearest fighters.

Bright red hair quickly came into view, and she sighed in relief. Sweat pebbled his brow as Rigel faced off against a tall, muscular soldier with a black moustache. Blood trickled from a slash on his left forearm, but he held his own, fighting through the pain of his injury. The soldier was domineering. He swung his weapon down swiftly, applying brutal pressure on the guardian. The man held strong until Rigel's arms began shaking. Her friend shoved the soldier back with all his strength, panting heavily.

Behind him, another man in a crimson coat leered over a body, blood dripping from the edge of his sword. A woman's chest rose and fell slowly as she stared up at the enemy. Her fingers twitched, one digging into the grass in search of a weapon that was not near enough. The other clutched a wound in her abdomen. Blood seeped through the spaces between her fingers. Her assailant shifted on his feet, and violet eyes found Serena. Madeline shook her head once, the motion so faint the man did not notice. Then her eyes closed.

A crooked smile turned away from his dirty work, fixing on Rigel's back. Her friend continued to fight, unaware of the enemy approaching from behind. The man reared his weapon overhead, but when he swung it down, the soldier did not meet Rigel's back. Serena's blade had blocked the strike.

The soldier's scowl waned, his shock evident. "It's shameful to strike a man from behind," she said, raising her brows in defiance.

Her opponent ground his teeth and shoved her back a few steps. "All's fair in war," he answered. His size was a benefit to his sheer strength. Speed and intellect would be her greatest weapons against him.

"If you say so." Serena grinned. The soldier swung his blade parallel to the ground, and she slid low on the ground, kicking up a puff of dust in her wake. The dirt was coarse and dry under her thin leather gloves. When she pushed herself off the ground, she tossed a handful of the gray soil in the man's face. He stumbled and hollered curses, pressing a hand to his eyes.

Now aware of the commotion behind him, Rigel turned and slashed through the agitated man while he was incapacitated. Serena grabbed her weapon off the ground and rushed his other opponent, eager to end this fight and get to their fallen friend. They parried twice, finding they were fairly matched in skill. Once Rigel stepped up on the other side of the soldier, the man stood no chance. They both dove into the fray, and it was not long before Serena managed to slice through his hand, disarming him. Rigel kicked the back of his legs, forcing the man down on his knees.

A deep voice cried out for retreat in the distance—one of Rexton's officers. Anger surged through her at the thought of any of these men escaping. She scanned her surroundings in stunned silence as several battered men raced away from the battlefield, abandoning their injured comrades in favor of the chance to see another day. They were cowards, every one of them.

Serena gripped Sannarvin tight in her right fist. As she stepped forward, a hand landed on her arm, holding her back. "Don't follow them. We've won today." Serena turned swiftly to face Rigel. Crimson splatter freckled his face, the smears a brighter red than his own hair.

"But they're getting away!" Serena yanked her arm away from him. "They are traitors. Murderers. They don't deserve to live."

Rigel nodded. "Look around, Serena. It's time to assess our own losses. Rest, recover. There are more battles to come."

She lowered her chin and loosened her grip on the blade's hilt. "And what about this one?" Blood dripped off the tip of her blade and soaked into the dry grass. A slow, deep breath helped to steady her pounding heartbeat. She had nearly died in battle, yet she remained standing. She always did somehow. No matter how many of Rexton's men tried to end her life.

"Wait," Rigel insisted as Serena lifted Sannarvin, intending to deliver a fatal blow. "We should take him hostage. See what we can learn about Rexton's plans." Serena blew out a breath and nodded. The guardian grabbed the man by a fistful of his hair and forced him to look up. "Your uniform. It's different from the border patrol. Why were you in the valley?" The soldier scoffed and spit in his face. Rigel clenched his jaw and worked to tie the man's hands behind his back.

Thomli clomped toward them, axe dragging the ground. Relief washed over Serena at the sight of another familiar face, though she was surprised the princess was not with him. "Taking this one prisoner, eh?" the dwarf asked. Serena nodded. "Allow me." The dwarf grabbed the man by the arm, dragging him onto his feet.

Serena watched as the sun sank beneath the horizon. All that remained was a faint orange hue that faded into the deep black night. The stars slowly flickered to life one at a time, and she wondered how many of their friends had joined their ranks. She looked around at the blood-soaked bodies from both sides of the battle before turning wide, frightened eyes toward her friend. "Will. Have you seen Will? Or any of the others?"

"Afraid not. We came farther in than most," Rigel said. He walked over to Madeline and pressed his fingers to her neck. "She's still here—barely. We need to find Crystal." His voice was ragged, his breathing heavy as he moved to lift the unconscious woman.

Blood still dripped down his left arm, trickling from his fingertips to the ground. "Wait. You're bleeding." His opponent had managed to slice through a leather bracer on his forearm. Serena peeled off the bracer and carefully rolled up his mangled sleeve. Thankfully, the wound was shallow. Not fatal. Not like the last time.

"I've survived worse. Mads is more critical," Rigel said glumly.

Serena wedged herself between him and their friend. "At least let me stop the bleeding, or you won't make it far." He sighed and shifted away from the body, standing upright. After sheathing her sword, Serena lifted the bottom of her leather vest and pulled out the hem of a plain cotton blouse. Using her teeth, she ripped a strip off the bottom of the garment. Her fingers shook slightly as she tied it tight above the cut on his arm.

"Let's find the others." He hoisted Madeline into his arms and nodded his chin in the direction of the wall. Or at least, what remained of it. That's where there seemed to be the most survivors. Not far ahead of them, Thomli escorted the soldier they'd captured, dragging him by a piece of rope attached to his bindings.

Broken chunks of brick scattered the ground. White dust from the wreckage smothered everything—the grass, the bodies, even the air. They passed dozens of unmoving bodies, their crimson uniforms nearly unrecognizable among the rubble. Moans followed as they searched the fallen faces, making their way to the area where their surviving comrades seemed to be gathering.

As they neared the group, Cole's voice rang out loud and harsh and tinged with fear. "Where is my wife?"

Serena's breath hitched, and her steps faltered. Rigel, however, took off in a run. When she came to her senses, she broke into a jog, terrified of what they might find when they reached the others.

Cole clenched the top of a soldier's uniform at the neck, nearly lifting the man off the ground. The enemy's hands were tied behind his back, and blood dribbled from his nose into his dark facial hair. The man chuckled darkly, further inciting Cole's rage. She had never seen him so unhinged.

"Why should we spare you if you won't talk?" Cole snapped. He dropped the prisoner onto his knees and drew a sword, pointing it at the man's throat. Gideon tried to pull him back, but the elf didn't budge. Something had broken in him.

"Would they take prisoners?" Rilura asked. She didn't look up from her seat on the ground as she wiped the blood off her axe.

"A fair trade's the only way you'll get yours back," the soldier said smugly, blood flying from his mouth to splatter Cole's face.

Again, Gideon restrained the elf before he could kill the man, and Ilrune moved to help. Cole growled as he thrashed in their grip. Commander Maynard stepped closer and helped pry the blade from the elf's hands as he screamed at the captive, "You think you're safe? You're a dead man! I'll kill every last one of you for touching her!"

A weary cry drew Serena's attention to another group huddled on the ground a few feet away. White blonde hair stained with the blood of their enemies caught the sun as Crystal leaned her head back and sobbed. Rigel and Serena approached cautiously. Neither of them had ever seen their Elven comrades so out of sorts.

Two dozen bodies had been gathered there—some still moaning in agony while others laid still. The two nearest to Crystal had been covered haphazardly with tattered cloaks. From beneath the nearest one, strands of black curly hair peeked out. The sight of a limp brown hand lying unmoving beside their friend made Serena's stomach lurch.

No. No, no, no!

Rigel laid Madeline with the other injured. Then he knelt beside the archer and gently touched her shoulder. "Crys…"

Bright blue eyes met his for a second before she plunged into his embrace. "You're alive," Crystal cried into his chest. "I couldn't save her. Blazing embers, there are so many injured, and I can't—"

Rigel wrapped his arms around her back and patted her softly, his watery gaze locked on the bodies beside them. "You can't save everyone," he whispered into her hair. The words brought her no comfort as she continued weeping.

Serena choked back the tears welling up. The tight feeling in the back of her throat kept her from asking what she desperately needed to know. Falling apart wasn't an option. Not yet. She still had to find Will.

She walked down a row of writhing bodies searching for his face among the injured. With each person she passed, she grew more worried. If he wasn't there, where else could he be?

Finally, Rilura hobbled over to her with a grim look on her face. "He isn't here," the dwarf said as quietly as Serena had ever heard the proud warrior princess.

"What do you mean? Where is he?" Serena asked. She grabbed Rilura's shoulders and screamed, her voice trembling, "Where's Will?"

The dwarf took a haggard breath and laid a hand on Serena's cheek. "I'm so sorry, Serena. I tried to get to him, but my leg…" She lowered her head in shame, tears springing into her bright blues. "I'm not certain where they've taken him, but he's gone." Rilura continued speaking but the words slurred into unintelligible slush in Serena's ears.

He's gone?

Serena's hands fell to her sides, her entire body going limp. She didn't feel it when her knees slammed into the ground. Couldn't hear what anyone said when they rushed over to check on her. All she could feel was the agony of her heart shattering into a million pieces in her chest. Like all the souls they had lost there were clawing at the air in her lungs instead of ascending to rest among the stars.

Though they had won the first battle, there were no smiles to be seen. Their hearts were heavy, their losses overshadowing their victory. No one had the strength for celebrations. Only weeping for all they had lost.

ACKNOWLEDGMENTS

Dear Readers,

Thank you for taking a chance on my Celestial Destiny Series. Writing and publishing *A Fox Among Flames* has been a long, emotional, and exhausting journey, largely due to welcoming a baby in 2025. There were times I felt like I would never finish writing this book. It is thanks to my family, friends, and readers that I found the strength to keep writing and complete this project. I hope you enjoyed the second part of this epic adventure.

Thank you to my family for your continued support of this longtime dream, especially my parents, my husband, and my sweet babies.

Huge thanks to Ramona Mihai, who completed the copy and line edits. I am so grateful *A Fox Among Flames* was entrusted to your skilled hands!

Special thanks to my alpha readers: Nikki, Kaela, and Blanca. Your feedback and reactions were exactly the encouragement I needed to complete this story and make sure the ending was satisfying (even as a cliffhanger).

Thanks to my Sparrows, my wonderful street team, and my ARC team! Your enthusiasm for my series is greatly appreciated! I hope you each found something to love in this story.

Special thanks to Briane Terry and Coco for helping to name new character Ryker Umbryon through the naming contest in fall 2024. He has the coolest name, even though he's a pain in the rear.

Lastly, thank you to all the friends and Internet strangers who have shown me support through social media during the craziest year of my life so far. I love having a group of friends, many of whom are in the same chapter of life–pursuing our passion for writing while juggling Mom life. You are all awesome, and I love being a part of our Author Struggle Street community.

About the Author

Sara Puissegur lives in south Louisiana with her husband Caleb and their two children. She has a Bachelor's degree in Communications and works full time. She has enjoyed taking her work experience and applying those skills in social media toward marketing her first fantasy series.

Sara has enjoyed writing original stories since elementary school, and her lifelong dream was to publish a novel. The Celestial Destiny Series has been a work in progress for over a decade, and the first book in the series, *A Sparrow Among Stars*, was Sara's first published work in August 2024. She is grateful that she gets to finally share part two of this epic saga with her wonderful readers.

Learn More & Subscribe
Sara Puissegur
www.sarapuissegur.com

www.ingramcontent.com/pod-product-compliance
Lightning Source LLC
Chambersburg PA
CBHW030350310726
48979CB00001B/250